The Journey Alone

The Journey Alone

John Jaie Palmero

And the Nile gave birth to a god, Greek by birth, eternal in death. And the Emperor of all Rome built a city to the god, Antinous, and temples to him filled the empire. And the visage of the god followed Hadrian everywhere in sculpture and dreams, but the emperor's life was now a journey alone.

To order additional copies of this book, contact:
Xlibris LLC
1-888-795-4274
www.Xlibris.com
Orders@Xlibris.com
133593

Contents

To all the shadows who led me to this place
and the light at the end of the journey.

Chapter One

The Mirror's Shadow

The morning sun took no notice of the events that occurred the previous day. No prayers to Ra, Apollo, or any of the other names for this invasive light could persuade it to stay away. The heavy silk that draped the high, bronze-grilled windows of the darkened room seemed to purposely separate just enough to allow harsh rays of light to penetrate the thick gloom of the massive chamber. Slowly, the rays traveled the room as if seeking the lodger that lay, barely breathing, on a ravaged bed covered with shredded linens. As the rays continued their search, they touched upon a sword, still sheathed and attached to its woven leather belt, lying in a pile of fragments that had only the day before been a rare, precious urn. Thrown there in a fit of rage, the sword had been followed by a gilt breastplate that the sun soon found at the foot of the great bed. As the journey of the light continued, it eventually found its way to the crumpled figure that had been watching its progress with lidded eyes. This was Egypt, and Ra was not to be defied. The eyes he searched for absorbed the joy in his morning rays, and there it died. Joy was not welcome here. Sorrow was the only occupant, and no amount of light could make it leave.

Great gods, let him walk into my chamber so that I may beg your forgiveness for the curses I laid upon you all last night! Hadrian watched the journey of that light for what seemed like an eternity. For the first time in his life, he wished for a permanent eclipse that would destroy Ra and all the other gods along with him. Morning brought truth with its arrival, and truth was not a friend today. What he had hoped was a horrific dream the night spirits had fed him became painfully real in the light of day. Once again, he felt an anguished groan swell up inside him, and he was powerless to contain it. Wearily, he sat up in the massive bed and surveyed the ruin that surrounded him. His rage was unrestrained that past evening, and the contents of the chamber silently testified to that wrath. The gold embroidery of the bedsheets still sparkled on the torn shreds of linen and silk. Feathers burst from gutted pillows like ripe seedpods, while the rare tapestries that had not been pulled down in his fits of anguish hung like tattered banners after a battle that had gone horribly wrong. Objects of gold and ivory lay dented and shattered, their precious stones, jolted from their settings, littered the floor. For a moment, the esthetic in Hadrian felt a vague pang of regret for this mindless devastation; but as his gaze turned to the empty space beside him on the bed, his renewed grief took hold and deemed the objects around him to be of little value. This was no dream. Somewhere in the vast temple of Ramses, the body of his beloved lay silent and cold. Hadrian rose from the bed and moved slowly to the washbasin near one of the covered windows. After splashing the tepid water on his face and hair, he looked up to catch his reflection in the polished bronze mirror that hung askew over the alabaster basin. A sliver of light that escaped from behind the silken drapery reflected in the droplets on his face, creating a constellation on a background of grief. He stood hunched over the basin, his hands gripping the cool stone, staring in the mirror at the tears that poured down his face. What had he done to the boy that could bring him to consider such an end? How was he to know that while he watched the lithe Egyptian boys dance and flirt before him at the final banquet, his beloved was surrendering himself to the Nile? Why did he not recognize the deepening sorrow in the boy as the days progressed? The youth had changed since their initiation at Eleusis, and the mystical effect the experience had on him held a darkness Hadrian could not, would not, see. Due to the draught that plagued Egypt this year, the Nile waters were shallow and sluggish. And besides, the youth was a fine, strong swimmer. Had the boy taken the prayers for a long life to heart? Was his death a final gift to his lover? Like knives slashing though his brain, these thoughts tormented Hadrian until he felt the vast chamber move in slow motion as a deep fog began to cloud his eyes. Somewhere in that fog, he heard his name being called. Was it Antinous? Had it all been a tragic dream sent to him to punish his pride and teach his ego a lesson? No, the sound was higher and timid, and there were two voices that echoed in the distance.

Two figures entered the chamber, their steps hesitant and soundless. Lucius Ceionius Commodus Verus and Pedanius Fuscus had not seen the emperor since he withdrew into the royal apartments two days earlier, but the sounds that emanated from there the previous nights still echoed in their ears. More terrifying was the silence that followed. As the morning shed its light on the situation, they knew it was time to face whatever dangers or horrors the bedchamber would contain. Hadrian remained hunched over at the immense alabaster washbasin, his hands still gripping the two carved lion heads on its sides. In the hazy reflection on the bronze mirror, Hadrian could barely make out the two figures approaching him. But the voices were familiar and shook him out of his grief long enough to gain control of his senses. He straightened up and turned slowly to face them, catching their look of shock as they surveyed the damage from the night before. Instantly, he was angered by his lack of control and the ruin it had caused. "I was not myself," he said simply. The sound of his voice caught their attention, and as they turned to look at him, they saw a face that betrayed the simplicity of his words. The ruin of the chamber was nothing compared to what they saw etched in his ravaged face. Hadrian never experienced a look of pity on any face that met his, and the experience shook and angered him. He suddenly felt he had lost face as well as control because of the death of his beloved, and that realization gave him the strength he needed to regain his composure.

Striding past the two startled youths he made his way to the vast private bath that was situated beyond the long gallery of soaring red granite columns crowned with capitals of carved and painted lotus blossoms. A bath would help him clear his head and think of how to approach the coming day, weeks, years. Stripping off his sweat-drenched tunica, he plunged into the steaming waters and sank deep into its soothing warmth. *How easily,* he thought, *the water seemed to offer consolation and escape. It would be over so quickly, and none would be the wiser.* But no. This was not the Nile, and there would be no deification for this act, only shame and discord within the empire. As he came up for air, his mind began to formulate the proceedings that needed to occur. He was the emperor of Rome with unlimited resources at his command.

Although the beautiful youth lay silent and cold in the temple, his name would become immortal and his likeness would grace the temples and baths of his empire. His beloved died in the Nile and now was being deified by the Egyptians. He would present Antinous as a god, even if it meant defying all of Rome and the rigidity of its religious and social mores. His likeness would grace the Pantheon and preside among the other gods. A temple would be built on the riverbank where the precious body was discovered. *No, not a temple but a city.* A city in the Greek style that would pay homage to his beloved and ensure his immortality. A cult would be founded and temples built for his worshipers to gather in. For now, the boy he loved was to be a god, and Hadrian would be his high priest. He fevered brain had caught fire.

Emerging naked from his bath Hadrian strode purposefully back into the bedchamber, a man reborn. The irritatingly servile Pedanius stayed in the shadows while the elegant Lucius had perched himself on a gilded bench wrought in the Egyptian style, his hands draped over the wide spread arms, his slender legs crossed at the ankles. There was a look of concern, mixed with something more. His posture was regal, the stool, thronelike. Silently, Pedanius made his way to Lucius's side, his gaze too showing more than just concern. The something more in his gaze looked too much like satisfaction to Hadrian's mind, and the remains of the grief and rage inside him made him want to grab the youth by the hair and beat the smugness from his face. Although his great-nephew was, in theory, the heir to Hadrian's throne, the emperor had no warm feelings toward the boy. Lucius was much more preferable, but that was a problem to be dealt with at a later date. More pressing issues were at hand, and the day was not slowing down for Hadrian's convenience. Lucius was suddenly at his side, holding a fresh tunica, the quilted *subarmalis* and the glided breastplate he retrieved from the foot of the great bed. As the youth bent down to buckle, the sandal straps around Hadrian's legs, a rush of familiarity threatened to overwhelm the man as memories of another youth, far more dear, filled his mind. How often Antinous would perform this task, much to his lover's amusement. For the youth, it was a gesture of affection and love—a gesture Hadrian had sloughed off and not truly appreciated until this moment. Regret and condemnation filled him to the point that he sank heavily onto the glided bench to gain control of his senses. Pedanius came forward with a formal toga from the cedarwood chest and began, along with Lucius, to drape the voluminous garment over the emperor. Brushing away Lucius's further efforts to help him, Hadrian rose from the bench and, after tightening the straps of his breastplate, strode from the bedchamber into the midday sun and the road to the future city of Antinoopolis.

Chapter Two

Whispers in the Shadows

The imperial entourage left Hermopolis as the morning sun was making its ascent. The empress had arranged a visit to the ancient city of Thebes on the upper Nile. Hadrian had never been this far south and, despite himself, was intrigued by the prospect. Sabina's objective was the fabled Colossi of Memmon, seated representations of Amenhotep III of the eighteenth dynasty. Julia Balbilla, in an effort to appease the empress, told her of the belief that if a piercing cry was heard coming from the statue in the early morning by those who stood before them, they would be favored by the gods. Sabina suggested the visit to Hadrian during one of his infrequent visits and now, because of the wait necessary for Antinous's embalming, the emperor agreed to the journey south. The barges would reach Thebes before sundown, and the royal party would remain in residence on the barges. The next day, small boats would transport the visitors to the mortuary temple that stood at the edge of the Nile flood plain.

Hadrian stayed aboard his barge the next morning as the small crafts arrived to take Sabina and her court to the temple and the great colossi. He had agreed to this journey despite his misgivings. The idea of leaving the body of his beloved in the hands of the priests did not appeal to him, yet there was little he could do if he had stayed there. He had seen, years ago when in Egypt, the embalming process and the horrors the corpse would be put through. He had no desire to witness the violation of the youth's perfection and felt it was best to return when that perfection was restored and intact. The emperor remained sequestered in his cabin for a number of days, as the women paid visits to the colossi in hopes of hearing its fabled song. On the evening of the third day, Julia paid Hadrian a visit, requesting that he accompany them to their final visit the next morning. "Perhaps with you present, the gods will show favor," she whispered. Hadrian leveled a scrutinizing gaze at the old woman to see if she was playing a dangerous game or was just senile. "After the cruel blow the gods have just dealt me, why would they now show me favor?" he asked incredulously. Nevertheless, he did reluctantly accompany the women to the shore the next morning.

There was a chill in the air, but Hadrian's dulled senses failed to acknowledge it. It was now nearly a month since that tragic day, yet the pain had not dulled, nor had the mist that surrounded him gone away. It was as if he was sleepwalking through all the diversions set before him, and he viewed everything as if drugged. It was the month of Hathor as well as the third month of Akhet, or what should have been the Inundation of the Nile. But Hapy, the god of the Nile, seemed unhappy with his people, and the river's life giving waters were shallow and muddy. *No one would enter these waters on purpose.* As that thought fluttered swiftly on sparrow's wings through his unconsciousness, its whisper was just audible enough to cause Caesar to wrap his cloak more tightly around himself. Guilt and bitterness, his now constant companions, would arrive with him when he reached the riverbank.

As he stepped from the deck of his barge to the small boat that waited along side, he looked across the river to the massive complex that was Amenhotep's memorial temple. For all his time anchored on the river, he had not once bothered to look out at the land beyond. Now, as the small craft approached the shore, the temple's reputation for magnificence became apparent. Stepping onto the once fertile floodplain, the emperor walked slowly to the massive statues that had been the destination of many tourists before him. They stood, or rather sat, impassively before the entrance to the monumental mortuary temple. Having seen the great temple at Karnak, Hadrian thought he had seen the apex of Egyptian temple building. But this cult center was more magnificent by far, defying its state of decay to remain a marvel to behold. Even the mountain that loomed in the distance seemed dwarfed in comparison to the twin figures flanking the view of its peaks.

Standing before the eastern colossus, Hadrian examined the reconstruction that had been done in earlier years by Roman engineers in an effort to restore the monolith. While the western statue was still intact, the eastern figure consisted of tiers of sandstone that showed some effort to restore the work to its original state. But it was the lower half of the sculpture that lured in the visitors. There, the reputed song of Memnon was hoped for; and as Hadrian stood before the massive pile, Sabina and her court gathered nearby in hopes of receiving the god's favor. Feeling diminished before the dispassionate figure, Hadrian began to tire of its overwhelming presence as he listened to a poetess in the empress's court, Claudia Damo Synamate, sing the praises of the great god in two elegiac couplets as the scribes wrote them down for future inscription on the Colossus.

> *Hail, son of Dawn, for favorably*
> *You spoke to me Memnon,*
> *For the sake of the Muses, to whom I am dear ~*
> *Damo, lover of song . . .*

"She speaks of herself as usual," muttered Hadrian, and as his mind began to wander, his gaze caught sight of another of Sabina's poetess—Julia Balbilla. Not to be outdone by her now-silent rival, she began a stream of spontaneous poems as she danced like a drunken maenad before the colossus. In the same Aeolic dialect as Claudia's couplets, they poured from her in a seemingly endless flow. Hadrian stood transfixed, not by Julia's impromptu performance, but by Sabina's frozen look of hate as she stared toward the dancing woman. He had seen arrogance, hostility, and even anger on that face. But he had never seen such loathing. Its intensity chilled him, yet it also sent through his dulled senses a rush of wild curiosity. For years past counting, Julia Balbilla had been the closest confidante to Sabina. Hadrian could not fathom the reasoning behind Sabina's hatred, nor its source.

But Sabina knew the reason for her disgust with Julia, and that, together with the loss of the boy, had left her in a state of turmoil she could find no way out of. From her window, she had watched Julia, a few days before Antinous's death, leave the palace compound by carriage. Sabina would later learn that Antinous had been with her, and they had gone to the city of Oxyrhynchus to worship at the shrine of Athena-Sophia, the city's patron goddess and muse of learning. But Julia had not brought Antinous to the city for its great library. Her reason was to finish the story she had started for him in Eleusis—a story of mysticism and sacrifice. According to ancient legend, the city was named after the spiky-nosed fish that was said to have devoured the phallis of the god Osiris after he was murdered and dismembered by his brother Seth. As she had in Eleusis, Julia filled the boy's mind with these lurid tales of death and rebirth, not realizing the effect they would have on him. For Antinous, the fate of Osiris would have meant little without his experience in Eleusis. But the mysteries revealed to him in the ancient temple, there opened his eyes to the significance of this visit and the meaning of Julia's tales. Here, he became resolute in the determination of his fate. *For his lover, he would become a god.*

Poor Julia knew nothing of the fevered plans in the impressionable youth's mind. For her, his attentions were simply due to her masterful telling of ancient tales. And that was all she wished for. She could not seduce him with beauty, wealth, or power. All she had were her words and her theatrical flair for presenting them. Little did she realize the power of those words and the destruction they would leave behind. Her mistake was to boast to Sabina afterward about the beautiful youth's fascination with her stories and the deep thought they seemed to inspire. Sabina had warned Julia about the youth's vulnerability to mysticism; he had revealed to her the darkness beneath his beauty during one of his infrequent visits to her palace. Hadrian's favorite had a fragility that worried Sabina, and she knew Julia had the power to shatter that. *And she did.*

Sensing her husband's watchful gaze, Sabina turned and quickly regained composure. She would not share with her husband her suspicions regarding Julia; his emotions had become more difficult to gauge, and she could not risk a backlash. She watched as the emperor turned and walked slowly to the temple, but before he had done so, Julia had begun to add a pentametered afterthought to her composition. *I, Balbilla, when the rock spoke, heard the voice of the divine Memnon or Phamenoth. I stood here with the lovely Empress Sabina. The course of the sun was in its first hour, in the fifteenth year of Hadrian's reign, on the twenty-fourth day of the month Hathor* . . . Julia too had caught the empress's look of hate, but unlike the emperor, knew its meaning. As the scribes looked up expectantly, Julia went suddenly silent, and the air suddenly chilled. Silence prevailed with only the dull sound of a wooden mallet striking a chisel as it etched away at the left leg of the Colossus, leaving Damo's inspired words for posterity. Julia's words too would appear there, beneath that of Claudia Damo's. *But at what cost*, she wondered. *What cost?*

It was an exhausted Hadrian that walked to the entrance of the temple looming before him. He did not have the strength or desire to enter the massive structure and so sat at the entrance and contemplated the crumbling foundation worn away by the Nile's annual visits. The god of Thebes was the ram-headed Amon, the equal of Jupiter. Leaving the shadowy darkness of Amon's sanctuary, his priests stepped into the morning light to greet the emperor who sat at their doorstep. The golden trays they carried caught new sun's pale glow, causing the newly washed figs and dates to glisten. Within a bowl of fine glass, fresh honey from the sacred hives of the temple carried its own golden glow, while crusty bread from the ovens of the temple compound lay still steaming in folds of crisp linen. *How the boy would have loved this small feast,* thought Hadrian. The memory of the youth eating heartily a meal such as this before a hunt easily brought tears to the man's eyes. The simplest things evoked memories not easily erased and wounds not willing to be healed. More out of courtesy then hunger, Hadrian partook of the offerings as a priest murmured condolences in a halting, belabored Latin. The antiquated formality of his language seemed strangely appropriate for the occasion and the words conveyed. Hadrian took comfort in the strange scene he was now the center of, a scene witnessed by Sabina and her court as they returned from the Theban Necropolis and their experience with the Colossus. Like noisy crickets on a summer day, the women chatted with shaken voices as they hurried behind the empress. She too looked unusually animated as she glided toward the temple steps and her husband. Hadrian could tell by the look on his wife's face that the gods had not disappointed her. "The son of Eos sang his sorrow as his mother rose in the sky," Sabina spoke between deep intakes of breath. "I did not believe this would happen, but we were favored by the tragic Memnon. Julia promised it would happen, and there we were . . ." Hadrian half listened to his wife's description of her mystical experience as his mind wandered to another time and place from not long ago. There in Eleusis, a beautiful youth described to his lover the mystical revelation he had been given during his initiation in the great temple. But as Hadrian revisited the scene, he suddenly saw the youth not as he had remembered him, but as he truly was. His body trembled from the power of the revelation. And his face. In it, Hadrian suddenly saw not just excitement, but also a deep sorrow. *How had he missed that?* In his own desire to elevate the youth, he introduced him to misconceived ideas he never should have experienced. Too young, Antinous's fragile psyche was no match for the ancient mysteries Hadrian had exposed him to. Now, with every day came new reasons for Hadrian to blame himself for the boy's death. He had hoped each passing day would be a balm to ease his pain. But instead, each day was more salt in the wound.

An ecstatic Sabina was still describing the sounds she heard emanating from the great cracked figure, when Hadrian suddenly rose from the steps and walked heavily toward the waiting boats. He had had enough of these ancient gods and their thirst for blood. Leaving a humiliated and furious Sabina behind, he made his way to the riverbank and settled himself in one of the boats that would ferry him back to the royal barge where he stayed, grateful for the dark solitude of his cabin. Later, when the veil of evening had settled over the desert, he watched the new star that sparkled beneath the protective breast of the *Aquila* constellation. The tutor, Chabrais, had pointed out this celestial sign to him during one of his dark moments and brought in the court astrologers to verify the finding. And at that moment, Hadrian named it Antinous and declared that it should be so. That he should reside beside the symbol of Zeus was all the better. The synchronicity of the new star between the Aquila and the realm of Capricorn gave it the natures of Venus and Jupiter—love and power respectively. The gods were paying attention, and the symbolism was impossible to ignore. That night on the Nile, there was no moon to compete with the star's brilliance. From his bed, the grieving Hadrian watched the radiance he called Antinous, until sleep finally took pity on him.

Chapter Three

The Preparation of a God

The temple priests had left Hermopolis at night, weeks earlier in hopes to arrive at the temple before daylight. The work they needed to do was best left for the darkness, and they hoped to begin the embalming process before the emperor had regained his senses. Day and night, priests and Alexandrian artisans who had been hurriedly summoned from Hadrian's entourage in Hermopolis, had occupied the Temple of Ramses to bless the body and create a wax likeness in the Roman tradition. While the Egyptian priests were far from pleased that foreigners were occupying the temple, there was little they could do about it. But as long as it was their religion that transformed the emperor's favorite into a god, they knew they had the most control of the situation. The light that shone in the emperor's eyes when the priests told him of the Nile's gift to those who drowned in its sacred waters created a pact that they knew would serve them well in the end. What that end would be was uncertain, but the generosity of the emperor was well known, and this situation would be handled with the utmost skill.

The priests returned to the temple just as the Roman artisans were finishing their wax image of the corpse. The skill of the artists shocked the priests as they viewed the naked images lying side by side, unable at first to distinguish between the sculpture and the actual body of Antinous. The meeting of the two cultures, one ancient, the other relatively new in comparison, had rarely been so poignant. The wax double was a perfect representation of the Ka or soul that was so important to the Egyptian process of body preparation. The priests continued the embalming process under the curious eyes of the Alexandrians, removing the organs and placing them in alabaster canopic jars before covering them with natron. After being swabbed with palm wine, the interior of the body was filled with spices, myrrh, and muslin pouches filled with cedar chips while natron mixed with water, oil of cedar, and palm wine was used to again bath the body. The Greeks watched with a mixture of awe and revulsion as the ritual, far more ancient than their own culture, proceeded.

The days had passed quickly during the eighth week of the embalming process, and on this morning, the sun was beginning to find its way into the dark recesses of the embalming chamber. The body had been restored, rubbed with oil and myrrh, and wrapped from the waist down in fine linen. The Egyptian priests had rubbed a powder of finely ground laurionite mixed with oil and beeswax on the chest, arms, and face that, mixed with ground carnelian, lent a healthy glow to the still supple skin. The hair glowed with fragrant oil mixed with a powder of lapis lazuli—the blue-black curls arranged in perfect patterns. The mouth, still full and slightly parted, was stained with pomegranate juice mixed with olive oil that restored its sensuousness. By the time the priests were finished, the entire group stood back in awe, not just because of the handiwork of all involved, but because of the vision of the masterpiece they had restored. Despite the steps they had to omit to comply with the time limit they were given, the youth truly looked as if he was merely asleep, and the affect was overwhelming to the point of miraculous. The warmth of Ra had begun to fill the room and completed the overall effect. His touch gave the lifeless form a glow that for a moment made it seem the sun god had returned to Antinous the gift of life. The gravity of this loss of life was suddenly made manifest, and the group bowed in reverence to their newly minted god.

Lost in their reverie, they failed to notice another figure standing in the shadows of the chamber. The figure, for his part, failed to acknowledge the living as he focused on the quiet figure lying on the granite table. Hadrian had prepared himself for a very different vision than the one he gazed at now. This was not the bloated, discolored corpse he had expected but a seemingly fresh, beautiful image of a sleeping youth. The wax image lying next to the body looked eerily like a twin of the youth, and the effect made the emperor swoon slightly. The straps of his cuirass groaned in protest as Hadrian caught his balance and raised himself to his full height. It was this sound that first caught the huddled group's attention, followed by the vision of the emperor in his gilded armor under a spotless white cloak banded in deep purple. Although they fell to their knees in his presence, they kept their eyes on his bearded figure as he made his way toward the body of his beloved. This was not the grief-stricken old man the priests had seen months before, but a rigid, majestic monarch visiting his personal god. Only his face betrayed the emotion he felt as he approached the twin forms of Antinous. The skills of the priests and artists were staggering, and he felt a perverse thrill at the vision before him. The perfection of the preservation would ensure the accuracy of the sculptures he would commission as well as the worlds knowledge of the boy's beauty. Standing beside the silent form of his beloved, Hadrian inhaled the scent of myrrh, lily, orange, and sandalwood that rose from the perfumed body. The boy never wore such scents. But then, this was no longer a boy, but a god. *His own god.* Yet even as he stood and admired the skill of the embalmers, he acknowledged that the life as he knew it was gone. This was a beautiful lantern with no flame. All the skills in Egypt could not restore that. His Beloved was dead, and there was still so much work to be done.

The soon after visiting the Temple of Ramses II, Hadrian crossed the river from Hermopolis to where the filthy mud brick village of Hir-wer once stood on the right bank of the Nile. It was on this bank that the body was discovered. And it was here that Hadrian was building a city worthy of his young god. As he made sure the boatmen who discovered the body were rewarded handsomely, he noted with a wry amusement that the four men who claimed to find the body now swelled to ten. But that was no matter. The village was soon razed to make room for the city, Antinoopolis, and the men needed their reward money to build new homes. From this humble place, Hadrian's architects and builders in his entourage began to raise a city of unparalleled beauty and culture. Hadrian's fevered mind projected images of pristine temples, baths, and theaters. Athletic events would join musical and theatrical competitions to create the Antinoan Games, while the new religion would be sparked with the imagination and funding of Hadrian. The priests who had traveled from Alexandria and participated in the embalming of Antinous were more than willing to remain here to found the temples of the new cult. As Greeks in Alexandria, they were considered outsiders. Here they would be among the elite. Hadrian would hand pick the priests of Antinous, and eventually, the epistles and prayers would also be of his own hand.

The next day, as Hadrian stood silently beside the scented and preserved body of Antinous, the priests and artisans remained prostrate before the emperor and his Beloved. From somewhere in the darkness of the temple, an ancient melody was being plucked from a solitary lyre. Years earlier, on the dusty shelves of the Alexandrian Library, a Hurrian hymn from Ugarit had been discovered during Hadrian's first visit. The tune had been composed about fifteen hundred years earlier and was played for the first time since then for the future emperor. Hadrian was so moved by the ancient melody that he had the Ugaritis script of the fragile manuscript copied and distributed to his personal musicians. The tune followed the emperor through out his wanderings and had found its way to this musty temple. Lost in his memories, Hadrian made his way to a gilded bench and sat in silent reverence. The priests rose from the cool granite floor and discreetly slipped away toward the temple's west-facing pylons. The shallow waters of the west bank of the Nile came close to the massive structure, and so, there the barge that carried the emperor to the temple complex and a small ceremonial boat waited to bring the body of the emperor's favorite to the palace at Hermopolis. Oddly, they found in the small craft not one coffin but two. Both were of gilt gold, but only one had a solid cover. The other had a lid set with a thick sheet of glass that would, from what the small group could discern, rest over the head and chest of the corpse. *But why two coffins?* As the carved figures of a worshipping Ramses II stared down from the outer face of the pylon walls, the priests removed, with great effort, the coffins from the small boat. Both the Egyptian and Greco-Alexandrian priests glanced at each other in confusion. Only the Alexandrian priests had a glimmer of an idea for the purpose of the second container. The wax figure would be, by Roman tradition, the image to be gazed upon by the mourners, while the actual corpse would be laid upon a pyre to be cremated. What made no sense was that the corpse had been embalmed with great ceremony and skill in the Egyptian tradition. It was obvious Hadrian had no intention to cremate the actual body of Antinous. Once again, two cultures were used for the grieving emperor's plans. With the coffins placed on the gilded wagon that waited on the riverbank, the priests wheeled them into the temple through the massive entrance between the outer pylons and past the Colonnade of the First Court. The wheels of the brightly painted cart complained under the weight of the two coffins, and their low squeal echoed off the forest of columns in the hypostyle hall as they reached the inner sanctuary. There they found the emperor seated at the foot of the wide granite table, drawing furiously on an array of papyrus sheets. Looking up, he motioned the group to come forward as he raised himself, with some effort, to his feet. He directed the priests to remove the covers of the coffins as he walked to the wax figure and its covering of fine linen. The dressing of the figure was identical to that of the actual body, and the dual presence was still disconcerting to Hadrian. But the drawings he had done while the priests were collecting the coffins had done much to clear his mind and set the future back in focus. Antinous was dead. There was nothing he could do about that. But Antinoopolis was coming alive in the grieving man's drawings and sketches, as well as the marble and granite used for the new city. As he handed the stack of papyrus to his chief architects who had been waiting the shadows of the vast temple, he felt a reentry into life. Although the pain of his loss had far from subsided, the ever pragmatic Roman knew when he had reached a situation that was beyond his control. Just as he had relinquished the provinces along the Euphrates when he realized they could not be adequately controlled, so too he released control of this tragedy to the gods and moved on to gestures within his grasp.

The gesture he was formulating was going to be a very grand, one that would reflect the vastness of his emotions. Emotions he had barely come to terms with at this point. He had long intended to gift the Greek Egyptians with a new city that would reflect the culture and heritage of their ancestors in a purer sense than the decadence of Alexandria. Now, he had found the perfect location and excuse. His beloved Greek boy would become the nucleus of a Greco river city that would preserve and honor his name. He knew the city would have to be built around the temple of Antinous and that the temple would have to contain the body of the new god. But how was he to part with it? How could he leave his Beloved even in death? As he gazed earlier upon the wax effigy lying beside the corpse, the answer made its appearance. Unknown to the Egyptian priests, it would be the coffin with the wax effigy that would journey past the seated colossi of Rameses and the Temple of Amon to the Temple of Thoth. There it would be blessed and rituals of deification would raise Antinous to realm of the gods. It would remain there, under guard, until his temple was finished and the coffin could be brought to his new sanctuary. There it would be sealed in a vast tomb where it would remain, venerated but unapproachable. As far as the world knew, the remains of Antinous would be interred in his temple in Antinoopolis. But in reality, the precious corpse would travel with Hadrian to Rome, to be interred in a tomb at Villa Adrianna.

Under Hadrian's watchful eyes, the Alexandrian priests gently lowered the body of Antinous into the golden coffin as it lay on the temple floor, then sealed the coffin with the glass paneled lid. The thickness of the glass sheet distorted the features just enough to make the Egyptians believe it was the wax image. They then wrapped the chest and head of the wax figure with linen in the Egyptian style, lowered the golden mask of Antinous's likeness over the face and placed it into the solid lidded coffin. The casket was being lowered onto the gilded wagon just as the temple priests were returning from their meal in the inner courtyard.

The wax figure, they were told, was in the glass-lidded casket and, in the Roman tradition, would accompany the emperor on his journey to Rome through Alexandria. The Egyptian priests, knowing little of what they considered a barbaric Roman ritual, accepted this explanation and proceeded to bring the gilded wagon to the Temple of Thoth. Once the wagon was safely far enough away, the Alexandrian priests carried the coffin with the body of the beloved to the small craft that waited on the river. Hadrian boarded the larger barge with his guards while the priests stepped aboard the ceremonial craft and pushed it away from the riverbank. The sun was setting into the vast expanse of the horizon as the strange procession made its way toward Hermopolis. But as the reddish light of Ra reached the gilded resting place of Antinous and covered the coffin, it cast an unearthly glow that radiated from the low craft. Except for the rhythmic slap of the oars that churned the thick water, no other sound could be heard. Even the ibis, feasting on the small frogs among the reeds along the riverbank stopped their feeding and gazed imperiously at the eerie scene before them. The sails of the barge that carried the emperor hovered protectively, close behind the small boat. At the helm was Hadrian, his watchful eyes never leaving the rose-colored glow that contained the body of his beloved. Despite all efforts to contain himself, he could not stop the flow of tears that now soaked his beard and made it glisten in the setting sun. The hypnotic splash of the oars lulled Hadrian as he contemplated the future that stretched before him. Yet before they reach the shore, the tears had dried; and the plans in his mind, conceived in tragedy, had reached their final epiphany.

Chapter Four

A Gilded Companion

I dreamt of a lighthouse
A beacon the likes of which
Alexandria had never seen.
It burned so brightly for a time
It angered the stars
And the constellations frowned down.
It blazed like burnished bronze in sunlight,
Then vanished
Suddenly.
In the unexpected darkness
I searched the sky for help,
And saw you
Blazing
Under the breast of Zeus.
I now dreamt of a lighthouse
Cold and sightless.
And in the darkness it no longer defied
I stumbled
Then drowned in sorrow.

The dignity with which Hadrian held himself was not unusual for the court, but the lack of mirth and wit was chilling. After laying the cornerstone for the new city and fine-tuning the layout of the many temples, baths, and stadiums that would be built there, the emperor began his return journey to Alexandria with its gossip and wild rumors. His interaction with the court was mechanical now because his mind was filled with memories and guilt. Even after all these passing months, he could not fathom the sacrifice he knew had been made in his name. His most cherished possession was taken away from him through misunderstanding and selfishness. The misunderstanding was Antinous's, and the selfishness was his own. He made his way through daily life, frozen not just in grief as many supposed, but in the knowledge that he had brought this tragedy upon himself. He had forced the boy's hand in a dangerous game, and both he and the boy lost. Hadrian would be forever the slave of a memory. And with an almost obscene pleasure, he tortured himself with that memory. Although the tears had dried, the salt that remained was still bitter. It flavored everything around him and smoldered in his wounds. Death, like night, could not come quickly enough. Yet the boy had removed death as an option with the sacrifice of his own life, and just as the youth's corpse was now merely an empty shell, so was Hadrian's. But one had the luxury of lying at peace in an ornate box, while the other had to go on as if living.

As the imperial entourage floated down the Nile toward Alexandria, the streets of the cities and towns along the way ran deep with malicious lies and half-truths about the tragic emperor. They filtered across the waters into the many barges that passed them until even the court of the empress Sabina caught wind of them. The empress herself was too lost in her own thoughts to acknowledge them, but her court was less distracted and caught bits and pieces of each rumor and wove their own tapestry of atrocious tales. The aging Julia Balbilla was especially keen to pass on the lurid tales in order to placate the empress's dangerous animosity toward her. She knew Sabina blamed her for filling the youth's mind with thoughts of noble sacrifice and the power of destiny. "How was I to know," muttered Julia into her veil, "the boy would be so susceptible to my own fevered fantasies?" After attempting to divert the empress's suspicions from herself to no avail, Julia slipped away in the dark recesses of the great barge and calculated her next move.

The great wound in Hadrian's life remained fresh throughout December, and the arrival of January did nothing to alleviate the ache. Stops at temples and shrines along the way down the river also did little to dull the pain. He was growing tired of the endless procession of lifeless likenesses of the dead pharaohs, their monumentality weighing down on him as much as the weight of the ache within. It was during one of these tedious visits that the wound was torn open again. After tiring from navigating his way through the endless columns of yet another temple, Hadrian sat at the base of a limestone sphinx that joined a long procession lining the entry route to the temple. As his mind wandered, he realized the end of December was the time of Antinous's birth. This revelation tore through him like an arid wind and left him breathless with mind-numbing grief. All the sorrow came flooding back to him as the tools he had developed to stem the tide failed him. As he gazed at the vastness that was Egypt, he realized the boy had been as enigmatic and unconquerable as this ancient land. *Just when one thinks there is submission and subjugation, the sands shift, and the image disappears.* Gathering whatever strength he could, Hadrian strode woodenly toward the waiting barge and climbed aboard, praying that the tears would hold until he reached his quarters.

Once there, they flowed, and the gilded box that lay silently in the corner of his cabin glistened from the tears he shed. Resting his head on the cool gold leaf, he whispered the name of his Beloved repeatedly until it became a mystical chant. A spasm of grief shook him as he clung to the coffin. "Merciful gods, will this ever end?" he whispered as the tears subsided and his strength drained from him until he lay crumpled on the wooden floor. For a while, he lay silent, staring at the fine inlay of the cabin floor as he struggled to will his mind to blankness. A moment of mindlessness, even if brief, was like a small death, a reprieve from the pain of truth. A deep breath shuddered through him as he lifted himself from the foot of the coffin. Tears still clouded his vision as the gold leaf shimmered like waves of liquid light before his eyes. He had finally found something more horrible than death—life undesired. There, under a slender cover of gilded cedar, lay his beloved boy. Yet for all the world, they were on opposite sides of the River Styx. He loved the boy for his body, and now that was all he had left of him. The irony slashed open another yet wound as a companion to the others. The love of this fatal boy would bloody him as no war ever could.

Drifting slowly toward the great desk that held his drawings for Antinoopolis still in transition, Hadrian saw the grandiosity of his plans and the ridicule those plans could expose him to. But this was the only weapon he had to continue his will to live. Plans, sculptures, and an embalmed body that would serve as a reminder of the great love he had wasted. Something broke in Hadrian at that moment. He slowly lifted the lid of the coffin and, for a moment, stared intently at the pristine figure inside. "You were my paradise while you lived, be now my hell in death," he whispered. He closed the coffin silently, and, with all emotion drained from him, made his way back into the sunlight.

Chapter Five

Brothers, Even in Death

Hadrian's reception upon his return to Alexandrian was muted, either out of respect or distain. With the Alexandrians, it was difficult to tell. Yet to all those present, the reception seemed to go unnoticed by the emperor. Riding directly to the palace in the Brucheum, he was greeted by letters of extravagant praise for the departed. The renowned writer, Pancrates, presented the emperor with an ambitious, if not lack luster, poem, the length of time for its composition belied its quality. It was what the work was written on was of more interest to Hadrian. A pale green cabbage had been cured, pressed, and dried to create a translucent parchment of a subtle hue. More subtle perhaps than Pancrate's epic rambling. The emperor stated absentmindedly at the parchment without truly seeing the content. Numerous other poets and writers littered his desk with their own attempts at glorifying the youth and justifying his death. To Hadrian's mind, they were the scribblings of the living audaciously attempting to explain the unexplainable. Hadrian suffered the feigned grief of the court in silence. The only group he truly believed was from the Greek quarters. They had lost one of their own, and their expressions of sorrow and consolation were far more endurable.

The coffin that contained Antinous remained onboard the barge. The emperor refused to subject it to the vulgar scrutiny of the masses or even the court for that matter. A delegation from Bithynia arrived at midmorning, and the emperor greeted them with some enthusiasm. They expressed their intent on building a temple in Antinous's honor, and Hadrian gifted them with the funds to do so. The problem of what to do with the body weighed constantly on Hadrian's mind. While the Egyptian priests lead the veneration of Antinous as Osiris and felt entitled to possession of the corpse, the Bithynians, understandable, also felt a sense of ownership. The idea of returning the youth to his birthplace was tempting. Yet Hadrian knew this could never happen. It was difficult enough to view the barge that carried the coffin from his chambers in the palace and feel a deep sense of separation. How could he hand over the youth to a province he would rarely see. No, he would soon return to Rome, and so would Antinous.

Lucius had remained alongside the emperor during the journey, a silent presence that seemed to offer little comfort. He felt his place was at Hadrian's side, yet he wished he was back in Rome and at the side of his new wife, now the mother of his first child. For Pedanius Fuscus, the days were long and uncomfortable. Since Antinous's death, Hadrian's distain for his great nephew was no longer cloaked in civility. The boy complained to the empress at first, but quickly realized she could do little for him. He contented himself with remaining in the shadows and watching the drama from afar. Even with Antinous dead, the presence of the emperor's favorite was still unpalatably strong. It permeated the air around Caesar and, as a result, the court. With Antinous's death, Fuscus hoped he could now influence the emperor and gain favor as the heir apparent. But it seemed as if a wall had been built around his great uncle, impenetrable by all except a select few. Lucius was one of those, as was the tutor Chabrais and the brothers Caesernii. The rest of the world, it seemed, was to be granted no access to the emperor on a personal level. As a result, a sullen Pedantus spent more of his time with the empress and bided his time.

The brothers Caesernii, Macedo and Statianus had acquired an unusual status in Hadrian's inner circle. Clearly beloved by Antinous, they were held in high regard in Hadrian's eyes. Handsome and good natured, they had brought a sense of calm and ease to Antinous's life while bringing out the boy that had never completely gone away. Yet while the presence of these two youths was comforting in one sense, it was disturbing in another. The sorrow in their eyes could not be denied, nor would it go away. They clearly missed their companion, and to see the two brothers bereft of the presence of Antinous became more painful for Hadrian as the days passed.

It was just past midday, two weeks into the court's stay in Alexandria, when Hadrian viewed the brothers from his window as they made their way to the docks below. Both carried a bundle of laurel and lilies bound together with vines of sweet jasmine. Their destination was clear, and the sight of the forlorn brothers on their pilgrimage tore into the emperor. Lost in his own grief, he had forgotten the impact the loss had on others. Slipping down a narrow passageway to the staircase leading to a small side street, Hadrian hurried to follow the youths to their destination. At this hour, the streets were all but deserted, affording the emperor of Rome a nearly invisible path to the docks. He noticed that not a word passed between the youths as they made their way to the barge that carried its precious cargo. The guards seemed so used to their presence that they were allowed to board the vessel without pause. Hadrian had followed so closely he could detect the scent of the fragrant bouquets as it trailed behind them. Yet he waited in the shadows until the brothers disappeared into the cabin before he made his presence known to the guards. The guards, startled by his sudden and unexpected arrival, saluted briskly but were unable to hide the shock in their faces. One guard asked permission to address the emperor, which was granted. "Great Caesar, the youths had been visiting every day since their arrival in the port city. I saw no harm in their homage, and," he added with some hesitation, "I thought you would be pleased by it." Hadrian said nothing, but while his smile was weary, it was warmer than any he had managed in months. He nodded and saluted the guards as he passed them and made his way to his private quarters. Quietly, he stepped to the threshold of the cabin and stood silent as he viewed the poignant scene in the shadows. The brothers knelt silently before the golden coffin, still clutching their floral offerings. It was the youngest, Macedo, who gathered the bouquets from the previous day, then rose to dispose of them through the grated window of the cabin as Statianus replaced them with fresh offerings. Turning from the window, Macedo suddenly froze in place. Reflected in the bronze mirror by the imperial desk was the emperor. Turning quickly, he faced Hadrian and fell to his knees. Statianus, still absorbed in the task before him, failed to notice the drama unfolding. The emperor walked slowly toward Macedo and embraced the youth with an emotion that was both painful and a release. "Dear brother of my Beloved, the Golden One watches over you with love," whispered Hadrian.

Overcome, Macedo said nothing as together they wept for their beloved companion and made their way to the coffin. The sun had already found its way there through the window and settled on the gilding, setting it ablaze. By now, Statianus had risen and bowed deeply to the emperor, who in turn embraced the youth with the same emotion as he had with his brother. Together, they gazed down at the slender coffin as the scent of cedar mixed with the floral offerings at their feet.

The sweet homage of the brothers suddenly filled Hadrian with shame and remorse. He had distanced himself from this painful reality while these pale youths faced the sorrow of the loss of their companion and paid homage to him every day. The emperor offered the youths chairs beside a massive table as he settled himself on one of its corners. He spoke as quickly as the thoughts came to him as he offered each of the youths a tribute for their loyalty and friendship toward himself as well as his beloved Antinous. He reminded the brothers that they were at the age when they were expected to marry and start families of their own. In a calm voice, he made an offer of land and considerable fortunes if they returned to Rome to continue their lives in peace. The brothers seemed hurt at first, but the sorrow in Hadrian's gaze made them face the reality that their presence only served as a reminder of Antinous and happier days—days Caesar would never see again. They could do nothing more than thank the emperor graciously before asking that they be allowed to remain in Alexandria until the emperor's flotilla returned to Hermopolis. With that agreed upon, the three disembarked from the vessel and walked silently toward the palace.

Chapter Six

Bound by Darkness

Another week passed before the emperor was ready to return Hermpolis. Along with the Caesernii brothers, Lucius also prepared to return to Rome and his new family. It was with mixed emotions that he left Hadrian. But then, he also left the nightmare this journey had become. Hadrian continued to drift in a haze of bitterness and grief, but Lucius noticed that these emotions were slowly transforming into something more lethal. Always mercurial, the emperor had always masked his harsher side with patience and wisdom. Lucius watched as those veneers slowly chipped away and a cold, bloodless man was revealed. He had witnessed Hadrian's streak of cruelty even toward his beloved Antinous. But that had been fleeting and quickly atoned for. Now, there was no one to maintain the balance, and the monster within was slowly stirring. Hadrian was becoming a victim of his own darkness; something Lucius did not wish to witness. His new wife and child were the perfect excuse for his return to Rome. With surprising ease, Hadrian consented to the departure, and a ship was prepared for the voyage.

As Hadrian watched Lucius's ship depart for Rome, he paused in the long columned corridor that lead to the empress's chambers.

The open-air passage allowed him to enjoy the same cool wind that filled the sails of the departing vessel and offered time to reflect on what his conversation with his wife would involve. Sabina had sent polite and dignified missives to the court in regards to the loss of Antinous. The court was not startled by her official recognition of the youth's death. They had known, as courts always do, the comings and goings of everyone in the palaces. The courtiers mutely observed the visits to Sabina by Antinous; they whispered among themselves but remained silent in the presence of the emperor. They had also noticed the lightened mood that prevailed after each of those visits; the warmth of his presence lingered, as would the fragrance of an exotic bloom. The court observed with great curiosity the effect Antinous had on the empress as her conversation, though still restrained, became somewhat more animated. Her eyes shone with a warmth she revealed to few, a warmth that continued for a time after his departure. She had found, as had her courtiers, an effortless and somewhat elegant charm under the youth's beauty. Without realizing it, she had become as beguiled by the youth as her husband was. And it was within the walls of her palace in Alexandria that she began to formulate the idea of Antinous becoming the heir to her husband's throne through adoption. While the impossibility of that happening always cut through the soft mist of her daydreams, the thought of it tantalized her just the same. Now, that dream was dust. And as she listened to the heavy thud of her husband's footsteps announcing his arrival, she found one more reason to resent and despise him.

Sabina had not seen her husband close up in nearly two months. Normally, that made little difference; but today, she was taken aback by his appearance. The robust swagger was gone, as was the haughty distain she normally saw in his face. In their place was the somber gait of an ageing man and a face that revealed the extent of his loss. Setting aside her ever-present sewing, she rose and, sweeping past her bowing servants, approached her husband and embraced him. Although startled by this sudden display of warmth from his wife, Hadrian seemed grateful for any affection afforded him at this point. "You honor me with your embrace, Sabina. And I might add, surprise me," Hadrian spoke quietly and with great effort to hide his grief. "I honor your Antinous and the pain of your loss," Sabina replied. Unnoticed by the emperor, the courtiers of Sabina's entourage remained in the shadows, riveted by the unusual sight of Hadrian and Sabina's embrace. For anyone unfamiliar with their relationship, the scene was that of two parents consoling each other on the loss of a child. And in many ways, this truly was the case. Hadrian's love for Antinous had passed from passionate lover to proud father. For Sabina, he was the child she would never have. Antinous's finer qualities had joined the two in a sense of harmony and mutual respect, even if they accepted this begrudgingly at times. Now it was his loss that bound them together, although each was to deal with that loss in their own way.

Hadrian accepted a chair that was offered him and seated himself next to his wife. It was then that he noticed the courtiers huddled uncomfortably in the shadows, which he acknowledged with a curt nod. Sabina, in an effort to assert her authority, turned to her court and dismissed them with a wave of her hand, saying, "Leave us. My husband and I wish to speak in private." She then reached down to retrieve her sewing. More of a habit than a desire, her handiwork helped her maintain her composure as this unusual scene began to play itself out. Hadrian, taken aback by the familiarity his wife rarely displayed, settled himself more comfortably in his chair and absorbed this brief domestic encounter. Silently, Sabina listened to Hadrian's description of the sarcophagus he had designed for Antinous, as well as his plans for the final resting place. Having seen the beginnings of the construction of Antinoopolis, Sabina was surprised to learn that the actual corpse would not rest there. *No,* she thought bitterly, *even in death, Hadrian could not relinquish the boy.* Antinoopolis, for all its beauty and grandeur, would be an empty tomb. Its namesake would be carried away to Hadrian's vast villa outside of Rome so that the lover and beloved would never be far from each other. Death had elevated the youth to a deity, and the simple boy whose presence she had come to cherish was gone. He was now a god to be worshiped and promoted to a level that suited Hadrian's purpose. He would let neither body nor spirit ever leave him. *And this will be his undoing.*

Lost in her own thoughts, Sabina failed to notice the silence stare of her husband. *As inscrutable as a sphinx,* he thought. *At least the boy had brought out her human side at times.* He was still unaware of the numerous visits she had received from the youth and so unaware of the depth of her sorrow. Yet her face betrayed a remnant of that emotion and it satisfied him. Suddenly, Sabina turned and stared at her husband. "Why?" The question came out in a hoarse whisper. "Why?" she repeated while continuing to stare at her husband for an answer. Startled by the question that sounded uncomfortably like an accusation, Hadrian turned away, unwilling to reveal to his wife the tears he could not hold back.

Regaining his composure, Hadrian rose stiffly from his chair and without a word bent down to kiss his wife on her forehead. He noted with satisfaction the quality of the cameos in her diadem and the somber strands of black pearls woven in her hair. She was always, if nothing else, appropriate and in good taste. Wrapping his cloak lightly around himself, Hadrian announced his plan to return to Antinoopolis while his wife would return to Rome. And as if finishing the last act of a drama, he bowed slightly and strode away with the uncomfortable feeling his silence spoke more than he had wished.

Chapter Seven

Leaving Antinoopolis

The imperial barge sailed to Hermopolis for the last time. Hadrian chose to remain on the barge, rather than use the ancient palace as he had done before. The memories in those halls were far too fresh and painful, even after all these months. And besides, the purpose of the voyage was to oversee the building of Antinoopolis, and that city's namesake lay silently in the royal cabin. Day after day, the emperor walked the broad streets of the emerging city, inspecting every building, fountain and obelisk. Crates of sculptures arrived almost daily from around the empire, and before the dust had settled after they reached the ground, Hadrian was prying them open to inspect the quality of each piece and designate their resting place. A number of portrayals of Antinous as an Egyptian god, one in basalt, the others in granite, were placed on a barge to be sent to Alexandria and then on to Rome. As he rounded the corner of the reflecting pool, he stopped momentarily at a tall circular temple at one end. Elevated atop a small knoll, the granite columns of the temple caught the setting rays of the sun and cast a shadow across the massive plinth it sheltered. Inscribed into the stone was the promise of a colossal statue of Antinous/Epiphanes by Fidus Aquila. Hadrian smiled at the thought of the frugal Aquila parting with what must have been a fortune in gold coins to erect this tribute in bronze. This gift to the city was meant to secure his position as the administrative governor of Antinoopolis, a position he coveted and was proving to be very adept at. While the priests chanted and burned offerings to the new god, Aquila saw to the emergence of the sacred city and the cult that would emanate from its walls.

The sun was already setting as Hadrian made his final walk of the day down the main thoroughfare. He turned and stared for a moment at the great jets of water that rose up from the reflecting pool that spread like a lake before the Temple of Antinous. Suddenly, as if as a sign from the new god himself, the jets ceased their upward flight, and the pool became deathly still. Disgruntled but too tired to bother with the problem, Caesar turned away and headed toward the bank of the river. As a small boat returned him to his barge, he sat with his back towards the days work, while the setting sun erased the deep creases in his face and silhouetted the building in progress, fragments of colonnades and temples that rose from a once desolate land. The inner sanctuary in the main temple to Antinous was finished and ready to receive the coffin that was in the possession of the Egyptian priests. For all its beauty, Hadrian knew the temple was an empty shell that would never receive the actual remains of the new god. And once the sarcophagus was sealed in the inner chamber, no one would ever know the truth. It would be a beautiful, fitting tribute, but in the mind of the emperor, it would be just another city. He would leave with the soul of Antinoopolis still in his possession and leave behind only marble images of his beloved.

From the barge, Hadrian continued gazing at the setting sun as it traveled down the newly erected columns. It was twilight in Antinoopolis, and hovering over the city was a veil of stars, reminiscent of the lapis tiled ceiling in Hadrian's bedchamber at the Villa Adriana. Memories of what transpired there for too few years filled Hadrian's mind and tore through his heart until he was forced to seat himself on the deck of the royal barge. As night fell and the vast Egyptian sky reflected off the dark Nile waters, he had never felt so alone. For over fifty years, he had led a life full of purpose; now there seemed to be none. All the platitudes that poured in from poets and writers throughout the empire fell short of their mortal subject that lay stiff and waxen in a golden box. There too, Hadrian realized, he had been selfish. Not able to let go, he subjected the remains of his beloved to unspeakable horrors in order to hold on to the image. Now it traveled with him, a tormented spirit to haunt him in both sleep and waking hours.

He had left enough carved likenesses of the youth in Antinoopolis and Hermopolis to keep the memory of Antinous eternal. The nobles, priests, merchants, and retired soldiers who arrived in Hermopolis to prepare for their occupation of Antinoopolis all reported that the sculptures Hadrian had ordered of the youth now flooded the empire. A cult had sprung up in Greece and Asia Minor, and a beautiful sculpture of the beloved had been enshrined at Delphi. The sculptures all originated from a likeness done while Antinous was in Alexandria. A particularly accurate rendering Hadrian had reproduced after the boy's death, and the reproductions were sent far and wide throughout the empire. With luck, these renderings were faithfully copied and would be waiting for him during his travels. Where there were acceptable images, he would build temples and baths to house them. The less skillful attempts would be placed in gardens where deep shade would cloak the image and the dappled shadows would fool the eye. No sign of reverence would be ignored or go unrewarded. The cults would be sanctioned and prosperous. The image and memory of the boy would be as eternal as the river that stole his life.

Chapter Eight

The Path to Rome

It was nearly a year since the event on the riverbank, and Hadrian was eager to leave the land of massive, expressionless colossi that boasted of power long vanished. What had once seemed exotic and novel, now felt simply outlandish, decrepit. Like a guest that had lingered too long in his host's garden, Hadrian felt the chill of having long outlived his welcome. With the exception of a short venture in Judea, he had remained in the vast land of Egypt to assure the foundation of Antinoopolis and the arrival of its residents. He oversaw the building of palaces for the new nobles and their families, as well as the baths, athletic sites, and theaters. He personally wrote the prayers and chants for the priests of the Temple of Antinous and arranged for annual games and theatrical events to be held in honor of the new god. It was only when he felt all was in order, that he was inclined to leave, knowing too well he would never return.

Yet for all his continued grief, Hadrian was pleased at the reception the Egyptians had give their new god. They had proclaimed a miracle in Antinous's name by crediting his sacrifice for the perfect inundation of the Nile on this, the year after his death. The reports from deep in the south of Egypt earlier in the summer were more favorable than had been hoped. The *Nilometers* or carved steps at the island of Abu were traditionally the first measurements to be dispatched, being that it was the first outpost where the rising waters gave an indication of their benevolence for that year. From the Temple of *Khnum*, the ram-headed god of the Inundation, Hadrian received reports of the rising waters, along with sheets of papyrus illustrating in jewel like colors the goddess of the flood, *Mehet Weret* embracing Antinous in his guise of Osiris. The importance of the Nile and the fertility it brought each year made the flooding vital to the well being of Egypt. For the people of Egypt, it was not much of a stretch of the imagination to connect Antinous's death to this year's favorable water level. They had proclaimed him a god, and as such, he interceded on their behalf for the gods to bestow their grace upon the people.

All this took place under the gaze of the dog star Sirius, and it was he that the Egyptians turned to as the herald of the flood time. This year, all the gods were in harmony, and soon, the flood would reach the desert, and flowers would bloom in the barren red soil. For Hadrian, the flooding this year had a more practical significance. The empire, and Rome in particular, depended on the grain shipments from Egypt. The favorable flood meant a plentiful harvest and a well-fed Rome. The news of this would make his return to the city more auspicious. But secretly, it was the inclusion of Antinous as the miracle for this bounty that pleased Hadrian even more, for it vindicated the deification of his beloved in the eyes of the empire. And when the cult statue of the youth finally stands above the last empty altar in the Pantheon, only the foolish will question its worthiness to be there. It would take courage to face down a certain senator in this matter. But it will be an old man's defiance, a currency of little value.

As he watched from the upper deck of his barge cabin, these thoughts flooded the emperor's mind as the new city grew smaller in the distance. The effect of the sun's shimmer on the desert sand gave an ethereal aura to the pristine whiteness of the marble buildings and the golden dome of Antinous's temple. The effect was unsettling. It was as if the sun had made a massive funereal pyre of the city as soon as its protector had left. No matter. The real treasure was with him in its cedar box. Waiting for him in Alexandria would be a carved alabaster sarcophagus that would hold the precious corpse in its final resting place. Soon, the gentle roll of the barge and the intensity of Ra's glow lulled Hadrian to a semi sleep. But it was not until he had conjured up the face of his beloved and embraced that vision in his mind did he truly sleep.

The imperial entourage's stay in Alexandria was a brief one. Hadrian inspected the crates of sculptures as he had done in Hermopolis and paid special attention to a pink granite obelisk that rested in its bed of straw. The emperor ordered the spire to be made upright so as to inspect the script that covered the four sides. On what would be the most important panel, the eastern face, Antinous was represented as being presented to the god Ra-Harakte with a long prayer of the now deified youth. The prayer praises Hadrian and the empress Sabina and requests of the god protection of these mortals. Antinous speaks to Ra as a father and prays to him as his son. All around the obelisk, the hieroglyphs proclaim Antinous as god and portray him being presented to three other gods of Egypt. As the priests translated the hieroglyphs just as Hadrian had transcribed, he felt the satisfaction of knowing he was bringing the perfect grave marker with him to Rome. But, being a suspicious man, he left the southern face blank, to be filled in when the obelisk was about to be put in place. Here, it would declare its purpose to all the residents and visitors to his Villa Adriana.

As the obelisk was gently lowered back into the wooden crate, Hadrian pondered the problems he would have in Rome regarding the youth's deification. While the rest of the empire willingly accepted the entry of a new god, Hadrian knew all of Roman society would be scandalized by the inclusion of this boy to the Pantheon of the empire's gods. By embracing the Egyptian deification as fact, it was easier to assimilate him to the Greek gods as the Greek provinces were eager to do. After Greece, Rome would follow. Antinous would not return to Rome as a dead ephebe, but as a god worthy of all the honors his grieving lover would shower upon him.

As the day grew to a close and the ships had received their precious cargo, Hadrian slowly returned to the palace for what he felt would be his last time. Age was making itself known to him daily and often. As he paused to rub his aching shoulders, his eyes caught the sight of the Eagle constellation. The star of Antinous shimmered brightly within the scattering of stars and seemed to ease the ache in Hadrian's shoulders, but not his heart. The heavy weight there would not ease with so much retribution still due. Knowing morning would come quickly, Hadrian climbed the steps of the palace and, with a weary salute to his guards, headed toward the comforting darkness of his chambers.

The morning's light had not yet reached the imperial bedchamber of the Alexandrian palace. Yet Hadrian was already risen and dressed, his servants scurrying about silently as they packed the rest of their master's belongings in camphor chests. A hanging oil lamp hovered over a small table that stood beside a gilt wood chair, a chair Hadrian slowly lowered himself into. On the table, in a shallow silver bowl, a single lotus shivered in the water. The movement of the chair had tapped the table and produced a ripple in the bowl. The rosy hue of the blossom, newly named the Antinoeios, was reminiscent of the parts of the youth his lover knew so well. The darker inner pedals resembled the full mouth Hadrian still hungered for. The outer pedals were the color of the boy's supple flesh, the taste of which was still such a vibrant memory. This was the color Hadrian preferred. The bluish variation resembled death, and he had enough of death for now. It pleased the emperor that the legend behind the color of the lotus was that the red of the bloom was from the blood of the Mauritanian lion he had killed in Libya, the beast that had threatened Antinous's life. The originator of that legend, the poet Pancrates, was duly rewarded for his creativity with a prized and lucrative position in the Temple of the Muses. Others quickly joined in the chorus of praise for the bloom, and Hadrian was pleased with their efforts, but less impressed. The lotus was a summer flower, and it was summer that Hadrian wished most to remember.

The activity of the servant had ceased, and Hadrian found himself alone in the soft glow of the lamp. But even those four flickering tongues of light were about to leave him. Having been burning all night, the oil was running low, and the flames were slowly dying. Leaning back in his chair, Hadrian gazed up at the lamp and saw more death. This had become, for him, a land of death he was eager to leave. From his chair, he could see the ships waiting to take him to Rome; and in less than a week, he would be back at his villa, the world of his design and his to control. So much had happened since he was last there. It was as if a dream had played itself out, its story ending cruelly where it began so brightly.

The servant returned to admit the prefect of the emperor's personal bodyguards, the Praetorians. The ships were ready for his sovereign's arrival, and Lucius Didius was there to escort him to the pier. Once in the service of Quintus Marcius Turbo, he began with Legion III Cyrenaica from the province of Cyrene. Hadrian had met him during a revolt in Judea in 117 when the legion was stationed in Alexandria. One of the emperor's most trusted guards, Lucius, personally oversaw five of the thousand man *cohorts* that were under the person command of the emperor. The remaining five cohorts, under the command of Lucius's second in command, Marcus Felix, had left earlier with the empress. Lucius had been with Hadrian during his travels with Antinous and witnessed the discovery of the beloved's body on the riverbank of the Nile. He had taken over for his subordinate, Fabius, whose cloak had been used to cover the youth's corpse. Despite the confusion that followed, Lucius had the foresight to assure the return of the captain's cloak, honoring the stern practicality of the man. It was then too that Lucius accepted Fabius's request for retirement and provided the five thousand denarii, grant of land, and military diploma due his long years of service. Lucius had seen much and said little.

Wrapping his deep purple cloak around himself with a single movement, Hadrian swept past the captain just as the last flickers of the lamp died out. As he strode through the vast colonnaded atrium and the frescoed vestibulum, he noticed the court on the pier waiting to board the ships. Chabrias waited at the foot of the palace steps, and Hadrian could sense Antinous's old friend and tutor was searching his face for some sign of his state of mind. But Hadrian was eager to board his ship and had no time for the old man's curiosity. Gripping him by his boney shoulders, the emperor guided Chabrias to the pier and up the ramp to the deck of the vast ship. The tutor's sense of loss was palpable and filled the air with a sorrow the emperor had tried hard to avoid. He would have to keep the old man at a distance during this voyage if he was to retain his sanity. After walking Chabrias to his cabin, Hadrian walked to the bow of the ship just as the oars were beginning their rhythmic splash and the ship glided gracefully from the pier. He purposely kept his back to the city he was leaving, his eyes fixed on the great lighthouse that loomed before him. *Such squalor amidst such grandeur.* He left all this with the best of what he learned engraved in his mind, to later embellish his personal world of the Villa Adriana. As he turned and headed toward his cabin, his mind whirled with the images of columns, temples, and a multitude of sculptures, all with the face of Antinous. Leaving this land of the dead, he was returning to a world of deceit and social scrutiny. But safe in the vastness of the villa, he will change the Rome that he was returning to. The axis of power would be shifted to the world of his making, and that world, whether Rome liked it or not, would include reminders of his beloved.

Chapter Nine

Respite at Sea

Hadrian was amazed that the lateness of the morning when he finally stirred from sleep. His servant had been in earlier to remove from the long walnut table, the remains of the previous evening's late dinner. Plates of half-eaten figs, fried veal, and boiled eggs were scattered amidst rolls of plans and drawings, as well as sheets of poetry and autobiographical scrawling. Hadrian had no fear regarding the man's discretion; he could neither read nor write. The sheets had been stacked in no particular order; instructions for the unloading of the treasures from Egypt as well as listings of grain shipments bound for Rome, mingled with outpourings of love and regret set in stanzas and parameters written late in the night. Scrolls were stacked according to size while pens and opaline glass inkpots stood in pleasing arrangements that had nothing to do with function. Strangely, one of the reasons Hadrian kept him on was the servant's blissful ignorance. Scholastically blind and mute, he could divulge no secrets that were written down. And his quiet tidiness pleased his master. Hadrian rose from his bed, tipping over an empty glass beaker that held wine from the night before, wine needed for the sleep that refused to come. The sound of glass hitting the silver tray by the bed brought the servant into the room as the emperor walked to the basin by the grated window of his cabin. The servant hurriedly left the cabin again and returned with a pitcher of heated water to pour into the empty basin. Gazing intently into the bronze mirror over the basin, Hadrian had not seemed to notice the lack of water in the basin, and the servant's swiftness prevented any delay in the bathing process. But a faint smile on the emperor's lips revealed the truth. The servant bowed deeply and, grateful for such a benevolent master, busied himself with the emperor's clothes for the new day. After helping the emperor into his tunic and cloak, he inquired if his master wished a breakfast of fruit, cheese, and thin pancakes of flaxseed flour or, due to the lateness of the hour, a midday meal. *In Mitulis*, or sea mussels prepared in briny Liquamen, leeks and white wine had been prepared as well as *Sarda ita Fit*, a mash of tuna fillet with dates, honey, wine, and oil garnished with quartered boiled eggs. A starter dish of *Gustum de Praecoquis*, a favorite of Hadrian's consisting of fresh, ripe apricots, white wine, Liquamen, honey, Passum, and mint cooked with a bit of oil and cornstarch was also offered. Although these dishes were very familiar to the emperor, at sea they seemed to take on a special flavor. Liquaman, the ever-present salty fish sauce entered much of the cooking, as did Passum, the sweet wine sauce. These dishes were tasty yet sat well in the stomach during these long voyages. Hadrian was suddenly reminded of the hearty meals he shared with Antinous during their journeys. The boy found very few foods not to his liking, and his appetite was one of the many things about the boy that filled his lover with awe. Even now, whenever Hadrian tasted a dish made with *Defritum*, a concoction of boiled fig and wine, he recalled the taste of the thick syrup on Antinous's lips. In so short a time, so many memories. And even in food, there was no escape.

The emperor chose the midday meal and wished it to be served outside his quarters under the vast purple awning that fluttered just outside his door. There he could meet with a steady stream of officers, courtiers, architects, and craftsmen who he knew were anxiously waiting to speak with him. The dry calculations of weights and measures, as well as the calculations of his wily courtiers would be a welcome respite from the emotions that filled the previous night. The questions and concerns of the various men were of some importance, yet the mood of the emperor had kept most of them at bay, unable to bare the sight of such grief. But Hadrian had brought his emotions under control, and what was left was a weighty weariness that he masked with a cordial indifference. His closer courtiers and companions knew how to lighten the conversation and did so with some success. Talk of Rome and construction at the villa always lifted the emperor's spirits. However, eventually the court noticed him withdrawing from the conversation and retreating into the darkness of his memories. Even the toast and salute of Viva Hadrianus brought with it a new and different connotation. The youth may be gone, but his spirit haunted every word and gesture. The darkness of Egypt seemed to be carried with the very wind that filled the sails of their ships.

Hadrian ate, with little relish, the small feast set before him. Even as he finished the meal with a small dish of dried dates stuffed with pine nuts stewed in honeyed wine, he seemed to lose interest in the conversations that swirled around him. As he absorbed the plans and drawings presented to him by his architects, the entourage grew tired of the pall that had settled over the court and hoped the emperor's arrival in Rome and all it had to offer would distract him from his grief. Certain members of the court purposely sent beautiful young pages to serve the emperor's meals in hopes of a spark of interest. It was a dangerous game they played. They risked the misconception that they were being disrespectful of the memory of Antinous. Many had forgotten the presence of the gilded coffin in the emperor's cabin and failed to recognize the gravity of their actions. But Hadrian barely noticed the dark-haired boys as they poured his wine and set plates of food before him. His was a world of few distractions and strong purpose; it was the only way he felt any control of his sanity. On occasion a dimpled cheek would catch his eye, but it only served as a pale reflection a greater beauty, now gone. As the ships sailed swiftly toward the coast of Italy, all the passengers had their own reasons for the journey to end. There would be days to go, then home.

Chapter Ten

The Cumaean Oricle

The imperial flotilla plied its way toward its destination, the port of Puteoli. This beautiful bay city was valued not only as a playground for the Roman elite but as a safe harbor of the unloading of costly and delicate items to eventually be shipped to Rome. Deep in the hold of the ships were many the sculptures of different colored marbles and granite destined for the Villa Adriana. Hadrian was taking no chances with these treasures, especially one of alabaster that rested in the hold of his flagship. Wrapped in thick cotton cloth and secured within a heavy oaken crate, this object was second in value only to the coffin and its contents in the emperor's quarters. The rose hue of the magnificently carved sarcophagus was shielded from sunlight and prying eyes. Only when it was ready to accept the body of his beloved would the world set eyes on its beauty.

Land was sighted just after mid day as the villa-lined coast of the Bay of Naples shimmered with the many marble homes of the wealthy, their private yachts bobbing happily beside long stone piers. Looking out from the deck outside his cabin, Hadrian could make out the Temple of Serapis nestled in the hills above the city. Nearby would be the Villa of Cicero, which he had purchased years before and where he stayed during his rare visits. From the entrance of the bay, Hadrian could also see the resort of Baiae—the quiet, ancient retreat he preferred. As the sails were swiftly furled into great scrolls of canvas, the oarsmen took to their task and guided the crafts neatly into their designated moorings. The great cranes and lifts were already in place to remove the many wooden crates that weighed down the ships. After a mishap with the cranes nearly two years before, which ended with many rare sculptures and columns resting on the floor of the bay, Hadrian refused to tempt fate and ordered the removal of the crates to begin the next day and under his supervision. The light was growing softer, and he had a destination to reach before sundown.

The first to leave the ship was the imperial horse, followed by the horses of the court. Hadrian was seen swiftly disembarking and mounting his horse as his companions scrambled to follow his lead. The pier was unusually crowded that day with richly dressed matrons and their entourages. The last visit was a frantic one, brought on by the mishap with the cranes. But it soon became the social event of the season with the first sight of the emperor with his young consort. Antinous lent a golden glow to the city and added to Hadrian's intoxicating presence. But this visit was not to be a repeat of that gilded memory. The emperor wore the black-banded purple of mourning and rode off alone into the hills above Puteoli. Having been forewarned of the emperor's dark mood since the death of his beloved, they assumed he was headed for his villa and wished to be alone. The court, however, made its way to the homes of friends or family and joined in the social whirl already in progress.

If Hadrian's hurried departure from the pier was meant to deflect attention from himself, it did just the opposite. Lucius Didius, the emperor's prefect, had quickly gathered a small contingent of men to follow their sovereign, at a respectful distance, to his destination. While most thought the emperor was headed for his villa, Lucius knew the man better than most. The Apollonian Oracle at Cumea was less than six miles from the waterfront of Puteoli. There, in the mist of sulfur that reeked from the cave of Cumaean Oricle, was the Sibylline Verses. Over the centuries, the Sibylline priestess and their cult had suffered from poverty and neglect. It was Hadrian's interest in the oracle and his restoration of the Temple of Jupiter that brought them renewed influence and respect; their gratitude showed itself in their verses. The last time Hadrian had visited was with the youth in tow. The verses flowed with praise and reverence for the couple, and Hadrian was pleased. But the youth was now gone, and Lucius knew what the emperor's question to the priestess would be. "Why had he not been forewarned of his beloved's death?" The priests of the Temple of Jupiter had always consulted them during dark times. Surely the predestined death of his beloved Antinous was worthy of a mention.

As Hadrian reached the mouth of the cave, believed by the Romans to be the entrance into the earth, he was well aware of the contingent behind him. Hearing footsteps coming close behind him, he turned to see Lucius carefully making his way along the rocky path, shrouded by the mist of the springs. Upon being seen, the prefect stopped and saluted his emperor. Hadrian nodded and gave the man a small tight smile. He noticed a sudden change in the man's expression and turned in time to see the vision of priestess emerging from the cave. Purposely standing upwind from the billowing fumes, Hadrian returned the deep bows of the priestess with a nod of his head. The head priestess could tell the man before her was not pleased, and she quickly assessed the situation. Tougher questions had been put to her in the past, but this man was dangerous, and the question was personal. Slipping to her knees, the priestess began a chant in the ancient language that for a moment held the emperor at bay. With the memories of the Eleusinian Mysteries conjured up by the shrill chants, Hadrian waited respectfully for the priestess to finish. As her mantra began to subside, Hadrian made his way closer into the sulfuric swirl and the swooning priestess. Looking down at the aged woman, he spoke softly his question. "Why could you not foresee?" Looking up into the eyes of her emperor and benefactor, she saw not the anger she expected but sorrow and pain. For a moment, she was taken aback. Her response was tailored for this question, but not for this emotion. Her red-rimmed eyes, half blind, the victim of years of sulfur fumes, now filled with tears of sorrow and humiliation.

She replied, "I have no soothing answer for you, my lord. The gods showed me nothing because, by then, Antinous belonged to them. He had offered himself to them long before he stood before me. He was a god even before he died. And as a god, he chose to divulge nothing to me." With that, the priestess turned and disappeared into the stench of swirling mist with the other priestess following protectively behind. Hadrian stood transfixed by the spectacle and the answer. He had lived with and loved a god without realizing it. And that god loved him in return with a love so fervent he gave up his life for him. Hadrian slumped to the hard earth, and the stark reality of his grief left him breathless. When he had chided the youth for his moodiness, he had no idea of the secret the boy carried within him. What a cruel, insensitive lover he must have seemed. Sensitivity was never a strong point for him, yet he demanded it from others. Weary and drained, the emperor of Rome raised himself from the mist-covered earth and stumbled down the rocky hillside to his villa. Following close behind, Lucius motioned the guards to follow. Night had come, and it would be a long and sleepless one. The next morning came fresh and clear. From his windows of his villa, Hadrian could clearly see the ships in the bay—filled with his treasures. The villa was a beautiful one: elevated on a small hill and surrounded by lush gardens, its colonnaded facade facing the sea. The view of the Temple of Jupiter from his bedchamber was soothing, but after a light breakfast, Hadrian knew it was time to head down the hill to the pier where the workmen were already positioning the cranes. The squeal of the pulleys mixed with the slap of the thick ropes against the oak beams and echoed throughout the sleepy port city. The wealthy residents of this lavish resort, still weary from their late night revels, called for their servants and slaves to draw the heavy curtains of their bedchambers tighter to keep out the noise. While the merchants and businessmen haggled over the value and cost of the luxury goods that had arrived the day before, the aristocracy dug deeper under their plump pillows to delay the sight and sounds of the morning's arrival.

Hadrian showed no sign of the debilitating grief he had suffered the night before. The morning light and the fresh sea air restored his spirits and filled him with a sense of renewal. The dark spirits that had tormented him the previous night hovered in the distance, but the light of day had powers of its own. Keeping a watchful eye on the workmen as they raised a succession of crates from the bowels of the ships, Hadrian made a mental note of each treasure as it sailed through the air with the help of mobile cranes and was settled skillfully on the horse drawn wagons that waited to bring these goods to Rome. But Hadrian was more interested in the crates that would be placed on barges that would have the Villa Adriana as their destination. There were powerful sculptures of Amazon warriors in marble, enigmatic sphinx's carved from basalt, and one particular obelisk of pink granite. As the light of day began to fade, the last crate, containing the alabaster sarcophagus, was lifted from the ship, and this was the sign for Hadrian to have the most precious item in his ship brought to shore. As he strode up the gangplank to the praetorian guards that waited on deck, he noticed the priests he had summoned earlier from the Temple of Jupiter were already gathered. The purple awning that had shielded the emperor from the sun during his meals had been lowered and draped over the façade of the cabin. The resemblance to a tomb was unnerving, and even the soldiers seemed subdued by its presence. As the head priest approached, the emperor the others began their litany of the dead, the smoke of their incense braziers billowing into the fading light of evening. The hinges of the awning frame complained slightly as the heavy canvas was lifted to allow entry. As the priests followed the emperor into the cabin, as slight rumble could be heard in the distance. It was as if they were disturbing the slumber of a god, and the apprehensive priests huddled close together, suddenly uncertain of their task. The oil lamps within the cabin were lit, and their light brought a soft glow to the slender golden coffin that sat quietly in the center of the chamber. To Hadrian's satisfaction, the priests fell to their knees, and their incantations continued with far more emotion and awe. In the presence of a god, their haughty demeanor had vanished; and their duties as priests took on new meaning, while another rumble was heard, this time louder and longer. After the priests draped the coffin with a black linen cloth bordered with a purple border heavily embroidered with laurel crowns done in silver thread, the soldiers lifted the box onto a litter and carried it from the cabin. Escorted by the priests and followed by the emperor, the soldiers walked across the ship's deck, down the gangplank, and to an awaiting wagon. Chabrais stood waiting for the disembarking of his former student and joined the procession that would lead to the Temple of Jupiter. There, the coffin would remain over night, watched over by the priests and a handful of guards.

Later in the night, the deep rumbling in the distance had turned to flashes of lightning and crashes of thunder. It was the Ides of October, and the traditional dedication of these Ides to Jupiter had begun before the arrival of Antinous's corpse. Now, watching from his chambers at the villa, Hadrian listened to the rumbling and watched the lightning crash over the temple. It was as if the great god was welcoming home his son. Just as Antinous was the son of Ra, Jupiter too claimed Antinous as *his* son. As Hadrian walked onto the colonnade outside his bedchamber, a blinding blast of lightning illuminated the temple and sent down a bolt that crashed through the great bronze doors searing a path to the altar of the high god and splitting it in two. Even from the distance of the villa, the sound was deafening. In the nearby villas, lamps were being lit and servants ran about, thinking an earthquake had started. But the rumbling had ceased, and an eerie silence prevailed. The emperor's servants rushed into the chamber to check on their master, only to find him already dressed and prepared to leave. Hadrian swept by them and came face-to-face with the prefect, Lucius Didius, who informed him his horse was waiting for him outside. Rushing down the steps, with the guards following close behind, Hadrian mounted his horse and headed, not toward the safety of his ship in the harbor but toward the temple. The thought that the lightning bolt had destroyed the body of his beloved filled him with terror. *Had he gone though all of this and come all this way, only to have the gods steal what little he had left?* He rode hard up the hill to the shallow plain that held the temple. His horse nearly stumbled as Hadrian reined him to a halt before the temple steps. The guards had not reached the temple before the emperor dismounted and strode up the marble steps. For a moment, he froze before the bronze door of the sanctuary, still steaming where it lay. Wrapping his cloak tightly around himself, he walked past the broken door and cautiously entered the sanctuary. Through the semidarkness, he saw the temple priests huddled on their knees in a corner. Upon seeing the emperor, the chief priest hurried from the group and fell to his knees before Hadrian. Lifting the priest up, he was shocked at the look of rapture on the man's face. The man began to whisper praise for the new god Hadrian brought to their temple. But as the priest rambled on, Hadrian's attention shifted to the great statue of Jupiter and the shattered altar at his feet. Yet in the dim light of the smoking lamps, there was no sign of a coffin to be found. Turning to the still whispering priest, Hadrian put his hand over the man's mouth and spoke quietly but firmly. "Where is the body of my beloved?" he asked the man. The trembling priest removed the hand from his mouth and led the emperor to a smaller sanctuary, a Roman style *aedicule*, off the main cella. There, behind a heavy curtain of embroidered silk, was the gilded coffin. Seeing the confusion on Caesar's face, the priest quickly explained that due to the fact that Hadrian had added the side sanctuary when he had designed and funded the temple's restoration, the priests felt this would be the appropriate resting place for Antinous. Hadrian gazed with disbelief at the darkly shrouded object that lay on the small altar as it absorbed the light of a multitude of bronze lamps. He walked hesitantly to the casket and slowly pulled at the thick fabric until the flames that hovered overhead illuminated the gilded carvings. The hieroglyphs seemed to come alive in the flickering light, as if attempting to speak their ancient prayers and assert the power of their god in this foreign land. The priests had not uncovered the coffin since its arrival, and the exotic nature of the object both disturbed and intrigued them. Hadrian walked to the cedar box and, for the first time in months, allowed himself to look through the thick glass window. The face was the same. Not a curl had been disturbed; the blush had not faded. He quickly replaced the heavy linen coverlet before the impact of that face registered in his mind. The fact that the body was safe was all that mattered. He had expected and intended the coffin to be placed at the foot of the main altar. Through a simple misunderstanding, the priests had saved the corpse from destruction. He would reward them handsomely when it was time to move on.

The following mornings arrived clear and bright. It was as if that night of terror was inspired by the gods to remind mortals of their presence. Hadrian woke early on the third day and had already issued orders for the journey to Rome. He had intended to prolong his stay, but it seemed the gods wished him to move on. And he had no intention of testing their patience. By the time he reached the temple, he was informed the coffin was already in place on a wagon, the flaps of its canvas covering neatly secured. The knots of the ties were pure army issue, and Hadrian found comfort in this simple gesture. Still, he could not help undoing the flaps to make sure what should be inside was. Upon inspection, Hadrian retied the knot to its previous handiwork and turned to enter the temple. Upon seeing him, the priests, fearful that the emperor blamed them for the events of that frightful night, fell to their knees. Hadrian went to the chief priest and, in a fluid gesture, removed from beneath his cloak a large gilded silver coffer and placed it into his hands. With a few simple words of thanks, he turned and left. As the emperor departed, the priest opened the silver box and gasped. There, arrayed in layers on a bed of padded silk, were many gold denari bearing, lest they forget the giver, the likeness of the emperor of Rome.

Chapter Eleven

The Pantheon's New God

Winter was making its arrival known before the imperial entourage found its way to the harbor city of Porta. But the air was still sweet as the spray of the sea mingled with the scented breeze from gardens of the villas that sprawled along the shore. The treasures from Hadrian's ships were unloaded and put on heavy wheeled freight wagons, to be eventually placed on barges for Rome or the Villa Adriana through a system of inland channels and canals. The goods of the emperor had been unloaded first and sent off when he left for Rome. The other ships would take a number of more days to unload, but their goods were not as important in the eyes of the emperor. Massive cargo ships containing measures of olive oil from Cyprus and modii of grain from Egypt were quickly sent off to Ostia to be then sent on to Rome. These goods were the property of the emperor and his gift to the citizens of Rome, and they would precede him there to help warm his return to the city. There was great curiosity among the crowds that gathered, regarding the carts that the emperor kept a watchful eye on. Only his entourage knew the contents of these heavily guarded wagons, and they knew the emperor would kill to protect those contents. It was near midday when the entourage had reached Ostia. To the great relief of the nobles and ageing scholars, barges were waiting to transport them the rest of the way to Rome. The jolting and dust of the road would be replaced by the scented luxury of the canal barges. On the largest barge, two great crates were carefully loaded as the Hadrian watched from the bank of the canal, unaware of the crowd that had assembled to view the emperor and his court. At the last moment, the emperor turned to briefly address the crowd before boarding the imperial craft. The excitement of seeing the emperor prevented the crowd from noticing his preoccupation with a darkly draped object that was being carried into his cabin. This was not the citizen's emperor who used to address the crowd at length and reveled in their cheers. The aging Caesar seemed to have little interest in the waiting crowd. Surrounded by his guards, Hadrian abruptly turned and boarded the barge before withdrawing into his cabin. His eagerness to return to Rome was swiftly vanishing.

Hadrian reappeared a bit later to join his closest companions at their meal. The conversation was light and innocuous, harmless chatter to dispel the silence. After the meal, a courtier produced a lyre and played light tunes that played with the rhythm of the splashing oars. Much to the court's relief, conversation ceased; and for a brief time, life had regained its former sweetness. As the sun move closer to the horizon, the sights and sounds of Rome made themselves known. The hum of the city seemed to vibrate in the water, and the court, long absent from this center of the world, was eager to rejoin its gritty, vibrant life.

Hadrian had busied himself with preparations for the sacrosanct items that shared his barge. While the court knew of the contents under the black drape, the impossibly cumbersome crate that had followed was a mystery. All they knew was that it had originated in Alexandria, was very costly, and required a special crane to lift in and out of the ship, wagons, and barge. As the emperor's barge neared the Tiber River, it would be a short time before it would reach the destination Hadrian had chosen—the pier by the Pons Aelius, a bridge that led from the Campus Martius to his mausoleum, which was still far from complete. This had been a consideration at first, that his beloved's tomb should be next to his for all eternity. But an unfinished tomb was not acceptable, and the distance of the mausoleum to the villa was far too great. Hadrian's destination was a finished masterpiece, the Pantheon, Temple of All Gods. Here, he would add one more. Antinous would rest here until a proper tomb was constructed at the Villa Adriana, and in the mind of Hadrian, the youth would be together again with his lover.

Special cranes were already in place when the emperor's barge arrived at the Pons Aelius. A pier had been built on this side of the Tiber for the delivery of materials during the construction of the Pantheon, and this same mooring would be used now for the installation of the body of Antinous. Directly across the river was an identical pier, used for the construction of Hadrian's tomb. The emperor looked with disgust at the lack of activity across from where he now stood, but that was a concern for later. His concentration was focused on the groaning crane that raised the large crate from the deck of the barge. Six workmen guided the crate to a waiting horse drawn wagon that would take the road to the temple. Another wagon, draped and curtained in deep blue muslin, would receive the coffin still wrapped in black. The emperor's steed had left the barge long before the crane had begun its work and was impatiently waiting for his master. Now Hadrian mounted the proud beast and led the wagons towards the temple. Only after he had taken the reins did the emperor notice the crowd that had gathered silently along the riverbank. He had hoped the location of their disembarking would discourage the idle masses from interrupting what he felt was a private matter. It had been two years since he was in Rome and one year since the Beloved's death. Hadrian was used to the constant scrutiny of the opinionated Romans. Yet today, it was their reserve that unnerved him. Presence of the *comitatus* and its massive household establishment of domestic personnel, chamberlains, ushers, and secretaries made the permanence of the emperor's stay clear to the crowd. The size of the imperial entourage was a spectacle in itself with the gold-embroidered hems of the knights' pure white togas, the Egyptian nobles and priests in gilded headdresses and leopard skins, as well as a vast array of civilian and military ministers in their finest attire. The guard itself numbered at about three thousand, and the cordon that had been formed around the emperor was formidable, yet it appeared to be unnecessary. While there were the obligatory cries of *Salve Hadrianus*, *Salve Pontius*, what was unclear to Caesar was the emotion that provoked these salutations; was it respect or distain that they were displaying? Knowing Rome as well as he did, Hadrian surmised they knew what at least one of the wagons contained. Gossip spread quickly in this city, but what was on the minds of the people remained a mystery. Yet as he led the procession of finely carved wagons behind a line of lictors bearing gilded *fasces* and surrounded by chanting priests and the three thousand of the Praetorian guard, the hushed crowd bowed in reverence, first for the their emperor, then as the blue draped wagon passed by. Behind the emperor, the Aquilifer carried the Aquila or eagle standard of the emperor's personal guard while a draconarius, wearing a lion's head and pelt over his helmet and body, carried a cloth banner that bore the ensign of a lion, woven into the fabric. Hadrian's gilt silver breastplate flashed like a beacon as his deep purple cloak flapped in the early spring breeze, while the pristine white tunics, scarlet cloaks, and polished red leather belts of the Praetorian foot and horse guards presented an impressive sight. The regal vision of their *Imperator* again evoked the crowd's cries of *Salve!* Praetorian Prefect Lucius Didius, riding along side the coffin, noted with a wry smile that the deep blue that draped Antinous's wagon was not quite purple, but the black drape on the coffin that could be faintly seen through the muslin, deepened the blue with its shadow, lending it a purple hue. Hadrian's true wish was whispered too faintly for the crowd to hear, too subtle to create a stir. What was accepted and revered in the rest of the empire was a scandal here in Rome. Yet the crowd, for now, showed respect. Was it the sight of their Caesar in battle armor, the chanting priests, or the number of armed Praetorians? Or perhaps it was the vision of an austere carriage, simply draped, carrying what they all knew was the emperor's greatest treasure now lost. Always a soldier, Lucius never fully trusted the crowd. But for the moment, he saw a people, out of respect and reverence for their emperor, mourn the loss of his Beloved.

Somewhere in the crowd stood three very different people who had a connection to the dead youth. Laberius, the head master of the paedagogium, the finishing school that Antinous had attended, stood quietly in the crowd and remembered the quiet sullen youth, too beautiful to be truly real. Looking back, he had felt an air of tragedy about the boy that seemed to enhance his beauty. *The gods are jealous and vengeful, even with emperors. What they gave slowly, they took back quickly,* he thought with some satisfaction. Also in the crowd was a young Greek man named Narkissos, a former classmate of Antinous and his first friend in Rome. The refinement of his bearing and fineness of his attire was a testament to how well placed he was within an aristocratic household. The same age as Antinous would have been, he was beyond the accepted age now to be an *eromenos* or beloved. Given a comfortable position in civic duty by his former lover, he was obligated to marry. He had been selected a mousey girl from a wealthy family who would make few demands of him. His life would proceed quietly, predictably, and without renown, but he at least had the memory of his beautiful friend.

Further down the long road to the Pantheon, near the Thermae Neronianae, a slender man in a fine woolen toga stood slightly separate from the crowd. The broad stripe on his *tunica laticlavia* distinguished him as a senator of considerable wealth. Galbius Soterianus, on his way to the Thermae Neroinane, had stopped to view the procession as it passed. He had heard of the death of the emperor's favorite over a year ago and had tried to push back the memory of the beautiful boy from Bithynia. Blissful nights he had spent with the youth remained fresh in his mind as he spent the years since attempting to find a close facsimile. As he walked closer to the procession to view the coffin in the passing carriage, he recalled the beautiful face, the magnificent body, and the fiery passion beneath it all. Galbius lost Antinous to an emperor, who in turn lost him to fate. It was as if a scroll had finished rolling and was now being slipped into its case, never to be read again. Galbius found himself drawn to the shrouded coffin and began to walk along side the carriage as it turned off the main road and began finish its journey to the Pantheon. Deep in thought, he failed to notice the intent gaze of the Praetorian prefect as he rode alone side the wagon. A mixture of curiosity and suspicion kept the prefect's attention on the man who began to follow the procession.

Lucius Didius watched, from his perch on the high saddle of his horse, a man in senatorial garb. Something in the man's face moved him, as if memories were flooding through his mind and reflecting in his eyes—eyes that refused to turn from the sight of the covered wagon. *A past lover perhaps*, thought Lucius. *Were there others before the emperor*? Lucius knew of the reputation of the paedagogium on the Caelian Hill as well as that of the boys who left there for placement in wealthy households. Well trained and above reproach, these boys were the crème of society, worthy of a high-ranking man such as this. It would appear this was just another heart broken by the beautiful Greek youth. Satisfied with his assessment, Lucius was about to turn his attentions elsewhere when his gaze met the eyes of the young senator. Something in them struck a chord and caused Lucius to shift uncomfortably on his mount. A memory whispered in his ears, and long-suppressed emotions began to rise dangerously in his chest. Clearing his head of all thoughts of the past, the prefect began to examine the crowd and thought ahead of what was to transpire once they reached the temple.

The procession ended at the steps of the massive portico of the Pantheon. The front row of eight magnificent granite columns dwarfed the priests and soldiers and even the emperor himself. The procession paused before the steps of the temple and was met by the temple priests bearing bowls of burning incense and garlands of laurel. As the emperor followed the priests into the temple, the soldiers removed the coffin from its wagon. The curious crowd, at first silent then conferring among themselves regarding the nature of the covered object, gasped as they caught their first glimpse of the coffin of Antinous. A sudden breeze had lifted off its cloth covering, and before it could be replaced, the full effect of its golden presence sent a shudder through the crowd. The exotic object, done in the Egyptian tradition, absorbed the sunlight, seeming to take on a shimmering life of its own. The soldiers quickly formed a wall between the crowd and their charge and with heavy steps entered the temple.

The gilded bronze door of the temple was already open in welcome for the Pantheon's newest god. The hobnailed boots of the soldiers clattered on the inlayed marble floor and echoed in the vastness of the temple space. In the center of the sanctuary, just under the oculus, was a smoldering incense altar resting on a large dark disk of porphyry. From its drum-shaped form carved with bulls heads and garlands of laurel, a great spiral rose up towards the cosmic eye of the dome. Hadrian was already at the altar when the soldiers reached him and set the coffin down on a thick carpet at his feet. Behind them came more soldiers pulling a great cart that carried the mysterious crate of enormous weight, its wheels wrapped in wool to protect the precious marble inlay of the temple floor. Upon the crate's arrival, Hadrian ordered the great door of the temple to be closed. Chabias the tutor, who had not left the emperor's side through out the journey, noticed the arrival of a senator who looked vaguely familiar and had been allowed in by the Prefect Lucius Didius. Galbius, using his senatorial rank, gained entry, hoping the Praetorian prefect would not object. To his relief, the prefect nodded his consent before moving on toward the altar and the large crate that was now being opened.

The rays of the sun had moved past a number of the great squares of inlaid marble floor before the object within the crate caught its first glimpse of light. As the soft covering that had protected it from the rough wood was removed, the first sight of the carved alabaster drew a gasp. Hadrian, impatient to reveal the work, unwrapped the rest of the stone object himself until the entire sarcophagus was visible. Even in the immense grandeur of the temple, the object overwhelmed. The reverence that greeted it was almost fearsome, as if the gods themselves had sent this object to earth, filled with their own divine power. Hadrian motioned for the priests to approach the Egyptian coffin, but it was here that he seemed to lose his certainty. The idea of removing the boy's body from its resting place of over a year seemed sacrilege. Yet gilded cedar was not worthy of the new god, and this masterpiece in alabaster most certainly was. It took the strength of four soldiers to dislodge the lid of the stone container, while the priests removed the body of Antinous amidst a cloud of incense. As Hadrian stood in the swirling mist and gazed at the youth's tightly wrapped corpse, the sun's light caught the gold-wrapped fingers and set them ablaze. Scarabs and other sacred charms could be seen through the many fine layers of precious linen as the priests carried the young god to his new resting place. The body had been wrapped up to the torso, leaving the great smooth chest and strong arms, the arms of a hunter exposed. The hands rested on the midsection with the fingers wrapped with thin sheets of pale gold, while the arms themselves were bound to the body with thin strips of finely woven linen embroidered with prayers of greeting to his brother, Osirus. But more importantly, and disturbingly, the face remained in full view. The features were more masklike now, but their magnificence was still evident. The famous curls glistened with rare oils, and the skin still retained the pigments and unguents that lent an eerily lifelike appearance.

The priests, still cradling the body in their arms, seemed frozen in place before the majestic sarcophagus, as if unable to relinquish the presence of the god. Hadrian too seemed immobile, unable to make sense of the emotions that raged through him. It was as if the entire world had grown silent, and even the sun had ceased its movement to gaze at the boy. Looking up, Hadrian saw an unexpected look of grief on the face of Lucius, but it was the distress of the man behind the commander that unnerved him. The face was familiar and the garb presented him as a senator, but why the look of grief? The senate cared nothing for the youth when he was alive and had only distain for his memory. The fact that there was a member of the senate profaning this sacred place was intolerable. But just as anger began to replace Hadrian's grief, he remembered the face. Yes, whenever the court was discussing the charms of the boys they had visited at the paedagogium on the Caelian Hill, it was this aristocrat, Galbius, who went strangely silent at the mention of Antinous's name. Had he loved him then? Did he love him still? *None of that matters anymore.* As the power of the youth transcended death and touched deeply the living, Hadrian turned numbly away and allowed the man the luxury of his memories and his own anguish.

The power of movement returned to the priests, and they began to place the body of Antinous to rest upon his silken bed within the alabaster tomb. The soldiers raised the thick slab of transparent rock crystal that formed the lid and, after the priests had applied a layer of tree resin as a sealant along the rim, laid the slab in place. The sun had resumed its journey, reverently touching the carved panels of alabaster and setting them aglow. A thing of beauty was now within another, and both now resided in Hadrian's greatest masterpiece. It was as if a long nightmare, emotionally as well as physically draining, had been sealed up. Hadrian knelt at the base of the boy's tomb, his heavy rings clicking along the panels as his hands caressed the carved memories of happier days. The intimacy of this scene was a clear sign for the court to leave the emperor alone with his memories within the Pantheon of the gods. As the last courtier exited the great door, Hadrian's spirit seemed to wilt as he slumped to the hard marble floor and rested his head on the cool alabaster of the tomb. Though grief remained, there were no more tears left to shed. He had done all he could within his power and would continue to honor the memory of his Beloved. Life would go on, but a piece of himself had been removed—the piece the boy had awakened in him. The ability to love and be loved took so long to reach him yet stayed for so brief a time. He was now just Hadrian, emperor of Rome, all-powerful, omnipotent. But like the great wooden cranes that stood in his harbors, all pulleys and gears. The human part of him was missing, and it would never return.

When Hadrian finally left the Pantheon, darkness had already settled over the city. His guards were still on the portico, waiting to escort him to the palace. He would remain in Rome for a few more days, then move on to the comforting peace and order of the Villa Adriana.

Chapter Twelve

A Change of Course

Hadrian woke suddenly, long before the sun gave thought of warming the sky. He had dreamt of his arrival at the Villa Adriana—a dream that carried with it a number of disturbing omens. In it, the emperor was arriving by barge, his favorite and most comfortable way to return home. Suddenly, the canal turned to solid ice, trapping his craft and shattering it in a great explosion. He escaped from the barge and walked a path of ice to the villa, entering a world covered with snow. Coal black crows flew overhead, screeching noisily and casting ominous shadows in the snow. As he passed what should have been the grand, completed gate of the villa, Hadrian watched it melt into ruin. Walking quickly now, he passed the gate and reached a colonnade, where it too melted into a shambles. Hadrian began to run toward the palaces, baths, and administrative buildings, each one dissolving from the shape of what it should have been. Attempting to catch his breath, Hadrian trudged though the icy whiteness as it began to grow deeper despite the lack of any snowfall.

The swooping crows grew silent and began to fall from the sky, disappearing into the deepening snow. As Hadrian stood motionless in the vast desolation that was once his magnificent

Villa Adriana, he felt the rest of his sanity and resolve to live vanish. Just as he was about to commit himself to the icy grave beneath him, he saw his horse, saddled and well provisioned. Steamy breath billowed from his flaring nostrils as his thick mane whipped about in the wind like black flames. As the steed impatiently pawed the ground with his hooves, the message became clear to Hadrian as he ran with what strength he had left toward the great beast and mounted him with a single bound.

When Hadrian finally awoke, the message of the dream was still vivid in his mind. The villa was clearly not to be his next destination, although what it was to be was uncertain. In his present state, he could do his masterpiece no good; he needed to cleanse his mind and continue his duties as emperor. As his dream evolved into detailed plans for travel, Hadrian walked the still darkened halls to the marble clad bath already steaming in preparation for the morning. In the light of a single twin wicked lamp, he sank into the tepid waters and released all thoughts from his mind. The day had not even begun, and he was already exhausted. It was the exertion of the dream, he thought, nothing more. And yet, deep in the quietest recesses of his mind, the whispered voice of his beloved Antinous floated like a breeze off the Nile, "I gave my life to extend yours. Use it wisely!" In the stillness of the marble bath, the sun began to peer through the small windows of the high ceilinged chamber. There it found the emperor of Rome as he rested his head against the sunken basin, eyes vacant and his face, yet again, wet with tears.

It was there that Hadrian's servants found their master, and as the emperor began to leave the bath, the servants hurried to put together the proper attire for travel to the villa, only to be told that was no longer the plan. With a thick sheet of soft wool wrapped around him, Hadrian sat at his desk of polished cypress and looked through the correspondence that had just arrived and sat, waiting for his attention. Waiting too was a centurion from the empress bearing a message for her husband. Not wishing for an extended intrusion, he addressed the centurion first and learned Sabina wished to be permitted to view the sarcophagus in the Pantheon. Remembering the warmth and fondness she had shown the boy, Hadrian was not surprised by her wish to visit. But the fact she requested the visit so formally struck him as odd, as if Sabina expected to see him there when she arrived. It was not a difficult request to grant as he had already intended to visit the temple before his departure from Rome. He dictated a hurried reply with the required salutations and sent the centurion off to the empress. As he settled into the stack of letters before him, his eye spotted a familiar hand. His close friend, Herodes Atticus, who lived in Greece with his young Athenian ephebe, was inquiring on the emperor's health and inviting him to stay with them during his next visit to Athens. The question as to where he should go when he left Rome was answered in this letter, and in his own hand, he replied to Herodes, announcing his departure for Greece as soon as preparations were made. Sending off the letter by messenger, Hadrian moved to the outer rooms of his chambers where his breakfast waited for him on the covered porch that overlooked the city. As he settled himself on the low couch that extended the length of the table before it, Hadrian looked out at the view before him and remembered why he had avoided this location since his arrival at the palace. As he watched from his porch, the sun unveiled the familiar view of the Caelian Hill and slowly illuminated the small villa that housed the paedagogium of Antinous's early days of learning. It was from here that Hadrian watched and dreamt of the day he would swoop down on the school and, like Zeus in the guise of an eagle, abduct his own beautiful Ganymede. Those golden dreams seemed so long ago, not just a few years past. *Too few.* Unable to bear the haunting view before him, Hadrian left the porch, leaving his breakfast untouched in the morning sun.

The imperial barges were ready to set sail one week later with Hadrian and his quietly disgruntled court in tow. They had expected to be comfortably ensconced at the Villa Adriana by now, not touring the empire again so soon after Egypt. The wanderlust of the emperor had its perks but also its shortcomings. Sabina chose to remain behind in Rome, grateful that her frail health permitting her a valid excuse. Her pilgrimage to the Pantheon weeks before gave her new insight into the nature of her husband, and what she saw closed what few doors remained opened in their relationship. As they stood before the sarcophagus of the dead Antinous, she saw the bitter guilt in Hadrian's eyes and the true reason for the boy's death. The realization that the sacrifice of this young life occurred for the sake of the emperor's was more callous than she could accept. At least now, the physical departure of her husband would allow her to resume her tranquil life, as it equaled the emotional distance she would keep for the rest of her days.

The plans for the royal journey were suddenly frustrated as affairs of state occupied the emperor for the following months. Uprisings in Gaul and Judea, as well as a drought in Egypt that slowed the supply of grain to Rome, required the emperor's attention. The Roman garrison Legio XXII Deiotariana was dispatched to Judea at the request of the Roman governor, Tinaius Rufus, and would join the Legio III Cyrenaica. While these solutions were somewhat easy to achieve, the drought was a different matter. In a flash of memory mingled with a desperate desire for luck, Hadrian sent a basalt sculpture of Antinous in the guise of Osirus with two Egyptian priests to the port of Alexandria. The hope of the emperor was the reenacting of the miracle of the rains that occurred as he visited the coast of Africa a few years before with his beloved. A coin commemorating the event still found its way among his belongings and would rest on his desk as a constant reminder. He hoped the young god would be merciful and the miracle would reoccur.

Nearly a month had vanished in a flurry of work and memories before the report arrived from Alexandria. The priests had remained behind with the cult statue, which had been greeted with great celebration. As stated in the report, the ship bearing the statue arrived at dawn, its sails bearing the insignia of the Lion of Antinous. It was said that as soon as the populous caught sight of the sails, clouds began to gather like a dark blanket over the city. As the ship docked and the crate with the figure was unloaded, deep rumblings could be heard in the distance, growing louder as the figure drew closer to the temple of Osirus. As per Hadrian's orders, the figure was placed beside the sacrificial altar that smoldered before the temple façade. Once the covering was removed and the fire stoked, the skies opened up to release a torrent that poured down and rushed through the parched streets. It was said that even the Nile swelled past its banks and reached the very walls of Antinoopolis, where it sprang up as a gushing fountain. While Hadrian could sense with little effort that this was a fabrication, the reports of the life giving rain throughout Egypt were acknowledged by the officials seals that decorated the document and accurate enough. The power of the new cult startled even the senate as it officially thanked the new god that had defied them and begrudgingly issued a coin in his name.

The barges that bore the emperor and his court down the Tiber had entered Portus by midday to great fanfare. Shunning the crowd's adoration once again, Hadrian was surprised to discover a pristine new ship waiting for him where his old ship, the *Felicitati*, used to be berthed. Designed and built in the great shipyard constructed by Trajan, the craft, also called the *Felicitati*, had been finished a few weeks earlier and furnished in time for the imperial journey. Berthed near the entrance to the vast hexagonal basin of the *Portus Traiani Felicis*, the vessel nearly blocked the view of the imperial palace that stood behind it. Larger and more lavish than the older flagship, this vessel promised a voyage of greater comfort than before. The multilevel stateroom of the imperial flagship was outfitted with all the costly trappings of an emperor's palace and afforded Hadrian with more space then he could possibly need. The massive canvas sails were bleached white instead of the usual dyed brown and were lined with purple borders that announced the imperial presence and matched the long slender banners that already snapped impatiently in the sea breeze. The ship would carry the usual handpicked assortment of knights, courtiers, scholars, and artisans, as well as the emperor's personal guard, who would follow their emperor as his memories chased him across his empire. As it rocked lazily beside the pier, the new ship dwarfed the small fleet composed of the vessels that escort the emperor in his journey.

Yet, despite the majestic beauty of the flagship, Hadrian had been content with his old ship and the memories it contained, seeing no need to contend with the expense of a new one. As the barge gently bumped along side the pier and was being secured, Caesar disembarked and, shielding his eyes from the sun's glare with his hand, began seeking out Lucius Didus and an answer to the riddle of the new ship. "Caesar," came a voice from behind him. Lucius's barge had been the first to reach the pier some time earlier, and the praefectus was waiting for his emperor to leave his barge. Hadrian turned and saw Lucius emerge from the stone guardhouse with a sealed packet in his hand. "This should explain the ship, Caesar. I believe your dear friends in the Senate are behind this magnificent gift." He spoke with a bemused tone but a neutral face. Without a word, Hadrian took the packet and, with an impatient snap, broke the large scarlet seal. He recognized the symbol of the three geese embossed in the wax and knew the sender before he opened the crisply folded parchment. Inside, the handwriting was unmistakably that of Marcius Turbo, and the brisk style of writing read more as a military report than a fawning gesture of thanks. Had the writing been florid, it would not have been truly from the austere Turbo.

The seal with the three geese was a perfect symbol of Marcius's value to the emperor. As with the ancient sacred geese that had alerted Rome of an invasion during the time of the republic, so too did Marcius alert Hadrian of the senate's subversive plans to undermine his authority on numerous occasions. Only on the subject of Caesar's Beloved did Marcius remain silent. For Turbo, this was an imperial prerogative and as such, not answerable to the senate or the people.

Other than the fleeting smile that brushed his lips, Hadrian gave no indication of how he felt about the senate's grand gesture. But inside, he felt a mix of emotions for the man who was both friend and praefectus, and the assemblage of men he knew better than to trust. He knew he never had the full support of the senate his adopted father had and never would. As he looked across the harbor toward the colossal statue of Trajan in military dress he felt a mixture of envy and defiance. While he had not only stopped the unbridled expansion of the empire, he had also reined in its borders to what they were before his adopted father's conquests. *I made a decision far more dangerous to myself than my people, unpopular perhaps but wise. I will leave Rome safer and more secure than you did, dear Father. And at the cost of my own legacy.* As he continued to gaze at the massive likeness he saw, as usual, an opportunity to erect yet another edifice; and after making a mental note to design and construct a temple to himself that would embrace the sculpture, Hadrian turned his thoughts to the journey before him.

"Preparations have been made for the blessing of the vessel," Lucius spoke to the emperor's back as he stood on the pier lost in thought. "What? Yes. Tradition must be followed," replied Hadrian just before the Praetorian was about to repeat himself." With that said, he proceeded toward the small altar standing in wait beside the oaken hull. As the elderly pontifex from the recently completed temple of the deified Trajan began evoking the protection of the gods, incense was piled on the mound of smoldering embers while a ewer of wine was handed to the emperor to be poured on the burnished bronze of the prow, a bronze cast of his own image covered in radiant gold. As the red wine ran down the meticulously sculpted portrait, a cloud thinly veiled the sun, and Hadrian felt a chill run through him as the bloodlike liquid covered the face. *Was this perhaps the way the senate wished to see him?* At this time in his life, he preferred the familiar; and in Caesar's mind this ship was a symbol of the senate's power, not its gratitude. But soon, the sun had rid itself of its veil; and Hadrian, returning the wine ewer to the waiting priest, shook off his dark thoughts and strode purposefully to the ramp that would bring him to his extravagant new quarters.

With the assurance that the *Felicitati* was at the ready, Hadrian began to board his ship when he suddenly heard a familiar voice over the din of court chatter. He turned in time to see Lucius Ceionius Commodus stepping from his litter and joining a retinue of nobles and young pages that scurried about him like baby ducks. Hadrian had not seen Lucius since he had left for Rome from Alexandria nearly a year before to be with his wife Avidia Plautia and his newborn son Lucius Verus. Born forty-eight days after the death of Antinous, the arrival of another generation held a special meaning for Hadrian. The child's father had long been a favorite of the emperor and had now returned to fill the void left by Antinous. He left his blond haired son in the charge of a favorite freedman named Nicomedes—a name filled with an irony that would not escape Hadrian. The emperor felt an odd sense of pleasure at the sight of his young friend, his coterie of youthful nobles, and their chattering pageboys. For the first time in almost a year, Hadrian felt life seeping into his blood and warming his bones. His magnificent new ship would be filled with beauty and life on its way to his favorite province in the empire. The message in his dream was true; it was too soon to retire to his villa and wait for the end of life. His Beloved's gift could not be wasted, and the empire would be once more preparing for the arrival of its emperor.

The sumptuous interior of the royal staterooms rang with the boyish laughter of pages as they followed their young lords from room to room. A lavish feast was prepared in Lucius's honor, and Hadrian settled back to absorb the beauty of the scene before him. With cups of diluted wine to dull his senses, he allowed a euphoric haze to envelope him as he sank into the lushness of the sights and sounds around him. The sumptuous dining chamber, with its gaily-painted walls, glowed from the blaze of massive bronze oil lamps that swung lazily from the lofty ceiling of carved cedar. The aroma of roasted meats mingled with the exotic perfumes of the guests and the wispy columns of smoke from the incense burners. As rose-lipped boys sang the popular songs of the day while plucking the strings of their lyres, the slender fingers of their companions slid beguilingly up and down flutes of ivory and rosewood. The lord chamberlain rushed about as quickly as his girth would allow, breathlessly giving orders to the serving slaves and wine stewards.

Lucius himself had overseen the preparation of a number of the elaborate dishes served this evening. These, along with the grand floral displays that poured from the porphyry urns or sat like islands on the massive low dining table, were of his own design.

Hadrian never tired of the young man's creativity or the elegance of his slender bearing. And despite being a husband and father, he still carried himself like a youth with no worries. "You still look much younger than the years you have seen, Lucius," Hadrian spoke teasingly to the golden-haired man. "How is that possible?" Lucius had settled himself in front of Hadrian and, after stretching himself lazily like a cat, suggestively ran his fingers along the fragrant citron wood finial that pierced the down cushioned couch, his gold rings clicking on the heavy carving. He had taken care to be shaven as closely as possible before the banquet, and not a shadow could be detected on his face or a trace of hair on his body. He had decided to forgo the usual dusting of gold in his hair that he knew amused Caesar but annoyed him in bed. Instead, rare oil had been worked into the curls, a light but beguiling fragrance reminiscent of another time and another youth. Tapping the wood lightly for good luck, Lucius laid back and, without a word, gently rested his head on Hadrian's chest and hoped for the best. For an instant, the emperor ceased to breathe, and Lucius feared he had gone too far. Then, with a barely audible sigh, Hadrian buried his fingers in the young man's thick locks and, after pressing a kiss into the golden mane, offered him his cup of wine to drink. The gamble paid off, and in the depths of the blood red wine, Lucius saw his carefully planned future unfold before him. As a young page leaped and danced to the music of the lyre and flute, his filmy gauze tunic twirling high above his waist, Lucius gently pushed himself against Hadrian, then turned to look into his eyes. Hadrian knew a subtle offer when he saw one and, taking the young noble by the hand, left the dining chamber, not to be seen again until the following morning.

Chapter Thirteen

Golden Lucius

By the end of breakfast two days later, the ships had entered the strait of Sicily and sailed past the port of Messina. Hadrian saw no need to visit this port, as the provisions onboard were more than enough for a direct route to Greece. The size of his vessels and the purple borders of his flagship's sails would announce his presence to both Messina and Reggio across the strait, but time was too short and life had become rather comfortable onboard. Sailing east past the southern tip of Italia, the ships headed toward the open waters of the Ionian Sea. Depending on the mood of the gods, there would be at least two more days onboard before reaching Greece. His flagship was sleeker than the others in the fleet and plied the waters swiftly as the rest of the flotilla struggled to keep up. The extra passengers were an unexpected addition to the load, but the strong Ionian winds would make up for that. The day passed quickly, and Greece would be on the horizon by midmorning.

That night, Lucius was not to be found in the royal bedchamber as on previous nights. In his place was a youth of about sixteen. Clad in a simple tunic of fine linen, the youth was standing in the center of the chamber, running his fingers over the inlay of mother of pearl, lapis, and gold in one of the massive bedposts. The soft light of the oil lamps was absorbed into the black wavy hair that flowed down the nape of his neck but reflected off the smooth pale skin of the back of his shoulders. Despite not seeing his face, Hadrian was instinctively drawn to the figure before him, and he walked silently toward the youth, still preoccupied with the delicate workmanship of the bed. Before he reached him, Hadrian could detect the faint smell of scented oil as well as the intoxicating aroma of youth. The boy finally became aware of someone behind him and turned to face the intruder. But the emperor was already close enough to prevent the youth from turning and with strong hands gripped the pale shoulders as he buried his face in the thick dark hair. There was the faint taste of sweat on the nape of the boy's neck as Hadrian's lips opened to gently nuzzle the smooth skin while his tongue met sweet salt. When the boy attempted to turn again to face his visitor, Hadrian nipped the boy's neck playfully, his beard tickling the pale skin and evoking a shudder and giggle from the lad. He finally turned the youth around to reveal his identity and watched the boy go slightly pale. Before he could respond, Hadrian covered the boy's mouth with his own and muffled any words that had come to the youth's mind. The beauty of the boy was too great to ruin with what might be a lack of intellect. Gripping the young man's tousled hair firmly with one hand, he watched the green gray eyes widen as the other hand explored the smooth skin, naked beneath the tunic. The small of the young man's back was slightly damp as Hadrian's hand traveled down to the firm mounds of flesh that followed it. The youth gasped as Hadrian pushed further and produced an arousal in them both. As if in a dream, Hadrian watched the fully ripe mouth move in speech, yet he heard nothing. Finally, a small voice revealed the youth's name. "I am Thanos, my lord." The whisper was barely audible, but its electric effect filled Hadrian with feelings he thought were long gone. The Greek boy's mouth, shaped like a Sythian bow, still moved in speech, but Hadrian heard nothing but what the youth's eyes told him. Taking the boy gently by the waist, the emperor led him to the bed and playfully but firmly pushed him down to the thick, down-filled cushions. Tunics were quickly tossed to the floor, and Hadrian was free to explore the lithe wonder beneath him. No thought was given as to how the youth got there or who sent him. And so neither player in this passion play noticed the eyes of Lucius Commodus upon them before he withdrew and, with a smile, closed the thick cedar door behind him.

Lucius Ceionius Commodus Verus was no stranger to the emperor's tastes, both in bed and at the table. As a very young noble, he had managed to find his way into Hadrian's entourage and eventually his bed, much to the chagrin of his father, Lucius Aurelius. The elder Lucius felt that as the descendent of ancestors of consular rank, including grandfathers on both his paternal and maternal sides, Lucius the younger was already in line for great things without having to pander to the tastes of an emperor of lesser pedigree. His son, however, saw things differently and preferred an easier and more glamorous route to power. His beauty was already quite renowned at a young age, and his entry into the inner circle of the imperial court was as glittering as the gold dust his hair stylists added to his already golden locks. It was a look his eldest son would take as his own years later.

Lucius Commodus had not been there in the garden of the Palace of Nicodemia on that fateful day in Bithynia. He had not witnessed the meeting of Hadrian and Antinous. And if he had, he would not have thought twice about it, so assured was he was in his own beauty and his power over the emperor. Lucius had been in Rome waiting for his benefactor and lover to return, which he eventually did do. But the Hadrian that returned was slightly different than the one who had left. Still affectionate and benevolent, but different. It wasn't until four years later that Lucius was to meet the reason for the change in their relationship. There, in a forest north of Rome, he met a beautiful god in a simple linen exomis that revealed strong arms and a finely sculpted chest. Although two years younger than Lucius, the youth had already developed the aura of a young warrior and an athletic quality the delicate nobleman could never hope to attain. Even Chabrias, the dour old tutor, took notice of the boy's unusual beauty. The dark eyes, full lips, and thick mane of blue-black curls left most of the hunting party that gathered in the forest speechless, but Hadrian was, as usual, fully in command of the situation. Or so everyone thought. Soon, the boy would steal the prize stag they hunted, right out from under the emperor's nose. But what would have been a fatal blunder for anyone else became a bonding moment for Hadrian and Antinous, and at that moment, Lucius knew he had a major competitor for the affections of the emperor. What he did not know at the time was that he, and every other courtier, was now out of the race for the title of Hadrian's beloved. The young Greek had conquered an emperor and would never relinquish him, even in death.

Lucius had married before the death of the Beloved One. He had been joined with Avidia Plautia, a wealthy noblewoman and the daughter of a senator. With his newly grown beard and his married status, he felt he had begun a new chapter in his life—a life without Hadrian. But the death of the boy changed that. Although Lucius had been traveling with the emperor's entourage before the death, he felt he was on the fringe of it as long as Antinous was alive. Their time in Alexandria was proof that the youth's physical powers still held sway, although Lucius sensed a decline in their effect. But by that time, he had already planned out his own life and was about to depart for Rome, just after the royal barges had traveled their fateful journey up the Nile. The Beloved's death altered his plans, and despite the birth of his first son forty-eight days after that death, he had returned to Egypt and his former lover.

Lucius's interests were extravagantly lavish. As he spent more time with the emperor, he realized his hold on him would depend on diversions to banish, or at least rebuff, the ghost of Antinous. During their journey to Greece, he had stocked the imperial yacht with the finest furnishings, drapery, bedding, and silver dinner service available. He carefully avoided a gold dinner service, knowing Hadrian's distrust of anything that echoed the excesses of past emperors. The gilt bronze lamps that illuminated the chambers barely passed the imperial scrutiny, but Lucius had a history of getting his way. As the flowers poured from rare vessels and the dancing boys whirled and swayed, Lucius took charge of the kitchens and began to orchestrate sumptuous but whimsical dishes. His epicurean masterpiece was presented the evening their ship entered Greek waters. He presented it to Hadrian as a *tetrafarmacum* after the Greek word for "four drugs." As the meats it contained unfolded, so did Hadrian's understanding of the joke. The cow's udder, wild boar, ham, and pheasant were all nestled in a flaky thick pastry that bled a luxurious sauce when cut. It was a lush and complicated creation that captivated the emperor and quickly became, much to the chagrin of his cooks, his most requested dish. The dishes that followed the dinner were of a different sort, served in a different room, yet just as rich and intoxicating as those from the kitchen. The exotic pages and glittering young nobles also, at times, captivated the emperor. Yet Lucius noted with regret the silent sorrow that shrouded Hadrian, even in the midst of the revelries. All of the young noble's efforts merely kept the Beloved's dark spell at bay, when he truly wanted it broken.

It would never *be* broken. The fire that had been smoldering for nearly two years was waiting for the next breath to give it life. And life it would have—a burning, crackling life that would consume everything that defied its existence. Wherever Hadrian would travel, the specter of Antinous would not be far behind, whispering both love and condemnation in his ear. As the *Felicitati* passed the Isle of Cephalonia and entered the Gulf of Calydon, Hadrian recalled taking in these same views not many years past. Then, the view included the vision of an excited, raven-haired boy at the helm. But as the Ionian Sea mellowed into the confines of the gulf, Hadrian too became calm in the face of his life without his Beloved. For the first time, he looked forward to the future and an extended stay in Greece. The ships sailed past small white homes clinging to the rocky hills of Naupactus as they glowed red, then pink in the setting sun. The narrow strait between Aetolia and

Achaia created a wind passage that urged the imperial flotilla on into the Gulf of Corinth. By morning, they would reach Corinth where they would replenish their provisions in preparation for the final stretch to Athens. As the last rays of sun began to vanish into the sea, their remnants slipped quietly into the stateroom and rested for a moment on a small votive image of Palaemon, the young dolphin-riding sea god whose subterraneous sanctuary was believed to exist near Corinth. This was the mythical child who, while in the arms of his mother Ino, was hurled to his death into the sea and as a result became a god. The significance of this legend was not lost on Hadrian, and the image of the boy god born of the sea stood silently by the image of another young god, born of a river. As a servant silently replaced the sun's rays with the flickering light of votive lamps that hung from the cedar rafters of the ship, Hadrian gazed at the two images before him. The gaiety of the dolphin boy contrasted sharply with the somber features of the beautiful marble Antinous, who seemed to gaze down sleepily at the smaller figure beside him. Taking a glass *balsamarium* of fragrant oil from beside the votive altar, Hadrian poured a small amount in his hand and began to anoint the marble figure. The pristine stone sparkled like snow as it absorbed the precious ointment. Hadrian's hands traveled the broad chest of the sculpted bust, his fingers finding their way up the sturdy neck to the broad features of the finely rendered face. Closing his eyes, he released his hands on a journey they had made so many times in the past—the solid jaw, the full, sullen lips, the deep-set eyes. As his fingers translated the features for his brain, his mind caught fire and released in the smoke all contact with the realities of the past and present. For one dazzling moment, the features were warm and alive and the horrible dream that now haunted this tragic life was dispelled. Taking his beloved's face in his hands, he kissed the slightly parted mouth with a passion he thought had been denied him forever. But his lips and tongue touched cold stone that could not return his desire. Opening his eyes, he saw nothing but the vacant stare of an artist's creation. The spell was broken, and reality tore through him like shards of glass. Numbly, he continued to anoint the sculpture, sliding his hands on the deftly wrought curls of the young god's great mane. The full lips glistened from the fragrant oil. How many times he had seen those lips parted as if to speak, yet no words were spoken. How many secrets had the boy kept from him? How many clues to his sadness were denied him? As Hadrian's mind traveled back to the many scenes in his travels with the boy, he recalled the days and nights in Eleusis and the prophecies that ravaged the tender senses of an impressionable youth. In his desire to gain a fuller understanding of the great mysteries, Hadrian exposed the youth to powers far beyond his ability to grasp. Even the priests warned him of the dangers he was exposing the boy to, but his ego would hear nothing of it. To Caesar, the boy was perfection and must be seen as such. For all the exposure the emperor had given him, Antinous could not be viewed as anything less; the obsession of an emperor could never be construed as misguided. Perfection had its price, but unknown to Hadrian at the time, the Nile was where payment would be extracted. And not a day passed that he did not remember the blame for that payment lay entirely at his feet.

Chapter Fourteen

The Grandeur of Corinth

The emperor's entry into Corinth was a momentous one, a fitting welcome for the ruler of the world. High above, on the rocky isthmus that separates the Peloponnese from northern Greece, the painted marble of the public buildings glowed in the winter sun. The severity of the city's grandiose architecture was softened by floral garlands and bore great banners of scarlet cloth emblazoned with the imperial eagle. One was hard pressed to find any remnant of the old wounds brought on by the Roman destruction under Lucius Mummius over two hundred years previous. The reconstruction by Julius Caesar that followed one hundred years or so later had been continued by Trajan, then Hadrian, and it reflected Corinth's place as the center of government for Southern Achaia. The wealth of Corinth was legendary, and today much of it poured out into the streets on the bodies of its citizens, eager to welcome and impress their emperor. This cosmopolitan swarm, always eager for a diversion, buzzed with anticipation as the royal entourage disembarked onto the docks.

From his seat on the ship's deck, Hadrian scanned the jagged terrain in an effort to view the ancient Temple of Apollo. Within the heavy Doric temple was the memory of a man and a youth embracing at the foot of Apollo's statue. What was a few years past seemed like a lifetime ago. But the memory remained fresh, the scar unhealed. Rising slowly from his chair, Hadrian's eyes remained fixed on the ancient temple until his prefect, Lucius Didus, interrupted his thoughts. Lucius too recalled the last visit to the temple by Hadrian, and was witness to the mystical moment when the Beloved caught his lover as he collapsed at the feet of Apollo's frozen image. How many times had Lucius been the silent witness to pivotal moments in the lives of the tragic couple? He had lost count partly because he was expected to and partly due to his desire to forget painful memories.

Hadrian had not even disembarked, yet he was already weary of Corinth and her boisterous inhabitants. The mingling of Greco-Roman freedmen with Jews and Christians lead to frequent brawls in the marble paved streets. The Christians especially irritated Hadrian, who considered them the spawn of the Jews and even more self-righteous. There was a time when, during his stay in Judea, Hadrian attempted to learn more about a crucified sophist, or Christus, the Christians worshiped. Once the word began to spread about his interest, bishops sought to convert him or at least convince him of the superiority of their beliefs, deluging him with their long-winded theologies. Used to the philosophic teachings of writers such as the aged and eminent Epictetus of Nicopolis, Hadrian was somewhat scornful of these arrogant, self-important bishops and their faith based doctrine of exclusion. Their persistent letters were both fawning and condescending; the emperor quickly tired of them and returned to his favorite works of Cato and Ennius. Their archaic writing style suited his stoic sensibilities. The Roman approach to religion was to include all gods to its pantheon and unite communities in the process. The idea of a single deity made no sense to the somewhat secular emperor, while the refusal of the Christians to accept his beloved Antinous as a god enraged him. Even here in Corinth, the Christians have been reported to be speaking out against the cult of the new god. As with Antioch, a city he truly despised, the Christian rabble was on the list for imperial scrutiny and scorn.

As always, roaring crowds and great fanfare marked Hadrian's entry into the city. The entourage was as impressive as with the last visit, but there was a star quality missing. The beautiful boy was not at the emperor's side this time, and missing too was the light that had shown so brightly in the emperor's eyes. The shining blue-gray had weathered to a cold metal, and the intellect, while still present in those eyes, had lost the sparkle of curiosity and had been replaced by a brittle, calculating keenness. This was an emperor of the sculptures, not the mortal whose joyful radiance flowed through his Beloved. Then, their frequent glances at each other, like bolts of lightning, electrified the crowd. The sheer beauty of their spectacle awed even the most jaded. Now, the austere majesty they witnessed chilled the masses, even as they cheered and tossed the pedals of ravaged roses.

The streets of Corinth had been romanized under Julius Caesar and were wider than traditional Greek roads. The principal platea, or broadway, that Hadrian and his entourage now traveled on had been widened from the twenty-four feet of its original Grecian dimensions to the more accommodating eighty feet, as suiting a city of this stature. The flanks of Praetorian guards filled the width of the marble-clad road as they clattered through the agora toward the palace and temples that awaited the arrival of the emperor. The narrow sidewalks lining the platea were crowded with the excited masses that jostled and spilled into the arcades along the street, stocked high with the good of venders from the many corners of the empire and beyond. In Corinth, as in most major Roman cities, silence never prevailed. The roar of the crowd, as they shared space with sedan chairs and litters, was replaced at night by the rattle of carts and groan of wagons burdened with goods for the next day's market. The wealth and significance of Corinth was unmistakable, making the city a worthy beginning, as it had been a few years earlier, for an imperial tour. This was one of Hadrian's many imposing arrivals into the city, and each had its own emotion for him. But today, he wanted nothing more than to reach the end of the main thoroughfare and disappear into the palace Trajan had built years earlier. As he gazed over the glistening flanks of his guards at the shining marble of the Roman-built forum and bustling agora, he realized there was little to add to this proud, luxurious city. He had restored the Peirene Fountain, the major source of water for the city, during his last visit there. He could just make out the frescos of swimming fish on the walls of the grand structure and, within the center niche, the statue of Perirene. The memory of a regretful moment with Antinous beside that fountain left him indifferent to the elaborate edifice he was once so proud of. How tempted he was to just toss a bag of gold coins onto the *bema* within the forum and move on. This raised public platform was used for public speaking and, more recently, the trials of troublesome Christians. On this site, nearly one hundred years earlier, a man named Paul had faced the Roman governor Gallio to contest the accusation of sedition. Paul was long gone now, but the foundation he had created for this sect still survived and remained a thorn in the side of the authorities. Hadrian was in no mood for the complaints of this common, sour-faced people and would not hesitate to expel them if they dared to disrupt the dedication ceremonies for the new temple to his beloved.

Entering the vast courtyard of the palace through an arch he had designed years earlier, Hadrian left the slowly subsiding cheers of the populace behind him. Making a mental note to have the slaves grease the creaking hinges of the iron gates that were closing behind him, the emperor dismounted and made his way to the portico of the palace. There, the recently installed governor Erastus Menos stood waiting to greet him. Erastus was a man of few words, and Hadrian silently thanked the gods for that. His usual quarters were ready for him, and they glowed from the polished stone of the floors to the burnished bronze of the many sculptures that lined the high walls. From the windows of his chambers, the Temple of Apollo could be seen, glowing in the setting sun as great masses of billowing clouds sailed by. The thick columns, only slightly shaken by a recent quake, stood defiantly on the rocky hill. Hadrian stood mesmerized by the view, unaware of the chattering pages in the next chamber, busily preparing his bath. As the music of the chatter and laughter subsided, Hadrian became aware of a presence behind him. He turned to see a youth standing silently between two of the slender pale columns that lined the entrance to the bathing chambers. Pale and slender too was the youth who, head bowed, lowered himself to one knee with a fluid grace that belied his age. For a moment, Hadrian was speechless. The fading light of the setting sun cast a warm glow to the already glowing youth, and the flickering light of the bronze lamps that hung above him added a luster to the thick mass of his hair. The contrast of jet-black hair and alabaster skin was a familiar one to Hadrian, yet it never failed to captivate him. He walked in carefully measured steps to the bowed figure, unsure of what he wanted the next move to be. As the youth heard the emperor approach, he rose to meet the man's gaze. With a glimmer of a smile, his eyes made clear to Hadrian the next step he should take. Following the barefoot youth to the bathing chambers, the anger and frustrations of the day slipped from Hadrian like a winter cloak on a warm spring day.

The décor of the bathing chamber was not surprising for a city known for luxury. But even for Corinth, the lavishness of this bath was astonishing. Hadrian took note of the finely crafted mosaics on the marble walls that convincingly depicted nonexisting rooms in the distance, creating the illusion of a room even more immense than it actually was. The floors of golden onyx were warm under foot, as was the water of the bath on whose floor mosaic dolphins danced around a bearded Poseidon. Small tables of gilded silver, supporting delicate Egyptian glass bowls filled with rare fruits, stood by low cushioned benches of camphor wood. Great cast bronze oil lamps hung overhead while tall torches supported by figures of satyrs blazed along walls embellished with bronze inlay and panels of semiprecious stone. Hadrian watched as the youth stood alongside a porphyry *tazza* that glowed with gilded bronze mounts, its handles in the shape of sea serpents. Hot water from the mouth of a bronze head of Medusa set into the marble wall flowed into the tazza, splashing over the delicately carved rim and down into the steaming bath. Naked now, the youth had already washed his face and hands and watched with curious eyes the approaching man. Droplets of water ran down the smooth musculature and clung to the boy's long black lashes. The full ripe mouth, slightly open, glistened. None of this was lost on Hadrian. Nor was the slightly seductive glint in the youth's dark eyes. *Beauty, standing naked before age*, thought Caesar. With the look of a man about to accept a challenge, Hadrian leaned over the basin to wash and, with a swift movement that belied *his* age, turned and pushed the youth into the bathing pool. *Age be damned,* thought Hadrian. *This is not my first time in the arena.* He smiled at the shock in the boy's eyes as he laughingly fell into the water. The sound of youthful laughter and the sight of the agile boy gliding effortlessly through the steaming water sent a rush of joy and bitter memories through the emperor. Removing his tunic, he pushed back the memories and, heading toward the splashing youth, reveled in the fleeting joy he was about to receive.

The sun had left the sky long before Hadrian left his chambers and entered the banquet hall. With a look of bemused satisfaction, he greeted his host and thanked him for his hospitality. He ate little and drank less. He had demons to meet in the Temple of Apollo, and it was to be an arduous climb. During the meal, the lithe young man who had beguiled the emperor earlier joined in the dances and did his best to engage the man once more. But Hadrian's mind had already left the festivities, and soon, he rose with some effort from his couch and, after thanking his host, left the hall for his chambers. The night chill had grown even colder, but his cloak would be sufficient for his journey. Besides, the exertion of the rocky climb to the temple would keep him warm. Slipping out of the courtyard behind his quarters, Hadrian kept cover under the vast colonnade that extended to a grove of olive trees. From there, he was able to vanish from sight and proceed toward the hill that over looked the city.

The full moon assisted the climb, but the treachery of the narrow path was present just the same. At one point, a bank of clouds covered the moon's face; and Hadrian, grateful for the excuse to pause, rested on what seemed to be a huge boulder. The noise of the city filtered up the hill through the thin night air, floating through the slender cedars and low-lying shrubs. Slowly, the cloud cover drifted away, revealing in the distance the Temple of Aphrodite sitting firmly on the rock of the Acrocorinth. Hadrian stood up from his resting place and prepared to continue his journey, when he realized that where he was sitting was not a boulder at all but a deeply carved section of the original temple. Whether deposited there by man or nature's fury, the marble fragment was now deeply lodged within the earth. Raising his head, Hadrian saw his journey was closer to its finish than he had realized. The rugged Doric columns loomed over him like great colossi, their fluted shafts playing with the moon's pale light. Gathering his cloak around him, the emperor strode toward the ancient portico and the great bronze door of the temple, uncertain of what he was to find.

Surprisingly, the massive door made no sound as he pushed his weight against it to gain entry to the cella. His keen sense of smell detected the scent of fresh grease on the hinges; a sign that his visit was not unexpected. As he entered the main vestibule, he was surprised by the amount of light that greeted him. Oil lamps hung from the massive beams of the ceiling, and great braziers blazed with abandon. The statue of the god, overwhelming in its beauty during the emperor's last visit, was grander now draped in fine linen and crowned with a wreath of golden leaves. It was obvious the princely sum the emperor had gifted the temple during his last visit had been used with abandon. He noticed the priests too were finely dressed and more portly than the previous visit. The emperor was not pleased. Yet something caught his eye that soothed his rising anger and proved the gold he had presented was not used without purpose. There, raised up in a coffered niche to the right of Apollo's altar, stood a life-sized statue of Antinous. Here too fine linen hung from the marble figure, and a radiant crown of gold leaves reflected the light of the votive fire at his feet. Silently, the priests made their way to the altar of their new god as the head priest reached out and pulled the linen drape from the glowing image. The fabric whispered in the air as it released its hold on the sculpture and floated to the floor. There, shining in the light of many flames, stood the exquisite form of his beloved. The marble form had not been painted as with the antique Apollo. Instead, a pale pink stone was used, its hue barely discernable, but it lent the naked figure the aura of a living being. Much gold had been sacrificed by the priests for a work this perfect, and in his heart, Hadrian know he would repay them in full. The face reflected the firelight at the sculptures feet, animating the soft features, the deep-set eyes, the heartbreakingly full mouth. Even cold stone warmed when fashioned to the perfection of his likeness. Lost in the sight of this masterpiece, Hadrian relived the anguish of his loss, the humiliating guilt. He did not have to go to Delphi to know the journey of his life. Here in the votive flames, he saw his future—to wander the empire worshipping his god, his Antinous. Forever on his knees before the boy he helped to kill his soul.

The morning light reflected off the snow-covered mountains in the distance and found its way through the ancient columns to the cella interior. There, Apollo cast his gaze upon the form that slept at the feet of his god. The feeble warmth was enough to waken the man from his slumber and cast his own gaze upon the face that looked down upon his. The features were motionless now. The soft warmth the fire had given them the night before was replaced by the chill of dawn. Rising unsteadily to his feet, Hadrian ached as he reached to kiss the foot of the sculpture. Behind him, he could discern the silent movements of the priests already at their duties. Having finished the ritual bathing of Apollo, they stood ready to administer the same solemn ritual with their newest god. They bowed deeply as Hadrian stepped back and made room for the placement of the oakwood ladder that would allow the priest to anoint the face and chest of the sculpture with holy oil. Lost in his own memories, the emperor's reverie was broken by the sight of a priest offering him the jar of oil and a soft linen cloth. After casting a wary eye on the ladder, he made his way up each rung and was soon face-to-face with the sculptor's skillful rendering of the young god. Pouring the rare oil over the finely carved head, he recalled the dense curls he ran his fingers through in the heat of passion. His fingers, dripping now with oil, ran a familiar journey down the forehead, the heavy brow, the broad jawline. As Hadrian wiped away the excess oil with the linen cloth, he left the perfectly carved mouth glistening. It was as Hadrian would always remember it, whether from a goatskin water bag, the remains of honey taken from a freshly harvested comb, or a kiss just left by his lover. The mouth of the youth was always shining, eager, inviting.

Tears made their way down his face as Hadrian continued to trace the lines of that mouth. Kissing it gently, he lowered himself down the ladder and returned the oil jar and cloth to the priest. Turning to leave, he saw the door of the temple was already open with the head priest standing silently in the winter wind. With a few words that promised a fitting gift to the cult, Hadrian left the temple for the last time. He found both comfort and sorrow at the sight of his god's presence here. They were emotions he would relive throughout his life's journey.

Chapter Fifteen

A Temple for Delphi

Hadrian was grateful to be leaving Corinth, that bastion of overindulgence and chaos. He longed for the mystery and shrouded secrets of Delphi, despite the fact that in his mind his questions had been already answered. The emperor departed with his private guard early in the morning, with the rest of his entourage leaving later to purposely confuse their hosts. Even his imperial chamberlain had no knowledge of his master's departure, not that the emperor consulted him in every aspect of his travels anymore. Since the death of the youth, Hadrian's movements and mood shifts had become even more erratic than usual. From the window of his own private quarters, Ophelos watched as the small band of Praetorian guards thundered off into the distance, while a smaller band made its way up to the ancient temple of Apollo, their horses burdened with bags of gold coin. With a promise kept, the emperor set off in the virgin light of morning to the still quiet port, eager to begin his journey to Delphi. A ship waited for him as the docks began to fill with merchants awaiting the incoming ships. The carts and wagons stood ready for their loads to be transported in the evening hours to the many storehouses on the city's perimeter. The imperial ship was berthed far from the merchant piers, and the arrival of the emperor that morning was both unexpected and unnoticed. That is, not until the more astute merchants noticed the familiar stride of a tall man as he boarded the ship. By then, it was too late to react. The ramps were not completely pulled aboard before the oarsmen set to work. Merchants and sailors alike waved what they feared would be their final salute to their emperor. The fortunes of the city depended on the beneficence of the emperor, and rumors told of a man in the twilight of his days. But for the emperor, the shrinking sight of the gleaming city was a welcome one. Within the hour, with the city of Sicyon visible on the port side, the sails of the flagship were unfurled into the too gentle winds. With the wind and the manpower at the oars, they should make the city of Crissa by late afternoon and with luck, Delphi by nightfall.

Lucius Verus had astutely assumed a redecorating of the royal cabin was in order. Hadrian noted with pleasure the reflection of himself in the chambers. If anyone knew him at all, it was his charming Lucius. As he surveyed the main cabin, his eyes set upon a low couch in the Egyptian style. An unintentional misstep on Lucius's part. What stood in nearly the same position in the former flagship was the gilded sarcophagus of Antinous. An Egyptian couch had replaced an Egyptian coffin. Both were a place of sleep—one temporary, one eternal. With a twisted sense of irony, Hadrian walked to the couch, removed his sandals, and laid down. A strange sense of tranquility washed through him like natron, and sleep descended. Morpheus sent him dreams of riding hard through the dense forests of Bithynia, his Antinous riding along side. But as Hadrian turned to gaze upon his beloved, he found the youth wearing the mask from the sarcophagus. Tears poured from the hollow, painted eyes and dissolved the mask, leaving in its place the head of Osiris. The Antinous-Osiris lashed the side of his horse and galloped off into the deep mist of the forest, leaving Hadrian drenched in steaming horse sweat.

With a jolt, Hadrian awoke from his troubled sleep covered in his own sweat. He rose quickly from the gilded couch and glared at it suspiciously, wishing it gone. After attempting to lug it from its place, the emperor went to the door of his cabin and called in the two guards who stood at the entrance. He ordered the men to remove the couch and toss it overboard. Unquestioning, the soldiers lifted the rare piece of furniture and, struggling under its weight, left the cabin. Soon after, a loud splash could be heard; and the emperor, with a grunt of satisfaction, walked to his desk and the pile of documents that awaited him. Chabrais, the old tutor, appeared at the door to inform his master that the towers of Crissa were visible from the fore deck. Hadrian smiled sadly at the old man, who seemed to have less hair than days left to his life. He had never really noticed the affection the tutor had for Antinous, when he was alive. In death, so much became clear. He kept the old man near for his company and his wisdom, but in truth, neither attribute was very apparent now. The man seemed mired in memories of the youth, and his mind was often clouded. Age had overtaken him.

Hadrian walked slowly with Chabrais to the main deck as a soldier rushed over with a stout oaken stool. Offering the elder tutor the seat, Hadrian paced the deck and looked out at the fading sun as it bathed the approaching city in warm light. Crissa, one of the oldest cities in Greece, had seen its share of turmoil. Located on one of the rocky spurs of Parnassus where the ravine of the

Pleistus meets the plain, the name of Crissa appeared in both the Iliad and the Homeric hymns. It had been rich, fertile, and arrogant due to its inclusion of the Delphi sanctuary within its territorial borders. But as Delphi grew in fame and the seaport of Cirrha rose in the Crisean Gulf, Crissa's importance faded. Hadrian preferred this ancient port city because it was used more by merchants than pilgrims, making his arrival less remarkable and his quick departure for Delphi less noticeable. As he had planned, the ship's arrival created little commotion despite its size due in part to the emperor's command that the royal standard be removed so as to not attract attention. As the emperor's troops and entourage waited for their horses to disembark, the emperor mingled with his architects and builders as they perused the many plans and drawings he had presented to them. Delphi was to receive a new temple as was Eleusis. Winter was late and mild so far, and the ground would still allow for digging. As soon as the horses reached the pier, the imperial entourage galloped through the outskirts of the city toward the mountains of Parnassus looming in the distance.

The road leading to Delphi was straight and paved in the Roman tradition, but filled with pilgrims on their way to and from the sacred city. As the sun began fading fast, Hadrian urged his men on as they trampled the low brush of the plain alongside the congested roadway. Hadrian had considered alerting the Delphians about his impending arrival but decided against it. He wanted to see firsthand what kind of honors the city had provided his beloved. In the past, he had always left the city and its temples far wealthier than he had found them. Now he would see how worthy they were of his generosity.

Passing a number of small villages in their path, it was some time before the lights of the city could be seen in the distance. The line of pilgrims had thinned the closer the imperial entourage came to the city, allowing for a more dignified entry. The emperor halted the group to allow the squires to wipe down the sweating horses and the shake off the dust of the plains from the cloaks of the men. After man and beast had caught their collective breath, they proceeded at a more leisurely pace toward the city. To their surprise, footmen began to appear along the road with torches to escort the procession and its regal leader. The city was aware of its visitor, and the shock of it could be felt even before the gates were reached. A number of emperors from Rome visited the city and its sanctuary, some welcome, some not. But the emperor who was arriving on this evening was more than welcome and watched as the great gates swung open and horns blasted the news of his arrival.

Over the centuries, Delphi had been plundered or gifted by Rome, depending on the nature of the emperor and the straits of his finances. Nero had plundered the treasuries and carried off over five hundred bronzes for his Golden Palace in Rome. Yet, despite plundering and the changes in religious movements and beliefs, the sanctuary continued to thrive and its rituals remained unchanged. And it was Delphic ritual and prediction this emperor was after, not gold. Gold was what he left behind. As he passed the many treasury houses that held the gifts of their respective cities to the sanctuary and its oracle, Hadrian noted with satisfaction that a construction of his own design stood tall and gleaming white beside the ancient Temple of Apollo. Within the cella, surrounded by massive Corinthian style columns, stood a votive statue of Trajan, his adoptive father. Pausing before the imposing edifice, he thought of paying tribute when a sudden rush of exhaustion overtook him. The day had been long and tiring. Motioning the group onward, they headed towards the villa of Arrian of Nicomedia, a Greek aristocrat he had known for many years. Though twelve years his junior, Arrian had applied himself to the Stoic philosophies and was older than his years. The fact that he was from Bithynia made him even dearer to the emperor, and he looked forward to spending the coming days with him. But as the procession approached the gate of the villa, the expression on the faces of the servants made him regret his unannounced arrival. An elderly man, still hastily pulling on his robes, bowed as deeply as he could manage before the emperor before informing him that the master of the house was not at home. Arrian was at his home in Athens, awaiting Hadrian's arrival there. An awkward silence followed before the old man helped both his master and the emperor save face. "But we will proceed as if my master was in residence, for surely his home is your home, sire," the man announced, as if to the entire city. Hadrian smiled and dismounted and, taking the man by the arm, walked into the villa for a welcome night's sleep.

The next morning was clear and crisp, and from his window, Hadrian could see snow high on the peak of Mount Parnassus. Mild weather would soon turn to cold, and the ground would not be as pliant to the spade. If there was building to be done, it would have to be immediate and swift. After a light meal, Hadrian, his architects, and his builders left for the center of Delphi. On the way, they were met by Marius Paulis, head of the legion for this province. With him were priests and members of the Delphic council, eager to show him the newest addition to the glories of Delphi. Striding past the theater and stadium, east of the Temple of Apollo, they began to reach the Kastalian Spring. Here, Hadrian had rebuilt the fountain house for the pilgrims to purify themselves before approaching the temples and the oracle. It was here that the city had intended to build a grand administrative building in Hadrian's honor—a tribute to his outpouring of support and protection. As the emperor approached the building site, he was startled by an elegant vision that rose from the piles of building marble and rubble. Without being told, he knew the purpose of this slender edifice. The morning sun had reached over the buildings of the city and now began to wash over the open space before him. As it did, the light began to warm the pure white marble of what Hadrian knew instinctively was the Temple of Antinous.

Taller and even more elegant than the ancient Tholos at the center of the sanctuary of the Athena Pronaia, the new temple stood proudly in the morning light. The advancing rays of the sun played with the deeply carved and gilded acanthus leaves covering the capitals of the twenty exterior Corinthian columns. As Hadrian walked slowly toward the entrance of the temple, he was startled by a radical departure in the mostly Greek architecture. There, crowning the ten interior columns that formed the inner circle, were capitals of a distinctly Egyptian order. This reference to the origin of Antinous's entry to the pantheon of the gods deeply moved the emperor. The connection of the youth's Greek birth and his Egyptian rebirth was a brilliant tribute. But more was to come. Entering through a tall bronze door, he immediately approached a cult statue of Antinous in pure Parian marble gazing down upon him. He was depicted as he was during the height of their time together, more a youth than a man. The great curls hung heavily around his face and the deep-set eyes set with jasper and ivory bore deep into Hadrian. Bathed in the morning light pouring from an oculus that opened the ceiling to the sky, the statue glowed with the vitality of the god when mortal. The votive image stood on a circular altar, and at his feet, a deep cavity was carved into the stone and lined with bronze for the burning of offerings. A mound of glowing embers competed with the light streaming from above, while a bowl of incense, resting in a bronze tripod, stood ready for the offerings of the faithful. Hadrian walked to the bowl and, gathering a good amount with a gilded silver spoon, made an offering to his god. The aromatic spices spit and flared as they hit the blistering coals, sending rising swirls of scented smoke; ghostly hands to caress the face of the statue. The form of the young god had been modeled with love and reverence. And as he examined the masterful carving, he took notice of the meticulously rendered hair around the youth's genitals, chiding himself with some humor for the tinge of jealousy it evoked. After a time, he turned and left the temple, deep in thought. *Beautiful and so close to perfection,* he acknowledged to himself, *but not real.*

Once outside, his mind cleared, and he thanked the priests and city magistrates for creating such a worthy tribute. But as they unrolled the diagrams and renderings that described the finished plans for the buildings dedicated to the emperor, Hadrian's mind began to formulate a design that would undo theirs. Inspecting the inventory of building stone, stacks of finished column drums, and finely carved capitals, Hadrian began to envision a different use for all this stone. Calling to his architects for parchment and ink, the emperor began to draw out the vision he had retained in his mind for some time. By requisitioning the existing materials, he could impose his own vision for the Temple of Antinous. Delphi had no need for another building in honor of an emperor, but what it must have, in Hadrian's mind, was a great temple complex dedicated to Antinous. As lines of ink began to cover the stack of parchment, the assemblage of architects and builders began to gather their drawings and diagrams with the knowledge that an emperor with a different objective and a powerful reason to reach it had supplanted their vision.

By February of the following year, the designs that flowed from Hadrian's brain to the pile of parchments littering the makeshift workbenches of the builders had become a reality. Working with the foundations that had already been installed, the workers constructed two semicircular colonnades of honey-colored marble that wrapped around the existing temple like great protective arms. Each colonnade was composed of a double rank of columns supporting a tiled roof. Corinthian capitals crowned the outer and first three inner columns while, in keeping with the decoration of the temple itself, the rest of the inner columns held capitals of Egyptian design. The twin structures were shorter in height to the temple so that the roof of that structure, now covered with gleaming tiles of gilt bronze, was visible over the roofline. A granite obelisk, imported at enormous cost from Alexandria, now rose at the mouth of the vast courtyard created by the colonnades and at times cast a shadow upon the temple itself. Surrounding the temple was a great pool fed by the nearby Kastalian Spring and dissected by a marble walkway connecting the two colonnades with the temple. The work had been done in record time due more to the watchful eye of the emperor than to the unusually mild weather. A weary Hadrian cast his gaze over his handiwork, knowing he had accomplished what he came here to do. During the rededication of the temple, he stood before the statue of his beloved as the thick smoke wrapping around the oiled marble spiraled out the roof's circular passage. Prefect Lucius, positioned in the shadows of the small temple, recalled another time he witnessed this scene in another much grander temple. In the filtered light, the emperor looked younger than his years; but Lucius knew that in the clear light of day, the years returned without mercy. He prayed silently to Mithras that this journey would resume soon so that the return to Rome would be still within the emperor's lifetime. And his own.

Chapter Sixteen

In the Arms of Athens

After the dedication of the Antinous's temple, Hadrian attended the dedication of a votive statue of the youth crowned with a circlet of golden laurel leaves in Delphi's great Temple of Apollo. These events had become nourishment to him, and a balm to ease the grief that continued to sear his heart like molten lead. In the haze of sacrificial smoke, Prefect Lucius watched, with suspicion and concern, Hadrian's willingness to accept with solemn dignity the mystic ranting of astrologers, spiritualists, and priests as they manipulated his preoccupation with death. Primordial incantations mingled with the clanking chains of bronze censers, their thick smoke billowing to the blackened cedar beams of the ancient temple. Time stood breathless here, immobile. Yet even as Hadrian worshiped before the altar of Apollo, Lucius realized the emperor remained strong willed and intractable. As the priests evoked the gods with their feats of luminosity and sound, a fleeting look of wry bemusement passed over the features of the emperor. Grief had not withered his resolve, nor his grip on reality. Hadrian saw clearly the intentions of the temple priests and used them toward his own means. All the power of his station would be put to use for the elevation of his Beloved as god. Power was Hadrian's medicine of choice—the remedy for an empty soul.

Lucius saw all this in his emperor's eyes as they left the temple; the old lion was gravely wounded but far from defeated.

The imperial court left Delphi for the journey to Athens. The emotional flagellation he had endured in the temples empowered him, but a visit to Eleusis on their way to Athens was far more than he could bear at this time. It was there that the seed of Antinous's demise was planted. And so as they rode out of the Cithaeron Mountains, Hadrian's guides chose a road that headed toward Marathon and skirted the mystical city. However, this would add two days to their journey, and Hadrian wished to enter the enlightened world of his much-loved Athens as soon as possible. The road chosen passed close to Eleusis and cut through the fertile plain of Thria toward Central Attica. From his horse, Hadrian could make out the acropolis on the high summit as well as the Sanctuary of Demeter on the flank of the lower slope. Memories of this beloved city rushed through him, and he turned away from the sight. Hadrian felt, at times, he would rather feel the pain of unfathomable sorrow than feel nothing at all. And yet, during weaker moments, he wished for numbness to overcome him. *Torture me, burn me with your memory. I light the flames of your altars so you may char my soul with their glowing coals.* It was a prayer of repentance he murmured at every temple that honored his Beloved, his god.

As the entourage advanced farther south, the sea air made its way past the low mountain range to the west of Eleusis and swept over the plain. For Lucius, it invoked a homesickness that grew stronger with every day. For Hadrian, the faint breeze pushed him on to Athens and from there, farther south. But something in his unconscious whispered to him. His Villa Adrianna stood waiting, unfinished, for his return. The uncertainty of his remaining years suddenly flashed through, provoking sudden urge to finish this journey. Spurred on by this unexpected revelation, Hadrian broke into a full gallop as the city of Athens came into view. His bodyguards, taken by surprise, recovered quickly and were soon by his side. Only Lucius was not startled. Over the years, he had come to know the man, and that sudden movements followed deep thought. The emperor too was becoming weary of the hunt and knew it was time to go home. But much was to deny them that goal in the meantime.

Athens had been prepared for the arrival of the emperor for nearly a week now. The Roman consul waited nervously at the Villa of Nero, the official residence of the Roman representative as well as the possible residence of the visiting emperor and his court. But Hadrian's avoidance of things connected with this infamous Caesar made this villa out of the question. Hadrian's friend since the emperor made him prefect of the Roman Provinces of Asia, Herodes Atticus had known for some time now that the emperor was to be his guest during his stay and had depleted a sizable portion of his massive fortune to assure a smooth visit. This was done at the urging of his new ephebe, Diodoros, and not out of need to placate Hadrian. Although born into a family of immense wealth, Herodes knew his friend well enough to realize his provision of great luxury was unnecessary for one who was, in truth, a stoic in nature. Herodes's suspicion was that his ephebe was using the imperial visit as an excuse to further embellish the villa and his own status. The fact that he heralded from one of Athens's most aristocratic families did little to appease his vanity. And Herodes, the wealthy, dotting lover of a much younger eromenos, could not find it within himself to deny him the slightest wish.

It was in Herodes's nature to please, yet without a hint of servility. His last encounter with the emperor was during his last visit to Athens, when Hadrian had stayed briefly before his pilgrimage to Eleusis, and the golden youth was by his side. Even Herodes, whose taste for beauteous boys was that of a connoisseur, was smitten by the intense aura of his friend's companion. He noted that Hadrian, usually so reserved and in control, was euphoric in the company of his spirited ephebe. But the nobleman had also noted a change in the youth upon their return from Eleusis. The experience seemed to have stolen away the innocence of the boy and replaced it with a brooding melancholy. Hadrian seemed unaware of the change and, from all reports, lived to regret it. His tendency to ignore or despise human frailties cost him dearly, and Herodes wondered silently as to what kind of man he would greet at the gates of the city.

The restorative power of youth in one's life was a tonic Herodes, even at the age of thirty-six, had come to appreciate. It was upon his return to Athens that a youth had come to gild his own life. Young Diodoros's bust stood on a simple pedestal in Herodes's study, and from time to time, Herodes would sit and gaze at the marble likeness. The boy was the philosopher's favorite pupil and, as many suspected correctly, something more. Herodes hoped to provide the same joy to his old friend and arranged for a scattering of elegant youths from the finest Athenian families to meet the emperor during his stay. The families themselves, eager for the prestige of imperial favor, groomed the youths to represent their peerage in the finest possible light. Many of the family patriarchs had met, or at least seen, Antinous during the last visit of the emperor and did not assume their sons could match the legendary beauty of the one who was now a god. But while a god reigned remotely from a marble altar, the mortal, seductive, and attainable could reign from an altar of down-filled cushions. Through his simple desire to accommodate his friend, Herodes had sent a frenzied ripple through Athenian society. It was too late before he realized what he had set in motion. But then, what would be the harm? If his friend retained even the slightest bit of his old self, the attention would be welcomed and the offers accepted.

The Roman consul greeted Hadrian's entourage as it entered the gates of the city; gates the emperor had restored during his last visit to the city. Cordial and perfunctory, the emperor acknowledged the salutations of the consul that were barely audible through the din of the cheering crowd. The obligatory phrases Hadrian returned as a greeting were enough to send a shudder of relief through the man as the emperor moved on and crossed the River Cephissus toward the Hill of Cronus. There he dismounted to embrace his old friend from Marathon. Although appointed prefect of the free cities in Asia seven years previous, Herodes had returned to Athens to marry, but instead became a teacher and was elected archon a short time before Hadrian's arrival. Although years younger than Hadrian, the bearded Herodes had acquired the patina of a middle-aged aristocrat that made him appear closer to the emperor's age. But the look of joy on his face as they embraced brought renewed youth and vigor to the man. Hadrian too felt the unaccustomed warmth of joy as he took the arm of his friend and walked down a winding path toward a magnificent gift from the grateful Athenians. Beside the still unfinished Olympieion, Temple of Zeus, stood a new gate in honor of the benefactor of Athens—the imperator of Rome. The gate joined the borders of the old city and those of the new city he had begun years previously. Inscribed in the polished Pentelic marble above the eastern side of the arc was the inscription "This is the city of Hadrian and not of Theseus." Hadrian stood silently on his horse for a time and took in the sight of this noble tribute, the pain and weariness he felt melting from him. The magnitude of the honor bestowed by the city he loved above all others moved him as few things ever have. The view he gazed at through the arch was the district of his own design, the Hadrianoupolis. Here he would gift the city with the plans he had begun years before, plans that would finish his final legacy and would include the Temple of Zeus Olympios, begun nearly seven hundred years earlier. The long walk with Herodes along the broad marble boulevard through the enormous Roman Agora felt refreshing after the tedious ride on horseback from Delphi and Hadrian reveled in the adoring cheers of the citizens who elbowed their way to a better view. The sight of ancient temples and sanctuaries that spread out before him in the distance never failed to overwhelm the emperor. As he passed the enormous Prytaneion, home to the priests who tended the many altars of the sacred precinct, he could smell the meat cooking as sacrificial offerings on the eternal flame of Hestia, goddess of the hearth. Sudden pangs of hunger urged Hadrian to hasten the pace of their stride. Above them on the Acropolis could be seen the Roman temple of Rome and Augustus among most ancient sanctuaries, the Temples of Hera, and the Erechtheum. They passed the Palaestra, a training site for the boxers, jumpers, and wrestlers. Their grunts and shouts of greeting to the emperor could be heard from the courtyard and upper chambers where spectators too added their own cheers of welcome. Passing the square Theikoleon or parish house for the temple priests, Hadrian raised his head to view the Parthenon that loomed in the distance. Hunger, however, distracted him from enjoying the sight of the sun setting along its massive columns. Silently grateful, he saw the sun was setting too quickly for a walk through the Agora to be feasible.

Herodes had planned well, and a line of steeds awaited the emperor and the court for the final distance of the journey. As the crowds cheered his arrival, the emperor's entourage turned up the tree-lined Via Kifissias, with a parade of elegant villas in the Roman style flanking either side. From the balconies of the villas, guests who had arrived for just this occasion cheered the emperor as he strode by. Waves of flowers poured from the upper rooms and fell into the shallow canals and flowerbeds that lined the streets below. Many of the guests were middle class Athenians who lived in comfortable but more modest dwellings in the less fashionable parts of the city. Knowing this was possibly their only opportunity to view the emperor of Rome, they rented rooms here for a view of the arrival. Children cheered from the balconies as a seemingly endless stream of flowers continued to pour.

Set far back from the Via Theseos and upon a small incline surrounded by lush gardens, the Villa Kifissia could finally be seen. Olive and fig trees as well as ancient oaks screened the villa from the main road. This northern suburb of Athens was the most prestigious and elegant residential area, and as Hadrian glanced at his friend for a moment, he saw the look of pride that beamed from his face. Without turning to look, Herodes sensed the emperor's gaze and, spreading out his arm to sweep the vision before them, stated, "My beloved's doing. He wished everything to be worthy of the emperor of Rome." This was said not without pride, an emotion he rarely displayed. Hadrian was amused by his friend's departure from the usual prim stoic he once was. What a difference the power of love makes.

Passing through an imposing gate of weathered marble, Hadrian dismounted and strode through this gate more robustly than his body actually felt. Entering the villa, he was greeted by Herodes's sister Claudia Tisamenis, who genuflected before him. A necklace of milky blue chalcedony and pale moonstones set in oval rings of gold circled her slender neck, but were no match for the radiant blue of her eyes. Reaching down, he took her by her slender shoulders and raised her up again. Refinement poured from the low soft voice that welcomed him to the villa, and as the enchanted emperor kissed her on her forehead, he thanked Claudia for her hospitality before turning back to his friend. It was then that he noticed the willowy figure of a boy who stood hesitantly behind his lover. Loose dark curls framed a delicate face with eyes that rivaled those of the radiant Claudia. With the smooth gesture of a Syrian presenting a carpet, Herodes swept Diodoros toward the emperor, and the overawed youth fell gracefully to one knee. Hadrian took the boy by his slender shoulders and raised him up for a better look. Herodes's boy seemed overwhelmed by the presence of the emperor as he murmured a rehearsed litany of welcome and gazed into Caesar's gray eyes. Hadrian was captivated by the radiant sprite before him, yet at the same time felt a sense of his own mortality weigh heavily on his shoulders.

Herodes sensed the tired man behind the gallant emperor and ordered his servants to escort the emperor directly to the private quarters prepared for him and from there, to the hot pool of the bathing chamber. On his way to the private suite, Hadrian saw the many rooms were furnished with a restrained splendor. The walls were frescoed with scenes from Greek mythology, landscapes, and architectural illusions. In the vestibule were fine sculptures, costly marble walls, and doors ornamented with silver, rare shells, and semiprecious stone. There were costly rugs from the East, while heavy silk draperies helped soften the overall affect, adding to the subtle beauty of the rooms.

The late afternoon sun strained to find its way through the slabs of alabaster set into the bathing chamber walls. The soft warmth of the light washed over the face of the emperor as he slept in the marble bath, his head resting on the thick softness of a folded cotton sheet. Sleep, dreamless and pure, was kind to this face; the brows were less furrowed, the lines of worry and grief wiped clean. It was a brief respite. As the light began to pass over him, the chill of its absence woke Hadrian, and the signs of age and life's tragedies returned to his face. Drying himself off, he entered the bedchamber where his steward waited with a fresh tunic and a toga of snow-white linen trimmed with a border of purple embellished with gold embroidery. Hadrian took a quick look at the garment and declared it too Roman. A wool *peplos*, the same bright white but without the embellishments, was unpacked from the cedar trunk and met with royal approval. While his steward was busy with the draping of the linen folds and fastening the corners of the cloth at the emperor's shoulders with simple gold fibulii, Hadrian stood gazing out of the window of his chamber at the distant view of the acropolis and, more clearly in view, the Athenian's gift to their benefactor. How fitting that this arch stood so close to the library he was finally seeing to completion. A grand staircase lead to the massive propylon or gateway that lead to the entrance of the complex. The grayish hue of the Eleusinian marble used in the propylon's construction contrasted with the Pentelic marble of the high, long west wall, which was flanked by massive columns of the Corinthian order. These walls were interrupted by protrusions that gave a hint to the spacious niches of the interior. Hadrian longed to inspect the interior and find the cedar shelves filled with countless rolls of papyrus and velum, as well as the clay tablets of the ancients. This was his finest gift to a city he had blessed with so many gifts.

The sun had nearly finished setting during Hadrian's contemplation of the massive edifice, but he had barely noticed. It was not until Chabrais made his presence known with a coughing fit that the emperor's reverie was ended, and the silence shattered. The royal chamberlain, standing next to the old man with a look of nervous concern on his face, announced that the host and his party were long awaiting the emperor's presence. Reluctantly, Hadrian left his place at the window and, taking the old man by the arm, followed the chamberlain to the banqueting hall. Torches lit their way through the rear of the vestibulum as they passed the inner courtyard of the villa, the spray from its elegant fountain catching the firelight. Laughter could be heard from the Roman-style dining room, and the emperor could see the flickering light of the hanging lamps and glowing bowls that sat snug in their finely wrought tripods. In the glow of that light emerged the somewhat gaunt figure of his dear friend Herodes and the slender elegance of his sister in a flowing chiton of blush-colored sea silk. With the look of a woman assured of her position in society, tempered with the warm refinement of breeding, Claudia welcomed the emperor with deep genuflection and a welcome smile. Her beauty was undeniable and her fashion sense impeccable. As Hadrian took Claudia's hand and entered the dining chamber, he silently appraised her apparel and choice of jewelry, suddenly taken aback by the necklace she had chosen to wear. A triple strand of large creamy pearls were joined together by two finely carved intaglio portraits in circular gold frames. It was an extremely costly piece for certain. But it was not the value of the necklace that captured Hadrian's attention; it was the subject of the two portraits. There, joined by the rows of precious pearls were facing portraits of himself as emperor and his Beloved. Modeled after a commemorative coin he had commissioned during his last stay in Athens, the portraits were meticulously rendered in disks of rare translucent jade. Claudia's face colored to the shade of her chiton as Hadrian continued to be mesmerized by the portraits. Finally, the emperor became aware of the tense silence that now surrounded him and, kissing Claudia's forehead, expressed his admiration for the necklace and his gratitude for such a loving tribute. The assembled guests drew a collective sigh of relief as Caesar walked toward the outstretched arms of his old friend and embraced him before taking his place of honor. At the sight of the majestic, toga-clad figure entering the dining chamber, the guests had risen in unison to greet their emperor and, more importantly, great benefactor. Hadrian's entrance signaled the music to begin, as well as the parade of servants bearing the first course on trays of silver. Boiled and pickled eggs prepared in a variety of ways sat nestled in lettuce leaves, while smaller trays of olives and marinated beans were passed around to excite the appetites of the diners. Hadrian suddenly felt the absence of any meal that day, and his hunger needed no stimulant. Herodes, reclining on a nearby couch, could hear the faint rumble of the royal stomach and motioned for the second course to follow quickly. In tight formation, an army of servants presented trays of sausage and apple-stuffed fowl swimming in a honeyed wine sauce, thin slices of rolled Egyptian beef filled with herbs and goat's cheese from Parthia, and fragrant fish cakes molded to resemble scallop shells and sprinkled with capers. On large plates of rare colorless glass, plump, wine-soaked cherries clustered around golden barley cakes dripping with honey and sprinkled with petals of lavender.

The combination of gnawing hunger, sumptuous array of foods, and the warmth and ease of Herodes's presence made the meal a rare joy for Hadrian. Over the chatter and laughter of the assembled guests, the musical clink of silver jugs against the rims of constantly refilled wine glasses could barely be heard. The musicians too were no competition for the celebrants. This idyllic setting was the combined presence of intellectual and aristocratic guests, as well as the young Athenian students of philosophy who Herodes instructed for free. A vibrant air of celebration prevailed, and for a moment, all was well in the world of the emperor of Rome.

The guests seemed to bask in the glow of the emperor, and their adoration filled him with even more satisfaction than the lavish meal before him. The overreaching coarseness of Rome could never compare to the glittering refinement of Athens. Here, his architectural achievements blended into the cultural fabric they derived from, while at the same time standing out as pristine examples of his ability to contribute to what was already a wondrous city. In Rome, his buildings stood like glistening jewels tossed into a pool of mud. Here, they stood proudly in a city worthy of their presence. As the night wore on and the blood of grapes continued to flow into goblets raised to the health of the emperor, Hadrian felt the pang of regret that he would have to leave this paradise for the reality of his duties. But for now, he reveled in the joy of friendship and the warm wave of gratitude. He was Athens's, and Athens was his.

The next morning, Hadrian and his court headed north through the Roman Agora, past the gleaming Parthenon toward the northern side of the Acropolis. His newly completed library complex was a sprawling edifice that glowed in the morning sun as they approached. Unlike the Library of Pantainos, built by a wealthy Athenian named Titus Pantainos during the reign of Trajan, Hadrian's structure combined a library with multiple rooms for philosophic lectures. The exterior columns, easily seen from a distance, gave no indication of their monumental size until one began to approach from this direction. Made of marble from the Euboean province of Karystos, they were capped by finely carved Corinthian capitals that spread plantlike under the architrave. An eager emperor strode impatiently up the massive stairs and parted the wave of scholars and onlookers that crowded the entrance. Having designed the structure himself and modeled it after the Temple Pacis he knew so well in Rome, Hadrian had no problem finding his way around the vast, multipurpose complex. An immense open-air courtyard and garden surrounded a central pool with splashing fountains that murmured happily as they echoed off the surrounding columns of Phygian marble. He noted with satisfaction that the floor was covered with mosaics of semiprecious stone and marble done in bold geometrics of his own design. Thick carpets, a gift from Herodes, absorbed the noise of footsteps and voices that rang off the many columns. In all, it dazzled the eye. The walls were lined with marble slabs, or frescoed, while the ceilings had exposed beams covered with ivory, gold, and frescoing. The lecture halls were lighted from above and received their illumination from these, and not through windows looking into the exterior. The windows of the rooms in upper stories facing the library were thick glass protected by bronze latticework to provide ample light for reading.

Sculptures of fine Parian marble were still being installed along the inner walls as Hadrian made his way toward the eastern end of the colonnade and its vast library. His broad stride halted suddenly, sending the courtiers at his heels into a disarrayed heap. Hadrian stood frozen at the entrance of the library, yet it was not the entrance that held his gaze. There, in a tall, slender niche lined with gray marble, stood an elegant statue of Antinous. Sculpted in the Greek style, the work portrayed the youth as a muscular god standing in front of a constellation of gilded bronze medallions embedded in the gray sky of Eleusian marble. The connection to Eleusis was not lost on Hadrian, and while he was enthralled by the mystical portrayal, the sting of memory wounded him. He soon felt the presence of a priest by his side, holding in one hand an alabaster bowl of Persian incense and in the other, an ewer of Egyptian glass containing rare oil. The cloying scent of the combined fragrances made Hadrian's head reel as the court stood silent, uncertain of what drama would unfold before them. But the emperor soon regained his composure and made his way toward the statue that stood quietly on its finely carved pedestal. The priest followed the emperor, and together they met his ecclesiastic brother who stood, draped in a leopard skin in the Egyptian manner, beside the statue. Hadrian reached for the ewer and then accepted the linen cloth from the leopard-clad priest. This allusion to the Egyptian rites chilled the emperor as he anointed the marble feet of the image. Using the linen cloth to rub the precious oil into the stone, he gazed up into the face of his beloved, rendered in pristine marble. How many images had he seen since the boy's death? Which ones were the accurate portrayals, and which were merely guesses? Somehow, the idealized portrayal here gazed at was a comfort to him. Though not totally accurate, it was godlike enough to be tucked safely away into his memory. As time wore on, the faults of the youth, if any, began to fade, and an aura of perfection took their place. It was enough, he felt, to justify his own adoration and obsession.

With the anointing of the sculpture finished, a somewhat shaken Hadrian resumed his way toward the library where the familiar smell of ancient papyrus and parchment drifted past the heavy drapes that framed the doorway. The scent of learning seemed to revive him, and as he entered, he noticed students were already utilizing the many works that filled the shelves or were busy scratching into clay tablets what might eventually be their own addition to the collection. While the students gawked in amazement at the presence of their emperor, older scholars and teachers went about their studies, ink stained and oblivious to the fact that they were in the company of their benefactor. As the emperor wandered amongst the scroll-filled niches of the vast hall, he examined the red-lettered titles of the cowhide-bound texts to the dull click of bone pens against the rims of bronze inkstands that echoed throughout the hall. Pausing to take in the scent of cuttlefish ink and burnt resin, Hadrian envied, for a moment, the simplicity of the lives of these hunched-over hunters of knowledge. But just for a moment. Silently, he slipped from the hall and joined his court as it stood at a respectful distance beyond the entryway. As he discussed with the complex administrators the oratories and lectures planned for the various rooms, Hadrian's eyes wandered toward the silent statue in its gray marble niche. The sun had shifted as it peered through the thick glass windows and found its way past the freshly oiled sculpture to the gilded stars behind it. Each likeness he came across opened a fresh wound, and from each wound poured grief. Suddenly, the echoing sound of voices and footsteps began to overcome him, and his head ached as it did earlier. Beckoning a member of his guard who held a handsome casket of polished cedar, he presented the casket to the senior administrator who appeared overwhelmed by the promising weight of the box. The emperor expressed his pleasure with the beauty and utility of the complex and brusquely pushed past the whispering courtiers into the fading light of evening. Uncertain of what protocol was demanded of them at this point, the court followed the emperor down the broad steps of the building. What was certain was that the specter of the dead youth had cast its shadow over yet another of the emperor's triumphs.

Chapter Seventeen

And His Wounds Bled

A year in Hadrian's life passed swiftly during his time in Athens. During that time, he had bestowed the city with numerous examples of his artistic endeavors. Wealthy aristocrats who had settled from Rome eagerly sought the emperor's input on the design of the villas they constructed on the hills outside the city walls. Baths, temples, and a massive stadium, many of which were begun years before, were finished during Hadrian's Athenian year. In a theater built by Hadrian into the Acropolis Hill, a chair of carved marble was reserved for the Priest of Antinous, while the actors had a shrine to the young god installed in a naturally formed niche behind the stage. But the land could hold only so much architecture, and space, as well as time, was running out. The court could sense the emperor was getting restless. His love of the hunt led him further away from the city confines and, more tellingly, from the temples that held the image of his beloved.

It was one of these hunts that lead Hadrian to the southern plain leading to Eleusis. During the pursuit of a wolf that had been terrorizing the local villages, Hadrian and his horse had followed the beast up a steep embankment of thick brush, and he found before him an unobstructed view of the sacred city. He could see the stream of pilgrims that traveled the Sacred Way that lead from Athens to the Greater Propylaia or outer sanctuary. In the distance, he could make out the Telesterion of Demeter, the great square temple where the secret initiation rites were performed. It was just more than a year before that he had traveled along side the Sacred Way, away from the city. Then he had avoided any contact, but now he was drawn to the site as if by Demeter herself. With the pursuit of the wolf forgotten, Hadrian ordered his entourage to follow him to the gates of Eleusis. They made their way toward the Sacred Way and, upon reaching a bridge built during Trajan's visit to the sanctuary, scattered the tired pilgrims, crossed the bridge, and entered the city with a minimum of fanfare.

It took little time for word of the emperor's arrival to spread through the surprised city and reach the temples beyond the rocky steps of the Acropolis Hill. Yet north of the Lesser Propylaia, in the priests' dwellings and the administrative buildings, the visit was no surprise. As the royal court strode through the great entrance built nearly two hundred years earlier by the Roman Consul Appius Pulcher, there was great activity in an underground temple dedicated to the emperor's beloved. At the top of the stone steps, the male priests of Antinous were joined in their welcoming of Hadrian and his court by the priestesses of Demeter. Behind them rose the billowing smoke of offerings that crackled on the altar before the cavern of Pluto. For the priests, the imperial visit was long overdue; their hopes had begun to fade. But for the priestesses, the arrival was expected and welcomed. Their long history with Hadrian, beginning before he became emperor, gave them a greater insight into the needs and desires of the man than the priests of the new god. Yet they knew it was the god Antinous that drew him here now, not the lure of Demeter and her ancient rites. By forming an alliance, the two orders created a united front before their benefactor—one by their worship of his beloved, the other by lending the aura of ancient mystery that gave that worship validity. As they escorted Hadrian and his closest circle down into the depths of the subterranean temple, the whispers of the ancients seemed to waft through the still air. Reaching level ground, they found a tomblike cavern, its high walls carved into columns and two great niches. In one, Hadrian saw a likeness of himself; familiar because he had gifted it to the Temple of Core, or Proserpina, daughter of Demeter. *Why is it here?* A look at the emperor's face prompted an explanation from the head priestess; the temple had been damaged a few years back by an earthquake. And while the statue of Core had taken refuge in the temple of her mother, the statue of Hadrian had been placed in the Temple of Antinous for safekeeping. A wry smile on the emperor's face led the court to realize he did not completely believe the explanation, yet he did appreciate the economy in the gesture. And the statue was perfect in its location. For upon following its gaze, one's own eyes fell upon a sculpture of Antinous. It was a somber portrayal, much like the statue at Delphi, but not rendered as well. The body was thin, with heavy draping that made it appear thinner still. This was not the body of the youth he remembered in Eleusis. It was quite clear that the body was rendered by a different hand than the head; itself not rendered well. *But well enough to provoke a reaction.* The godlike quality of the Delphi sculpture was missing, and in its place was a frightened boy. Furrowed brows hung over eyes that revealed fear and apprehension. And sorrow. The hair was rendered not in the tight curls favored by other artists, but limply as if damp with sweat. The mouth, while still full and lush, seemed vulnerable, bruised. The cloak that hung heavily from the shoulders of the body was clearly not his own. This was a portrait of a boy who saw things he should not have, and standing before him was the reason why. Hadrian was silent before the votive form. He did not feel the earth as his knees fell upon it, nor the tears that ran down his face unchecked. All the guilt he felt inside himself was portrayed in that face. All the faults he found in the rendering were his own. All his sins had been carved into the marble that stood before him. "Cover it," he whispered, no longer able to bear the condemnation of its gaze. "Cover it!" he said again, this time as a hoarse command. His choking voice echoing in the subterranean chamber. One of the priests, as pale as his companions, quickly removed the heavy linen cloak he was wearing and covered the silent image with shaking hands. The three priests fell trembling to their knees before the emperor, still on his own knees at the feet of the shrouded image. The priestesses of Demeter, however, remained standing upright. With eyes as cold as the waters of their ancient spring, they stood detached from the scene before them. They had been there when the emperor brought his boy to the Telesterion for the initiation rites. They had warned him that the youth was too young, too impressionable to absorb the gravity of the rites and bear its weight. But at Hadrian's insistence, the youth remained, at a cost none but the presciently gifted priestesses could imagine.

An arm appeared within the emperor's line of vision. The bronze wrist cuff was familiar to Hadrian; it was that of his prefect, Lucius. Reaching up and grasping the man by the shoulder, Hadrian raised himself up and stood silently before the draped figure. After an abrupt bow to the priests of Antinous, he turned and found himself face-to-face with the priestesses still standing in the shadows, barely touched by the flickering firelight. They said nothing yet their eyes burned through him, exposing his soul and tearing open every wound he had carried with him since that fateful day. Unable to take anymore, Hadrian turned and stumbled out of the gloom of the cavern temple. With the feeling he had escaped from hell itself, Caesar welcomed the blinding light of the afternoon sun as it burned away the chill that filled him. Eleusis was as ancient as the gods themselves, and the gods were not kind. He would find no sympathy here because it was here that his sin was witnessed. When he reached the bottom of the great stone steps of the temple, he mounted his waiting horse and sat for a moment. Reaching into his saddlebag, he retrieved a chunk of wrapped cheese and a link of hard sausage. Slinging his water bag around his shoulders, he motioned for his Praetorian guards to move on. The court followed close behind for their silent return to Athens.

Chapter Eighteen

Another Brief Respite

The experience of Eleusis soured Hadrian's desire to spend more time in Athens, or in Greece itself. Herodes provided diversions for his moody friend, including a masked party with the most beautiful young aristocrats he knew of. The youths were dressed as garlanded shepherds in gauzy tunics that fluttered seductively behind them as they danced around the pool in the massive courtyard. They were the sons of the finest families in and around Athens—educated and refined, yet full of life and merriment. As the wine continued to flow, the laughter of the youths began to drown out the music of lyres and flutes. Before long, the young nobles of Athens were splashing about in the pool wearing only their garlands, their gauze tunics scattered about on the mosaic pavement of the courtyard. Herodes left his friend in this lively company after seeing the glitter of life had returned to his eyes. As he entered his private quarters at the far end of the courtyard to join his eromenos, Herodes turned in time to see his friend leave his couch in the company of the two most splendid youths. With a slight smile, he marveled at his old friend's endurance and closed the door behind him.

Hadrian followed the naked youths as they danced eagerly to his bedchamber. After tumbling into the overstuffed cushions of silk and gold embroidery, two pairs of large brown eyes watched him as he paced the marble floor of the chamber. *I am far too old for this*, he thought, with a hunger that had become more of a habit than a need. The spoiled little aristocrats were lithe and limber as they began to giggle and wrestle each other on the massive bed. Hadrian had hoped the wine would have slowed them down. Instead, it energized the youths, making them impatient to be prizes for the emperor of Rome. Through the layers of frothy gauze that draped the posts of the cedar bed, Hadrian could see their shafts were already erect and glistening as they paused in their horseplay and again cast their eyes on him. As they lay back on the silk and linen pillows, Hadrian observed that one was more athletic in build than the other. *Apollo and Eros,* he thought with some amusement. In the face of such intoxicating beauty, the master of the world never felt more mortal. Yet as he searched for his goblet of wine to give him strength, he recalled the words of the poet Ovid. "Prescribe no more my muse, nor medicines give / Beauty and youth need no provocative." As he parted the sheer curtains and gazed at the wonders before him, he realized the true aphrodisiac lay naked on this bed. Removing his belt and tunic, he sighed and joined his reward for being the imperator of Rome.

The next morning came quickly as misty light crept through the window beside Hadrian's bed. The two youths, whose names he could not recall, lay sprawled on their stomachs amongst the plump pillows. Plump too were the pale mounds he had reveled in the night before. As he gazed at the young sleeping gods, Hadrian felt secretly pleased with himself and a performance that had lasted nearly until the early morn. As insatiable as the youths were, he had persevered. True, he was leaving the bed somewhat more slowly than usual on this morning, but his aches were a worthy price for such a night. The rare wines served the night before had served their purpose, and for a time, reality was swept away.

Loosely draped in a light woolen cloak, he made his way to the outer chamber of his suite, where he saw a large platter of fruit and cheeses tucked into long leaves of Kos lettuce had been placed on the long alabaster table, as well as a basket of bread so fresh it steamed in the cool morning air. On another tray stood a ewer of finely crafted silver filled with fresh spring water, along with goblets of thin rippled glass. Three goblets. *How astute of Herodes*, thought Hadrian. A slight scraping sound on the marble floor alerted him to the presence of his chamberlain, already poised to receive the orders of the day. A toga of thick white linen sat folded on a low bench at his side; a reminder that the frivolity of the previous night had no bearing on the new day's duties. As Hadrian took a fig and a handful of plump grapes, the chamberlain hurried to the table and poured water in one of the goblets. The emperor finished the fruit, devoured a large chuck of the soft, fragrant cheese and downed the water in nearly one gulp. A slight shadow of a smile passed over the face of the chamberlain as he witnessed the emperor's unusually youthful hunger. *Perhaps he truly is immortal*, thought the old man as he began to drape the intricate folds of the emperor's toga to prepare him for the day's events. Opening a great cedar chest that stood against one wall, Hadrian picked through various golden objects and pieces of jewelry. After choosing a number of pieces he felt showed adequate appreciation to the youths for the previous night, Hadrian placed the gifts on the table and instructed his chamberlain to present them to the youths when they awoke. He then walked somewhat stiffly from the chambers and into the warm morning light.

Herodes and Diodoros were seated in the courtyard garden, the splash of the fountain masking the approaching footsteps of their guest. Hadrian's sudden appearance startled his hosts, who rose quickly to greet him. Seating himself on a thronelike garden chair, Hadrian looked every bit the emperor of Rome. A glass of mead was presented to him, and a tray of fruit was silently placed beside him. Caesar felt the amused eyes of his friend observing him as the oblivious Diodoros chatted in the soft, melodic voice that captivated Caesar from the start. Hadrian shifted his weight on the hard marble seat as Claudia joined the intimate group, and the talk soon turned to the planned journey to Herodes's birthplace. Marathon was on Attica's eastern shore and an easy departure point for Hadrian's eventual voyage to Bithynia. Through the promontory of Geraestus and past the island of Andros, he would head north through the Aegean Sea, toward the Hellespont and the birthplace of his beloved Antinous. The imperial ships were already docked at Marathon and were being prepared for their extended voyage. Provisioning the ships would begin upon the emperor's arrival into the city and be finished the following morning.

As Herodes discussed with Claudia the issue of comfort in the wagons that would transport her and the servants to Marathon, Hadrian pondered the details of the coming journey. He was eager to depart Athens and continue his tour of the eastern empire.

Rumblings were being heard in Judea, and the reports from the legions stationed there were not encouraging. The emperor had expected to leave earlier than in a few days, but the logistics involving Claudia's and Diodoros's comfort and the number of wagons needed for their luggage had become more complex than a major military campaign. As the number of days needed for planning began to grow in number, the emperor decided he had enough. Explaining to Herodes the need to depart earlier, Hadrian ordered his chamberlain to prepare his own entourage, ready to leave Athens the next morning.

That evening, a banquet was given in honor of the departing emperor. Now that the plans were finalized for his journey, he was eager to begin his trek across the eastern plain to Marathon. The next day would begin before daybreak, and Hadrian left the festivities early to supervise the packing of the many gifts he had received during his stay. Precious cups of delicately carved jasper were carefully packed in trunks, their thin translucent stone protected against heavy gilt silver ewers and ancient Attic pottery. Jewelry in finely wrought gold set with cabochons of carnelian, turquoise, and milky aquamarine lay in leather cases and awaited their eventual presentation to the empress, alongside ropes of creamy pearls and strands of exquisitely carved beads of amber from the far north. All worthy tributes for the imperator of Rome, who always left Athens wealthier and more beautiful than he had found her.

As the emperor wished, the journey began before daybreak. As the courtiers stumbled grumbling into their carriages, the emperor had already mounted his steed and discussed travel plans with the praefectus, Lucius Didus. Herodes, Diodoros, and Claudia had risen early to wish their illustrious guest a safe journey and to assure the provisions provided for the entourage were sufficient. If they were perturbed by the emperor's abrupt departure, it did not show on their faces. The visit was a long, exciting, and somewhat grueling one, and the young beloved as well as his older lover welcomed the silence that would descend on the villa upon Hadrian's departure. As the sun began to show itself at the horizon, the imperial party began to move to the sound of creaking wheels and the dull thud of horse's hooves. This commotion as well as the clatter of the Praetorian guard echoed through the elegant streets and woke the many dogs that guarded their master's possessions. With the rising sun beginning to peer into their eyes, the royal entourage made its way past the Arch of Hadrian and through the main gate of Athens. As he left the gate behind him, Hadrian could not rid himself of the premonition he would never see his beloved Athens again.

Chapter Nineteen

The Balm of Friends

The journey across the plain was swift and uneventful. They had avoided the shorter mountain route because of the wagons and took the flatter southeastern plain. The travelers could smell the sea before they reached it as the scent drifted through gaps in the lush forests that spread out before them. The tile roofs of the temples and baths of Marathon came into view by late afternoon, while the heady aroma of fennel mingled with the sea air. The setting sun lent a golden glow to the ancient city as the imperial party began their entry. A messenger sent the day before had alerted the officials about the imperial visit, and the city was dressed for the occasion. Herodes himself had sent an announcement of the imperial arrival the day before the royal messenger, and his family villa was prepared for the momentous occasion. As Hadrian rode down the broad central avenue, the crowd threw bouquets of wildflowers, creating a fragrant carpet that cushioned the sound of the horses' hooves. The cheers of the frenzied masses warmed the emperor and lifted the fatigue that had dogged him throughout the journey. A coterie of city officials lead the visitors through the winding streets and toward an exquisite villa set in the center of an idyllic garden. Herodes's family homestead was not as grand as his Athenian villa, but more refined in its simplicity. Still within the city walls but set apart because of a vast landholding, the villa gave the impression of a country estate. In this home, Hadrian saw more of his old friend's personality, and the warmth he felt already assured him of a pleasant stay.

Once the imperial entourage was settled and the horses were in their stalls in the massive stable, Hadrian took a small band of his courtiers to visit the bath built by Herodes a number of years earlier. Set amongst temples from various eras, the pristine marble glowed in the light of the full moon that had risen over the city. The Greek citizens, unused to the sight of an emperor bathing with commoners, gaped in awe and not a small amount of discomfort. But his easy manner assured them and they found him to be more of a soldier then the soft, effete emperors who had visited in the past. Handsome youths introduced themselves as the emperor held court in the vast marble hall of the caldarium surrounded by sculptures of both ancient and recent origin. As more torches and braziers were being lit, Hadrian could slowly make out the features of a larger-than-life-size statue across the pool flanked by twin braziers carried by tripods in the Greek manner As a warm breeze cut through the vast bathing chamber, the curtain of steam from the heated pool parted momentarily, and the face of Antinous appeared before him. The emperor's abrupt silence quieted the chatter of the youths, and soon the entire chamber was eerily still. Even the splashing fountains seemed to grow quieter as all eyes looked toward the direction of the emperor's gaze, and the reason for his silence became clear. The apparition seemed to have put Hadrian into a trance, cutting short the frivolity of moments ago. Suddenly, a beautiful youth took hold of the emperor's gold goblet of wine and, raising it up and toward the marble sculpture, broke the silence and declared, "Ave Antinous!" While the older men in the crowd gasped, appalled by this breach of etiquette, Hadrian was moved by the tribute. Taking the cup from the youth, he drank deeply and repeated the salutation. Taking their cue, the rest of the assembled bathers did the same, and soon the din that echoed off the walls of polished marble was a vociferous as before.

The burial mound for the 192 fallen but victorious Athenians at the Battle of Marathon nearly six hundred years earlier could still be seen on the coastal plain, a marble stele declaring the Greek victory over the Persians. A short ride on horseback brought Hadrian to the site still revered by the descendants of the fallen heroes, and in reverence, he draped over the stele the wreath of laurel he brought with him. The priests Hadrian also brought along with him for this visit set down bronze bowls of incense that was soon flickering and billowing smoke. The ghosts of the fallen heroes were palpable as the living paid homage on the breezy plain. The enormity of their sacrifice moved Hadrian as he silently wondered why there was not a more fitting tribute on this sacred site. Yet as he gazed out over the plain toward the sea, he slowly came to the realization that nothing more was needed. The sea air mixed with the fennel plants running riot over the massive mound, creating incense without smoke. Hadrian could imagine the deep taproots of the foliage mingling with the ancient bones as tiny yellow flower heads bobbed in the ocean breeze. Sitting at the foot of the mound, Hadrian contemplated the stele that bore witness to the glory of the fallen. As he did so, he contemplated his own life, his own sacrifices. There suddenly seemed to be so little time left to complete his own legend, and that he knew would have to be done in Rome, because Rome was immortal. And as Rome was, so would he be.

Despite the woolen cloak he had set down first, a chill cut through the emperor as he sat on the damp ground. With some difficulty, he raised himself up, his officers knowing better than to offer assistance. His thoughts drifted back to the villa, and Hadrian was ready for a hot soak and a meal. With the salt air at their back, the entourage returned to the city and used the ancient gate that stood close to Herodes's villa to avoid the main road. Hadrian returned the greeting of his old friend as they met at the villa's entrance and did not bother to hide his pleasure and surprise. Herodes had changed his mind after. Walking through the colonnade, Hadrian could also hear Diodoros's giggles and Claudia's soft, throaty laughter as it played against the more brittle laughter of the other young men. Herodes had brought the party with him it seemed, and his sister was there to assure moderation. Smiling at the thought, Hadrian welcomed a repeat of his last night in Athens, although after his walk, he wished for nothing more than a hot bath. As they crossed the massive peristyle with its columns of Nubian marble, the fountain in the shallow water basin competed with the laughter from within. Hadrian avoided the public rooms and abruptly turned down a long hall to enter the state apartments, leaving his friend to join the others alone. It was a rude gesture to be sure, but age was making itself known, and all Hadrian could think of was the hot water that would sooth his ache. Strangely enough, Herodes did not seem disturbed by this decision and smiled warmly as Hadrian made his hasty departure. The emperor's chamberlain was already present in the bedchamber busily laying out the robes for the night's festivities. Hadrian stripped off his light armor and tunic as the Ophelos drew back the heavy curtains that led to the bathing chamber. As Hadrian strode the short walk down the corridor to the bath, he found it odd that his chamberlain did not follow to attend to him. Yet as he reached the bath, the reason, in all its enticing glory, became clear. Standing there, with bold brown eyes and skin with the radiance of alabaster, were the two youths from his last night in Athens. One carried a bowl of beaten gold while the other stood with a matching ewer of water, all at the ready to wash the hands and face of the emperor. The suntanned Hadrian was a stark contrast to the pale smoothness of the naked youths. Wisely, after they had politely addressed him as Caesar, the boys introduced themselves again as Aeolos and Demetrios, in case the emperor had forgotten. After washing his hands and face, Hadrian stepped into the steaming waters of the bath and sank gratefully into its warmth. Soon, his body acclimated to the heat, and his aching joints began to respond to the soothing water, allowing the emperor to turn and examine the naked youths, one of whom was now seated at the smooth edge of the pool. There was a look of innocence and knowledge in the eyes of the youth as he dangled one foot in the warm water, creating small ripples that mischievously made their way to Caesar. Rejuvenated now, the emperor slapped the surface of the bath and sent a stream of water that splashed the boy and sent his surprised laughter echoing off the marble walls. Tugging the dangling foot, Hadrian pulled the still laughing youth into the water while motioning for his companion to join them. The peaceful, soothing bath Hadrian had planned was not to be, but surrounded by these sleek, seal-like beauties, he knew this would play out to be something far more enjoyable.

Refreshed from his bath and dressed for the night's festivities, Hadrian walked past a series of elaborate rooms and joined his hosts in the banquet hall. The walls of the hall were decorated in the Roman style with colorful frescos that imitated the gardens that could be seen past the terraced courtyard just outside the dining chamber. The terraces held carved stone dolphins that sprayed water into a sunken pool. The sober, restrained exterior of the villa belied the extravagance within.

Claudia too was decorated in the Roman style as she floated across the marble mosaic floor toward the emperor. Set amongst the elaborate dark curls of her hair was a simple diadem of embossed gold set with a cameo of Venus done in sardonyx and surrounded by pearls. The simplicity of her diadem was off set by a lavish necklace of woven gold braid generously set with blister pearls and emeralds ringed with gold beading. Hadrian was especially pleased to see the necklace; it was a belated birthday gift he had presented her during his stay in Athens. A heavy gold ring set with a massive emerald completed her adornment, and she wore the entire collection with distinction. Over her tunica of bleached white linen was a stola of pale yellow silk gathered in pleats at the shoulders with simple ribbons, while over this she draped a scarflike palla of faded rose gauze trimmed with small pearls that fluttered like wings behind her. The simplicity of her attire was offset by the luxury of the materials.

Hadrian was pleased his chamberlain had chosen the purple toga bordered with an acanthus design embroidered in heavy gold thread. On his head, he wore a circlet of golden laurel branches, their leaves studded with pale topaz cabochons that glistened like the sky reflected in dewdrops. The branches were tied in the back with cords of purple silk, their ends capped with golden lion heads. The image he presented as he entered the banquet room astonished the assembled guests. Even Claudia hesitated in her greeting and slipped elegantly to one knee. The majestic apparition in the doorway left Herodes somewhat ill at ease. Yet he had to concede that while his friend was a fellow stoic, he was also the emperor of Rome and needed to look the part. With a sudden flush of pride, he bowed in welcome to his powerful friend. Hadrian's eyes sparkled with amusement at the awed faces of Aeolos and Demetrios, the two youths who had only a short time ago known the man as mortal. Now, standing before this vision, clothed in imperial raiment, they saw the Roman Caesar of legend. For most, it would be a sobering sight; but for the youths, there was pride and excitement in the thought that they had pleased the emperor of Rome. As the evening took on a glittering aura of anticipation and intrigue, Herodes, for once, took comfort in his status and began to settle into what he knew was the beginning of a memorable dinner.

Chapter Twenty

A Final Gift of Gratitude

After a few more weeks at Herodes's villa, Hadrian knew it was time to resume his travels through the empire. It was becoming far too enticing to remain in the presence of his perfect host and the diversions he thoughtfully provided. Aeolos and Demetrios too proved to be an addiction difficult to relinquish. But the time had come for this idyllic time to end. And while he was tempted to recruit the youths to accompany him, to be truthful, they were more exhausting than he wished to admit. Antinous too was passionate and demanding in his desires, but two at the same level of craving would surely do him in. The beautiful youths were far too devoted to each other to be separated, so both would be left behind. Instead, Hadrian selected lavish gifts for the boys and honored their families back in Athens with positions of privilege arranged by Herodes. The people of Marathon also benefitted from the imperial visit with the emperor's financial support of new temples and administrative buildings, as well as the repair of the ancient buildings, crumbling with age. By the time he finished his last good-byes, he was considerably lighter in gold but filled with golden memories.

The ships and their crews were waiting patiently at the docks as the emperor made his way down the rocky path to the harbor of Marathon. The imperial banner snapped briskly in the wind, a favorable sign for swift sailing. But the ship that bore the banner was not the senate's gratuitous gift. Beautiful, yes. But not one he had seen before. It was massive yet more streamlined than the Roman flagship he arrived on, as it barely nodded to the waves that slapped against it. A centurion from the garrison at Marathon stood at the entrance of the stone pier that tethered the great vessel. As Hadrian approached, the centurion saluted and presented the emperor with a large packet sealed with blue wax and embossed with the insignia of two entwined dolphins. Sliding his fingers beneath the seal and giving it a tug, Hadrian opened the parcel and found blueprints for the ship that loomed above him, along with a note written in Herodes's hand on translucent parchment.

> *Accept, Great Caesar and dear friend of Greece, this vessel as a symbol of the people's gratitude and my own. May it carry you to your destinations in comfort until your wanderlust subsides. Your humble servant and friend, Herodes.*

The *Adriana Augusta* was to be the imperial yacht and a gift from Herodes and the people of Greece. Only the Greeks, with their seawater for blood, could build such a masterpiece. Sleek and powerful, it had originally been designed and begun a year previous and now bore the royal standard of the intended recipient proudly. Built of enough costly wood for two ships, the detailing of the design was such that Hadrian could truly appreciate;

crafted of oak from Bithynia, cedar from Lydia, and fitted with an armor of iron with bronze embellishments. The rostrum at the bow was decorated with dolphins and mermen, carved in wood and gilded. Bronze and iron spikes in the Greek style elongated the profile of the bow and gave the ship a formidable appearance. Alongside the enormous mast stood armaments that included cranes with grappling hooks for clamping on to hostile ships, a giant catapult of the ancient but still deadly design of the great Greek *Archimedes*, and rows of weapons' racks that contained handheld catapults, spears, and grappling hooks. While it was doubtful these formidable weapons would ever be put to use in the *Mare Romana*, their presence lent a certain air of substance that countered the lavishness of the design. *Form and function,* thought Hadrian. *How could I ever thank Herodes and Greece properly?* Never had a gift moved him more. From his place in the shadow of the columns that lined the pier, Lucius Didus took note of the emperor's reaction to the gift and the delight that showed on his face. Once more, the Greeks outplayed their conquerors and blazed brightly in the eyes of the sovereign of all that was Rome.

As the last of the provisions were loaded on, the *hastati* prepared their oars for the navigation of the ships through the islands and into the Aegean Sea. Taking a commanding position on the ship's ornate rostrum, the scent of the sea rejuvenated Hadrian as he finally began to look forward to the arduous trip to the eastern end of his empire. The main sail had not yet been unfurled, its loose riggings tapping a lazy rhythm against the mast in the light breeze. The oars began to beat a measured tempo in the water and gradually thrust the great yacht away from the pier toward open waters. By midafternoon, they had entered the promontory of Geraestus; and soon, over the leeward deck, the ancient city of Carystus could be seen on its rocky perch, its still colorful temples shining in the blazing sun. Soon, they were gliding through the promontory of Caphareus into the Aegean and were swiftly headed toward the Hellespont as the waves bathed the gilded lion head.

As the sun became more intense in its gaze, Hadrian left his perch at the bow and strode along the starboard rail toward the staircase that led below deck. There he found corridors leading to the guest suites, a lavish bath, and a library with a mosaic floor of semiprecious stones. The walls and ceilings were covered with elaborate wood inlays and carvings illustrating scenes from Greek mythology. The officer's deck had shared staterooms, its own bath, an airy gymnasium, and a small but lavish shrine to the god Mithra. On this level too was the kitchen area and a massive bronze freshwater tank. Hadrian examined, in wonder, the detail and skill that was poured into this magnificent vessel.

Not wishing to deal with his inner court as they lounged in their suites, Hadrian silently returned to the main deck and made his way to the royal staterooms. The great sail was unfurled now, and one of them shaded the aft deck with its purple-trimmed expanse, putting this suite of rooms in their shadow. Saluting the two Praetorian guards at the entry, Hadrian entered the chambers past the carved cedar and ivory door held open by his waiting chamberlain. Tall, narrow windows filled with glass shutters and decorated with bronze grates illuminated the interior. A huge bronze fire bowl, situated in the center of the main stateroom to drive away the chill of damp days at sea, was cool and silent now, its purpose unneeded. The floors were inlaid with a variety of wood and stone to mimic the great marble floors of a lavish villa, polished with beeswax and buffed to a deep glow. The emperor's eyes wandered to the columns that supported the oaken beams—thick, solid, and carved of the same Bithynian oak as the great ship's masts. As he circled one of the fluted columns, Hadrian realized that peering out from the gilded acanthus leaves of the capital was the image of his beloved. The face of Antinous gazed down at his, as it did in countless statues in countless temples. *Dear Herodes and his eye for detail*, thought Hadrian. The furnishings were of the highest Roman quality in both their ornate design and materials, while the gilded bronze oil lamps that hung from the rafters were a study in Grecian restraint. Order and balance. All was well here.

Upon entering an adjacent room that was to be his study, Hadrian seated himself at a vast marble topped desk and perused the pile of manuscripts before him. Pushing it all aside, he reached for a plate of his familiar favorite dried sausage and, together with cheese and bread from a basket of woven silver, silently ate his lunch. The chamberlain appeared with a ewer of wine that Caesar waved away, reaching instead for the glass pitcher of water that stood on his desk. *There was too much to be done for any indulgence in wine*, he thought to himself. The courier packets were from the legions III in Petra and XXII that he had dispatched to Judea to discourage an uprising there. From the contents of the letters, XXII was not doing well in that regard. Hadrian had no desire to cut short his visit to Bithynia, yet the Judean situation was quickly becoming as violent as the Kitos War under Trajan. Hadrian thought back on his edicts regarding the banning of circumcision. Then too was the renaming of the city to Aelia Capitolina, when the governor of Judaea, Tineius Rufus, narrowly escaped assassination by one of the burgeoning rebel groups. By then, Hadrian's initial sympathy for the Jews vanished. He responded to the assassination attempt with the building of a temple to himself and Jupiter on the site of the temple of the Hebrews, destroyed under the order of Titus in retribution for the uprising under his father's reign. Tensions continued to grow and Hadrian's desk was littered with ongoing reports.

The Legion XXII had not fared well during the Kitos War, only the arrival of the III prevented an outright slaughter. With that experience behind them, Hadrian was led to believe the new commander had rebuilt this legion, and its strength was adequate for suppressing the current revolt. Yet the latest dispatches seemed to say otherwise. With stylus in hand, the emperor personally wrote an order for the Legion III to join the XXII in the hopes of preventing another drawn out and costly war. *Should it come to that,* thought Hadrian, *I will wipe clean the city of Jerusalem and start anew.* These people had been a thorn in the side of Rome since the beginning, and it was time that thorn was removed.

As the imperial flotilla crashed through the waves between the southern tip of Euboea and the Isle of Andros, the sun had made its way to the west, and its glow was slipping under the closed door of the main stateroom. Hadrian watched Apollo's rays slide across the polished floor as they ventured toward his study. Feeling suddenly weary and alone, he pushed aside the packets of mail and rose from the massive desk. The chamberlain, hearing the emperor moving about, appeared at the doorway to announce a bath was waiting for him. Hadrian moved on to the inner chamber to disrobe, submerging himself into the steaming water. The roomy bronze tub was a thing of wonder, but its practical function was far more meaningful for the emperor at this moment than its visual attributes. The hot water, heated safely outside the staterooms and piped into the bathing chamber, was a welcome respite for Hadrian's aching body. His time in Athens was idyllic but tiring for the aging man. Now, as the great ship gently rolled and listed, the water's warmth lulled the emperor into a deep sleep.

The sun had long since set before Hadrian awoke with a start, the water having gone uncomfortably cold. Calling for his chamberlain, the emperor stood up in the cold water and swung his legs over the high rim of the tub. The chamberlain hurried in and handed his royal charge a linen sheet to dry with and a woolen wrap to chase the chill. Hadrian left the bathing chamber for his sleeping quarters. The euphoria from his stay in Greece was slowly wearing off, and the reality of the problems in Syria and Judea was taking its place. The great bed with its down-filled mattress draped with purple watered silk beckoned. Hadrian moved slowly to the bed and fell into its thick comfort. Other than the gift of the *Adriana Augusta*, the day had offered nothing good, and its end was a welcome feeling. As the flotilla passed the moonlit Isle of Scyros, Hadrian passed into a deep slumber.

Another day and a half had passed before the Isle of Tenedos, at the mouth of the Hellespont, could be seen. Soon after, Hadrian's secretary entered the study and announced the sighting of the ancient city of Troy perched on a high plain in the distance. The crash of waves was of such force they battered the banks of the narrow inlet and made the great ship shudder in their wake. It was the part of the sea voyage Hadrian always disliked. As they reached the port city of Percote, the emperor had run out of patience and ordered that his yacht be docked there so that he might disembark and take the land route to Bithynia. After unloading the horses and hastily assembled provisions, the courtiers who wished to join the emperor disembarked, preparing them for the arduous journey through Mysia to Bithynia. There would be rivers to cross and mountain ranges to traverse before they reached the gates of Nicomedia. Only the hardiest and most adventurous members of the court joined the emperor while the rest remained comfortably at rest in the imperial ships. Chabrais watched regretfully as the emperor's entourage disappeared into the thickets beyond Percote. Age had rendered him too weak to undertake such a grueling journey, and the comfort of the ship proved too enticing. Hadrian was relieved at the old tutor's decision; to lose his old friend now would be too great a blow. And it he could cover far more ground in less time without him.

After the imperial party had reached and crossed the first river, Hadrian felt his old passion for the hunt revive within him. The wooded hills and mountains held great promise, and by the time they had reached city of Dascylium, just within the border of Bithynia, the amount of prize game they had encountered was staggering. They entered the port city with little fanfare and startled their hosts with their appearance and the number of boar and deer they carried with them. As they dined with the city magistrates, they could see the imperial flotilla passing by in the setting sun. The immense size of the *Adriana Augusta* was evident even from shore as it dwarfed the other vessels in the flotilla and created a sensation amongst the citizens. Unusually calm winds had slowed the fleet, and there was now the possibility that the emperor and his companions would reach the city of Nicomedia before his small armada. Spurred on by this challenge, the emperor roused his fellow travelers before dawn and left the city before it was awake. Hunting was no longer on the emperor's mind as a new game was afoot. By the end of the day, they had reached the lake city of Nicaea and were within a day's journey of Nicomedia.

The great forests of Bithynia filled Hadrian with bittersweet memories. Before meeting Antinous, this had been a place of great resources and fine hunting for Hadrian as it had been for scores of Roman emperors before him. But after the fateful meeting, and especially after the death of the youth, this had become sacred ground. Although only four years had passed since his last tour with the golden youth, it seemed like another time. As he rode toward the walls of Nicomedia, tucked deep within the ancient harbor, memories preoccupied his mind, and his silence kept his court at bay. The royal flotilla had reached the city before them, and the proconsul and dignitaries gathered on the docks to greet their emperor. But Hadrian and his entourage entered through the eastern gate and traveled the empty streets. The rhythmic clatter of the horses hooves echoed loudly off the vacant buildings, their residents having gone to crowd the shore to welcome their emperor. The Praetorian guard had left the ships, and the court that had remained on their vessels disembarked to the fanfare of trumpets. Confusion began to sweep through the assembled welcoming party as no sign of the emperor could be seen. Suddenly, the imperial guard assembled along either side of the main road of the metropolis as trumpets resumed their announcement. To the amazement of the crowd as well as the dignitaries on the dais, Caesar Traianus Hadrianus Augustus, emperor of Rome, paraded through the hurriedly parting crowd and rode toward the welcoming nobles. Startled and confused, the nobles regained their dignity and, after some rearranging of position according to rank, continued with their tribute as planned. Although he had not arrived before his fleet, Hadrian's self-satisfied smile showed that, at least in his mind, he had won the game.

Hadrian entered the nearly four-hundred-year-old palace of Nicomedia and was confronted with ancient shadows and scents that had not changed since the time of Julius Caesar's visit, let alone the time of the Beloved. The layout of the rooms was still familiar to the emperor, as were the great columns that had remained untouched from the earthquake more than twelve years earlier and towered over the central courtyard like the trees of the Bithynian forests. The ancient spring, still rippling within its stone confines like liquid silver, remained as it was on that fateful day. Nothing had changed, yet nothing was the same.

To his surprise, Arrian waited for him in the garden courtyard. Lucius Flavius Arrianus was a native of this city and a lifelong friend, having studied under the same philosopher teacher, Epictetus. He had joined Hadrian at Eleusis for the initial indoctrination to the Mysteries and at an early age had become a priest of Demeter and Kore at their temple in Nicomedia. Having served as consul in Rome for two years and having been there at the time of the death of Antinous, Arrian was trusted and loved by Hadrian. It was he who, along with Sextus Julius Severus, kept Rome in order during the emperor's travels. The irony was that Julius, whom Hadrian had dispatched to Britain a year before, was at this moment being sent yet another dispatch from the emperor that would transfer him to Judea to suppress what was being called the Bar Kochba rebellion. Hadrian hoped Severus's success in Britain would be repeated in Judea; he had no desire to deal with the Jews himself.

Arrian and the emperor made themselves comfortable on the cushions that covered the stone chairs under the ancient Cyprus trees. The sparkle of the spring continued to distract Hadrian, and in its blinding glare, he imagined the boy of twelve that once sat there years earlier. "The boy's beauty was more blinding that the sun's reflection," Arrian mused as if to himself, but aloud. The sound of his voice stirred Hadrian from his reverie as he suddenly remembered Arrian was also present that fateful day. There was comfort in that voice as well as the fact that here was another soul who understood his infatuation. From here, he had swept up the youth, as Zeus with Ganymede, and brought him to the center of the Roman world. But he had left the boy at a boarding school and kept his distance. Despite the boy's beauty, he was at an age that did not warrant Hadrian's attentions. Had he seen the future, he would have kept the boy close to him and enjoyed the pleasure of watching him grow to the godlike youth he would become. But the future was kept hidden, and Hadrian was deprived of precious years.

I envisioned myself as Zeus

To your Ganymede.

But my talons ripped your flesh

To bone,

And pierced your heart.

Like tears shed in the dark

Your supplication went unnoticed.

Your fears remained hidden, masked

By a face of tranquil, godlike beauty.

Caught in the web of my own grand design

I failed to see the danger, the future anguish.

My tears are futile now.

I was always

Unworthy.

Again, his mind had wondered off, and the stirrings of Arrian repositioning himself on his cushions brought him back to reality.

Turning to him, he said, "Forgive me, old friend. The past intrudes more and more these days." But Arrian, knowing his friend, needed no apology and told him so. As they sat together and gazed into their own pasts, the amber-hued sun slipped behind an endless stand of cedars in the distance.

Chapter Twenty-One

Unrest in Judea

It was during his stay in Nicomedia that Hadrian received word from Sextus Julius Severus that the Judean uprising was far more widespread and popular than first reported. Hadrian's policies, including among other things the ban on circumcision, which he viewed as barbaric, had been viewed by the Judeans as anti-Jewish and had sparked discontent almost immediately. Severus had been in command for nearly a year, and that year had not been kind to Rome. The rebels, led by zealots named Simon bar Kokhba and Akiba ben Joseph, had made the Roman legions pay a heavy price for the emperor's edicts. The skill of the Judean forces has improved since the emperors Titus and Trajan's confrontations with them, to the point that an entire legion, the XXII Deiotariana, had been systematically wiped out by the rebels. The Bar Kokhba revolt had escalated to an all-out war.

Hadrian sent an urgent dispatch to the brother legion of the XXII Deiotariana—the Legion III Cyrenaica stationed in Petra. This was the legion of Quintus Marcius Turbo, the prefect of the emperor's personal Praetorian guard. Hadrian sent the dispatch with Lucius as well as the staff of command that would announce him as the Legatus Legionis of the Legion III. Lucius was eager to rejoin the disciplined and well-trained legionaries and was grateful for the emperor's gift of equipment and heavy armor to be presented to the legion upon his arrival. After briefing his handpicked replacement as prefect of the imperial guard, Gaius Vitellius, Lucius joined his personal Cohort of 480 men and set off for Jerusalem by way of Petra.

It was Hadrian's intent to wait for the reports from Legatus Lucius before descending upon Judea. His sympathy for the Jews had led him to rebuild the city of Jerusalem, but his desire to rebuild the city as a Roman metropolis did not sit well with the local citizenry even during his stay. The Legi VI Ferrate had been stationed there, and a Praetorian, Tineius Rufus, was installed as governor. But growing tensions had fermented and spilled out as a carefully planned revolt. The restoration of the Judean state had progressed to the extent that a large quantity of coinage was minted, struck over foreign coins. Many were being circulated in the form of a tetradrachm that read "To the freedom of Jerusalem." One of these slipped out from the folds of the dispatches Hadrian had removed from the packet sent by the Primus Pilus of the VI Ferrata, Marius Lollius Urbicus. The writings of Urbicus sat unread on the massive desk as the emperor examined the symbol of a restored sovereign Jewish state in his hand. The coin had been an Egyptian one, commemorating the founding of Antinoopolis. With a wry smile Hadrian observed a crudely made die had nearly obliterated his portrait with an image of the destroyed temple of the Jews. But the smile vanished quickly when he turned the silver piece over. On the reverse, a portrait of his Beloved had been defaced with the symbol of a palm and Hebrew script. Hadrian felt a rage build within him as he stared at the desecration of his young god. It was time to pay these Judeans a visit, and this time there would be no sympathy or restraint in his dealing with them. The revolt would be crushed and the populous driven into the desert, the name of their land wiped off the map. Summoning his chamberlain, Hadrian made hasty plans for his departure from Bithynia as he watched the idyllic visit he had planned turn sour, with little time to savor the beauty he had created in his Beloved's honor.

The cult of the god Antinous was a radiant light in Bithynia. His people revered the youth, and like jewels in a breastplate, the land was dotted with temples and shrines to the emperor's favorite. Hadrian himself added to their number by constructing a magnificent bath with an attached temple in the youth's home city of Claudiopolis. The emperor visited the site of the Antinous's birth and erected a lofty, elegant temple of his own design. Thirty Corinthian columns stood on a raised circular dais formed by ten rings of marble steps. The gilded capitals reflected the sun as they bore the circular entablature, its carved reliefs telling the story of the young god's life. The cone-shaped roof ended with a gilded bronze finial in the form of Zeus as an eagle abducting Ganymede. The interior of the temple was clad in local green marble and held a sculpture of Antinous that Hadrian had commissioned in Athens during the youth's lifetime. It was to be a reminder of the youth's beauty long after that beauty had faded. Now, it served as a cult figure for a god whose radiance would never fade. As the setting sun washed over the silent form and sank into the deep green walls, the translucence of the Parian marble went from pale white to rose. Just outside the temple, highly carved and placed on a raised platform of marble, was the sacred altar where Hadrian was to be the first to set a sacrificial blaze in the pristine stone's recess. As he poured the sacred libations that sent a plume of smoke to the heavens, memories began to overwhelm him; and once again, he moved as if sleepwalking. In the shadow of shadows past, he moved beyond guilt and grief and performed a proper homage to his dead eromenos. As he stared into the marble basin containing a newly tapped spring that bubbled and spilled over onto the temple steps, the liquid silver of the waters forced him to shield his eyes. It was a small miracle that excited the crowd of worshippers but pierced the emperor with shards of grief. The circle of their lives together had been closed, and the story ended at the steps of a temple. The next day, as the emperor gathered his court of knights, scholars, and courtiers and set off for his journey south, he felt as if another piece of his life had been burned away and joined the dark cloud of ash that threatened to consume him.

The travelers made their way through Mysia toward the fertile valley of the Caicus and city of Pergamum. Their stay in that city was a short one, due in part to Hadrian's aversion to the large Christian sect there. Self-righteous and opinionated, these people had objected loudly to the presence of the emperor and his favorite during their visit. The emperor's response was to have their meeting places burned and the leaders of the cult imprisoned, never to be heard from again. Now, his return to the city, accompanied by his three thousand Praetorian guard was a cause for consternation and fear among these people, and they remained in the shadows during the extent of the imperial visit. For Hadrian, Pergamum was a city of past glories; the great sculptures of Galen were antique, the massive marble altar to Zeus was in disrepair, and the great library, once second only to the Alexandrian Library, had become a part of that collection over a hundred years earlier. Pergamum was a city with a faded history, and with the Christians wandering its shadowy alleys, it possessed nothing to hold the interest of the emperor of Rome.

Chapter Twenty-Two

A Hunt and a Haunting Memory

After a too brief respite, the imperial court followed their restless emperor south toward the port city of Ephesus. In the province of Lydia, on the road to Ephesus, were great expanses of densely wooded forests that stretched along the River Cayster. These woods had been known for many hundreds of years as the playground of wild boar so wondrously fierce that, according to legend, the city itself was founded specifically for the hunting of this beast. Upon crossing the Cayster, Hadrian could see the bustling city in the distance, but the dark forest of tall oaks beckoned the hunter in him—an invitation he could not ignore. Not since the death of the youth had he hunted, as all of his challenges since had been on parchment or in stone. He had not felt enough life in himself to be up to the task of taking one. But as the imperial court grew nearer to the shadowy woods, he could feel the hunter's instinct coursing through his blood, just as it had in younger days.

Sending the wagons of provisions and servants ahead to the city, Hadrian gathered his closest circle of companions and headed for the evergreen labyrinth of paths trampled flat by snorting beasts. The sun's rays struggled, with little effect, to pierce the canopy of mighty oaks. As the horses of the emperor and his court padded along the soft, moss-carpeted floor of the forest, small creatures darted overhead from branch to branch while birds went about their business of nest building. The tranquility of the woods belied the danger of the razor tusked beasts hidden within. The musky scent of boar permeated the tangled maze of paths as freshly torn branches, scattered leaves, and deep hoofprints on the pliant moss gave proof of the recent presence of at least one of the creatures. As the scent grew stronger, the horses began to whinny in anticipation of the coming conflict. The dogs too sensed the approaching confrontation; their growls and short barks growing more urgent as their fur stood stiff on their backs. The court was assembled in whatever space was allowed behind the emperor. For some, safety was more of an issue here than vanity.

Suddenly, a shaft of sunlight reflected off a wicked, bloodshot eye in the darkness; and just as suddenly, a rampant hulk shot out from the cover of dense underbrush. Deep, violent snarls and snorts shattered the placid silence of the forest. Startled, the horses reared back in fear but recovered quickly at the command of their masters. Uncertain to run or stand his ground, the ragged beast paused for a moment, scarlet eyes blazing with indignant rage and drool dripping from its hairy muzzle as well as from tusks the size and shape of a Scythian dagger. A single swipe of these tusks could gut a horse as easily as a man. *Only Hades could conjure up such a beast*, thought Hadrian as he sat in his saddle, alert and taut as a bow, spear raised in preparation for what he hoped would be a fatal blow. From high on his mount, he could clearly see the beast's flaring nostrils as well as the glint of treachery in the piercing eyes that glared back at him. After seconds that felt like an eternity, the boar made up his mind and, tearing the tender mounds of moss under his hooves, boldly charged the object of his rage. Hadrian's horse reared at the sight of the unleashed fury that thundered toward him but, in turning slightly, gave the emperor a clear aim at the trophy he was to claim as his own. With a strength he had thought himself no longer capable of, Hadrian hurled his spear and sent it whistling through the air toward the oncoming beast. The razor-sharp bronze of the spearhead found its mark, sending the boar's blood-chilling screams of rage echoing through the forest as it pierced its side. Suddenly, silence. The creature stood unsteadily before Hadrian and his horse, his eyes blinking as if bewildered by the searing pain from the shaft now lodged in his body. With blood filling his lungs, a deep gurgling sound could be heard; and soon, with a muted grumble, the beast's hind legs gave way, followed by the front. After a short time, as if resigned to his fate, a barely audible sigh escaped the boar as his massive head fell between the fearful hooves, the once blazing eyes now dull with death.

For a time, the forest stood eerily hushed, as if reverently mourning the death of a king. What was so powerful and fearsome moments ago was now suddenly lifeless as Hadrian slipped quietly from his saddle and strode toward the bloodied corpse. Kneeling beside the once great beast, he felt none of the past euphoria that came with a kill. Here, within this great basilica of ancient trees, it felt all too prophetic. Despite all its majesty and power, in the end this creature could do nothing to change its fate. Suddenly weary, the emperor stood up and, with a few words of praise for the magnificent creature, returned to his horse.

Upon returning to his mount, Hadrian gave orders to the squires and slaves to proceed as usual after a kill. The assembled court, recovered now from the drama that had exploded before them, praised the emperor for his mastery and skill as well as his fortitude. Hadrian accepted their praise graciously but with feigned enthusiasm. For him, the hunt was no longer a celebration of life, but a mournful reminder of his own mortality. The trophy had become a souvenir death had left behind. As his courtiers chatted amiably behind him, Hadrian whispered a prayer to his personal god, "Oh, sad Antinous! My joy and companion in the hunt. Is this what you intended for me? To be sent on my life's journey alone with only reminders of death to keep me company? Was I so cruel to you that you should curse me so mightily? Was your heart so broken, there was no room left for pity?"

The mood of the emperor made the journey to Ephesus a silent one, save for the occasional grunt of the slaves burdened with the corpse of the great beast that now hung upside down from a thick wooden beam. Their arrival into the city created a festival atmosphere for the people as they marveled at the fearsome trophy claimed by their emperor. But the cheers and adulation went barely noticed by Hadrian as he went through the motions of his station. In his soul, he knew nothing good was to come of the rest of this tour. Darkness descended over him, and sleep, an old man's favorite but most elusive medicine, was the only remedy.

The temple of Artemis appeared to Hadrian in a dream. The multi-breasted goddess sat in regal splendor in her great home and glared down at Hadrian as he stood in worship and offered to her the wild boar as a sacrifice. This feral goddess of unfettered things sat in judgment of the emperor's sorrow and bitterness as he traveled his empire. Her strength and sensibility overwhelmed him as wandered through his own anguish. She had no use for sorrow and regret, Hadrian's constant companions. Her massive temple had survived earthquakes, fires, and lootings, yet remained standing. In this dream, a garland of flowers trembled on her many breasts that loomed over the tightly skirted legs ornamented with great beasts. Lions, griffins, stags, and bulls mingled with flowers and bees in a mystic concert of Olympian proportions. Never had he seen such majesty and grandeur. The Athena of the Acropolis was nothing compared to this ancient goddess. In the mist of the dream, Artemis continued to glare down; but instead of gathering strength, Hadrian felt nothing but the chill of sorrow. Suddenly, the corpse of the beast burst into a flaming mass; and when the inferno subsided, the beast was nothing more than a shadow of ash to be swept away by a bitter wind. To the ancient eyes of Artemis, Hadrian's all was nothing.

Hadrian woke just as the morning light was beginning to slip into the gardens of the interior courtyard outside his private quarters. The open windows had a decorative iron grating that kept out intruders but did nothing to deny entry to the early morning chill. But the clay pipes beneath the stone floor brought warmth with the hot water they carried throughout the villa. As he sat on the high ornately carved bed, Hadrian examined the elaborate frescos that ran the length of the walls over a high band of green and yellow painted to resemble carved-stone panels. The hanging oil lamps that had burned so brightly the previous night were now sputtered weakly. He had stayed here before and shared this chamber with his Beloved. He hadn't noticed the fading frescos before, nor the chill in the air. Life was sweeter then; the light was warmer, and love was a truth to be believed in.

This villa was a gift to the emperor upon his entry to the city. Ephesus knew how to thank a generous benefactor, and they provided him with a villa on the highest of the three terraces along the lower slope of the Bulbul Mountain. As he walked through the gardens of the silent peristyle and reached the main loggia, a startled slave sprang from his low bench and, bowing low, opened the heavy cedar door to the outside. From the portico, Hadrian could see, across from the hill, the final elements of construction of a small elegant temple built in his honor and dedicated to Artemis and the people of Ephesus, the façade with its four Corinthian columns and wide curved arch easily recognizable. Surrounded by his personal guard, Caesar made his way through the city as it slowly woke and soon found himself at the junction of Curetes and Marble streets where before him stood the three-story gatehouse he had built years before. Sprawling and elegant, the wide center entrance was flanked by two side entrances capped by finely carved architraves. This gate was one of the many designs he brought with him from Rome, and its positioning here, in pristine marble, was one of the most perfect and satisfying. Oblivious to the stares of the merchants and tradespeople who followed his every move, Hadrian made his way to the Agora and arrived at the steps of the Prytaneion and its sacred flame of Hestia. This was the mystical heart of Ephesus and had been embellished by Hadrian during his first stay there, and while the size and scope of the city never failed to amaze the emperor, as he mounted his horse and galloped back to the villa, he realized there was nothing else left to do here. More urgent packets arrived from the legion in Judea containing messages that soon ended the emperor's stay in the city. It was time to move on.

Chapter Twenty-Three

This Blood-soaked Land

Hadrian had the foresight to order his small flotilla to meet him at the port of Ephesus in anticipation of the situation in Judea becoming more critical. His court was informed of the change in plans at midday and set off for a sea voyage the next morning. Sailing between the mainland and the island of Samos, the ships navigated their way between the scattered islands for a day and a half before they made their way past the Isle of Rhodes and the open sea. Two days would pass before the lighthouse at Paphos on the Isle of Cyprus could be seen on the port side of the ships. Two more days would pass before the their destination, the harbor city of Caesarea, would be spotted on the horizon.

From the deck of the *Adriana Augusta*, Caesarea was a marvel even to Hadrian's eyes, and the most complex and masterful aspect of the city was its harbor, Sebastos. Rivaling Cleopatra's harbor in Alexandria, Sebastos had been built on a coast with no natural harbors and where the sea was harsh and unforgiving. It was nearly two hundred years earlier that Judea's King Herod called The Great built this harbor in defiance of the sea and as a symbol of his power and ego.

The legend of the king was that of a voracious and wicked ruler who was despised by the Jews and held with an ill-concealed contempt by his Roman lords. But the names of Herod and Caesarea were immortal, and Hadrian had more interest in the construction of the harbor city than the political and moral aspects of its creator. In so many ways, Caesarea was a wonder to behold. Considered as large as the Athenian harbor of Piraeus, it was the official residence of the Roman procurators and governors. To appease his Roman masters, Herod named his new city Caesarea; and about eighty years later, the emperor Vespasian declared the region a colony and renamed it Colonia Prima Flavia Augusta Caesarea to reflect its rise in status. During the reign of Titus, the destruction of Jerusalem changed the capital of Judea to Caesarea; and after the Jewish revolt had been suppressed, the Caesarea Maritima was the scene of the slaughter of over two thousand rebel captives. Hadrian hoped, as he gazed over the bow of his ship, that history would not have to repeat itself during his own reign. From his place at the bow, the emperor could see Herod's great double aqueduct that extended from the foot of Mount Carmel coming into view. Hadrian had attached additional channels to the original during his time as procurator under Trajan. Visible too was the hippodrome he had rebuilt as a theater during that same time. As he watched from his stateroom, the *navae tabellariae*, or herald ships, circumvented the rugged breakwater in the distance and docked at the port to great rousing cheers. Hadrian felt his contributions to the empire soothe his soul as they also fed his vanity. As he returned to his reports that littered his desk, he smiled bitterly. *Yes, even in this quarrelsome land, there was civilization to be found.*

During his last visit to Caesarea, Hadrian had planned to return to study the complexity of its construction with his own engineers and use that knowledge to improve the Roman harbors of Ostia and Puteoli. The moles or breakwaters Herod's engineers had built far surpassed those at the Roman ports to such an extent that a tsunami that battered them two years earlier left little trace of its violent power. Even today, as the rolling waves of the sea crashed mercilessly against the concrete moles and sprayed the marble columns of the bronze roofed stoa, the city stood proud and defiant in the face of Poseidon's fury.

But the revolt that was raging around Jerusalem changed those plans, and Julius Severus's dispatches were becoming more urgent. The revolt had spread from Modi'in, in the Modi'in Valley, and spread eastward toward Jerusalem, threatening the rest of the province. The rebels were much more tenacious and professional than the insurgents of last insurrection nearly sixty years earlier, and the Roman legions were suffering their wrath. The Roman garrison of the Legion XXII Deiotariana had been disbanded under Severus after its near destruction; Severus included a request for a replacement of his commandership in the last dispatch. As the royal flotilla entered Sabastos, Hadrian was still in his staterooms pouring through the reports from Judea. Publicius Marcellus, the Tribunus Laticlavius Hadrian had appointed as the second in command of the Legion III Cyrenaica, had sent his own dispatch to the emperor, a brazen move, but one Hadrian could appreciate. The Judean governor, Tinaius Rufus, had been given the title of Legatus Propraetore Augusti or imperial legate as well as praetor, but Hadrian was considering a true, seasoned Praetorian for the command of this troublesome province. Publicius Marcellus was looking like the ideal prospect.

The emperor's personal guard was already waiting on the pier as the imperial court disembarked. More dispatches from Tinaius Rufus arrived from Jerusalem, and they were added to the stack already boxed and loaded onto the saddle of the emperor's secretary. The emperor's distain for the Judeans was growing with each report, and by the time he had reached the lavish Promontory Palace, his plan of attack was solidified in his mind. He realized his plans to build a Temple to Jupiter on the foundations of their old temple was an affront to these people, and his abolition of circumcision was against their sensibilities. But Roman rule came at a price—a price set by the emperor. Hadrian was determined to root out the rebels and bring the province under control, even if it meant exiling the Judeans from their own land. The land of Judea would become Syria Palaestina and the *Pax Romana* would prevail.

It would be another three bloody years before the Pax would come to fruition, and Hadrian would no longer have to deal with this arid, bitter land. In his attempt to cleanse the land of Judaism, which he saw as the root of the discontent that haunted the province, Hadrian renamed Judea, Syria Palaestina after the ancient enemies of the Jews—the Philistines. In addition, he rebuilt Jerusalem as *Aelia Capitolina* in the Roman ideal and after his family name. The Jews were expelled from the city, and it would be another seventeen years before they were allowed to resume burying their dead in Betar, deep in the Judean Hills. This was the last of the fifty fortified towns to fall as the legions finished off the rebellion. In all, it was reported that about 580,000 Jews were killed in the rebellion, which also took the lives of thousands of Romans. The long, tedious war had further embittered Hadrian's opinion of the people and lead to drastic moves to assure the peace. He prohibited the Torah and the native calendar and, in addition to Bar Kochba, executed leading members of the Sanhedrin and Judaic scholars to prevent any further spreading of the religion. The rebellion was crushed, and the county was no more. But as Hadrian held a small coin that commemorated the Aelia Capitolina, he recalled the losses his legions had suffered and his disgust with this land that still lay smoldering. From his seat under the vast colonnade of Promontory Palace, Tineius Rufus, governor of what was now Palestina, watched cautiously as the emperor paced the marble portico clutching the small coin he had handed him a short while ago. Suddenly, the emperor stopped his pacing and hurled the coin into the crashing surf. Turning, he strode past the now pale administrator; and with a glare that withered any resolve in the man, Hadrian disappeared into the darkened chambers.

Sextus Julius Severus and Publicius Marcellus sat in the anteroom just outside of the throne room of the palace. The fact that Hadrian had not used Herod's throne room once during his stay here, and in light of their brief but disturbing conversation with Tineius Rufus, the two men waited apprehensively for an audience with their emperor. They had expected a warm welcome, but were met instead with cool silence. Prefect Lucius Didius of the Cyrenaica Legion was already with the emperor when the two men arrived, and that had been nearly an hour ago. Suddenly, there was a muffled knock on the great gilt bronze doors, and they were quickly opened by the two Praetorian guards standing motionless in front of them. The lord chamberlain hurried out and with a stiff, barely perceptible nod, motioned the men to follow him into the chamber. The afternoon sun reflected off the pool that overlooked the sea and cast odd shafts of light into the vast throne room. Prefect Lucius was standing beside the throne and turned to the men as they approached. With his back to the light, they could not see what expression he wore. Behind him sat the emperor, clothed in the full purple toga of state. At his feet was a recognizable pile of reports regarding the conclusion of the rebellion. The two men saluted the emperor and stood before him for what seemed like an eternity. With a movement that was both regal and weary, Hadrian rose and descended from the dais. He first embraced his old friend Severus and then Marcellus. Leading them to a large table of rose and deep purple porphyry, the emperor reached into a large cast silver coffer and removed two packets of fine calfskin. Handing one to each of the men, he turned to seat himself on a marble bench beside the table. Severus and Marcellus slowly removed the contents of the packets, and in the reflected light, each read his own reward and future. Severus was to return to the province of Moesia in the Balkans where he had been governor before his time in Britain. He had taken a Dacian wife who followed him reluctantly to Britain and then Palestina. A return to Moesia was a welcome reward for his service and an example of Hadrian's astute nature. A vast estate along the Black Sea as well as the funds to build a villa worthy of his station was also part of his payment. The emperor knew how to reward an old friend, even if that friend had not lived up to his expectations.

Publicius Marcellus had spread the velum sheets before him on the cool stone and stood silent after reading their contents. Besides the gold and honors granted him by the senate through the emperor's intersession, he had also been given the title of Legatus Propraetore Augusti. As imperial legate, a vast store of funds was also at his disposal to rebuild the province in the Roman ideal, with three legions to assure a smooth transition. Still dazed, Marcellus walked slowly toward the emperor and, foregoing the soldier's salute, sank to his knees. "Ave Hadrianus . . . Ave Caesar . . . Ave Pontificus." Although rarely an emotional man, he was too moved at this moment to utter much more than these words. Hadrian too was moved. He stood and raised up the man before him, noticing that in contrast to the immaculate white dress tunic underneath, he could see the dried blood and sweat on the leather straps of the man's cuirass. Marcellus wore with pride his battle-scarred armor for this audience, to prove his active participation in the victory over the rebels. Hadrian was bemused and pleased by the man's silent message. Rather than a senate-appointed politician, he now had a true soldier to administrate this province.

The sun's light had shifted, and the shadows of the columns along the atrium were sweeping like a sundial along the marble floor of the chamber. Hadrian was weary of this land and its religious zealots. Although the Christian sect had not been involved in the insurrection, Hadrian despised and distrusted them just the same. To Hadrian's mind, they were spawn of the Jews and would eventually prove to be just as troublesome. *Thank the gods that will happen long after I'm gone,* he thought to himself as he gazed out at the sea. He was to visit Aelia Capitolina only once after the war, and that was to consecrate the statues of Jupiter and himself at the Temple of Jupiter on what was once the site of the Jewish temple. In an apse along the side wall of the temple was an altar to the twin gods Hadrian had worshiped all his life. Deimos and Phobos, the sons of Ares and Aphrodite, stood painted and lifelike in their grandfather's temple. The daunting gods of fear, panic, and terror had used their influence, in Hadrian's mind, to rout the rebels and restore the peace. Together with their father, the god of war and sacker of towns, they had done well for Rome. As the emperor stood beside the great granite altar in front of the temple, he watched the flames of his sacrifice smolder, the smoke rising to enter the nostrils of the gods. His gaze wandered to the façade of the temple where colossal columns, carved in the form of bound prisoners in Judean costume, supported the roof and pediment of the temple. Hadrian had commissioned these when his sympathy for these people vanished in the wake of their insurrection. These columns served as grim reminders to all enemies of Rome, as did the smoke that still rose from the rubble of the homes of the vanquished.

Now, as he stood in the shade of the massive pillars of Herod's palace, Hadrian wanted nothing more than to leave here and return to the glory of the Villa Adrianna. At the age of fifty-nine, he was ready to spend what was left of his life in a world of his own making.

Chapter Twenty-Four

A Floating Oasis

The *Adriana Augusta* was a welcome sight for the emperor on this particular morning. Although he could view the same sight from his private chambers every day during his stay in Caesarea, on this morning as he surveyed the provisions being loaded in preparation for his journey home, there was a sense of relief in his heart. Hadrian observed with amusement his chamberlain, who sat limply on a low stool, exhausted after a morning of preparation and orchestrating that started long before dawn. The once portly but elegant Ophelos had become thinner, along with his hair, in the service of an energetic emperor. Hadrian recalled the old man's almost slavish devotion to Antinous and that his hair seemed to go quite white after the youth's death. Not, in all probability, of grief, but because his vanity gave out, and he no longer saw a reason to dye his thinning locks to keep up an appearance of youth. Hadrian knew he should have retired his old servant when they returned to Rome from their last visit to the east, but he was too much a part of the past to let go. Now Hadrian was resigned to release his old retainer when they returned this time to Rome. The emperor would reward his faithful servant with a comfortable villa outside Rome. *Two old men*, thought Hadrian, *retiring to their homes in the country.*

A vast array of chests and crates had been loaded on the emperor's ship during the night and the following morning. Some of the chests contained items the emperor was already familiar with. But others were curiosities to him. Like a child on the morning of its birthday, Hadrian watched with great anticipation as the chests disappeared one by one into the hold of the ship, waiting to be opened during the voyage home. One item he especially wanted to hold again was a two-handled silver cup with two scenes of an erastes and eromenos during the act of love. It had come to him from the treasury of the Promontory Palace and was a parting gift from Tineius Rufus. This, and a nearly four-hundred-year-old cup made of chalcedony that came to Caesarea by way of Egypt. Supposedly commissioned by Ptolemy II Philadelphus, it was artfully carved with Dionysiac scenes that almost magically absorbed any light that found it. As he recalled the cup, Hadrian touched the cameo set into the *fibula* that fastened the ends of his woolen cloak. Carved from a flawless amethyst of the deepest purple, it portrayed a profile of Antinous with a laurel crown and was included at all times in whatever the emperor was wearing. As his finger continued to trace the profile of his beloved, Hadrian's mind began to reach far beyond Caesarea and this land he was eager to push from his memory.

The city of Caesarea too had wearied of the imperial presence. Their coffers had been considerably lightened by the scores of legions who were either stationed there or had passed through. This was a province at war, and it was expected to pay the cost of its own defense. In the past, Hadrian had been gracious to the conquered. But in this case, the cost of victory was too great and the deaths of his legions too dear. These were a people who needed to be scattered to the winds, and there was no imperial benevolence to be found. As Hadrian watched the shores of Caesarea fade in the distance, he knew it was the last time he would see the sight of it. And to be honest, he really did not care.

Hadrian could sense the guards too were eager to return home to Rome. Their congenial chatter was unusual when he boarded the ship, and he reveled in a soldierly camaraderie he had not experienced since Britain.

As the polished bronze of his cuirass faced the mid morning sun, it flashed against the iron armor of the guards that, worn smooth with years of wear, caught the same light and illuminated their faces. Hadrian could not help but notice that from time to time he would catch sight of one of the guards eyeing the mask of Antinous on the cast panel of the imperial breastplate. Gilded and set with pale jasper for eyes, the visage was arresting despite being surrounded by scrollwork, dolphins, and an array of grotesques. From the farthest reaches of the empire to the person of the emperor himself, there was no escaping the memory of the youth. Yet Hadrian saw nothing judgmental in the gaze of his Praetorians. Here on this massive ship surrounded by his handpicked guards, Hadrian felt at peace for the first time in years.

As something brushed his sleeve, he turned to find his chamberlain bearing a tray holding a jug of wine and low gilt silver cups. Knowing the difficulty the old man would have in balancing the tray while pouring the wine, Hadrian stopped his attempt with a raised hand and then proceeded to pour the blood-red drink into the cups himself. The guards look on as if this were a religious ritual and accepted with gruff reverence the offering of their emperor. Raising his cup to a cloudless sky, Hadrian toasted Rome, his peerless legions, and the successful end to a brutal war. After a few gulps, one of the Praetorians raised his cup again and, caught up in the sudden emotion of the moment, gave his toast. "Ave Hadrianius. To our god emperor and the god Antinous." Hadrian, startled by the spontaneity of the tribute, seemed to hesitate before drinking. At first, the guard feared he had spoken out of turn, but the glistening in the emperor's eyes told him otherwise. The guards took up the toast and, along with the emperor, drained their wine in a single swallow. For a few seconds, Hadrian stared briefly into the vast nothingness of the open sea, absentmindedly running his thumb along the cup's gilt band of ivy leaf before he returned the cup to the tray, saluted his guards, and turned toward the fluttering awning that shielded the entrance to his staterooms. The two guards there, having witnessed the ritual that had just taken place, saluted crisply as one reached to open the heavy oaken door for the emperor. The Praetorians, still affected by the scene that had played itself out on deck, watched wordlessly as Caesar disappeared into the shadows.

The staterooms of the imperial yacht were cool and dark when Caesar finally made his way to them. The reflected light from outside glowed on the newly polished columns and the inlaid floor. The hanging lamps were full but silent, their fluttering whispers reserved until the sun's departure. On a low table of polished camphorwood, the royal chamberlain had already set up a lunch for the emperor. A shallow silver tray held a small oval loaf of fresh bread as well as a mound of soft cheese pierced with a small silver knife. As with the wine, the pale cheese was part of the provisions brought from Greece along with the bowl of deep purple olives and small round honey cakes that sat stacked like coins on a footed silver tray with goat head handles. Plump figs lay nestled in bunches of grapes that flowed over the side of a footed glass *tazza* of Egyptian origin, as a ewer of the same fine craftsmanship held wine, rich as blood, glowing deeply in the ray of light that found its way through the partially shuttered windows.

Hadrian sat heavily upon the low couch and picked at the meal before him. His headaches were becoming more frequent, and he knew more food and less drink was the remedy. He had never cared for the heavy drinking of wine, and in the past, he imbibed only to please his mentor, Trajan. But now he found it gave him what little sleep he could manage, and more sleep meant less time to ponder the direction his life's journey had taken. Still, he pushed away the cup before him; and as he ate, he tried to piece together the past years since Antinous's death, his thoughts turning to the sheets of velum that lay hidden in a leather case, their contents known only to their author. These memoirs were vital to history's understanding of his reign and would put to rest the rumors and slander he had endured over the years. Tearing off a chunk of the bread and using the small knife to scoop a portion of the cheese, Hadrian left the couch and made his way to the vast desk near the entrance to his sleeping chamber. Littered on his desk were scrolls with architectural plans stacked safely in their tooled leather cases. As Hadrian reached for a gilded leather case that sat off to the side, the movement sent the stack of scroll cases careening off the table and clattering to the floor, their deep thuds followed quickly by the sound of their metal fasteners clicking loudly on the polished wood as they rolled across the room. The chamberlain materialized with a swiftness that startled the emperor as the elderly man began to chase the scroll cases that were still meandering around the room due to the slight listing of the ship. The sight of the old man's boney legs beneath his elegant tunic and the sound of his loose sandals flapping with every step was quickly becoming more than Hadrian could bear. "Enough, old man!" Hadrian's words came out more sharply than he had intended. In a softer voice, he continued. "Send for a page to take care of this. Go back to your rest, old friend." The chamberlain, humiliated by the first command but mollified by the change in Caesar's tone, hurried out of the stateroom and headed toward the lower level of the ship to find a suitable page. As he reached the door of the stateroom, he turned to bow again, in time to see the emperor retiring to his bedchamber.

As Hadrian entered the sleeping chamber, the only light came from a bowl-shaped lamp of cast bronze secured like a small jewel into a well in the marble altar. Its three wicks illuminated an alabaster bust of the Beloved tucked into a richly carved niche in the cedar-paneled wall. Hadrian was drawn to the portrait, its features skillfully carved from life and closer to the boy's likeness than any other portrayal. There was no personification of another god here, no garland crown of glory, no Egyptian allusions; only the perfection of the mortal boy as he was. The curls of his hair were deeply sculpted, not in an orderly pattern but in the dense disarray of their natural state. The eyes were the almond shape of the originals; their expression frank, not downcast or questioning. In life, they spoke more than those full lips, the color of watered wine, ever did. But when those lips did speak, they relayed an intellect one did not expect from such beauty. The sturdy neck and broad solid chest were rendered simply but with great care, to the point that Hadrian could not resist running his fingertips over the rose-colored nipples. The head was not turned and bowed in submission as future artists were wont to do, but straight facing so that the unflinching eyes met the viewer's. The portrait was dynamic yet tenderly contrived. Although one of many portrayals, its hypnotic realism made this sculpture the emperor's most treasured possession after the youth's death and had made its sculptor a rich man.

The lamp's flickering tongues of flame illuminated the stone from within and warmed it to the touch. The effect was startling. The texture of the stone and the warmth it absorbed from the flames recalled a flood of memories with one touch. Hadrian caressed the broad chest to release those memories. He needed sleep, and he wanted that sleep composed of merciful dreams. With a sigh, he turned and walked slowly to the richly appointed bed that stood like an island in the middle of the room. Collapsing on top of the coverings of rare silks and linen, he cast his eyes once more on the glowing figure in the wall. As his eyes grew heavy, tears, so familiar now they went unnoticed, blurred the image and gave it an eerie sense of movement. And with that last vision, he slept.

As the *nauarchus* of the imperial fleet, the captain of the emperor's *quinterime* set the course for the rest of the flotilla. He had conferred with the emperor days before the voyage to review the list of ports they would visit and set a time schedule. He then met with the *trierarchi* of the other ships to inform them of the fair weather course they would take as well as the alternative course these captains would take in the event of storms. On the morning of the voyage, he set off for open water, bypassing the ports of Cyprus and heading, as planned, directly toward Crete and the port of Cnossus. In the morning haze, the sea was a sheet of blue ink while the sky took on the color of milky chalcedony. That night, the sea absorbed the light of the full moon as it reflected off the foamy tips of the rolling waves. As Posiden slumbered, the great fleet parted the waves and sped toward Cnossus.

The ship Hadrian's friend Herodus of Marathon had gifted him was mostly Greek by design, but also had the characteristics of a Roman warship. It was larger and far more luxurious than any ship in the Roman navy, and although this was a time of peace on the Mediterranean, the *Adrianna Augusta* would prove a formidable adversary if attacked. With ten banks of oars and three masts, it was a swift, well-armored yacht that could run or hold its own with ease. But with the flotilla surrounding the vessel and the imperial standard snapping in the wind as a warning, no one in their right mind would ever attack. The ship was built for the comfort of an old friend, and Herodus's gift was doing what it was meant to do. The waves of the "Roman Lake" were well mannered during this voyage, and the gentle listing of the great ship lulled its imperial passenger into a deep sleep.

Chapter Twenty-Five

A Diversion

The sun had long begun its decline before Hadrian woke to the sounds coming from outside his door. Forgetting for a moment the recent conversation with his chamberlain, he thought the old man was still chasing after scroll cases. Hadrian's irritation vanished when he entered the room and found a page had carefully stacked the cases and was now arranging the pens and inkwells in neat rows. On the desk was a tall lamp stand in the shape of a tree with the slender form of Eros standing beside it. From the tree's branches hung a cluster of six oil lamps, four of which the youth had burning. It amused Hadrian that the youth was so absorbed in his simple task he failed to notice the naked man before him. It was not until Hadrian had reached the desk and lit the last two lamps himself that the boy looked up with wide, startled eyes. "Forgive me for waking you, Majesty. The boy's whisper was soft yet deep. By then, Hadrian had made his way to where the boy stood behind the desk. "There is nothing to forgive. When I heard the sounds, I thought perhaps my ship was a host to rats." The lamplight caught a gleam in Caesar's eyes as he added, "But I can see from your tail you are certainly not a rat." The youth stood still for a moment, then when he comprehended the jest, he smiled shyly, the lamplight betraying the blush on his cheeks even as he

turned away. Charmed by the youth's profile, Hadrian sat himself
on the edge of the desk and gently touched the youth's chin,
turning his face to his own. The tousled hair was slightly damp
from his scurrying around with the heavy scroll cases, and some
tendrils hung down over his eyes. His long lashes nearly reached
the dark line of brows that hovered over deep eyes that now
absorbed the lamplight. Lifting the youth's chin slightly, Hadrian
ran his thumb over the full soft mouth that opened invitingly
at his touch. Rising from the desktop, he saw the youth was of
average height for sixteen, slender but solidly built. This was not
the descendant of aristocrats but from the bloodline of soldiers.
In time, the features will coarsen, and the body will thicken. But at
this moment, he was nearly perfection. Hadrian's fingers wandered
down to the gilt sliver bulla around the youth's neck. The amulets
that were contained in it to ward off evil spirits rattled softly as
Caesar playfully tapped it. The quality of the bulla and its chain
of braided silver showed the boy's family was of estimable wealth
and the youth was well bred. Hadrian had no recollection of the
boy being brought into his entourage, but that was of no concern
right now. He softly asked the youth's name, and the same soft,
low voice from before answered, "Marius Gaius, my lord Caesar."
Bending slightly, Hadrian tasted the lips of the youth with his own
and then pulled back to appraise the reaction. The pleasure in the
youth's eyes lead to another kiss before Caesar took Marius into
his arms. As he pulled the thin linen tunic down off his shoulders
and to his waist, Hadrian reveled in the pure, smooth paleness
of the youth's skin. Marius trembled as the man slid the garment
off him completely, leaving nothing between each other's flesh.
Hadrian could hear the urgent breathing of the youth as the heat
of his pliant body warmed Caesar's. The youth's eagerness was

felt as his hardness pressed insistently against Caesar's own and proven as he lay back on the massive desk and wrapped his slender legs around Hadrian's firm waist, surrendering himself completely and with surprising ease. The scent of the youth made Hadrian's head whirl, and suddenly, the world that burdened him no longer existed, let alone mattered. The only reality was here in his arms, and as the youth began to return his kisses with increasing fervor, Hadrian's own half-forgotten desire grew. With a small gasp, Marius accepted Caesar's penetration, and the world for both vanished in a haze of passion.

Unlike the Greek youths in Athens, Hadrian quickly found that in his sixteen years, Marius had learned little about the expression of sexual desire. As was often the case, the emperor found himself in the role of teacher; and as the night wore on, his student became more willing and eager. Quick to learn, Marius's innocent exuberance was a revelation Hadrian had experienced only once before. And for fleeting moments, memory and the present collided until both were blurred. Even as the morning sun found its way through the shutters of the bedchamber, the youth's ardor had not been quenched. The same could not be said for the lamp in the niche. It had sputtered out shortly after Apollo made his appearance in the room, but its absence did not go unnoticed.

From his nest of pillows on the great bed, Marius watched as his emperor slept. The slashes of light cutting through the darkness found their way to Hadrian's face revealing all the lines and creases of advanced age in the unforgiving light, and Marius saw more silver than dark in the curls of the man's hair and beard. But the previous night's revelry was not the performance of an old man; even Marius had enough experience to recognize that. As the youth sat and gazed at this powerful man, he was torn between the desire to wake him for more pleasure and letting him continue a well-deserved sleep.

In the corner of his eye, Marius caught the last remnants of smoke rising from the oil lamp as it danced in a beam of light before disappearing into the darkness. The youth quietly slid from the bed and, after retrieving a small ram-shaped lamp still flickering on the side table, made his way to the niche. He had noticed the sculpture the night before and knew at a glance it was the god Antinous. He had listened to stories about the emperor's favorite and his deification in the Nile, but much of what he heard was beyond his comprehension. Until now. Sharing the same bed brought him closer to the stories he was told and a better understanding of the consequences. As he stood before the sculpture, it was impossible to see clearly the features of the famous ephebe. Running his fingers along the surface of the altar, he found what he knew would be there. His hand struck a small bronze *balsamarium* containing the precious lamp oil; it tipped over with a dull clank. Retrieving the container, Marius found its opening with the help of a shaft of morning light that now washed over altar. He poured the fragrant oil into the lamp and, using table lamp from the bedside, lit its three spouts. The altar lamp sputtered, then blazed brightly while the ram-shaped lamp he held flickered out in deference. The intensity of the blaze from the fresh oil startled the boy, but not as much as the face that appeared before him. The carving was more realistic than any he had seen before; the flawless alabaster glistened as if living flesh. For a time, Marius stood in awe before the young god that stared back at him; and without warning, tears began to flow freely down the boy's face.

Hadrian, stirred from sleep by the sound of the balsamarium hitting the marble of the altar top, had been watching the small drama that was unfolding before the shrine of his Beloved. The beautiful youth he had found much joy in a short time ago, stood at the altar, his tears shining in the lamplight. Hadrian was not sure what had lead to this moment, so he had watched in bewildered concern. Leaving the bed slowly so as to not disturb the sacred moment, he stood behind the youth who was now gently touching the face of the portrait. Two beauties faced each other. One Greek and made of stone, the other Roman and very human. Hadrian stepped closer to Marius and gently placed his hands on the youth's hips. The youth was startled out of his reverie at first, but allowed the now-familiar hands to slide to his chest as strong arms followed and embraced him. "Why do you weep for Antinous?" Hadrian whispered into the boy's ear. The youth was hesitant to express his feelings at first, but the emotions that filled him loosened his tongue. "He was my age when you first brought him to your bed. And in two years, he was a god. Are you truly that powerful?" Hadrian was startled by the youth's simple but direct observation, and the innocence of the comment contained a painful confusion. Did the boy mean he was responsible for the death or for the deification? "It is not everyone who can create a god out of a man. You must truly be a god yourself." The boy continued, "How did he die?" Hadrian quickly grasped the youth's thoughts and found them far more benign than he first imagined. *And much simpler.* Marius knew only the stories that created the legend, not the sordid rumors that poisoned them.

But his question was painful just the same. "He fell into the Nile," was Hadrian's somewhat gruff reply. He repeated what he had written in his official memoirs. He had meant to write more of it, but could find no words he could share. How could he explain what happened when he himself was not sure? In his dreams, he is responsible, a great black bird sending the golden youth to his doom. Not Zeus with Ganymede as he had always imagined, but the death god Thanatos, forcing the youth into the river Styx. No, there were no words to follow the single line he wrote. *Nor would there ever be.*

Hadrian continued to hold the youth close against him, and he inhaled the scent of the dark curls that tumbled over his face. The slightly sweet taste of flesh on his tongue helped dispel, somewhat, the power of the stone image that stared from its altar. "Come. Let us greet the morning in a more human way," Hadrian whispered in the youth's ear. The lad giggled, and a slight shudder of desire ran through him. As they returned to the great bed, Hadrian turned briefly toward the silent figure still glowing in the lamplight. *Release me, boy. Give me some peace in the short time I have left,* was his bitter prayer.

The sky face of Aether was clear and cloudless that morning, as if Africus, god of the southwest wind, had blown them all away while filling the sails of the imperial fleet. Hadrian greeted the new day with a vigor that amused his chamberlain as he returned to the kitchen once more to replenish the emperor's breakfast. His guest from the previous night had discretely left at dawn, but the signs of the youth's presence were evident in the scattered pillows and ravaged bed. Hadrian paid Ophelos no mind as the chamberlain busily restored the room to its formerly pristine state, all the while wheezing and clucking his disapproval. "Your Majesty needs a full night's rest at his age," the old man ventured when he realized his sounds were being heard. "And our chamberlain needs to mind his own business," was the emperor's reply. But a slight smile warmed the reply. They had been through too much together to keep secrets now. Ophelos could have called servants in to do the bending and lifting needed to restore the room, but the devoted servant had become more possessive of the emperor since the death of the Beloved. Word of the night visitor would spread soon enough without the gossip of servants speeding it along. Returning from the kitchen, Ophelos noticed Marius looking out dreamily over the deck railings. *Perhaps choosing this one to look after the emperor was not so clever after all,* thought the old man as he watched the boy who seemed to be dreaming of a golden future. He thought better than to set the boy straight. *It is better to let the emperor choose the tune to this dance.* "Boy! Take this tray to the emperor for his breakfast. I'm too old to be carrying such burdensome things," the chamberlain commanded. Marius, eager to return to Caesar's side, bolted from the railing and with admirable agility plucked the silver tray from the man's grasp. With a self-assured smile and a graceful turn, he headed toward the royal stateroom.

Marius's reception was not quite what he expected. While the emperor smiled at the sight of the youth, he went on with the work before him without another glance. Placing the heavy tray on the desk, Marius picked up the wine ewer and the glass water jug, deftly mixing the two in a goblet of chased silver. All the while, the emperor seemed to take no notice. Marius took a bolder approach and stood beside the emperor, placing his hand lightly on his shoulder. "There is a time and place for all things," was the curt response. Stung by the brusque dismissal, Marius blushed deeply, bowed and turned to leave. Hadrian looked up from his correspondences just in time to see the blush and tears that began to fill the youth's eyes. Reaching out, Hadrian grabbed a handful of youth's tunic. *One of his finer ones*, he observed. With a tug, he pulled the boy backward and onto his lap. Ashamed of his behavior and his tears, Marius could not look at the emperor. "Forgive my boldness, my lord," he whispered. Hadrian gently turned the youth's face to his and looked into his eyes. "Forgive *me*, little one. Your presence is far too much of a distraction when I have so much work to do. If you stay, the only thing that will attended to will be you." With a kiss, he released the youth. Marius smiled shyly and bowed again before the emperor. "We will dine together later on, Marius. Then after, we will see what more pleasures we can come up with." Marius bowed once more and, his hurt feelings restored, walked slowly from the stateroom, certain a pair of eyes were following his every move.

Another night had passed, and the flotilla had sailed beyond the scattered islands of Carpathos and reached Crete by early morning. Hadrian had been at work since before sunrise, and the sun peering through the window of his stateroom was competing with the cluster of lamps on his desk. The cases holding reports from all over his empire littered the floor as their contents lay scattered over the cedar tabletop. Much like the empire itself, the reports were in a state of controlled chaos. Hadrian knew the contents of each stack and what was required to get those stacks back into their respective cases. After Crete, he had a precious few more days before reaching Syracuse and the delegation that would be waiting for him there. And beyond Syracuse, Rome. After the violence and backstabbing politics of Syria Palaestina, he was well prepared to face the city that was truly the beating heart of the empire. It was from there that the Villa Adrianna waited for him to return like Olympus waits for Zeus. But it would be an Olympus without Ganymede.

At the thought of his Beloved, Hadrian's gaze wandered to the next room, still sheathed in darkness. There, the youth slept off an evening of sweat and passion. If nothing else, Marius was the tonic needed to relight the fire within. The energy Caesar felt during the past days was more than he had known in the past years. As he gazed at the gradually disappearing stacks of vellum, he could still smell the scent of the youth on his skin and offered a silent prayer to his personal god for sending him the strength to overcome his slowly fading health. It was as if he drew energy from the youth in the other room and let it fill him like wine from a jug. But like wine, there was a such thing as too much. While Marius's need seemed to be unquenchable, Hadrian's thirst was satiated earlier in the night and not renewed until the morning. But it was morning that felt the loneliest. In the silence of the new light, the emperor felt the weight of the empire and all the years he had given it. Then, as if to answer the silent prayer made earlier, the sun poured forth through the grated window and warmed his shoulders, a cloak of light from Aurora.

Hadrian turned toward the sun-filled window in time to see, to his surprise, the lighthouse of Itanos. Africus must have summoned his Greek brothers Notus and Eurus, the south and east winds, and together they had outdone themselves. As they passed the Isle of Dia, the dark staterooms of the ship became awash with the blinding white reflection of the city walls. The light woke the sleeping Marius and drew him from the comfort of the royal bed. He walked naked to the chamber the emperor now sat in, gazing out the window toward the approaching city. Settling himself on the seat near Hadrian, Marius peered out the window, full of curiosity and excitement. The nearness of the youth was too tempting for Caesar, and with a quick kiss on the back of his neck, he sent the youth back to the bed chamber to dress. The day would be long, and Hadrian knew he could afford no distractions.

Chapter Twenty-Six

An Idyllic Kingdom

The swiftness of the ships startled the Cretan procurator as they appeared on the horizon a day before their expected arrival. Despite Crete's ancient and glorious history, visits by Rome were few over the past hundred years or so since the island's defeat by Marius Caecilius Metellus during the time of Pompey the Great. The most recent visit was during the reign of the emperor Trajan, when the Legion VII Claudia trampled Cretan soil on their way to put down the rebellious Jewish population in Cyprus. Those diasporic Jews arrived there after the destruction of Jerusalem by Nerva over sixty years earlier and then after Trajan's war against them over forty years later. The Judeans never reached Crete, and by the time Hadrian sailed into the harbor of Zakros, the province had returned to being a simple backwater that saw few imperial honors. As the oarsmen guided the flotilla toward the pier, the Hadrian could see that the reflection filling his staterooms radiated from the whitewashed walls of the old royal palace that served as the residence of the Roman procurator governor. Ancient Cnossus, a small but flourishing city that boasted a grand palace ruin, was too far inland along the valley of the River Platyperama to warrant a visit. Clearly, the stay would be short, and barring any promise of a good hunt, the governor would be enough to visit on this antiquated island.

The procurator governor, Sextus Marius Fabii was a younger man than Hadrian had expected. *Or,* thought Hadrian, *is it that I am at an age that considers any man too young for his station?* Slender and elegantly attractive, the man was well suited for a province that had not seen conflict in over one hundred years. The ancient palace of Kato Zakros was far more immense and comfortable than at first glance and, although considerably newer and smaller than the famed Palace of Knossos, exuded an aura far older than Rome itself. The floor plan was like a small city with an immense central court. Hadrian took his scribes to write down the endless details of the palace and sketch their details. A bath in the Roman style took up an entire wing of the palace while another wing was devoted to the royal stables with an enormous grassy courtyard behind it. As Hadrian watched his favorite horse, now free from the confines of the ship, run with abandon on the lush grounds, he suddenly longed for his villa. A staircase off the marble-clad bath lead to the imperial guest chambers, with fresco lined corridors and ceilings set with glass panels to provide natural light. The scribes were still busy with their assigned duties when Hadrian entered the guest quarters, which overlooked a rocky cliff and the sea. His chamberlain was already present, presiding over the servants as they moved chests into position and emptied their contents. Hadrian walked to the long-columned porch that stretched the length of the suite and offered a view of the sea and the low mountains in the distance. Looking around the rooms, Hadrian noticed an absence, but thought better than to mention it. He left the chambers and proceeded to the banquet hall, where the sounds of youthful laughter redirected his thoughts.

The vast banquet hall was off the throne room, which had been decorated with the imperial standards and insignia. As Hadrian passed through a small corridor, he noticed a light burning in a marble-lined room, its tall double doors opened just enough to allow passage. As he neared the great doors, the strong scent of lilies filled the air and dizzied his senses. Intrigued, he walked through the doors to a sight that both pleased and chilled him. The high walls of the small square chamber were clad with a pale gray marble while six pilasters of rose-colored marble lined up along the rear wall. The six pilasters flanked an exedra or apse pierced with long, narrow windows dressed with bronze grills in a "Greek key" pattern. Dark gray marble capitals in the Corinthian order sat on cushions of gilded bronze and crowned the slender pilasters. The pale walls were studded with gilded bronze rosettes and raised the eye to a semidome covered with a brilliant mosaic of hunters surrounded by fanciful beasts. All this was unexpectedly beautiful, yet it was what stood surrounded by all this magnificence that made Caesar's heart hesitate. There, on a plinth of rose granite, was a life-sized sculpture of his Beloved. Carved from a block of the finest Parian marble, the Antinous image glowed in the shafts of light pouring in from the narrow windows. Bearing a hunter's spear in his uplifted hand, he gazes down at a faithful hound, so reminiscent of the hunting dogs he cherished during his life. Still, for all of the beauty in the form, it was the face that captivated the emperor. The features were finely modeled; the expression wise yet tender. It was a look Hadrian had seen so many times and was still haunted by in his dreams.

Who the artist was and how he knew the youth so well was a mystery. And the fact that is was here, on this tired, ancient island amazed him even more.

The heady scent of lilies drifted from bowls set before the plinth, lavishly filled with the favorite flower of Crete. The blossoms were of so great a number that the air nearly tasted of their scent. Carved in the granite plinth was a verse that, with its first few lines, seemed so familiar to Hadrian. As he read further, he recalled the Hymnus of Kourion, at the Temple of Apollo/Antinous on the island of Cyprus. The portrayal there was a lithe Antinous from his earlier years and not as well rendered as the sculpture before him now. But the verse was memorable and odd to find again, here in this chapel of gray marble. Hadrian read on, savoring each graceful line:

We praise the Adonis of the Underworld

Whom we formerly called Antinous.

Grant harmonious divine melodies to me

The radiant-haired lyre player

Has lured me alone to this place,

The singer of songs, to sing for you.

It is for you that I strum the barbitos,

It is for you that the cythera sounds

At the untouchable altar of Hylates.

It is for you that I have assembled a chorus.

To call upon the sons of Phoroneus,

The sons of Perseus, who single-handedly

Chose this loftiest city above all others.

It is at your instruction that I sing to the Cythera,

You with the curls of violet-blossom-locks,

Beautiful haired youth, blessed Bithynian,

Whose face is full of grace

Offspring of the Golden Winged Goddess.

Continually running his fingers over each word carved in the hard stone, Hadrian remained in the temple-like chamber for sometime. So much time, in fact, that his chamberlain came looking for him, his face a mask of restrained worry. When he saw what had captured the emperor's attention, he stood silent, awed by the sight. Together, wrapped in their own thoughts and memories, master and servant stood in reverence before the image of the young god. As the sun began to slowly shift and the glow of the marble began to fade, Hadrian turned to leave and caught sight of two figures lost in the moment. His chamberlain stood tragic and tear stained, his memories written in the lines of his face. Behind him, framed by the double doors of the chamber, stood his tribune prefect, Quintus Marcius. Nothing could be discerned from his expressionless face, but his eyes were a different matter. A strange glimmer shone in them, as if he too recalled a special time in the life of the youth. Hadrian moved again, and both men recovered from their reverie. The chamberlain bowed and suggested they continue to the banquet hall, while Lucius saluted and inquired on the emperor's health. Hadrian was somewhat bemused. *They expected to find me dead on the floor*, he thought bitterly. *That time will come soon enough, but not now, not here!* Brushing past the chamberlain and returning the Praetorian's salute, Caesar strode through the great doors and made his way to the banquet hall where laughter could be heard, even from here.

A vast stone staircase flowed from the upper stories into the broad corridor that lead to the hall. Massive carved bulls, ancient and fierce, stood at the end of the balustrades flanking the marble steps, and Hadrian stopped for a moment to examine their craftsmanship. As he turned to study the graceful sweep of the stairs, a lithe figure with a wisp of blond beard was gracefully descending the steps. His dear Lucius Ceionius Commodus came toward him with a sly smile and open arms. "You've ruined the surprise, my lord!" he admonished the emperor. His voice was deeper than Hadrian had remembered, but his movements were as light as ever. "I would not survive a surprise greater than this one, my boy," the emperor replied. "How is it possible that you are here in this forgotten land?" Commodus's answer came with a laugh. "I could not wait for your arrival in Syracuse, let alone Rome. I know how you tend to dawdle when Rome is your final destination." It was Hadrian's turn to laugh. It was true, and Commodus was a frequent witness to this. "How is your wife and child?" he asked, changing the subject. "Well enough," Lucius Commodus replied. "But enough of that. How are you, and what kind of adventures have you been up to?" There was a wicked gleam in his eyes, leading Hadrian to conclude the man knew more than he pretended. Yes, a man now. Physically, the boy had vanished, although he seemed to remain in his movements and wily tongue. Hadrian again changed the subject, but his thoughts shifted to Marius, who had made himself scarce since they arrived at Cnossos. The couple walked arm in arm to the banquet hall with the lord chamberlain shuffling behind until they reached the entrance. There, Prefect Quintus Marcius stepped forward and announced the presence of the emperor of Rome. The crowded hall rose in unison as the emperor passed through the heavily draped doorway and took his place of honor. This was the cue for a great cloud of floral petals to descend from above onto the assembled diners as the musicians took up light and spirited tunes. *For what is considered a backwater by Roman standards, these people know how to give a proper welcome,* thought Hadrian as he reached for a cup of finely wrought gold. It was just beyond his grasp, however, but within Commodus's. The young man took the cup from the table and presented it to the emperor with both hands, reliving the past in a gesture. As Hadrian drank, he peered over the jewel-encrusted rim just in time to see the boy Marius handing a cup to Sextus Fabii. The emperor now understood the reason for the boy's absence.

As Hadrian lowered his cup, the youth turned, and their eyes met. The youth's blush could be seen even across the vast distance of the hall, but Hadrian merely raised his cup in salute and turned to Commodus's ongoing conversation. If Lucius noticed the youth, he made no mention of it. There were plenty of attractive youths to distract the emperor, and this boy, though beautiful, was just one of them. If the emperor was interested in this one, Commodus would know soon enough.

As the night wore on, the music began to irritate Hadrian, as did the constant laughter. Early on, Hadrian noticed the absence of women at this event. Their chatter was replaced by the lilting laughter of flirtatious dancing boys and the deeper voices of their prey. Hadrian watched in amusement, as various dramas unfolded while others were resolved with a whisper in the right ear. Many of the youth's whirled by Caesar in hopes of catching his eye, but most knew of the beautiful sculpture in the temple-like chamber and the golden boy that was Caesar's. Hadrian studied the cup in his hand and refused the refill he was offered. The gold of the cup was actually a cladding for an interior of polished agate set with carnelian. Egyptian in design and craftsmanship, it was quite ancient and rare. The procurator had carved out a sweet life for himself in this forgotten land, and the treasures he amused his guests with were a testament of the wealth that lay hidden in the endless labyrinth of rooms.

While Hadrian continued to examine the cup, Marius, seeing that Lucius had wandered off to mingle with another group of young men, made his way toward the emperor's couch. "Majesty, I pray you are not angry with me for not attending to you earlier," he spoke earnestly and with deep trepidation. Hadrian looked up and into the pale gray eyes of the boy. He was tired and suddenly homesick for his Villa Adrianna. This boy, though beautiful, held little interest for him now. The youthful god in the marble-clad room still filled his thoughts and even in stone eclipsed the boy before him. "Does Procurator Fabii please you, little one?" Hadrian asked with a slight edge of sarcasm. The boy blushed again and nodded before adding, "But I am the emperor's servant, my lord, and his to command." *Damn right!* thought Hadrian bitterly. And even though he had decided to release the youth sometime ago, he was like a cat whose paw was still on the mouse's tail, unwilling to end the struggle. Calling his chamberlain to the couch, Hadrian instructed the man to bring the governor to him. Sextus accepted the summons with some alarm and sailed hurriedly across the vast hall, sinking to his knees before the emperor's presence. After formally thanking him for the banquet in his honor, Hadrian spoke plainly to the still kneeling man. "It appears my young companion, Marius Gaius, has caught your eye, Procurator Fabii." Hadrian affected a stern manner to see how the procurator would react. "Forgive me, Majesty!" the man replied. He had grown quite pale as did the youth who was the uncomfortable subject of the conversation. "I did not intend to offend you or take what is rightfully yours." For Hadrian, the night had grown late, and this game was wearing quite thin; a quick resolution was in order. "As it is with the ancient tradition of the Greeks, the boy is free to choose his own lover," was Caesar's bemused reply. "And if he wishes to be with you, I am pleased to offer him to you as a gift with my blessing." The man looked up suddenly, his worried look replaced by astonishment and relief. With a furtive look toward the youth, he thanked the emperor for his kindness before returning hesitantly to his feet. With his hand on the small of the boy's back, Hadrian gently guided Marius off the couch and toward Sextus, his smile a sign of the blessing he had offered. The two bowed before turning to wander off toward the lively group they had left, with Sextus's hand now where the emperor's had been.

A slight movement caught Hadrian's attention, and he turned to see Lucius standing at the head of the gilded couch, a wry look on his handsome features. Hadrian said nothing as he rose from his couch and, with a brief nod to his former companion, walked past the bowing members of the court. The day had been long and tiresome. And there would be, he mused bitterly, many more to come.

The next day, Hadrian attended an elaborate ceremony in the high-ceilinged throne room. Light poured into the chamber from an upper gallery where a faction of his imperial guard was standing at attention. The throne room was still decorated with the imperial standards and insignia, and a billowing canopy of purple silk hovered like a dark cloud over the ivory-and-jasper-mounted throne. The emperor made his way to the dais, pretending not to notice the chests and coffers of various sizes at its base. As he settled in the cushions of the ancient chair, the sunlight caught the gilding of his bronze breastplate and cast a spray of golden light across his face. Sextus Marius froze for a moment at the sight of the emperor of Rome seated in majesty and surrounded by his knights and squires, before he approached the throne, dressed in his whitest toga. It was difficult to fathom the emperor's mood as he sat, his signet ring flashing as a finger tapped impatiently on the carved head of a lion. Sextus knew of Caesar's wanderlust and sensed he was eager to move on. The final act of this drama had better be a good one, or Sextus could easily lose command of what had become his home and haven. Speaking in Greek, which he hoped would please the emperor, Sextus praised his Roman lord before signaling for a parade of youths to approach the chests before the throne. In unison, they opened the heavy lids as one by one the sun's light revealed their contents. Even Quintus, the Praetorian prefect was momentarily distracted by the shining glow before him. Each youth gathered up whatever golden gifts he could carry and presented them to the emperor. Soon, at his feet lay a ransom's worth of treasure: golden ewers and bowls, fine caskets studded with precious stones, and rare books bound in heavy-tooled leather and mounted in gold and ivory. A sizable coffer spilled over with gold and silver denarii that bore the newly minted likeness of the emperor. Sextus himself presented a great bull's head cast in silver with golden horns and eyes of glowing rubies. Over a thousand years old, it was the rarest object of all and not easy to part with. But the pleasure Sextus saw in Hadrian's eyes assured for him the wisdom of his choice.

After the presentation, the emperor stood and motioned his scribe to bring to him a slender case with the imperial seal. The cracking of the wax seal echoed in the vast hall. Such was the silence that had descended on the court. Hadrian removed the thin sheet of bronze that bore the engraved edict of proclamation:

Emperor Caesar Trajan Hadrian Augustus, son of deified Trajan, grandson of deified Nerva, pontifex maximus and holder of tribunician powers bestow the title of Legatus

Propraetore Augusti upon Sextus Marius Fabii, Governor of Crete . . .

The edict went further, but Sextus was too numb to hear all the honors being bestowed upon him. The visit of the emperor had become far more than he had ever imagined, and the imperial benevolence was overwhelming. Stepping up to the dais to accept the edict, Sextus caught sight of Marius; the joy on the youth's face sending a rush of warmth and emotion through him as he fell heavily at the feet of the emperor. Hadrian felt a strange sense of brotherly compassion for this man who had carved out his own little kingdom in a province that had been largely ignored. Deep inside, he envied him for the simplicity of his life as he yearned more than ever for the rarified world of his villa. It was not the golden treasure laid at his feet that led to these honors, but the small elegant chamber clad in somber gray marble and the glowing tribute to his Beloved. Lifting Sextus up from his knees, Hadrian presented the edict and embraced the man. Clutching the bronze plaque to his chest, Sextus walked, as if in a dream, to the curule governor's chair beside the dais. For Caesar, it was a sheet of bronze with the inscription of lofty but relatively meaningless titles. Yet for Sextus, it firmly secured his position and brought to fruition a lifelong dream.

The banquet that followed was a riotous affair that Hadrian quickly tired of. He made his way to the imperial chambers and the opulent private bath that was part of his suite of rooms. Passing a table of inlaid stone, he paused to peruse the pile of drawings and descriptions of the sprawling palace his scribes and engineers had produced for his future use. Gathering a handful of drawings,

Hadrian continued to the bath. He spread out the carefully inked vellum sheets along the side of the sunken tub and slowly entered the tepid water. He could hear his chamberlain issuing orders for the slaves to stoke the fires that warmed the water, and soon the temperature reached a level of warmth that was soothing to his ageing bones. As he examined the drawings, he envisioned their placement among the existing buildings of his villa, and his mind raced with the architectural possibilities before him, his body complained bitterly from lack of rest. Soon, the steaming water lulled Hadrian's mind, and he turned away from the work of his engineers to examine the room around him. The colors of the bold geometric patterns in the marble walls blended in the heavy steam, while the sculptures that lined the walls seemed to sweat. As the weightlessness of his body began to relax his mind, Hadrian reflected on his life's future. He suddenly felt like a great ship in a vast, silent sea. No destination was charted, no ports held interest. The vessel was still majestic, but its crew was slowly disappearing, leaving it bobbing aimlessly in the steaming water. Hadrian leaned back against a stone dolphin half-submerged beneath the water's surface and chuckled softly at the nautical image of himself he had conjured up. Clearly, it was time to hoist the sails and go home.

Chapter Twenty-Seven

On to Syracuse

The imperial flotilla left the port during early morning, Hadrian's favorite time to begin a journey. The sea air was fresh and had blown away any remnant of clouds, leaving the sky a pale blue topaz. The crispness of the new day energized the crew, and the ships slid majestically away, their heavy oars slapping the water in unison. Marius watched the departure silently from the colonnaded pier, his fingers toying with a pear-shaped black pearl that hung from a woven gold chain around his neck. Sextus stood watching too—but the boy, not the departing fleet. *Could it be he regrets his choice of lovers?* thought Sextus. He was even more smitten with the youth now than when he first laid eyes on him. The treasure he had gifted the emperor with was enormous, but the nights made this energetic young beauty well worth the price. The emperor needed to save face, and Sextus needed Marius beside him. Somehow, in the end, Caesar proved to be the more generous. As the Praetorian governor watched the boy gazing out at the vanishing fleet, he wondered if he had really won the prize he paid so dearly for. The boy's pale slender face betrayed no emotion as he continued to gaze out at sea. With the fleet disappearing into the shimmering light of the sun's reflection, Marius, his fingers still clutching the large rare pearl, turned to face his new lover. With a shy smile, he wrapped his arms around the man's neck and kissed him lightly. But while these gestures were shy and gentle, the light in his dark eyes spoke of something profound and passionate. And as Sextus drew the youth close and held him tightly, he felt the complete submission that body offered. And he knew without a doubt he had won the best prize after all.

Hadrian had retired to his stateroom aboard the *Adriana* long before the little drama on the mainland had played itself out. As he studied the chests and coffers of golden objects, he felt a pang of regret. The taciturn glitter of these treasures was a cold comparison to the comfort of the youth he had traded them for. But he had done the right thing by giving the youth to the younger man. In truth, the boy's passion was too demanding for a man his age. And there was no room for another Beloved. Sextus Marius Fabii had proven his worth with the elegant temple to the Beloved he had created in the ancient palace. His veneration on the young god was worth more to Hadrian than twice the gold that now sat silently in the shadows of his quarters. The high price Sextus paid for the youth was not expected or necessary. But Hadrian was not one to turn down a gift. The governor did well by this royal visit—a beautiful youth and a sheet of bronze filled with lines of archaic but status-filled titles. After dealing with the rebellious zealots of what was formerly Judea, Hadrian was thankful for a peaceful, secure spot in his empire. Crete was not an Egypt, Britannia, or Germania, but then neither did it have the problems and worries for the emperor that these provinces gave him. Let Sextus happily rule his ancient little kingdom, this pocket of peace and tranquility in a troublesome empire. And with him, a beautiful eromenos that

Sextus will surely treat with more gentle kindness than Hadrian had done with his own.

Hadrian had strolled to the ship's bow just as the lighthouse at Itanos came into view. Notus, the south wind god, was alone this time and pushed the flotilla around the cape without any sign of his east wind brother. The spray of the sea and the warm dry wind were an invigorating combination that lulled the emperor and quieted the barrage of worries that filled his head. Opened letters from Rome lay strewn across the desk in his stateroom, read but unanswered. Status reports from his *tabularii* or administrators at the villa made him glad for the golden hoard from Crete. The expenses seemed to be mounting at a greater rate than the work was progressing. Drawings of finished buildings mingled with lists of merchants who had received payment. But the drawings of his chief *toparius* or gardener pleased him, and here he saw money spent well. Beautifully painted landscapes covered sheets of velum as the toparius's neat handwriting identified each specimen. Each piece of correspondence made the return to the villa even more attractive, and Hadrian prayed to Eurus, the east wind, to join his brother and make the return to Rome a swift one.

Hadrian returned to the stateroom and picked through the still unopened letters. Among the many scribe-written packets was a familiar scrawl. Uneven and coarse, it warmed his heart just the same. Dear Germana, his elderly wet nurse from his childhood, was writing to him as always. Her writings were, as usual, filled with little nothings that soothed him and brought back memories of his youth. Big boned and buxom, she had been his friend and confidant long after she had fulfilled her duties as his nurse. Upon becoming emperor, he had freed her from her slave status and provided a small suite of rooms at the Villa Adrianna. Once there, he provided her with a tutor who taught her to read and write as she requested. Her endless stream of letters began as a source of amusement for Hadrian, yet deep inside he was extremely proud of her progress. And as the years progressed, the content of her writing became more profound. Germana's finest letter, written after hearing the news of Antinous's death, was always with the emperor. Her words held no judgment, only emotions of sorrow and praise for the youth she too had come to love. He had read the letter so many times he eventually had a scribe create copies of it so that the original could be tucked safely away. There, in a small gold-and-ivory chest, beneath a braid of the Beloved's hair, the letter lay neatly folded. As was the tradition, the braid was one that hung down the nape of Antinous's neck and severed on the day of his eighteenth birthday. How prophetic that severed lock became. Little did Hadrian know that at that moment the Fates too were making a cut of their own. One life severed, another diminished.

As if taking a cue from Caesar's darkening mood, the sky too became clouded and ominous. When the brothers of the wind had retired for the night, the storm gods Aeolus and Tempestas joined forces and sent the chamberlain hurrying into the staterooms to light the lamps that swayed from the ceiling beams. The threat of a storm made the table lamps too dangerous to burn, but Hadrian would be working deep into the night in hopes of clearing his desk by morning and needed the lamps to be burning brightly. From the corner of his eye, he could see his loyal servant moving slowly from lamp to lamp while trying valiantly to retain his dignity on the polished surface of the shifting floor. Hadrian's near exasperation was relieved by the appearance of two servants bearing a bowl and pitcher for washing, as well as his dinner. After they had found a place for the heavy silver trays, he sent them to assist the chamberlain with his task. Before long, the stateroom was ablaze with light, and Hadrian sent them all away with a brusque movement of his hand.

Despite the storm, the ship barely listed, and the only sound to be heard in the stateroom was the occasional pop of an oil lamp and the cracking of wax seals securing the contents of letters from Rome. The packets with ominous black wax were given special attention. These were from the Frumentarii, Hadrian's secret police. Originally composed of collectors of wheat in the provinces, the emperor found them useful in that they could infiltrate the communities without raising suspicion, while gathering information that could be useful in keeping control of the provinces. But the Frumentarii became so skillful in their role as private agents for the emperor that they were allowed to gather information from the deepest recesses of Roman society, including the imperial household.

Hadrian's mood darkened further as he read a report of a Praetorian guard's perceived familiarity with the empress. Years earlier, his spies had reported an affair between Sabina and his historian and secretary, Suetonius, while the emperor was in Britain. It was Suetonius's high birth and talent that saved his life, but without a word to his wife, Hadrian exiled the scholar whom Sabina was never to see again. Now it seemed Sabina was still capable of being indiscreet, and her weakened state of health was just a guise. Yet it appeared that only the Furmentarii knew of the affair while the Romans, who reveled in good gossip, saw only the regal Augusta she chose to portray. Hadrian would deal with this after his arrival into Rome and not before. He refolded the report, put a corner of velum to the flame of the closest oil lamp, and allowed it burn to a sheet of ash within inches of his fingers before he allowed it to flutter silently to the hard-polished floor. The rest of the reports were dry and monotonous, requiring the skills of a clerk rather than an emperor. Putting his head down for a moment's rest, Hadrian sighed and, with the gentle rocking of the ship, was soon sound asleep.

The flotilla made good time despite the storm, and by morning, the lighthouse of Diktinna, at the western tip of Crete, stood proudly in the clear light of the new day. The ships passed close enough to the shore for the legion garrisoned there to acknowledge the passing ship of their emperor. The purple-bordered sails reflected the morning sun as the imperial standard snapped in the wind. From the shore, the soldiers could make out a red-cloaked figure at the bow of the flagship. The proud tall stance made the identity of that figure unmistakable. The soldiers cheered as some removed their own cloaks and waved them in an enthusiastic salute to their emperor. They saw the distant figure in red raise his arm in salutation as the soldiers roared their own salute of praise. The wind-filled sails speeded the ships quickly out of sight, and the emperor left the bow to return to his overburdened desk. It would be another day or two before they entered the Bay of Syracuse, and Hadrian needed to make good use of the time before then.

Chapter Twenty-Eight

A God in Syracuse

Other than a number of visits from court officials and occasional dictation to the scribes, Caesar was left alone during what was nearly a two days journey from Crete. All the correspondence had been answered and lay in leather-bound boxes of finely carved cedar to be delivered upon arrival in port. Two years had passed since Hadrian had been near Italia, and Hadrian's feelings regarding his homecoming were as dry as the desert wind from Africa that blew over the arid island of Sicilia. He knew the festivities planned in his honor would be long and tiresome, but unavoidable. As the flotilla neared the piers of the great city, garlands of laurel and lemon leaves studded with orange blossoms trembled from the roar of the crowd as they draped the marble villas that lined the port. Dressed in his parade armor, diadem, and heavy purple cloak, Hadrian looked every bit the emperor of Rome as he mounted his steed and rode down the ship's oak ramp to the waiting dignitaries. The aged praetor stood on a raised dais clothed in a snow-white toga and nervously rehearsed his words of welcome. He had not seen the emperor since the death of the Beloved, and he was told that this was a different man he was welcoming today. The stories that reached his ears told of a wise, benevolent ruler who had become the scourge of Judea, as well as a short tempered and bitter man. In its eight hundred years of existence, Syracuse was used to greeting formidable guests, but this guest was the only one the praetor was concerned with today. He had been careful to honor not only the emperor but also his eromenos, Antinous, having ordered a Syracusan tetradrachm to be struck with the image of the emperor facing the likeness of Antinous. The reverse bore the representation of Zeus in the form of an eagle as he abducted Ganymede. Bronze coins were minted for the masses while silver and gold were struck for the imperial entourage. A temple had been raised by the fledgling cult of the new god, which the praetor had personally encouraged and funded; a gesture based on his regard for the beautiful youth and a wise political gesture. As the emperor dismounted and strode toward the dais, the praetor carefully made his way down the steps and lowered himself, with great effort, to his knees. Hadrian had reached the elderly man before he had completed his supplication and stopped what was obviously a painful gesture of respect. While old and thin, the praetor was still the same height as the emperor; and when Hadrian had lifted him to full height, he was able to look directly into the cool gray eyes of the man. "The city of Syracuse humbly welcomes his imperial majesty, Hadrianius Augustus, divine master of all Rome." In his nervousness, the praetor had forgotten all the formal names of the emperor, but Hadrian pretended to take no notice. "You honor us, Aulus Licinius Priscus. The city of Syracuse and the province of Sicilia have done well under your administration, and We are extremely pleased." Hadrian returned the greeting with his own, saluted the assembled court, then turned to address the cheering crowd. His gift of oratory overcame his fatigue, and the crowd stood silent, enthralled. The desert wind that had followed him from Crete found its way under the imperial cloak and lifted it in a swirl around the emperor to a dramatic effect. It was pure theater, and Hadrian found himself swept away by his own grandeur despite his original misgivings. Praetor Priscus stood erect and proud by the emperor's side, basking in the glory of his august guest. Priscus never subscribed to the belief in the emperor as demigod, yet today, as he stood in the presence of Caesar, the plausibility of such a belief was possible. The bitter, capricious man they had whispered about in court was not evident here. While the warmth Hadrian conveyed during his last visit with the beautiful youth in tow was no longer evident, this tall elegant man who held the unruly crowd's rapt attention with his golden oratory transcended that mortal form and was the living embodiment of a temple god. The summer sun shimmered on the gilt bronze of Caesar's breastplate and illuminated his face with an ethereal light while the golden leaves of his crown blazed like divine fire. The crowd reacted as if they were witnessing a miracle, and the power of their adoration was intoxicating. A wisp of cloud drifted beneath the sun and brought Hadrian back to reality. Although the crowd remained fixated, the spell was broken for him. He used his role as *pontificus* and bestowed a blessing on the assembled masses, who bowed their heads in reverence, then roared their approval. Saluting the praetor, Caesar left the dais, mounted his horse, and paraded slowly down the broad avenue toward the island Citadel of Dionysius. There, the seat of Roman rule, as well as the official residence, stood at the end of an ancient bridge on the banks of a narrow strait that separated the mainland from the sacred island of Ortygia. The wave of adrenaline that had washed through Hadrian as he addressed the crowd was wearing off, leaving the feeling of fatigue he had felt earlier. Numbly, he saluted the frenzied crowd that parted for him, as well as the lectors, priests, knights, and nobles surrounded by the three thousand Praetorian guard that seemed to shake the earth as they passed. The midday sun seemed to cook the emperor's body within the heavy metal of his breastplate and intensified the scent of the dye in his cloak. Even the occasional gust of wind did nothing to alleviate his discomfort. As he passed the grand homes that lined the vast boulevard, Hadrian wished for nothing more than to return to the sanctuary of his ship.

Despite the crushing heat outside, the interior of the Palace of Hieron was cool and inviting. Even the desert wind was tamed to a gentle breeze that carried with it the scent of jasmine and orange blossoms. *My praetors live in more comfort than their emperor*, Hadrian silently mused as he walked the marble corridor leading to the imperial apartments. The dryness of the region was countered with lush frescos of floral gardens that covered the walls and the splashing of fountains that sang to him at every turn. The centurion guards left him at the doorway of the rooms prepared for him, vast and airy with a sweeping view of the sacred island and its magnificent temples to Athene and Artemis in the distance. As with the walls of the corridors, the rooms were decorated with artful depictions of garden scenes and fountains frozen in mid splash. Naked youths with flowing scarves and floral garlands evoked a memory of Marius and pang of regret.

But the boy on Crete was quickly a distant memory, washed away by the sight of a bust that sat silently on a pedestal by the heavily carved bed. Sculpted from pale pink marble, the portrait of his

Beloved seemed to hold the breath of life as it stared at him from the shadows. Like Narcissus drawn to his own visage, Hadrian was captivated by the image across the room and, shrugging off his heavy wool cloak, made his way slowly towards the likeness. It was sensitively wrought, and the purity of the stone intensified the realism of living flesh. As always, familiar pain began to build in his chest as his fingers traveled the lines of the face that haunted his dreams. But while the stone was the color of life, its touch had the chill of death. The world went still as his mind swam in pools of memory.

Caesar was still gazing at the image when his servants silently entered the chamber and began positioning the trunks and cases of the royal suite as unobtrusively as possible. The bravest of the four approached the emperor and began to unbuckle the leather straps of his breastplate. As if returning from a dream, Hadrian stared blankly at the servant and mechanically went through the motions of undress. In the distance, the sound of water could be heard over the voice of the chamberlain as he issued orders for the bath. As reality returned, the pain disappeared, and Hadrian prepared to bathe. The mundane was a balm for the soul, the chaser of memories.

As he entered the bath, he reveled in its warmth and settled in to study the random patterns of inlaid stone of the walls and ceiling. Hadrian smiled slightly at the parade of quail that seemed to dance in a long line across the walls. Knowing that Ortygia was Greek for quail, an abundant bird on its namesake island, he was amused by this subtle joke narrated in inlaid stone. He laid back into the water to get a better view of the vast array or marbles and semiprecious stone was used to create panels and ribbons that spread across the walls that wrapped around columns of cream-colored marble. The capitals were of a warm brown marble, skillfully carved in the Corinthian manner and resting on a collar of black granite. All of this was washed with the sunlight that seeped through the thin sheets of alabaster that studded the walls. The colors used here were restful and inviting; they lulled Hadrian into a state of semi-sleep. And in the thick steam that rose like smoke from a sacrificial altar, he conjured up the image of his beloved Antinous. Hundreds of images of the youth floated before him, but the flesh and blood eluded his memory. Yes, it was time to go back to Rome, where under the great dome of his Pantheon, his Beloved lay beneath a sheet of rock crystal. There he would see the true face of the boy, and his mind would regain its memory.

The next day brought slightly cooler weather due to an infrequent rain that had soaked the land the night before. After donning a himation in the Greek fashion, Hadrian strolled to the grand portico that overlooked the small harbor. There, Aulus Priscus was already at his place by a finely carved table of cedar and ebony, but rose at the sight of the emperor. "The people of Syracuse praise you, Caesar, for the rain you have brought to our land," the praetor spoke in a soft, shaking voice. The banquet held the previous night had taken much of what was left of his strength after the welcoming ceremonies. Hadrian motioned for the elderly man to return to the comfort of his couch and took his place of honor beneath a statue of Apollo. "Jupiter has favored us, and we are pleased your city could benefit from his benevolence," replied the emperor. The air was fresh and filled with the sound of the surf slapping the rocky shore. Hadrian told Priscus of his plans to visit the forum in Achradina, one of the cities that made up Syracuse. There too was the magnificent Temple of Jupiter Olympius, where he would give thanks for the gift of rain. He had gifted this temple as well as various others during his last visit to this province. Sicilia and Syracuse in particular had suffered under the mismanagement of Gaius Marius Verres, a Praetorian governor over two hundred years earlier. The remnants of his plundering were still in evidence when Hadrian had visited for the first time during the reign of his uncle, Trajan. The island's Greek origin and prevalence for all things Greek made it dear to him, and later, as emperor, he restored many of the ancient temples, while adding buildings of his own design. Although not Greece, it was close enough.

The morning meal went quietly as the sun traveled across the portico. Hadrian finished the last of his mead and wordlessly left the now dozing praetor to his dreamless sleep. Joining the entourage that had already mounted up and waited in the outer courtyard, Caesar set off for the sights of Syracuse. Crossing once again the ancient stone bridge, the imperial party soon found themselves at the outer gate of the city, the Portae Agragianae, and then at the tomb of Archimedes. Just beyond the tomb was the massive fortified Pentapyum, and opposite that edifice, the forum. The *prytaneum*, one of many victims of the voracious Verres, was once more lavishly adorned; an inscription on the pediment attested to the city's gratitude to the emperor. Surrounded by porticoes constructed by Dionysius the elder, the agora adjoined a temple to Jupiter restored by Hadrian nearly twenty years earlier. Climbing the steps hewn from one of the many stone quarries of the *Cappuccini* outside the city proper, the emperor stood for a moment to examine the workmanship he had paid for. While this was not the more celebrated temple of Jupiter—that edifice sat proudly on a hill some distance from the city—this sacred site was the one Hadrian preferred. Done in the Doric order, this structure was far older and now bore the emperor's handprint in its reconstruction. As Hadrian walked silently past the forest of thick columns and entered the shadows of the cella, the cool air of the temple interior, scented as it was with incense and floral boughs, washed over him. The only illumination was from an opening in the roof and the great iron brazier that burned before an ancient sculpture of the divinity.

The interior of the temple smelled strongly of burnt offerings and old priests, with ancient columns blackened with centuries of smoke. But as Hadrian paid homage to the father of the gods, the priests seemed preoccupied with another matter and not the offerings of the emperor. With a deep bow, the youngest of the priests stepped forward and spoke to the emperor haltingly in Greek, asking that he follow them to an outer courtyard. Passing through a door at the rear of the cella, they entered a long, narrow courtyard lined with open porticos flanked by columns in the same order as the temple. At the end of the courtyard stood a small temple of pristine white marble. It stood gleaming in the sun like a younger version of the ancient temple. A tall, slender bronze door inlaid with ivory panels and rosettes of silver with gilded leaves stood slightly open—a hesitant welcome.

After ascending the broad polished steps and walking past the double row of columns, the priests bowed in deference to the emperor and motioned him to enter. As he did so, Hadrian paused to examine the fine carving of the door panels. There, in rare African ivory, was rendered the arrival of the emperor and Antinous on the shores of Syracuse. Densely carved in great detail was the imperial flagship with the emperor and Antinous descending the ramp from the ship and being greeted by the ancient tyrants of Syracuse, Dionysius I, Timoleon, and Hieron. Another panel portrayed Jupiter, Artemis/Diana and Minerva gesturing toward their restored temples in the distance and casting their blessings on Caesar and his consort. The delicacy and skill in the carvings captivated the emperor; he made no effort to resist running his fingers over the warm, smooth ivory figures of himself and his Beloved.

Hadrian turned to examine the second door and the two panels it contained. One portrayed a boar hunt that occurred near the Lysimelian Marsh on their way back from the Shrine of Cyana. It was an event Hadrian had all but forgotten, and the memory rushed back to him with alarming clarity. The second panel portrayed the great banquet given in their honor, with the emperor reclining on a couch, finely carved and inlaid with carnelians, behind a reclining Antinous. Their hunting dogs lay at the foot of the couch as a parade of young servers offered great platters laden with food. Like a journal without words, memories carved in the cream-colored ivory stood before him and revealed what was waiting for him inside. With some trepidation, Caesar walked past the magnificent doors and entered the darkened temple. The design was similar to the temple of Jupiter but without the soot-covered columns and ceiling. And here the devotional object was not hundreds of years old, but radiantly new as it sparkled in the light that poured from a small grilled opening in the roof.

As in the temple room at the palace in Crete, this sculpture on its richly embellished plinth was exquisitely carved and Greek in origin. The pose and expression was what sculptors had settled on as the perfect depiction of the new god—both powerful and modest. As he positioned himself under the statue's gaze, he looked up into the deeply carved eyes and reached out to touch the smooth sculpted legs. The priests stood silently in the shadows as they watched the emperor's reaction to their tribute to his famous love. In the sunlight, his upturned face revealed both admiration and sorrow, as memories continued to flood his brain. The form was that of a younger Antinous—softer, lithe. The broad chest was fleshy, not the firm hunter's chest he would eventually develop. *This was the youth just before his prime, the height of his life,* thought Hadrian bitterly, *a time that would be a brief memory.* The priests shifted on their feet, uncomfortable with being witness to the emperor's still existent and painful devotion to the youth. Yet they understood, for they had seen the boy themselves and marveled too at his astounding beauty and sublime manner.

The sound of a large gilt spoon on the rim of an incense bowl brought Hadrian out of his silent reverie. In front of the statue was a low altar that was being attended to by the priests, and the smoke was already spiraling upward when Hadrian finally turned his gaze from his beloved's image. With all the many likenesses he had seen in his travels, why was it that they each had the same profound effect? Even efforts less successful than this portrayal stopped time for him. These images were as essential to his life as air, painful as they were. Caesar now noticed the priests who had escorted him to this temple had been joined by four younger men of about eighteen to twenty years of age. Each was handsome, athletically built and wore a golden medallion with the image of the young god around his neck. The older priests bowed before the sculpture, then to the emperor, before turning to leave the temple.

The young priests of Antinous stood still, each bearing a golden bowl and spoon with an offering to the god. As Hadrian made his way toward the altar, one of the priests stepped forward and presented him with an offering. The bowl was finely crafted of gold and studded with large moonstones surrounded by gold beading. Inside were small sticky chunks of precious myrrh, their dark golden hue absorbing the light from above. Filling the bowl of the spoon, Hadrian released the myrrh onto the glowing embers. A serpent-like hiss emanated from the coals as they devoured the spice and sent a plume of earthy, bitter smoke to the sky. The next priest stepped forward with an offering in a rock crystal tazza engraved with acanthus leaves and inlayed with cabochons of pale aquamarine. Small grains of amber resin filled this one, and they soon joined the myrrh into the flames. A beautifully rendered balsamarium, bearing the image of the young god, was filled with the oil of frankincense that joined the other offerings on the glowing embers. Two more offerings followed in bowls of equal beauty, matched only by their bearers.

Surrounded by the young priests as he stood before the altar, Hadrian gazed up at the marble figure now shrouded by thick smoke. A breeze had whispered in through the still open doors, took hold of the fragrant column that rose from the sacrificial altar, and wrapped it around the silent figure of Antinous. The bitter aroma of the rare offerings mixed with the scent of the priests, creating a heady mix that lifted Hadrian to a euphoric state. He was overwhelmed by the devotion shone to his new god, the beauty of the structure and ceremony that filled it. He was not prepared for such an exalted tribute and would certainly reward the temple priests for the experience. It was sometime before he reluctantly turned to leave the temple and its votive image, leaving the priests behind. A thought passed through his mind, and he turned to look once more at them. Yes, his intuition was correct. The four priests were obviously two couples as they stood together flanking the still billowing altar. With a slight smile and a nod, he turned once more and left the temple before his emotions could betray him.

He returned to the courtyard and his courtiers who were seated under a billowing canopy, having just been served a small repast. At the sight of him, they rose and hurriedly joined him as he strode though the side portico toward the main street. What seemed like hours was less than one, but one filled with joy, sorrow, and amazement. Once again, he understood why this city enjoyed such a glorious reputation. Their devotion to the gods was as magnificent as the architecture they housed them in. As Caesar and his the court headed toward the forum and the baths, the emperor acknowledged the adulation of the crowd, yet all the while his mind could not help but wander to the villa that waited for him outside of Rome.

The next day was a time of festivals and oratory; first in the ancient Greek theater, then the Roman built amphitheater. While the Roman theater celebrated the life of the emperor with gladiatorial games that glorified his lineage and name, the Greek theater celebrated with poems, dance, and music the life and deification of Antinous. Hadrian sat through the gladiatorial games with some discomfort that was caused more by the senseless violence and bloodshed he abhorred than the heavy breastplate and cloak he wore. For the Greek events, he changed into a short tunic and draped over that a himation in the archaic Greek style. Upon his arrival at the theater, the crowd acknowledged the tribute the emperor paid the Grecian origin of their city with a great roar of approval. For his part, Hadrian arranged for garland-draped youths to walk the aisles and toss handfuls of silver coins to the crowds; the sight of them flickering in the sunlight was like a summer rain.

Joining the emperor at the Greek theater was the Praetorian governor and his wife. Although her given name was Agape Eileithyia, her elderly husband began to call her Amaltheia after their marriage, a Greek name that meant "to soothe." As he watched Aulus Priscus being tended to by his much younger wife, he understood the reason he had changed her name. Her tender attentions were admirable in that they were loving yet discreet. Simply dressed and jeweled, she was like the air in her movements, and Hadrian was greatly moved by the sight of her. At her side was her mother Damaris Elektra. Upon introduction, Hadrian smiled warmly, not out of admiration as with Amaltheia, but in a somewhat wicked amusement at the mother's name. He knew well that in Greek, her name meant "heifer" and "bright or shining." And a shining heifer she was too. Her colorful chiton barely contained her ample form and strained at the decorative fibulae that kept the delicate fabric from bursting. Long earrings of sapphires and dusty gray pearls set in gold constantly tapped a similarly adorned necklace that seemed to have a strangle hold on her thick neck. A costly sapphire cabochon intaglio hung heavily from the necklace and matched in color the inlaid fibulii that held her linen chiton together. The enormous cabochon was carved with the image of Antinous in the guise of Hermes, and Hadrian found it difficult to take his eyes from it; the likeness was too much to realistic for comfort. But his reverie was interrupted by Damaris's collection of bracelets that clicked and clattered with every movement of her hands, which fluttered with each spoken word and accentuated her many woven gold rings adorned with precious gems. A rope of pearls and rare Egyptian glass beads flecked with gold glistened in her elaborately plaited braids at the back of her head, while small jewel-headed pins adorned the curled headdress that draped nearly to her brows. All of this would have been rather repulsive to Hadrian were it not for her eyes. The luscious blue of her sapphires was no match for the depth of their color, nor her words, their liveliness.

As Hadrian studied Damaris more intently as one would a rare bird, he began to see through the artifice, sensing a woman who mourned the flight of her youth and resented the fact that it had deserted her. *Youth is brief and cruel in the silent swiftness of its departure,* Hadrian mused bitterly. Yet he thought better than to tell her so. He suddenly felt a wave of affection for this strange woman, and the more they chatted, the more her intellect revealed itself. In her face, he saw the beauty that once was, yet her voice still held a resonance that must have beguiled many men during her prime. For Damaris, the seemingly rapt attention of the emperor helped her forget her age and justified her choice of apparel, a choice her daughter seemed to find appalling. But she had dressed for the imperator of Rome who appeared to be pleased by her, and that was all that mattered to her at this moment of victory.

The day passed quickly for Hadrian, as did the remainder of the work filled week. The grandeur of Syracuse was beginning to pale for him, and the reports from Rome were taking on a renewed urgency. Prefect Quintus Turbo had been in the city for nearly a month and had settled most of the intrigues that plagued the senate and the empress's court. But not the Empress Sabina herself. Being her only peer, it was Caesar who would deal with his wife.

Chapter Twenty-Nine

A Welcome Wears Thin

Hadrian's last public event was an assembly on the steps of the administration building in the forum where he presented the *Lex Hadriana*, a law that enabled the province's permanent tenants, mostly Greek in origin, to develop land. This was an extension of the Lex Marciana from the Flavian dynasty, which dealt with the development of the North African provinces. The wealthy Greek families who had arrived in Sicilia after the Roman occupation were finally, after hundreds of years, vindicated. Hadrian's law was applauded in that it was simple and direct without the usual oratory trappings that could create future loopholes. Truth be told, he really hadn't the time to elaborate and embellish the directive. After meeting with the Greek families, one of whom was Amaltheia's, the emperor reworked the Lex Marcianna and presented it at the forum. This, combined with the silver coins bearing the image of the emperor that were showered upon the crowd, left the people with an exultant memory of the imperial visit and stories to tell for generations to come.

It was early morning, and the flotilla had been made ready for the final leg of its journey to Rome. Hadrian had risen before sunrise to make his way to Hiero's *Ara*. The immense, ancient altar was now nearly four hundred years old and, when new, had been visited by the great mathematician Archimedes. It had suffered greatly during the three-year Roman siege that ended in Rome's acquisition of the city. During Hadrian's first visit, he had funded the reconstruction of the altar and with that gesture created a foundation for the love the Syracusan's had for him. Hadrian now stood at the steps of the monumental structure and watched the great bronze sculptures he had placed there catch the slowly rising sun.

The great altar was actually an austere marble building with a massive staircase rising to the uppermost level. Once there, one was faced with a pantheon of gods that spanned the ages in their renderings. Hadrian reached the top of the altar just as the sun appeared in its newborn splendor on the horizon. The priests had already arrived and were busy preparing the many altars for the day's rituals, yet Hadrian was here for one reason, and that reason was quickly visible. Painted in the ancient Greek style and draped in silken cloth and floral garlands, an image of Antinous stood radiant and lifelike in the light of the emerging sun. The young priests fussed with the silk draping; the fabric, sheer enough to reveal the naked form beneath. The white marble body glowed golden in the morning light and reflected in the painted eyes that stared down at him.

Preoccupied with their devotional tasks, the priests were startled to suddenly find the emperor of Rome, clad in a simple himation and cloak, beside them. They turned and fell to their knees before him, looking up in awe. As he bowed slightly in return, the sun caught the gold of his diadem, which flashed on what they could clearly see was a massive cameo portrait of Antinous carved in amethyst; an intaglio of the god set in the gold-beaded fibula securing his cloak. The lone jewel absorbed the morning light, and its purple glow seemed to take on a life of its own. Set in the fastener by Grecian artisans, the gem was a gift from Sabina shortly after her husband's return to Rome. Both the beauty of the craftsmanship and his wife's gesture had moved him. He rarely wore a jewel of this size, yet he was pleased that his chamberlain had set this one out for him earlier that morning. The weight of the stone felt reassuring, and the effect on the priests was profound. Taking the bowl of incense offered to him, Hadrian paid homage to the image before him. For sometime, as the smoke rose up to the wisp of clouds that passed overhead, Hadrian stared at the face of his Beloved. Then, without a word, he turned, walked toward the broad marble stairs, and disappeared.

As he left Hiero's great altar, he found Chabrais waiting for him along with a cadre of the Praetorian guard. The elderly tutor seemed to grow smaller and weaker with each day. Yet the inner strength of the man still emanated from within. *We are both nearing the end of our journey, old friend*, thought the emperor. But Hadrian's end was not to be as soon or as peaceful as Chabrais'; a young life given to the Nile had seen to that. And as the men walked slowly toward the harbor, both pondered the fact that neither one knew what the future would bring.

Aulus Priscus waited at the pier along with his wife to watch the emperor's departure. Amaltheia wore a simple himatian in soft yellow with a simple necklace of blue topaz beads and small golden seahorses. Earrings that matched her necklace hung demurely, as a circlet of seahorses danced around her slender forearm. Her hair was pulled back simply, wrapped by a single thick braid intertwined with delicately carved florets of white agate. Damaris Elektra was not with her daughter and son-in-law; the sun and heat was far too intense for her to bear them another day, and she lay in a state of dispirited exhaustion in the darkness of her lavish villa. But she made her presence known with a parting gift to the emperor. Her daughter carried with her a golden coffer that was crafted to look like a small circular temple. At one point, curiosity gained a hold of her, and she decided to see the contents for herself before presenting the gift to the emperor. Nestled within the box, in a silken pouch, was the costly sapphire intaglio the emperor seemed to be so impressed by the day before. Amaltheia was startled by her mother's generosity but said nothing. She had no knowledge of what transpired between the emperor and her mother, but the gift was clearly a token of great affection.

Hadrian arrived at the pier a short time before the sun had reached its highest point in the sky. He had changed into his parade armor as well as the gold-embroidered cloak of imperial purple, and with the heat becoming more intense, he was eager to reach his staterooms before midday. After a short salutation to the crowd that had gathered along the harbor banks, the emperor presented Aulus Licinius Priscus with a proclamation of honor and a *corona civica* or civic crown, a chaplet of oak leaves. No one in the crowd knew that this was to be Priscus's last day as praetor; an honorable retirement had been negotiated the day before, making his final days ones of privilege, comfort, and respect.

In the shade of an umbrella of embroidered silk, Amaltheia presented the emperor with the small round chest, her mother's gift. The emperor, in an uncharacteristic rush of curiosity, opened the gift immediately. When the large sapphire dropped out of its pouch, Priscus and his wife were reassured by the emperor's unexpected gasp of surprise. "Your beloved and noble mother has honored us deeply," Hadrian said softly to Amaltheia. "We will treasure this as a token of our friendship and will always hold her in the highest esteem." Amaltheia genuflected before the emperor, and as she rose, he grasped her slender shoulders and kissed her forehead. "We will offer my own token of friendship to her before my departure," he added, before turning to board the *Adriana*.

Once onboard the ship, Hadrian disappeared into his staterooms for sometime before reappearing again with a young page wearing a Phrygian cap in tow. He stood at the balustrade as the page walked swiftly down the ramp and with a deep bow presented the daughter of Demarius Elektra with a folded packet. Its soft leather folds contained a letter from the emperor and a medallion with his image in gold set in lapis, surrounded by diamonds and sapphires, hanging from a chain of woven gold. It was originally meant to be a gift to the empress, his wife. But Hadrian felt he had met a much more deserving recipient. The page bowed once more and returned to the ship as Caesar, still standing on the wide-planked deck, saluted the cheering crowd. As trumpets blared tribute, the oarsmen announced the ship's departure with a loud splash that sent a great wave toward shore. The rest of the flotilla was already at the mouth of the harbor, waiting for the imperial flagship to lead them on their journey. The visit to Syracuse had been much sweeter than Hadrian had ever thought possible. The anger and bitterness that followed him for the past years had lay hidden in the shadows of this arid land. Now, as he returned to his staterooms, he knew they waited for him there.

Chapter Thirty

A Mind in Flames

It was nightfall, and the lights of Rhegium could be seen in the distance and, soon after that, the lighthouse of Messana. It was here that the Ionian Sea turned into the Tyrrenhean as the flotilla sailed through the strait that ran between the main land of Italia and the Isle of Sicilia. The lamps in the emperor's stateroom were already burning and could be seen from the other ships. As the knights and courtiers dined and laughed, emperor was hard at work finishing the last of the correspondence. But Hadrian was not alone. The young page that had delivered the gift packet to the wife of Aulus Priscus sat barefoot and bareheaded on the polished floor of the emperor's study, his sandals and Phrygian cap tossed carelessly in the corner. Absorbed as he was with the task of organizing the emperor's letters and proclamations in a leather-bound courier case, he was not aware of Hadrian's gaze as he sat behind his desk. The evening was warm, and the page had slipped off the one shoulder of his linen *exomis*, exposing a scattering of freckles on his pale shoulders. Being from the Thracian city of Regio near Byzantium, the reddish brown hair of his people contrasted with his pale skin, and both reflected beautifully in the abundant lamplight. The son of a Thracian knight, the boy was named Sabos after his family's cult god, Sabazios. One of the god's symbols was tattooed between the youth's shoulder blades, a bursting pomegranate within a full sun. The symbol was a sign of the youth's ancient Hittite roots, as well as his connection to the region of the southern Thracians. Sabazios, the god of fully ripe vegetation, had been extremely kind to Sabos. Although not yet as tall as Antinous, his body had the same supple skin, the soft fullness, the tender, intoxicating scent of youth.

At the entrance of two servants bearing the evening meal, Sabos dropped the stack of packets he was arranging and in one nimble movement was standing to eagerly inspect the meal. More amused than offended, Hadrian let the boy pick through the royal dinner with abandon. With his back to the emperor, Sabos stood beside the low table bearing the silver platters of food, and Hadrian noticed the youth's tunic did nothing to hide his obvious charms. The exomis had ridden up over the boy's belt while seated on the floor, and now from under the embroidered hem of the thin linen garment peeked the youth's buttocks, snow white and plump. Hadrian was both shocked and intrigued. The youth seemed oblivious to the impression he was making and was happily munching on a quail leg when he turned in time to catch sight of the emperor observing him. Glancing at the half-eaten leg in his hand, the boy suddenly turned even paler than usual. Hadrian laughed as he waved toward the food and told the boy, "Eat, little one. You need it more than I do." "But from the way you've outgrown that new tunic so quickly," he added, "you may be want to eat a bit more slowly." Hadrian rose from the desk and walked over to the table where Sabos was still standing but had turned back to continue devouring the platters of food. As he reached down to help himself to yet another leg, a yelp followed the sound of a slap from the emperor's hand on the youth's barely covered buttock. "But you must learn to ask before eating Caesar's meal," he whispered sternly. "Forgive me, Majesty," the boy whispered in return, "I was so hungry." The chastened youth dared not turn around, and from the sudden redness of the boy's ears, Hadrian realized his feigned anger was misplaced. Hadrian hugged the youth while placing a gruff kiss on the pomegranate tattoo. Ordering the servants to bring another meal for himself, Hadrian remained with his arms around the youth's slender waist. Sabos made no effort to dissuade the emperor's gesture, eager as he was to find himself in this situation. *Asking the washerwoman to soak the new tunic in boiling water was a brilliant idea after all*, he thought to himself and a giggle escaped him. Hadrian, thinking the boy was being coy, bit him slightly on the neck, which produced a shiver and a deep laugh as the youth turned to face his seducer. As Sabos pressed himself against the emperor, Hadrian could feel the excitement he had inspired in the youth. The thin tunic did nothing to stand in the way of his hands as they caressed the warm mounds of flesh. Sabos wrapped his arms around Hadrian's neck, his gaze almost brazen in its heat. The full mouth was still shining from the grease of the quail he had helped himself to, and it was far more appetizing than any confection the royal chef could produce.

But before Caesar could avail himself to the sight before him, the servants returned with another set of laden trays. Irritated by the intrusion but suddenly hungry, Hadrian motioned for the trays to be placed on the now-empty desk. The flustered servants hurried to set down their burden, nearly tipping over the wine flask of Egyptian glass in their rush. Without waiting to be told, they bowed deeply and scurried out of the room, closing the heavy door quietly behind them. Hadrian turned to the youth still in his arms and put a finger to his lips. "You must eat, lovely one. And I must also," he softly told him. "I have a feeling we'll have a sleepless night."

There was no sleep to be had that evening. But not because of the reasons Hadrian had prepared for. It took quite sometime to accommodate the youth's appetite, but once sated, he slept soundly for the rest of the night. Hadrian slept fitfully at first, then not at all. His sleep had been filled with dreams of moving earth and falling buildings as everything he had accomplished was diminished. Leaving the bed, he found his way to the small-windowed alcove behind his desk. Settling himself on the thick cushion tucked within the curved wall, Hadrian looked out at the full moon as it reflected on the open water. The pale light and gentle rolling of the ship lulled him into a shallow slumber, that place between conscious and unconscious.

It began with an immense map of his empire, spread before him like an infinite plain. He could recognize the handiwork of his reign from the sprawling wall in Britannia and the gleaming white marble architecture of Rome, to the still smoldering city of Aelia Capitalina in Palestine, his temple to Jupiter rising from the ashes. As he gazed at the land of Egypt, a glow emanated from a section of land along the Nile. Hadrian knew this plot of land well, a sacred site now called Antinopoolis. The death of his Beloved turned a village of mud huts into a radiant city of marble temples, broad boulevards, and proud granite obelisks that pierced the sky with prayers to the new god. It was a grandiose tribute to a simple ephebe, born from grief and guilt. Antinous was a spirit of the forest and rivers, not this metropolis of cold, polished stone. Once again, as before, the lover misunderstood the beloved and projected his own ego upon the boy's fragile memory.

As Hadrian continued dreaming, the city that rose up from the vast map, the city he built to immortalize his fallen favorite, burst into flames. The vellum of the map began to sizzle and blister as the flames spread from the blessed site toward the four directions of the empire. The emperor watched helplessly as his world, portrayed as it was with this massive atlas, burned out of control. Black smoke billowed skyward and filled his nostrils with its putrid fumes. He could smell burning flesh and the lime of incinerated stone as the landscape turned into a blanket of fiery ash. Only the Villa Adrianna stood untouched, with an obelisk of pink granite glowing like a beacon in the distance. His home, and site of the final resting place of his Beloved, was all that remained of his world. Suddenly, a strong gust of wind blew in from the east and scattered his smoldering world to oblivion. Then, all was black.

Hadrian awoke, chilled and shaken. Wind blew in from the grated windows and scattered the few documents left on his desk to the floor. He left his seat by the window and quickly closed the heavy shutters to the wind and sea spray. The days at sea were taking their toll, and not even the lovely form of Sabos could ease their oppression. The new day could not come too soon. But the morning sun was slow to rise this day, and in its feeble light, Hadrian could make out the villas on the Isle of Capri and the bay of Neapolis behind the scattered islands. Along the northern shore of the bay was the deep water port of Puteoli and its gleaming marble villas that were already catching the sun's hesitant rays. Hadrian had little interest in the social obligations forced upon him during his visits here and was relieved that autumn had arrived, signaling the end of the resort season. The fashionable aristocrats, nobility, and courtiers, as well as the sycophants that clung to the hems of this glided society, had returned to Rome and left the city to the merchants and businessmen who were the lifeblood of the empire.

The emperor had sent an order for the fleet to dock at Puteoli. A number of ships already secured at the piers were unloading sculptures, columns, and architectural pieces from Greece and Egypt as well as jewelry and fabrics from Persia and beyond. The presence of the emperor, as well as the departure of the well to do, made the merchants eager to broker deals for their goods. Hadrian had purchased Cicero's lavish villa a number of years ago and was still making it worthy of an emperor. Connected to the harbor by a long colonnaded walkway that snaked its way up the hill, the villa stood proudly on an outcropping that had a commanding view of the surrounding villas and temples, as well as the bay itself. The villa had remained empty since the orator's proscription by the emperor Augustus, his exile from Rome and his eventual murder near his family villa at Formiae.

As Hadrian walked through the massive gated entrance and the gardens that lead to the restored villa, he sensed the mystery and decay that marred his first visit years ago had dissipated; yet a shadow still lingered. Before he entered the villa, Hadrian stopped to gaze at a bust of the aged Cicero that had been discovered, half buried in rubble by Antinous during a brief visit here. The inquisitive youth found the ruins of the villa a playground filled with treasures meant to be unearthed. The bust now greeted visitors from a pedestal in a small garden, under a delicate temple-like structure in the Greek style. Both the old philosopher and the golden youth would have been pleased.

It was Antinous's unabashed joy and sense of wonder that lead Hadrian to restore the villa, rather than demolish it and design his own. Cicero's love of Greece was evident throughout the structure as it followed the floor plan of the many villas Hadrian had visited there. His last visit to this lodging was while the youth was still alive, and as he stood on the vast portico overlooking the bay, he recalled the boy carefully examining his lover's plans for the restoration and additions. Turning his gaze to the now-flourishing gardens in the courtyard, he recalled the movement of that dark head of curls as Antinous poured over every detail and impatiently asked question after question. Whereas the Villa Adrianna overwhelmed the youth, this villa was, though lavish, on a more human scale the boy could understand. The weed-choked courtyard was resplendent now, with roses, lilies, and poppies contained within hedges of myrtle, box, and yew, while elegant cypress and spreading oleanders provided dignity and shade. Ancient marbles from Greece, their paint long worn down to a subtle memory, gleamed from their plinths in the autumn sun as a magnificent bronze fountain splashed in the vast pool at the peristyle's center. From the ashes of ruin and misfortune, a paradise emerged.

Walking along the path that extended from the massive porch to the dining room, Hadrian stopped to examine a small lizard that dozed lazily in the sun on an acanthus leaf poised precariously over the sparkling water. Leaving the creature in peace, Hadrian continued toward the dining room and, running his hand through the well-tended herbs planted in carved marble urns that lined the walk, was met with the aroma of thyme, mint, savory, and bay leaf, as hyssop and deep green basil carpeted the ground and spilled over the steps to the chamber. A veil of a cobwebs, reaching from the shutters to one of the marble urns, trembled with the weight of the few remaining jewels of morning dew. Moss crept out from the dampened shadows and cautiously spread an emerald carpet along the stone steps that led to a worm-eaten gate and the lower levels of the estate. The steps of worn tufa, nearly black from the dampness of the years, were the sole witness to the villa's melancholy past. From the sunny gardens of the upper terrace, Hadrian could see through the wooden shuttered doors that were opened just wide enough for him to make out the frescos of the darkened dining room, depicting plants and animals more familiar to Greece than Rome. *When Romans leave Rome, they become Greek*, thought the emperor with a wry smile. In country estates and seaside villas, Greek was the language of choice for Romans who wished to appear refined and well traveled. The rough and tumble Romans still looked to Greece for education and polish.

Entering the dining room, Hadrian found the furnishings to be sparse but elegant. The lively mythological scenes, framed in bands of bold vermilion and ground lapis, gleamed through the half dark in the reflection from the great pool. Hadrian moved from room to room until he reached a bath suite, situated opposite the main bedchambers. This would be used by residents and guests of the villa and was lavish in the use of marble inlay, the patterns of which were from designs the emperor recalled from his travels. Traveling the portico that led away from the guest suites, Hadrian found himself in the private apartments. An intimate garden contained in a walled in *viridarium* lead to the sitting room of the suite, which in turn lead to the high-ceilinged bedchamber. Painted with architectural features that contained varieties of birds and wild animals, the decoration was perhaps a bit too stimulating for a bedroom, yet was very much to the taste Antinous had developed for himself.

Despite having never seen the finished work, the spirit and shadow of the youth permeated the entire villa. Walking through this airy room, Hadrian was able to see the bay through a private peristyle garden surrounded by another colonnaded portico. Off to the side was a two-story circular tower with windows set with thin slabs of cream-colored agate—the private bath suite Hadrian had designed for two. A sudden breeze from the sea scented the air ruffled the proud heads of the fiery red poppies as they balanced themselves on slender stems. Ferns waved from the shadows under the oleanders, and the entire garden appeared to dance to a joyful tune the emperor was deaf to. All was in place, but for Hadrian, the joy in it all had long vanished.

Hadrian spent four nights at the villa before boarding the *Adriana Augusta* for Rome. His days were filled with meetings with administrators and officials who had traveled from Rome. They provided the emperor with updates on the senate's activities as well as his own wife's comings and goings. None of the reports made his homecoming any more pleasant. Only his meetings with his *villicus* afforded him any pleasure. These meetings took place in the freshness of the morning, and the estate manager showed Hadrian plans for further building as well as sprawling gardens to envelop the villa and further isolate it from the surrounding estates. Concise and full of beautifully painted illustrations, these plans reignited Hadrian's interest in the estate and renewed his intent of making it his permanent retreat.

The emperor's meetings with the Roman administrators and officials were not without their pleasant side. Walking through the grove of Plane trees, just as Socrates might have done, Hadrian knew he was following the footsteps of the villa's former owner. Cicero had followed the model Crassus had used at his Tusculan villa, and he in turn had used the Greek model as his own. Dotted along the pathways were benches of dark brown marble carved to resemble rustic wood seating, where the emperor would sit in silence to absorb the flow of reports. It was typical of him to walk with three or four officials at a time and reply to all of their reports in succession while a scribe for each would struggle to keep up with his flow of words. Pausing at the great portico Cicero had made famous, its sweeping colonnade extending the length of the western façade of the villa, Hadrian looked out at the setting sun as it turned the bay a fiery orange. Something deep inside told him it was not just the sun that was setting. This arcadian setting, so tranquil and remote, was a far cry from the power and majesty of the Villa Adriana. Yet, while tempting in its simplicity, to remain here would mean turning his back on the empire and handing power over to those who wished him ill. Lucius Commodus was not yet named his successor as Hadrian had planned, so the reins of power still must remain firmly in his own hands. *It was time to withdraw from this place and set things straight in Rome.* With that final thought in mind, Hadrian entered the villa and ordered the preparations for his departure for Rome.

Chapter Thirty-One

Distant Memories, Opened Doors

Hadrian stood at the helm of the *Adrianna Augusta* with a silver cup of warmed *mulsum* in his hand. He felt the honeyed wine traveling his entrails and soothing the ache in his head at the same time. A few pancake biscuits and dates were all he could stomach for his breakfast on this morning. It was not the movement of the ship that ruined his appetite but his proximity to Rome and her ravenous society. After each visit to the ancient lands, Hadrian would return with an even lower opinion of Rome; that brutish upstart on the world's stage. But the world had come to respect power and might, not cultural finesse. And with the reign of the Nervan emperors, a certain polish had come to Rome by way of Greece. Hadrian, for his part, had seen to that personally through his architectural endeavors and his patronage of the arts. His plans for another Greek school in the center of Rome were finished and tucked safely away until his arrival. In two years, his *Athenaeum* had become the success he had wished it to be, thanks in part to the combination of Greek scholars and Roman administrators. He had not seen it finished and was eager to plan the official dedication upon his return. Finishing his uncompleted projects could take more time than he actually had. But at this time in his life, posterity was all.

The imperial fleet was not entering Ostia for its return to Rome. The emperor decided instead to enter the cargo port of Portus, which his uncle, the emperor Trajan had enlarged and embellished to rival Ostia's aging seaport. The straightforward entry to the Tiber and a deep, spacious basin designed for heavy cargo ships made Portus a more comfortable berthing spot for the *Adriana Augusta*. Here too was a lavish but comfortable palace Trajan had built toward the end of his life, together with an amphitheater to the east of the palace that held his private gladiatorial games and reenactments of famous sea battles. Although this pastime was a great pleasure for Trajan, Hadrian did not share his uncle's taste for sea battle, simulated or not. Nor did he look kindly upon the waste of human life in gladiatorial combat. Upon his adopted father's death, Hadrian had the amphitheater filled in with earth and a vast garden, surrounding hundreds of fountains, planted to provide a restful view from the private quarters of the palace.

There were no memories of Antinous here. The youth had never seen Portus or explored the many rooms of the palace. *This path is unknown to the boy,* thought Hadrian. *Perhaps his shadow will not haunt me here.* And with that thought, Caesar disembarked and headed down the colonnaded walkway toward the palace. He would spend the night here while the ships were being relieved of their burden and the barge that would bring him to Rome was being prepared.

The palace of Trajan did hold memories of a different kind. It was here, many years ago, that a nineteen-year-old Aelius Hadrianus came to know Plotina, his second cousin Trajan's wife, more intimately. The wife of the then future emperor had always held a warm spot in her heart for the youth since his arrival from Espania. Sturdy and athletic, the raw youth from the country held a certain allure in the jaded confines of Rome. Having bedded only youths of his own age at this point, the lusty society wives in Rome were a new experience for the young provincial. Plotina, in her wisdom, corralled Hadrian before he could do damage to his reputation and, as a result, his future. Acting as both mother figure and lover, she nurtured the young man, teaching him the finer aspects of societal behavior and diplomacy. His extreme fondness for the hunt brought him closer to Trajan, and he was soon treated as a son. Having lost his own father at the age of ten, Hadrian had great affection for this man he was now a ward of.

That is not to say Hadrian was above being seduced by his mentor's wife. Shortly after being made one of the ten judges of the inheritance court and later, tribune of the Adjutrix or Second Legion, Hadrian was invited to Trajan's summer villa at Portus. Unknown to the young man, Trajan was stationed in Upper Germania, and Plotina was at the villa with only her most trusted entourage. The week Hadrian spent at Portius cemented a relationship that would last until Plotina's death. Later, when Trajan was emperor and the senators Palma and Celsus fell under suspicion of eyeing the throne, Plotina pushed Hadrian further toward her husband; and there, in what was now a palace in Portius, assured a second consulship, this time in Syria. It was in Syria that Hadrian learned of his adoption by Trajan, and there that he learned of his adopted father's death.

All of these old memories came rushing back as Hadrian sat in the great garden that had once been the amphitheater. The strong and learned Trajan was still no match for his formidable wife. Hadrian's marriage to Trajan's niece, Sabina, was desired even less by Trajan than by Hadrian himself. Plotina was the advocate of this arrangement and, as usual, got her way. As Hadrian thought back on his relationship with Trajan, he recalled the thorn in that relationship was always the same. His taste in youths was far too similar to the older man's, and more than once they nearly came to blows over the affections of a beautiful boy. Leaning back in a marble chair beneath a spreading pear tree, Hadrian recalled these times and smiled. All the while he had known the prophecy of the Sybilline Verses; his future was assured all along, and Plotina was the vessel of that prophecy. Through her came his adoption by Trajan and eventual succession. And through her, very possibly, came the deaths of the four senators who had questioned that succession and were accused of plotting his murder upon his entry into Rome. This had darkened the beginning of his reign, and he had to work hard to overcome the stain of suspicion that was on the minds of a hostile citizenry. Even to this day, his relationship with the senate was laboriously civil at best. The honors they bestowed on him they gave grudgingly. Hadrian was diligent in his timing for the acceptance of honors, never wishing to seem eager to receive them before he was deserving. Plotina had taught him well, and her lessons lived long after she had become divine.

The evening had passed in a dreamless sleep, and Hadrian awoke at dawn refreshed and prepared for his entry into Rome. After a light breakfast, he and his court made their way to the pier where the barges sat ready for their journey up river. The cargo barges, loaded with sculptures, furniture, and chests of treasure from the emperor's travels, had already set off for the Villa Adrianna, their final destination reached by way of canals that branched off the Tiber.

The court could not make out the mood of the emperor. He spoke to the crowd that gathered at the pier, but more briefly than usual. When a centurion approached Caesar to announce that the royal barge was at the ready, Hadrian saluted the crowd and abruptly departed for the riverbank. Lucius Commodus had been watching the emperor's mood from afar and noticed he stroked the great amethyst intaglio of Antinous, a habit he had developed when something was agitating him. Commodus knew the return to Rome was not a joyful event for Hadrian, and were he able to, he would go directly to the Villa Adrianna. But the senate awaited him, as did, more reluctantly, the empress. And the dilatory pace of his return had set both on edge.

Hadrian's entry into Rome was more of a social event than a victorious return. There had been no military victories to commemorate; the resolution of the Bar Kokhba Revolt in Judea was at such a massive cost of lives that during the crises, the emperor did not include in his reports to the senate the customary salutation "I and the legions are well." It was a conflict that had a bitter taste to its victory and one he wished to forget. But if the fanfare that surrounded the imperial party had a hollow ring to it, the crowd barely noticed. Coffers of gold and silver coinage had preceded his arrival and was now being scattered over the masses. The recent delivery of grain was the largest in years, and the autumn weather was balmy and as clear as the waters that poured from the aqueducts. All was well in Rome, and the image of their Caesar on horseback, his golden crown and gilded parade cuirass flashing in the afternoon sun, was enough to bring the voice of the crowd to a mighty roar.

Rome had not seen their emperor in nearly four years. And in that time, the *praefectus praetorio*, Marius Marcius Turbo, had proven to be the perfect representative of the emperor. Turbo's political and military influence helped him maintain the peace between the senate and the emperor, but did little to contain the intrigues that surrounded the empress. Those he would leave for the emperor. Now, as he strode down the steps of the Temple of the Deified Trajan and Plotina to meet the emperor, it was with mixed emotions that he watched his command draw to a close.

It was part of Turbo's prestigious *Misenum Fleet,* the *Castor, Pollux,* and *Heraclea* that traveled with Hadrian throughout his voyages, and it was to Turbo that Hadrian gave responsibility of the first *Adriana Augusta*. The fleet's shadowy past was cleansed during Marcius Turbo's first tenure as commander. Upon becoming praefectus years later, he resumed the command of the fleet and this responsibility, together with the praefectus, kept Turbo in constant contact with the emperor, but left little time for a private life. Now that Caesar had returned, Turbo feared he was to slip quietly away into obscurity.

As he mulled over these thoughts, a golden aquila came into view, its outstretched wings spread proudly on the tall staff that bore it. Bearing the gilded eagle was an Aquilifer, an *Optio ad spem ordinis* Turbo remembered from his tenure as the Danubian Command, when he, along with the emperor, divided Dacia into two regions with the hopes of making the province more compliant to Roman rule. It was the success of that venture that led to his return to Rome. Turbo was surprised to see the Optio had the *phaleri* or military decorations of a centurion he had been groomed to be, yet he stilled carried out the duty of an officer of a lower rank. His surprised vanished when he noticed this aquila bore Caesar's royal insignia. This honor was beyond measure, and it showed slightly on the man's otherwise stoic face. The arrival of the Aquila heralded the arrival of the legion that served as the imperial bodyguard and so, the emperor himself. Marcius Turbo ran the hem of his cloak quickly over his numerous bronze phaleri, an almost unconscious gesture that polished further the shining decorations. As the emperor came into view, their eyes met; and Turbo, even with the distance between them, could see something disturbingly restless in the gaze that met his.

Chapter Thirty-Two

New Intrigues, Old Wounds

The procession from the pier eventually reached the Clivus Palatinus, under the Arch of Titus to the Basilica in the forum where Caesar was to meet Marcius Turbo; the route seemed to be endless. Looking over the heads of the populace, Hadrian could make out the many temples and public buildings he had left in Rome. No scaffolding could be seen, meaning Marcius had attended to the building projects with the same diligence he brought to all his other responsibilities. The city seemed to have an aura of order he had not felt before, and as the procession neared the temple of his adopted father and mother, Hadrian noticed the crowd cheered almost as loudly for the emerging Turbo as they did for their emperor. Hadrian glanced at Lucius Commodus and the bemused look on his handsome features seemed to legitimize Hadrian's sudden dark thoughts.

Perhaps he had been away too long. He had no reason to doubt Turbo's allegiance, nor his pure intent, and Hadrian had known the man for too many years to not recognize his true nature. Hadrian had first met Marcius as a young man twenty-two years before during the reign of Trajan. It was his first time as commander of the Misenum Fleet, a great honor that heightened the audacity of his youth. He had taken the fleet east to fight in Trajan's campaign against the Parthian Empire. It was also at this time that the second Jewish revolt posed a serious threat to the stability of the eastern empire. Turbo proved himself so well in Parthia that Trajan sent him to Egypt to protect Rome's lifeblood—the region's grain supply. Turbo left the fleet and became the military prefect of Egypt until the death of Trajan and the succession of Hadrian. It was then that they reconnected, and Turbo fought a military campaign along the coast of North Africa alongside the new emperor. When Hadrian left to deal with another uprising in Parthia, he left the command of most of North Africa in the hands of Turbo. After this was the Danubian Command, then Dracia. It was after the success of Dracia that Hadrian knew who he could trust to represent him in Rome.

Had he been wrong? There was never any indication of misconduct or even ego in the reports Turbo sent in a steady succession. But he had seen many before this who had succumbed to the heady elixir of power wealth and public adoration. Yet, as he watched the tall elegant soldier descend the marble steps of the temple and take his place beside the marble altar, he saw nothing different from the man he knew years ago. His armor and phaleri were gleaming in the autumn sun, but even from this distance, Hadrian could see they were worn with the years, and Turbo had not had the silver awards gilded as many had done. No, this was a soldier still. Unsullied by the prestige his emperor had burdened him with, Turbo wore the responsibilities as comfortably as the scarlet cloak that draped his broad shoulders. Would he find it difficult then to relinquish these duties? Has the potent taste of authority left even the shadow of an addiction? *Perhaps not,* thought Hadrian. And as he surveyed the cheering, riotous crowd, he realized it was this fickle mob he should be wary of and not his praefectus. With a salute, Caesar descended from his horse, strode up to the raised altar, and greeted his trusted friend.

A soldier had followed the emperor to the dais, bearing a packet of supple goatskin, which he quickly unfolded when the emperor turned to him. Hadrian removed from the sheet of leather a gold *phalera* of considerable size and, after a brief oratory, fastened the sculpted disk to the breastplate of his loyal praefectus. The decoration flashed in the sun as the crowd cheered with even greater enthusiasm. Unseen by Hadrian were two senators who had come from the crowd and ascended the steps to greet him. Both carried with him a purple cushion, one bearing the *corona triumphalis* and the other an ivory baton inlaid with gold stars and topped with a golden eagle. The first senator presented the golden laurel-wreath coronet to the emperor with great flourish. Looking directly into the eyes of the man, Hadrian searched for any sign of mockery, but found them instead, glistening with emotion and pride. The second senator was a different matter. He presented the baton with less enthusiasm, almost begrudgingly. There was arrogance and a thinly veiled hate in the eyes of this one. While there was always something about Servianus Hadrian did not trust, it took a change of plan concerning the royal succession that had finally brought out the truth.

Lucius Julius Ursus Servianus was the widower of Aelia Dominitia Paulina, Hadrian's eldest sister. Although never close, Hadrian had long treated Servianus with significant honors and had once considered him to be the first in line for the succession. When

Paulina died in the beginning of the year of Antinous's death, she was deified as due her position and to add prestige and legitimacy to Servianus's succession. As the years progressed, however, Hadrian began to reconsider his choice due to his brother-in-law's increasing age. Now in his nineties, Servianus's reign would be far too brief to be of any value, despite his capabilities. So Hadrian turned his attention to Servianus's grandson Gnaeus Pedanius Fuscus Salinator. Hadrian began to groom his great-nephew and bestowed special status upon him in his court. For this, Servianus was spared any bitterness for being passed over and was pleased that his grandson would someday succeed as emperor.

But as time unraveled, so did the true personality of Pedanius Fuscus. Hadrian watched as his choice of successor soured into an immature and petty monster before his eyes. It was after the death of Antinous that Hadrian changed his mind and turned his attentions to his former eromenos, Lucius Commodus. As rumors grew that Hadrian intended to adopt Commodus as his son and heir, the senate grumbled with impotent indignation, but Servianus and Fuscus seethed with anger. It was this resentment and rage that the emperor saw in the glare of the baton-bearing senator. Hadrian ignored the glare, but could not ignore the warning that sounded in his hunters mind. There was a dangerous beast in the forest, and its eyes were on him even now.

A small cadre of temple priests had arrived at the altar with a prepared offering for Hadrian to present in honor of his deified adopted parents. Soon, thick smoke swirled up into the autumn sky as Hadrian recited the verses that sent praise and prayer to the deified Trajan and Plotina. As the burning began to subside,

Caesar turned and strode down the steps to his horse that had been straining impatiently at the reins. Marcius Turbo acknowledged the centurion who had brought along his own horse and mounted the steed before taking his place just behind the emperor and Lucius Commodus. The regal image of the emperor in his armor and golden crown once again awed and excited the crowd. His rigid figure on the purple draped horse was more reminiscent of a living sculpture than a mortal man. Turbo maneuvered his own horse further into the center of the procession and wisely made himself less visible to the masses. He was still puzzled by the enigmatic gaze of the emperor, but the memory of those stone gray eyes chilled him despite the warmth of the autumn sun. The atmosphere in Rome was quickly changing with the presence of the emperor and his court. Old intrigues reborn, old wounds reopened. Marcius Turbo felt this chapter in his life was drawing to a close. It was time to return to Epidaurus, in his homeland of Greece, and leave Rome to the Romans.

Hadrian did his best to match the enthusiasm of the crowd as he acknowledged their cheers. He had done much to pave the way for his return, knowing as he did the extent the senate had gone to poison their minds against him. But bread, games, and silver spoke louder than senatorial rhetoric, and the majesty of his presence dazzled the masses. The allegiance of the people was easily bought and their memories, fleeting. The silver coins rained down upon the crowd carried Hadrian's portrait, a blunt reminder of who was truly the master of Rome.

Continuing on the Clivus Palatinus through the forum, Hadrian strained to see the massive dome of his favorite building in the distance. The gilded bronze tiles of the Pantheon gleamed under Apollo's gaze, and the shimmer appeared to blaze like golden heat. With a bitter smile, he recalled Trajan's favorite architect Apollodorus's dismissive comments on Hadrian's designs for domed buildings as pumpkins. Despite Hadrian's dislike for the arrogant master, he still felt pained that he was blamed for the man's untimely death. The architect's great tribute to Trajan, the magnificent column with its winding frieze, earned Hadrian's own grudging respect. And despite having banished the man for the disrespect he showed to the new emperor, Hadrian knew in his heart he could never have ordered the death of such a genius. As the emperor's gaze reached past the great column and settled on the gleaming dome of the Pantheon, he could not help recall with satisfaction the tomb he designated for the dead architect. There, in an unmarked space under a dome of Hadrian's design, lay the ashes of Apollodorus.

The imperial procession had passed under Augustus's great arch, then abruptly changed course and turned right, toward the Palatine Hill. Publicus Urbicus, commander of the Frumentarii, had made his way toward the front of the procession and, pushing his way past Lucius to the emperor's side, spoke directly to him. After a brief conversation, Hadrian turned and motioned Lucius and Marcius Turbo to ride along side him. Their conversation ended with frozen faces, but with a shadow of concern on Lucius's, anger on Marcius's and a smug satisfaction on the face of Urbicus. Only the emperor seemed at ease and somewhat amused at the subtle drama that had unfolded. The procession changed course without much notice; so smoothly did Turbo maneuver the crowd as Lucius directed the guard and mounted court. As the procession melted into the trees and vegetation of the Palatine Hill, Hadrian's head of the secret service remained at his side. The frumentarius had many more stories for the emperor, but those would wait until Caesar was settled in the Tiberianna Palace high on the Palatine.

Far from the emperor's entry procession, two men waited on the tiled roof of the Temple of the Caesars. Both were skilled archers, and both were waiting for their quarry; however, each had a different idea of how the day would end. Aulus Vibullis Nigrinus was a member of an ancient aristocracy whose family had resented Hadrian's claim to the throne since the day he entered the city to occupy it. When he was a child, Aulus's father, Avidius Nigrinus had been murdered alongside three other consuls accused of attempting a coup against the new emperor even before he took the throne. Nigrinus, as the governor of Dacia, had resented Hadrian's rejection of Trajan's expansionist policies, which would have enriched him even further. Added to this was his belief that he should have been chosen as Trajan's successor, which led to the thwarted assassination. As he waited on the warm clay tiles of the temple, Aulus burned with a desire for vengeance that had not dissipated after all these years. His hand clutched an iron-tipped arrow more firmly as he caught sight of the emperor's purple-cloaked figure high atop his steed. There was a pause; the procession seemed to waver in the haze of the heat that rose from the marble pavers. Then, as if in slow motion, the procession turned and headed toward the hills of the Palantine. Aulus stared in disbelief as he watched his plan unravel. He turned to his partner and suddenly saw the truth.

Salvius Lupus Palma had also been waiting for the imperial procession to pass by the temple. But unlike Aulus, he knew it would never happen. He had known Aulus since childhood and loved him despite his flaws; the most tragic of which was his undying hatred of the emperor. Salvius's father, Cornelius Palma, had also been murdered for the same reason. Yet Salvius knew it was more probable that the senate had ordered the killings at the instigation of the Praetorian prefect Attianus. The fact that Attianus was later held in high esteem by the new emperor did not help squelch the dark rumors that surrounded the throne. But there was never any proof that Hadrian was personally involved in any way in the murders of the men who stood in his way those many years ago. However, that made no difference to Aulus and his thirst for vengeance.

As Salvius returned Aulus's look of hatred with his own steady gaze, he knew their old friendship had suddenly ended. Nothing could make Aulus forgive this betrayal, but then nothing could make Salvius allow this treason to occur. As they sat frozen on the temple roof, the silence was broken by the sound of the brittle tile shattering under the heavy boots of the Frumentarii guards. As Salvius glanced at the guards, then motioned to his former friend, he recalled a story his Christian wet nurse had told him many years ago. He could not recall the names of the two men, but he recalled the betrayal. As the guards hauled Aulus roughly toward the heavy wooden ladder they had used to gain access to the roof, Salvius felt a piece of his life slip away.

I watched a lamplight flicker
Valiantly in the wind.
But the wind was strong
The wind was old.
The flame did not know
It had no chance.
I watched the smoke
Of an extinguished lamp
Rise.
Heaven is filled with the smoke
Of dead lamps.
And offerings
To disinterested gods.

Salvius stood before the altar of the Caesars and offered up the sacrifice he had just made. Another life had been given to preserve the life of the emperor. But Salvius had known another truth that led to the betrayal. Lucius Ceionius Commodus, the favored member of Hadrian's inner circle, was the stepson and son-in-law of Avidius Nigrinus. Salvius's connection with the imperial court and the prestige that connection brought with it was going to be severed if Aulus was allowed to go through with his plan. Salvius could not reveal Aulus's intentions without jeopardizing Commodus's future, and, at the same time, his own. No one would believe Aulus alone was capable of such a plot, and their own friendship would have ended had Salvius attempted to expose him. All that was moot now. And as Salvius left the temple, he gazed thoughtfully at the ground where Aulus lay dead; the Frumentarii long since vanished. Salvius walked from the shadows of the temple and summoned two legionaries walking toward the baths. With a great deal of distress, more real than feigned, Salvius reported his friend's tragic fall from the temple roof. A family honor was preserved and his own future ensured.

Hadrian had dismounted from his horse upon entering the tree-lined street leading toward the Domus Flavia and the Domus Tiberiana. Eager to be alone, he veered off the street and took a wooded path he had known since childhood where the scent of rosemary and fennel mingled with wild roses. Scarlet poppies danced drunkenly in the breeze as Hadrian entered the palace compound through a forgotten gate. A line of stately Cypress cast long shadows across the garden courtyard that led to the private suite Trajan had arranged for himself years ago. A shallow pool glittered as thin ribbons of water fell lazily from the bronze lion heads set into a marble urn. Golden fish wandered gracefully among the rose-red Nile lotus that bobbed as gilded fish fins brushed against them. They were descended from the lotus flower the poet Pancrates had presented to Hadrian during the emperor's first visit to Alexandria after the death of Antinous. The color, Pancrates told him, was from the blood of the Libyan lion Hadrian had killed in defense of his Beloved.

As the broad-petaled *Antinoeios* bobbed hypnotically in the pool, Hadrian sat and recalled the youth whose mouth matched the color of these radiant blossoms. It seemed like a lifetime ago that the youth sat on this same spot and chased the plump fish before sharing with them the seed cake that was part of his favorite morning meal. All that was good in the world died with him that night in the Nile. Like the lotus itself, Antinous was pulled from the muddy river, untainted and pure. As a cloud passed in front of the sun's face, it stole the sparkle from the water; and with a sigh, the emperor released his memories and rose slowly from the hard marble of the pool to walk slowly into the cool shadows of the ancient palace.

In another palace, the Domus Augustana, the empress sat quietly in the shade of her colonnaded courtyard. A shallow fountain splashed here too, but the sun was already sending long shadows across the garden, leaving only the sound of water and none of the shine. Sabina had arrived weeks ago from Putoli, where she expected to meet her husband upon his arrival from the east. His abrupt change of plans was never shared with her, and as a result, she and her court waited for nothing. The disregard shown by the emperor was the final humiliation that culminated in her unceremonious return to Rome. But her survivor's sense told her there was something more to the slight. Hadrian usually made an elaborate public show of their marital harmony whenever he had the opportunity, and this humiliation was not his style. There was danger in the air, and the now-aged empress had little desire to do battle with her bitterest enemy.

Sabina's nervous tension left her ladies-in-waiting on edge. She was dressed in an unusually formal manner; her elaborate hairstyle had taken her ladies over an hour to create to her satisfaction. The plaited braids that coiled around the back of her head extended in fat rows to the front and were met by a towering headdress, arched and adorned to resemble a diadem. A band of gold set with moonstones defined the line of her forehead, while long earrings set with matching stones and large pear-shaped pearls swayed heavily with each move of her head. Around her neck, Sabina wore a heavy chain of beaten gold links that was met in the middle by a large carnelian intaglio with a portrait of her great uncle, Trajan. Swinging from the gold mounting was another costly pearl that Sabina now rolled nervously between her fingers.

The pale aqua stola the empress wore was in stark contrast to the elaborate jewelry in its simplicity and lack of detail. Made of tightly woven linen, it puddled around her as she sat on a low-cushioned stool. A bust bodice in pale rose was draped over one fragile shoulder but did little to ward off the chill autumn air. As was her habit, the heavy rings Sabina had chosen to wear that day were resting on a small bronze table as her fingers slowly worked the golden embroidery of a silk veil. From time to time, she would interrupt her sewing and, after signaling her slave to cease with his lyre, would raise her head expectantly while again clutching the massive pearl that hung from her great uncle's portrait. When no visitor could be heard, Sabina would return to her sewing and the slave to his music.

Julia Balbilla too was working on embroidery, hers on a pale yellow veil. But her sharp eyes were busy watching the silent drama. The expected guests were far from unfamiliar, but the purpose of their visit was of great importance. Julia had distanced herself from the empress as she watched Sabina's mind became more deluded by her own fury as well as the influence of two vengeful players whose scheming was taking on a more sinister tone. The years had worn down Sabina's sense of propriety and caution; two gifts nature had given her that she was unwisely discarding. Julia was no stranger to intrigue, but the game Sabina was playing could prove deadly, and Julia's own sense of survival warned her to remain in the shadows.

The silent thoughts of all assembled beneath the colonnade came to a halt at the sound of heavy footsteps. The small court readjusted their garments and jewels as they prepared to greet the long-expected visitors. Sabina put aside her embroidery and replaced the heavily jeweled rings. It was while she was sliding on the final ring that she looked up expectantly. But the sight that greeted her was not what she was prepared for. Instead of her brother-in-law and his grandson, she looked up at the figure of her husband. The court too was taken aback, despite having no knowledge of who exactly was expected. Only Julia Balbilla remained nonplussed, her "oracle's sense" having warned her something unexpected was about to happen.

Hadrian was not dressed in the simple tunic and cloak he would usually wear for such a visit. No, the emperor of all Rome arrived in full regalia—a gold-embroidered toga picta of imperial purple over a tunica of the same color and also heavily embroidered in gold. In his hand, he carried the ivory baton of state he had received earlier in the day from his brother-in-law on the temple steps. The sun of the previous summer had exposed the reddish streaks in his hair, and they mingled with the ever-growing spread of gray. All this was an imposing sight as the sun further disappeared, and the slaves were busily lighting lamps along the colonnade, crashing into each other as their lamps revealed the icy presence of the emperor. The increasing lamplight revealed a golden diadem set with the massive sapphire intaglio bearing the likeness of the golden youth as Hermes. There was something surreal and blood chilling about this presence, further heightened by the presence of Marcius Turbo and the head of the Frumentarii, Publicus Urbicus.

It was the presence of Urbicus that drained the blood from Sabina's face. With a strength and composure that defied her age, the empress rose to greet her husband and with some difficulty bent to one knee in deference. "We welcome your long-awaited return to Rome, my lord." Her voice wavered slightly but remained strong and clear. Hadrian stared down at his wife for what seemed like a silent eternity before responding. "*We* as in yourself and your court? Or has my wife taken on the royal prerogative for herself?" "I consider it my due, my dear husband," she replied dryly. A sharp intake of breath could be heard from the shadows, and Hadrian noticed the figure of Julia Balbilla looking eerily like an ancient Delphian Sybil. Hadrian's attention returned to his wife who remained prostrate before him. "You seem to have found much to be your due," was his terse reply. Sabina looked up in time to see the face in the sapphire catch the light of the many lamps now burning, as if to bear witness to the humiliation her court now watched with guarded interest. Sabina moved her gaze down from the diadem to Hadrian's eyes and saw an all too familiar glint in those gray shadows. It was there when he removed from office Septicius Clarus, the prefect of the guard, and Suetonius Tranquillus, the imperial secretary, for conducting themselves with less than proper etiquette in the presence of the empress. Did he know the truth then but choose to ignore it to save face? His excuse then was weak and petty, but the truth would have put the two men to death. Did he know the truth now, and would he take stronger measures in the face of conspiracy? She found the answer to this riddle with the arrival of Servianus and Fuscus in the company of four guards. Her brother-in-law's face was pale but blank, while Fuscus appeared as if he were about to wet himself. By all indications, the Frumentarii had been vigilant and had done their duty well. With the knowledge that the plot had been unraveled, Sabina rose and walked silently toward her husband. Putting two fingertips to her lips, she raised them and touched the intaglio of Antinous/Hermes, saying simply, "You did well to place this gift to you into a crown." And with that, she bowed deeply and swept past the emperor to the dark interior of her palace. The guards, as well as the court, stayed frozen in place until Hadrian finally acknowledged them. "Tend to your mistress" and, with a wave of his hand, dismissed the court. His thin smile was cold but held a strange degree of humor. "It would appear the empress has deserted you." Hadrian turned and addressed Servianus without a glance at Fuscus. "She is tired and getting on in years," was the elderly man's only reply. "As are you. These days, the old seem reluctant to die," was Hadrian's icy reply. Turning toward two of his guards, he spoke, "See this old man safely to his home. And make sure that he does not leave there." To another two guards, he said, "I am told this one still has his eyes on my throne. Remove him to the Tullianum Prison where he will be able to see nothing but his own future's dwindling light." After they had gone, the emperor looked around at the flickering lights of the palace, then strode angrily out with Marcius, Publicus, and his own guards following close behind.

Chapter Thirty-Three

The Price of Greed

The next morning, Hadrian looked down from his palace at the Tullianum Prison in the distance. In the clear autumn light, the ancient building on the Capitoline Hill looked almost benign; its rugged stones warming in the morning sun gave no clue to the stench and horror below. Hadrian's thoughts turned to the dimwitted Fuscus, the latest *carcer* to be lowered into the dark pit of the dungeon that in its seven hundred years had held worthier prisoners. He was related by blood, true. But the blood was thin and tainted by an overly ambitious grandfather who, even in his nineties, felt worthy of the succession. Fuscus was a foolish young man whose pride and overreaching ambition negated any qualifications he might have had. Servianus had poisoned the boys mind, with the assistance of Sabina to be sure, against the emperor. Even in the presence of the Beloved one, he hadn't the decency to hide his arrogance and sense of entitlement. It was Fuscus's rude behavior to Antinous that Hadrian began to recall. Even his dear Lucius Ceionius Commodus, resentful though he was of his replacement by Antinous, had enough sense and respect to bury his feelings. But Pedanius Fuscus was goaded by wicked, ambitious minds, for which now he would pay the price. To Sabina, Hadrian could do little. He had burnished her public image far too well to send her into exile. Let her sulk and snarl in the darkness of the Domus Augustana, deprived of the processions and ceremonies that she had come to expect as her due.

As for Servianus, the man was as old as the seven hills and just as tough. Hadrian had tried over the years to embrace the senator as a friend and ally, but the man had shown his true colors too often, from years ago in Germania when he unsuccessfully attempted to prevent Hadrian from announcing the death of Nerva to his uncle Trajan, his manipulation of public opinion regarding the deaths of the four consuls that sullied the beginning of the new emperor's reign, and the reports from the Frumentarii that Fuscus was being groomed as heir apparent by his grandfather. And although it was Hadrian himself who brought to Servianus the idea of Fuscus as heir, the emperor's observations of the youth during his travels came to prove there was little to recommend him for the succession. His change of opinion had greased the wheels of dissention and traitorous malice, and sent a ripple through a long-simmering cesspool of resentment and hate.

The memory of the murders of the consuls Nigrinus, Palma, and the others at the beginning of his reign tempered Hadrian's emotions and delayed any action in regards to the three he held in suspicion. Fuscus could rot in the Tullianum for all he cared. Servianus was under house arrest, and Sabina would be carted out for an occasional public viewing to prevent any rumors of her death. An appearance of domestic bliss was, as least while in Rome, essential. And besides, Sabina was becoming more fragile as the days progressed; and Servianus, despite his opinion to the contrary, would not live forever. Perhaps the gods would take a hand in this dilemma and end it all for the good.

Winter was making its arrival known early in Rome. The gray sky was darkened further by the smoke of countless fires that did little to warm the Roman people from the smallest brick hovel to the grandest villas perched high on the hills. It had been six years since the death of his Beloved, years that rang hollow like a wine cup once full. Hadrian made his way on foot toward the outskirts of the city, and as always, the early walk made memories come alive. As he walked toward the Tiber, his enormous, but as of yet unfinished, mausoleum rose up from the gardens of Domitia in the distance. The situation of his three treasonous relatives weighed heavily on his mind, and the inevitable resolution that would transpire chilled him. The thought of their deaths reminded him of his own mortality. But a glance up at the sky put aside those thoughts and urged him to quicken his steps in order to reach the shelter of the outbuildings before the clouds released the downpour it was promising. He strode purposely across the vast Pons Aelius that lead to the tomb, defiant of the sixty years his body had weathered.

As he approached, the foremen and workers who had been gathering their tools with the intent of heading toward the shelters stood frozen at the sight of the purple-clad figure that came toward them. The wind had picked up and brought life to the heavy toga, pushing it tightly against the emperor's body and sending it flapping behind him—a male Nike in purple wool. Despite the mud puddles from the previous rain, the workmen fell to their knees in homage and the legionnaires stood ramrod while saluting with a throaty "Ave Imperator, Ave Hadriannus.: The reverence of their salute trumped Caesar's initial annoyance at the sight of the men seeking shelter from a simple rainstorm. Hadrian lifted his toga slightly and muddied his boots as he proceeded toward the carved doorway of his final resting place.

Descending a staircase, Hadrian traveled a corridor that lead to a large niche holding a statue of the emperor in his parade armor. Walking the white mosaic pavement past walls of travertine paneled with Numidian marble, the emperor reached the square basement of the tomb, the clicking sound of a chisel chipping stone breaking the vast damp silence. Climbing a wide inclined spiral way leading up to the central chamber, Hadrian found the source of the distracting noise. A massive funerary basin, of red porphyry, stood in the center of this chamber and glowed in the light of blazing torches as a craftsman, crouched in a corner, carved away at its capstone. The sarcophagus had been carved on-site and portrayed in deep relief Hadrian's journey through life. At the sight of the emperor, the craftsman ceased his work and moved from the small wooden stool to his knees. Hadrian walked over to lift the awed artisan from his prone position. "Show me the work you've done on my final resting place," he said softly. "Caesar honors me beyond measure," was the man's reply, as he removed a torch from its iron holder and followed the emperor. Holding the crackling light close to the sarcophagus, the stone changed in color from deep rose to blood red. As they circled the massive repository, Hadrian ran his fingers over the scenes so masterfully carved and told the story of each. His library in Athens, the miracle of the rains in Africa, the Judean War, the Pantheon—all here in meticulous detail. Suddenly, his fingers stopped at the carving of a youth mounted on a steed. Beside the youth was a bearded man, also mounted, who was engaged in the act of thrusting a spear into an enraged lion. The lion hunt in Libya, carved in blood-red stone. The youth looks to the man for help as the man shields him from danger with an arm across the youth's broad chest. *Was this truly how it happened?* thought Hadrian. His Antinous about to be devoured by a lion. It all seemed so long ago and distant. The youth was haunted by this event for the rest of his life, and now it was here in Egyptian stone.

A raised panel followed this scene; a blank space left for the writing of the final chapter. Hadrian gestured to the basin, saying, "They will see this and know whose ashes lie within. I do not need my name in stone. Carve here, instead, an image of the golden youth, the god Antinous. He will guard my ashes with his gaze." The craftsman bowed and replied, "It will be done as you say, Majesty." With that, the emperor turned and began to ascend the steps to the great circular hall above. Before he had reached the stairs, he noticed on a small wooden bench a covered jar. Picking it up, he examined the jar, exquisitely crafted from a single piece of honey-colored chalcedony with handles carved in the form of masks of Pan. The surface was covered with vine branches and clusters of grapes in high relief while the foot of the jar rested in a nest of acanthus leaves. The cover of the jar was of the same stone, carved in the shape of a lotus flower in a pool of water surrounded by a band of laurel branches in gilded bronze. Holding the jar to the torchlight, Hadrian marveled at the translucent quality of the stone and the masterful workmanship, while unaware of its purpose. Replacing the jar to the small bench, Caesar turned to begin his climb up the stairs, leaving behind the receptacle destined to someday hold the burnt remains of the emperor of Rome.

During the emperor's inspection of the lower chamber, the soldiers had removed the woolen coverings from the sculptures that had been finished and awaited placement. They were standing around one piece in particular when Caesar returned. At the sound of his boots, they turned and stepped away from the object. The sight that met Hadrian startled him. A sleeping faun greeted him, legs splayed, one arm wrapped around a tree trunk to support his sleeping body as the other supported his thrown back head. With closed eyes and open mouth, he dreams of things mortals would dare not do. At first, Hadrian thought it was the Hellenistic piece he had seen in Athens. But he knew the Athenians would never willingly part with a work from the Pergamene school, and only the emperor could convince them to do so. As he drew closer, he saw it was a recent work, a Roman copy of the highest quality. So recent was the carving that upon examining the powerful head, Hadrian blew softly on the slightly open mouth, releasing a cloud of marble dust into the air. Although he questioned the appropriateness of the piece for his tomb, he gazed at the sculpture in fascination; its blatant eroticism made it difficult to turn away.

Hadrian eventually did turn away and began to tour the massive hall to examine carved capitals, giant urns, and a terra-cotta model of the monumental bronze that would stand in the gardens atop the completed mausoleum. A bevy of gilded bronze peacocks stood in a silent cluster along the wall and joined an array of stone sculptures, their smooth marble surfaces shining in the torchlight.

The building itself was nearly complete, but the adornments alone would take the majority of a year. Hadrian suddenly felt weary of it all, the oppressive grandeur was more suited for the dead than the living. He longed to return to the energy and perfection of the Villa Adrianna. He would take Sabina and Servianus with him and provide an elegant house arrest, while Fuscus would be left rotting in the Tullianum.

The next morning, as the imperial household roused itself to prepare for the journey to the Villa Adrianna, Hadrian was already on his way to the Pantheon. Despite his ban on riding on horseback within the city walls, Hadrian rode his steed down the Via Agrippae, the reappearance of an old leg wound having made the long walk impossible. Preparations had begun the day before for the removal of the alabaster sarcophagus of Antinous from the Pantheon to its final resting place at the villa. Hadrian had sent his plans for the burial complex to his architects nearly a year earlier. When the emperor had returned to Rome, he received word that the temples and tomb for his Beloved had been completed and were awaiting the final element, the presence of the god himself.

As he rode around the Thermae Agrippae, Hadrian caught sight of the bronze roof tiles of the Pantheon, their gilding shimmering in the early morning sun. The same sun warmed the gleaming white marble of the temple façade as well as the columns of gray Egyptian granite. Dismounting, Hadrian stood silent for a time before the façade, then walked slowly up the broad flight of steps to the portico, where he was dwarfed by the massive columns. He gazed up at the bronze ceiling of the portico, then to the niches that held the statue of Agrippa and two emperors—Augustus and

Hadrian. This was the only visual connection to the building he had allowed himself, but it was enough. He walked toward the massive bronze door, with the sun already splashing across the gold adornments with a blinding brilliance. The door opened slowly and relieved the glare in emperor's eyes as he entered the dark interior of the cella.

The morning sun was not yet high enough to make an impact on the rotunda, and the heavily draped sarcophagus sat silently in the semidarkness. The soldiers had already placed the casket on a low wagon with thick wooden wheels wrapped in wool to prevent damaging the vast mosaic floor. As they began building the sides of the crate that would contain and protect the tomb during transport, the rhythmic tapping of the iron hammers against iron nails brought a sense of panic to the emperor as he all but flew toward the workers. The soldiers, preoccupied with their task, did not notice the emperor coming toward them; his sudden appearance both shocked and unnerved them. It was only when Hadrian was satisfied the covering around the coffin was thick enough to protect the carved alabaster did he allow the soldiers to resume their labor. The clanging of metal against metal continued to echo throughout the cavernous temple as the crate's wooden cover was lowered into place and the morning slowly peered in from the oculus. The soldiers who had accompanied the emperor to the site joined the soldiers with the cart to help move it slowly through the colossal bronze portal of the temple. Once outside, a ramp led to twin oxen that stood waiting for their burden.

Hadrian had remained behind and watched the procession move slowly toward the door before turning to gaze at the marble image of his Beloved that stood in its shadowy niche of gray marble. As he made his way toward the statue, the shuffle of feet could be heard as the temple priests hurried over with oil lamps that hung on either side of the altar. The gilt bronze of the lamps glowed in the tall flames that flickered from each spout, and the freshly oiled image seemed to come to life in the dancing light. The priests stood still and silent as the emperor moved toward the sculpture and, as he did every morning since his return to Rome, kissed the foot of the Beloved. With a nod to the priests, Hadrian walked past the now-smoking altar that stood just beneath the oculus and made his way out of the temple in time to see the oxen leaving with their precious burden. By now, the city was awake and already aware of the emperor's departure.

Hadrian had not yet reached his horse before seeing Marcius Turbo coming toward him with a look of solemn concern on his face. That look did not bode well. With a salute that was less brisk than usual, he drew closer to the emperor in order to give him news that was, for now, for his ears only. "Majesty, the empress is dead." Such simple words spoken only as a soldier would utter them. But simple words filled with meaning and consequences. The simplicity of the soldier speak cleared from Hadrian's mind the thoughts that had occupied it only moments ago. Quick thinking required a clear mind, and the gravity of this sudden situation needed to be handled deftly and astutely. With his grand nephew Fuscus in prison and his brother-in-law Servianus under house arrest, malicious tongues would soon be wagging with tales of intrigue and, more dangerously, murder. Seeing that Turbo had brought his horse along with him, Hadrian instructed him to mount and accompany him to the Domas Agustianus.

"Who else knows of the empress's death?" he asked Turbo. "It is not known beyond the palace walls, Caesar," came Turbo's reply, half believing it himself. "I learned little of the particulars when I arrived to escort the empress to the barge. From the reaction of the servants, I assumed it had just been discovered when they went to wake her to prepare for the journey." Turbo's clipped speech told Hadrian the man knew full well the potential scandal that could ensue if this was not handled properly. Turbo went on to add, "I posted guards along the perimeter of the estate to prevent servants from leaving with the news." As always, Turbo was quick to assess the situation and prevent the theatrics that usually follows an event such as this. *Few things were more untrustworthy than a servant with a secret*, thought Caesar. Marcius took a quick glance at the emperor as they rode up the Palatine Hill, but as was always the case in situations such as these, from behind the beard the features were inscrutable. Only the discovery, years ago, of the dead Antinous along the Nile banks broke through the emperor's stoicism—a sight and sound Marcius tried but could never forget. They arrived at the palace in silence and were met with a darker silence. By now, the court was already in mourning; and servants sat huddled in corners, low moans emanating from bowed heads. Julia Balbilla emerged from the private chambers and bowed low at the sight of the emperor. The aged woman's voice was a crackled whisper in the silence. "I saw the omens yesterday in the entrails of Isis's sacrifice," she whispered hoarsely. "And in the smoke of Antinous's altar." Hadrian's attention suddenly shifted to the woman, and he shuddered at the realization of how much she resembled the Medusa on the breastplate of his old armor. But this was a living Medusa before him, wrinkled and wild haired, but with eyes that still pierced the mind. He could feel those eyes on him as he brushed past her and entered his wife's private quarters, where the courtiers who had clustered around the body parted at the sight of the emperor. He walked to the bed and looked through the embroidered gauze curtains at the still figure that lay on the other side. Parting the curtains, he looked down at Sabina and strained to find some emotion befitting a dead wife from her husband. Reed thin and gray haired, she resembled one already mummified. Sabina wore no jewelry, save a slender gold bracelet that had been in her family for generations. The same bracelet Hadrian had been unwise enough to taunt her with years ago by giving it to Antinous to wear. Seeing it on her now, he knew it was her last vengeful retort. Even in death, she hated him.

A voice interrupted his thoughts as he stared down at the corpse. "She too visited the golden youth." It was Julia standing beside him. Hadrian turned and glared down at the woman with a look he hoped was indifference. Something about her always chilled his blood. "She did what?" he asked, not wishing to converse with her, but needing to know what she meant. "Sabina too visited the tomb of Antinous. Even when you were away, she paid homage to the boy. When you returned, you visited in the mornings under the cool gaze of Aurora and stayed until Apollo's light poured through the great eye. Sabina visited long after Hespera had spread her cloak and night fell under the watchful eyes of Thoth, the same god that witnessed Antinous being embraced by the Nile." Hadrian resisted with great difficulty the urge to slap the woman. The audacity of this hag to let the name of his Beloved pass her lips. "She placed flowers before his votive image and burned incense on the altar of the Pantheon." Unlike the rest of Rome, she worshiped your young god in scented shadows."

Hadrian listened to Julia in frozen silence, unwilling to believe her words, but the pleasant taste of truth showed too clearly on her face. "Last night, instead of white smoke, I saw black plumes rise up to the face of Thoth and reveal his form as a great beaked Ibis. Tendrils of vapor rose like snakes through the eye of the temple and caressed his face until they blotted out his light. The incense smoldered but would not flame. A life was to soon depart this world. It was Sabina, and now she has joined the golden boy on Olympus!" Without warning, Hadrian's hand flew out and smashed against the wizened face of the old woman, sending her hurling toward the stone floor. "One more word, old witch, and you will follow my wife in death. And trust me, it is not on Olympus she sits!" Julia glared up at the emperor as she wiped the blood from her dry, broken lips. Although he nearly regretted his rash action, his face betrayed no emotion.

Without another word, Hadrian turned to Sabina's corpse once more and removed the offending bracelet from a pale wrist, before turning to leave the bedchamber. Julia had already risen from the floor and composed herself, her face a mask of dignity barely hiding her rage. She flinched slightly as the emperor walked toward her and took her chin in his large fingers. He examined her bruised mouth, still glistening with blood, and grunted regretfully. Taking his wife's old friend by the hand, he paused before wrapping the fateful bracelet around her wrist. "I have given instruction for the preparation of the body and the proper sacrifices in her memory," he informed her. "You may observe, but be silent." He gazed down at her for a moment before leaving the room and heading toward the barge that waited to take him to the Villa Adrianna.

Upon leaving the palace, Hadrian motioned for Marcius Turbo and Lucius Didus to join him, along with the commander of the Frumentarii. Publicus Urbicus was dressed in a simple woolen toga without a border of any kind. Nothing in his appearance betrayed his station or his power. Hadrian dispatched Urbicus to the Tullianum Prison to release Pedanius Fuscus and escort him to the villa of his grandfather, Servianus. "Marcius and I will go to Servianus's villa to announce the death of his sister-in-law, the empress." I wish for Fuscus to arrive while I am still there, as a sign of my goodwill," instructed the emperor. With a bow, the commander of the Frumentarii slipped into a waiting sedan chair and vanished into the crowd. "Lucius, go to the river landing outside the Porta Tiburtina and make sure the barges are prepared to sail," the emperor instructed, almost as an aside. Lucius hid his surprise well and trotted off toward the pier along the Tiber, his horse whinnying in the chilled morning air. The praefectus caught on quickly what plan the emperor had in mind. The barges had originally been docked at the Pons Agrippae, but the Porta Tiburtina was closer to Servianus's villa, making for a quick and silent escape after the emperor's visit. Lucius was not surprised that the emperor was leaving Rome despite the empress's death. With the remains of his Beloved settled on a royal barge set for the Villa Adrianna, there was nothing left in Rome to keep Hadrian there.

One could almost smell the gossip brewing over the breakfast tables of Rome's aristocracy, but the allegations were groundless and would wither away to nothing in due time. Hadrian's administrators had things well in hand, and the Frumentarii would keep any suspicions to a whisper. As he neared the mist-covered river, Lucius wondered how much longer his services would be required. With Marcius Turbo in the emperor's inner circle once again, Lucius's position was inconsequential at best. He sensed the decline of Hadrian's reign and his own career as well. Part of him welcomed retirement, while another part longed for a past that would never return.

Chapter Thirty-Four

Reprieve

The arrival of the Imperator Caesar Traianus Hadrianus at the gates of the Domus Aurea sent a wave of fear throughout the villa. Hadrian had not stepped foot within the walls of the ancient villa since the death of his sister, Paulina. He had remained on friendly terms with his brother-in-law after the death and had honored Paulina's memory at the newly rebuilt Temple of Venus and Rome. But since the emperor's return to Rome, relations had gone sour with the old man. Hadrian's decision to bypass Servianus for his grandson was simply a more graceful way to take out of the line of succession a man Hadrian felt was too old to rule. The emperor had originally looked at Fuscus as a viable successor, until he had a chance to observe the youth's arrogant, callow behavior. After the years of prudent rule, Hadrian was not about to hand over the reins of power to a man with the temperament of a spoiled boy. Intrigue and treason met the emperor's arrival into Rome, and he wasted no time in issuing justice. The sudden death of the empress changed these plans or rather, delayed them. Hadrian's visit to Servianus was meant to offer an olive branch; one would soon wither and die.

Ursus Servianus met the emperor on the steps of his villa. Still robust despite being in his nineties, he looked every inch the aristocrat. His pale gray eyes look directly at his brother-in-law as he dismounted in the leaf-strewn courtyard. "The gardens have gone untended since my sister's passing," Hadrian said to Servianus, forcing some warmth into his voice. "You should take out your aggressions on your servants to keep them in line." The fact that Hadrian said "sister" rang with a familiarity that eased some of the tension out of Servianus's face. Also, the sight of Marcius Turbo and not Publicus Urbicus accompanying the emperor sent a rush of relief through the man's body. Servianus returned Hadrian's forced warmth with his own as he descended the steps and clasped the man's hand and arm. "May I offer my condolences for the loss of your wife, our empress?" the old man purred. Hadrian froze at these words and returned Servianus's clasp with such a force that the man winced despite his best efforts not to. "You are, as always, well informed," Hadrian replied stiffly. "But this time, ill advised. You play a dangerous game poorly old man." Servianus bowed with difficulty as age betrayed his physical state. He motioned for the emperor to enter his home, as behind him a young groomsman tended to the horses. Hadrian's attention was diverted for a moment by the sturdy youth, but he quickly turned away and strode past Servianus toward the portico of the villa.

The Domus Aurea had been a wedding gift from Trajan to Paulina and her new husband. It had a patina of ancient nobility that was familiar to Hadrian's sister and pleasing to his new brother-in-law. Paulina quickly took control and transformed the tired villa into a lively gathering place for Roman high society. The villa's gardens were the pinnacle of Roman horticultural style and design, and Hadrian had made use of many of his sister's plans for his own villa. The interior had suffered over the years since Paulina's death and Hadrian suddenly felt the presence of death. To relieve himself of the shadowy pall on the interior, Hadrian seated himself on a marble bench in the inner courtyard. Water in a marble basin supported by lead griffons trickled dismally into a shallow pool that stood in a weed-choked garden. The sound of the dry leaves, scratching the travertine pavement as they danced in the breeze, filled Hadrian with a sudden melancholy. Everything here seemed to be at the verge of death, and he fought an urge to quietly leave before he was absorbed into its brittle demise.

Hadrian discussed the plans for Sabina's funeral and deification as he traced with his finger a large crack that cut through the face of a satyr carved into an arm of the bench. He said nothing regarding Servianus's future or his house arrest. *Let the old man stew in his own bitter juices,* Caesar thought angrily. *There are plans even his spies have no access to.* Just as the strained conversation was becoming unbearable, the sound of heavy boots rang through the villa. Servianus went pale as Fuscus suddenly appeared in the light of the courtyard with Urbicus and two legionnaires behind him. The youth that stumbled into his grandfather's arms bore no resemblance to the spoiled aristocrat Hadrian had last seen. The Tullianum had aged the youth, his pale skin turned ashen and eyes sunken. A wicked sense of satisfaction warmed the emperor as he viewed his handiwork. Humbled and humiliated, Fuscus lay crumpled in his grandfather's lap. But the spark of hate had not died; dark eyes blazed as they peered out from behind a filthy sleeve of his tunic. The stench of human waste and moldy earth that rose from his body was such that it reached the nose of the emperor even at the distance where he sat. Servianus called for servants to bring the youth into the bath and find him fresh garments. As they led Fuscus away, Servianus turned to gaze curiously at the face of the emperor. It was void of any emotion as Hadrian rose from his seat and took his leave. "I have arranged for Sabina's funeral and dictated when it takes place. And after, at my leisure, I will return from the Villa Adrianna to acknowledge her deification," Hadrian spoke dismissively. "Do what you wish with your life, but remember, I will know your every move." Servianus watched with a mixture of fury and relief as the figure of the emperor disappeared into the darkness of the villa; all plans, for now, on hold.

Before Hadrian left the villa, he walked to the *unctuarium* where the servants had brought a still sobbing Fuscus to clean off the stench and grime of the Tullianum. Slaves had already removed the soiled and tattered tunic that lay in a heap on the marble floor and were scraping down the oiled the youth with a bone *strigil*. From his vantage point beside a smooth granite column, Hadrian smiled ruefully at the sight of the servant's faces as they reacted to the filth dripping from the youth's thin body. The soft fleshy youth that entered the prison was no more. The boney shoulder blades and clearly defined rib cage gave the emperor pause. As much as he had come to despise Fuscus, he had not intended the punishment to be this cruel. The youth's stupidity and an emperor's anger brought Fuscus to this state. Had Sabina not died, the youth would have languished in that ancient hole, never to be seen again. The slaves had scraped the remaining oil from the young man's body, and the servants were now leading him to the *caldarium* for a soak. As the youth was lead to the bathing chamber, he caught sight of the emperor. Tear-filled eyes glared at Hadrian with a hatred the emperor knew would never die. Hadrian's loathing for Fuscus was quickly rekindled, and he returned a glare that made the youth's bowls turn to ice as he quickly turned away. As the youth sank into the steaming bath, Hadrian left his place by the column and with his guards left the villa, deep in thought. A dark pledge whispered in his mind. *When that boy crosses me again, and he will, I will show no mercy. And after him, the old man.*

Hadrian left the villa and, after a few words to Urbicus, parted ways with the man who seemed to vanish into the mist that still rose from the river. It was a short distance down the Via Navalia to the riverbank and the Porta Tiburtina, a distance made shorter by Hadrian's determined stride. He had remained in Rome far too long and wished only to scrape the stench of this rotting metropolis from his skin. As he neared the banks of the Tiber, he could hear, but not yet see, the barges that waited for him. Soon, the red horsetail crests of his Praetorian guards came into view as they saluted and boarded the crafts with their horses upon the arrival of the emperor. Lucius Didus was already onboard the emperor's barge and stood protectively by the shrouded crate that contained the sarcophagus of Antinous. *Even in death, the Beloved is protected by his loyal praefectus*, thought a bemused Hadrian. It was as if he had been blind to all the devotion that surrounded the youth during his lifetime, a devotion so evident now, even in the thick morning mist. This same shroud of fog shielded Caesar from the masses who would have formed along the banks had they known of this presence. Silently, Hadrian gave thanks to

Auster, the god of clouds and fog for providing him with good cover. Torches blazed along the riverbanks to assist the boatmen in their safe passage for the royal barges as they made their way slowly up river toward the canals that lead them to Hadrian's world of his own making—the Villa Adrianna.

Chapter Thirty-Five

Bright Pasts, Uncertain Futures

Braziers had been lit to ward off the chill and dampness, yet even with their blaze and his heavy woolen cloak, Lucius Didus could feel the oncoming winter. While he wished the direction they were going was south to the resorts of Baiae or Puteoli, a glance at the emperor's face affirmed the purpose of this journey. Despite the chill, Hadrian stood at the helm of the barge and looked out as far as possible into the distance. From time to time, he would turn and study the rhythm of the oarsman, as if willing them to increase their speed. After all these years, he was eager to return to the only place he truly considered home. He had hoped to send Lucius Ceionius Commodus, soon to be called Aelius Verus Caesar, ahead of him to prepare the villa for his return; but Aelius remained in Rome, too ill to be moved even by litter and barge. Yet while this plan seemed to be unraveling, it mattered little to Hadrian now that he was on his way to the Villa Adriana with the remains of his Beloved. Lucius Ceionius would be well enough for his adoption in December, and all things would proceed as planned.

The thick mist eventually began to melt into the river as the flotilla passed the Flaminia Wall that concluded the northern confines of the city. The rhythm of the oarsmen was altered as the barges merged into the Aniene that flowed from the northeast. For Hadrian, this change always meant the villa was close, with only a canal to separate them. Hadrian paused in the middle of his dictation to his vigilant *notarius*, whose shorthand always pleased the emperor. He stopped to watch the remaining fog swirl around the base of the massive aqueduct that channeled precious water from the Aniene to the villa, then onto Rome. Over the slapping of the oars, Hadrian could hear the rushing water from the distant conduit as deer scampered beneath its massive arches. The procession of barges veered slightly into the great canal deeply carved from the tufa that was abundant here. The great amount of this limestone was removed then used, along with brick and pozzolana cement, for the creation of the villa. Hadrian's mind continued to wander as he observed the number of plants that made their home in the porous rock along the canal banks. Small crabs that had wandered from the connecting riverbanks scurried over the low flora in their search for food. Hadrian suddenly recalled Antinous's fascination with the crabs and often, on their travels to the villa, would ask that the barge be brought closer to the bank so that he could capture some of the crabs in a basket he had brought along with him for that purpose. The descendants of those crustaceans still haunted the watery depths of the villa's Canopus, where the youth had deposited them.

The emperor was distracted from his memories by the sound of his notarius sharpening a bone stylus, more out of boredom than necessity. Hadrian marveled at the young man's skill and eagerness to fill the many volumes with the emperor's thoughts, but the journey was drawing to a close. The canal soon ended at a great open pier lined with simple Doric columns and flanked by a guardhouse on one end and an accountant's office on the other. Hadrian had designed the canal for the safe delivery of building materials and fine artworks, but later found it a peaceful mode of transportation as well. As the barge glided toward the limestone steps, the boatmen threw out the heavy lines to the slaves who stood waiting to secure the vessels to the iron rings that hung from thick stone piers. Lucius Didus was the first off the emperor's barge, as from the vessel behind it, Marcius Turbo could be seen leaping to the broad steps before the ramp could be secured. Hadrian smiled at the competitiveness of the two men, cloaked in civility but evident just the same.

There was no need. Turbo had managed Rome brilliantly in the emperor's many absences and was respected by the populus. Lucius had been at the emperor's side from the time before Antinous to the present, commanding what was probably the finest Praetorian guard that ever served an emperor, including Trajan. Hadrian felt a greater affinity toward Lucius because of all they had been through together, as well as his protective nature towards Antinous that continued even after the youth's demise. His devotion became evident after the deification of the Beloved. Hadrian noticed the praefectus began to wear a ring with a portrait of Antinous masterfully carved in carnelian. It was one of the many votive items created to honor the new god, but the quality and accuracy of the likeness moved the emperor. It gave the aura of something that was carefully chosen—a personal talisman, a divine connection.

Marius Marcius Turbo, for all his mastery in the administration of Rome's political world as well as his brilliant military career under

Trajan, held a lesser regard in the eyes of the emperor. Along with his skills came a thinly veiled arrogance and opportunism. Having made him praefectus praetorio, the emperor ranked him higher than Lucius and had always treated him as a close friend and confidant. But the man was too close to Hadrian in temperament, and his military successes made the increasingly suspicious emperor question his loyalty. The reports from the Frumentarii uncovered nothing to give merit to these suspicions, but an exit plan for this man was already forming in Hadrian's mind. There could be no competitors casting a shadow over the throne of the next emperor.

As the small procession made its way toward the main buildings of the villa, Hadrian noted the morning sun had moved along the long containment walls that ran from the Roccabruna to the Accademia and settled on the small bath. Returning the salute of the soldiers who guarded the complex from the high walls, Hadrian and his entourage eventually reached the main entrance of the vestibulum, via the long double road. They passed an austere grouping of structures in pristine white marble, but the emperor's eyes remained fixed on the building ahead. While the court was dismounting before the steps of the vestibulum, the emperor had already reached the columned porch and was entering the great open courtyard. The courtiers who had settled at the villa earlier in the day were noisily assembled among the gardens and fountains before the emperor suddenly appeared before them. The chatter ceased as the court bowed and saluted their Caesar, whose presence already energized the atmosphere of the villa. Once he had acknowledged the court and visiting dignitaries who had left their comfortable lodgings to greet him,

Hadrian and his band of courtiers proceeded toward the small baths as the rest of the legionary guards headed toward the Great Baths. Pausing for a moment before the entrance to the *exedra*, Hadrian gazed out past the south porch toward the direction of the shimmering water of the *Canopus*. The court paused behind the emperor who seemed lost in thought, the sun's reflection off the great canal absorbed in his gray eyes. It took little imagination to know what thoughts ran through the emperor's mind, what memories misted his eyes. Suddenly aware of the courts prying gaze, Hadrian turned abruptly and strode through the north garden toward the nymphaeum and doors that would lead him to the comfort of the small baths.

Young slaves from Germania had scurried out from the service tunnels and waited within the baths for the arrival of the emperor and his court. As always, the emperor's chamberlain had reached the baths before his master and had oils and linen towels at the ready. The courtiers, tired after their long journey, made their way through the entrance corridor, passed through the palestra, and poured unceremoniously into the *frigidarium*. Dividing up, they entered the water basins that flanked the main chamber and splashed in the cool clear pools. Hadrian left the court behind him as he made his way through the *Tepidaria* to the soothing warmth of the *Caldarium*. The vast oval water basin was lined with slabs of creamy white marble inlaid with a bold acanthus leaf design rendered in brown marble mosaic. Brown and black marbles from Gaul covered the walls, their broad, deep veining creating its own magnificent pattern that needed no assistance from man. Lapis-and-blue-glazed tiles covered the ceiling, and as Hadrian settled himself in the basin he gazed up at the constellations portrayed by polished bronze stars set into the blue tile. There, in the center of the eagle constellation of Zeus, flickered the Star of Antinous. The light of the massive hanging oil lamps seemed to enable this star to radiate more brightly than the rest. After a moment's reflection, Hadrian realized his Beloved's star had been gilded, rather than simply polished. *A clever, subtle touch* thought the emperor. He made a mental note to inquire about the artisan, then closed his eyes and let the trickle of the wall fountains lull him to sleep.

Lucius Didus sat on a low marble bench in the Great Bath and stared down blankly at the riot of diminutive tessella that formed the intricate mosaic floor of the tepidaria. He could not shake the feeling that his career was at its final chapter, and its closing moments would be brief. The emperor had changed radically since the death of Antinous; the most telling proof was the destruction of Judea. Gone was the temperate ruler of Rome, and in his place was a capricious Hadrian who could also be bitter, suspicious, and cruel. His devotion to the mortal Antinous was eclipsed by his obsession with Antinous the god. Wherever one went in the vast villa, reminders of the young god were visible. On his way to and from the *sudatio*, Lucius passed a life-size sculpture of the youth on a granite plinth in the center of the colonnaded *tholos*. The circular hall bore an ornate astrological floor design copied from the Tholos of Epidaurus in Greece, and the inclusion of the youth's portrait where the statue of Asclepius stood in the original tholos reflected the taste and obsession of the emperor. Especially when one realized the larger than life-size statue of Caesar that stood in the frigidarium was positioned to look directly upon the young god. In art, as in life, the emperor dominated the boy.

Lucius leaned back on the stone bench and, as he often did, absentmindedly ran a fingertip over the portrait stone in his ring. The carnelian image was beginning to blur from years of this meditative gesture, and Lucius tried to break himself of the habit. Now, with his eyes closed and his body relaxed from the heat of the caldaria, he used the ring to evoke memories of the golden youth. From the east porch of the Great Bath, the boy would run naked along the Praetorium Esplanade toward the Canopus, darting between the many sculptures that surrounded the long canal before leaping into the water. His laughter caused a wave of music in the air just as his body caused waves in the still water.

From his perch on the esplanade, the Praetorian Lucius Didus secretly longed for the youth that, even then, seemed more god than mortal. To desire so deeply something so forbidden was an anguish Lucius lived with during the youth's all too brief a time with the emperor. When Antinous drowned in the Nile that tragic autumn, Lucius too mourned his passing. But unlike Hadrian, his grief remained hidden, silent. Yet the intensity of that emotion and the forbidden memory it cloaked seeped out of him like blood through a wound, and the aura of it reached the sensibilities of the emperor, creating an unspoken bond that traveled with them throughout their continuous tour of the empire. Now, in the safety and security of the villa, Lucius felt his services were no longer necessary. Perhaps it was time to retire and return to his homeland. Greece had always beckoned him, even when many miles away.

Lucius was still evoking his memories when Marcius Turbo entered the tepidaria. The Praetorian didn't wish to disturb the man he considered his biggest rival after Servianus and was about to leave when a group of chattering slaves entered with towels and refreshments. Their voices ceased when they noticed the resting Lucius and the look of annoyance on Turbo's face, but it was too late. Lucius opened his eyes and saw a somewhat uncomfortable Marcius standing before him. Nodding slightly, Marcius took his place on a bench along the glistening wall of marble. Lucius had assumed Marcius had followed the emperor to the small baths and would be spared any interaction with this man. Ironically, Marcius had thought the same about Lucius, and this meeting caused discomfort to both men. After a few words of forced conversation, Marcius suddenly faced his rival and spoke with a startling directness. "What is to become of us now?" The voice was low and conspiratorial, but still echoed in the vast chamber. "I have been here pondering the same question," replied Lucius. "It was never easy to read Caesar's intentions, but now it has become impossible." Marcius leaned back against the cool stonewall and spoke quietly again, "He did not even acknowledge Antinous's new tomb as we passed the *termenos*. Unlike you, who seemed to be unable to turn away." Marcius turned to study the Praetorian's face for a reaction, yet found none. "The complex is quite beautiful in a severe way. And it is the tomb of a god I had known as a mortal. How many of those have you seen in your lifetime?" replied Lucius. He spoke coldly, yet felt he had already betrayed too much. Lucius tactfully changed the subject and continued. "I feel our duty at the villa is to protect the emperor, as always. Yet I doubt he will leave here often, so I would think you would be sent back to attend to things in Rome." *One can only hope*, was his unspoken thought. Marcius was silent, then sighed deeply as if surrendering a piece of himself and replied, "My days as administrator are finished. Doing one's duty too well is not very welcome these days. Rather than being of service, I am a suspect." "And," he added, "I would rather leave on my own two feet."

They were both aware of Hadrian's suspicious nature—a character flaw that had become more prevalent since the death of the youth. Fuscus had barely escaped death and Servianus's security was in doubt. The number of courtiers, artisans, and hangers-on had swollen, yet was swallowed up by the vastness of the ever-expanding villa. And the growing number of senators and other public officials lodged in the lavish guest suites led both men to the conclusion that the center of Roman power would soon no longer be Rome, but the Villa Adriana. Here, they were in the world of one man's creation and that man would not need an official administrator, nor would he wish for the presence of someone who carried with them a spectator of the past. As both men sat in the silent chamber, they could sense their part in this long running drama was about to end. But how would it end? That was the question lingering in the humid air.

A great banquet was planned that evening for the emperor's return. As the low dining tables and couches were being positioned in the *triclinium* of the imperial palace, Hadrian was sitting in the inner garden of his small island palace listening to his servants unpacking the many chests he had brought with him from his travels. The curve of the inner porch was already lined with sculptures that had arrived over the years, pieces Hadrian knew well and mentally recalled the past of each. As the servants began to leave the *tablinum*, Hadrian rose stiffly from his stone bench and headed toward his favorite room, its shelves lined with volumes of ancient works and stacks of his own drawings. Most of these drawings had come to fruition and now stood in gleaming marble within the villa complex. Before he entered the study, he stopped to gaze at the life size sculpture of his Beloved in the guise of Hermes. The accuracy of the piece was due to the fact that it had been done during the youth's stay at the villa. It was a portrait of Antinous in his prime, before Eleusis, before Egypt, before the Nile. As Hadrian passed the figure, his hand reached up to run his hand over the smooth hard surface of that noble chest. But the cool stone was a cold comfort.

Both Lucius and Marcius shared the Praetorium Pavillion, yet the vastness of the structure assured that their paths would rarely, if ever, cross. But it was the distance from the imperial palaces that caused the men concern. Philosophers, libraries, and theaters were in closer proximity to the imperial presence than the emperor's two praefectii. Even old Chabrais had a suite in a section of the original palace in an area close by a private latrine as the aged tutor had requested. Lucius knew that neither the imperial palace nor the winter palace would see much of the emperor's presence. These residences would function as a stage for official business as well as guest quarters for visiting dignitaries. The royal court itself was lodged in various buildings that clustered around the imperial residences. No, the true center of the villa, the nucleus, was the small island palace that Hadrian always retreated to. It was a place of business before the youth, a temple to passion during his lifetime and a place of refuge and dismal isolation now. As the years progressed, Lucius watched as the emperor became a hardened, bitter recluse. With the glory days of the emperor all but gone, he wished for nothing more than to be released from duty and allowed to return to his family's estate, south of Rome or his birthplace in Greece.

Marcius shared the same unspoken prayer. His wish was to return to Greece with his wife and children and live out his days in peace. The rigors of Rome had worn him down, and his only desire was to leave behind both friends and enemies he had acquired over the years. As he left the Praetorium Pavillion on his way to the banquet, he caught sight of Lucius descending the stairs from the upper floor. Once again, both were surprised at the physical distance the other was from the emperor. "It seems in this glided world of Caesar's creation we are mere ornaments," Marius spoke ruefully as he waited for Lucius to reach him. "And aging ornaments at that," Lucius replied. "I don't need a clock to tell me my time is just about up." "There comes a time when a man must accept his fate," said Marius, as if to him self. "I speak of my own fate of course. In this day and age, I would not assume to know the course of any other." "As dissimilar as we are as men, our fates are like twins," replied Lucius with a smile that belied the irony of his words. Marius halted suddenly and looked unflinchingly into Lucius's eyes. "I never knew you as a man, only as a distant adversary," he said quietly. "That, it seems, is my loss." Startled by this sudden revelation, Lucius assessed the man's cool gaze before replying. "As men, we let our minds rule and not our hearts, which is usually wise. But at the end of the day, it is our heart's choices that keep us warm." His reply was cryptic, too much so perhaps, for the gruff Marius who simply grunted and then began to make his way down the tree-lined path. As the setting sun cast an amber glow on the façade of the pavilion, the two men accepted the fact that the sun was setting on their careers as well. It was with this common knowledge in mind that they walked as silent comrades through the Garden Stadium, toward the light-filled imperial palace.

Chapter Thirty-Six

Visitation and Distraction

The island palace was suddenly quieter as the last of the servants crossed the swing bridge and scurried to the tunnels that served as connecting passageways between buildings. This was the world of a people whose station in life was to be always accessible but silent and unseen. Their sudden absence told Hadrian his refuge was finally his own, yet he was not alone. Spirits floated through the lingering shadows and the many columns of the porches and atrium. As Hadrian listened from his tablinum to the many fountains that splashed into the water basin that separated him from the rest of the complex, he suddenly heard laughter and the sound of dancing feet. The sounds were of different timbres, light and dark, nimble and heavy. In the fading light, Hadrian saw, through the columns of the inner porch, the image of a woman, her dainty chiton of pale yellow flowing like faint plumes of amber smoke behind her. In her dark hair, he could see a golden circlet set with pale blue chalcedony ovals whose milky essence caught the fleeting light, while from her ears, heavy drops of the same pale stone swung from side to side in time with her swirling dance. Her graceful neck glistened with strands of pale white pearls and shimmering beads of topaz the color of a clear morning sky. Hadrian was startled by the youthful image of Sabina—the

Sabina he first knew so many years ago before she became bitter and vengeful. As he watched her dance gracefully around a slender fountain of blood-red porphyry, another shadow slipped from behind the fluted columns and joined her. In a joyful duet, they danced and swirled through the trickling water and fading light of the evening sun. Hadrian sat spellbound at the sight of the mass of black curls, the broad chest, skin that matched the creamy white pearls around Sabina's neck. It had been so long since Hadrian had seen such a look of radiance on Antinous's face; having become so used to the somber downcast gaze of the many portraits he had filled his empire with, he had forgotten the mortal he had loved.

Unable to turn away, Hadrian braced himself for the look of condemnation that was sure to appear on their faces. He had wronged them both for different reasons and with different intent. But when the dancers ceased their movement and came to rest before him, Hadrian saw a look that chilled him. It was not censure, or even anger that stared back at him but pity. Pity for the broken old man they had left behind. Suddenly, as if summoned by celestial music, the spirits took up their dance once more and floated past Hadrian, across the blue-tiled canal and the outer porch toward the red marble Faun that stood silently in the marble clad exedra. They floated through the semi-dome of the alcove and disappeared into the darkening sky, leaving Hadrian shaken and covered with sweat.

The deep clang of a bell revived the emperor's senses, and he moved slowly through the inner porch toward the rotating bridge. There, his new chamberlain stood, frozen and uncertain until he saw his master in the dim light. Accompanied by centurions with torches, the chamberlain announced the arrival of the guests at the banquet and their eagerness to pay homage to the emperor. With a sharp tug of the iron chain, Hadrian sent the bridge sailing over the still water and connected his refuge with reality. The servant moved cautiously across the bridge and followed the emperor into his bedchamber. After working his now-thinning beard into the customary curls with fragrant oils and beeswax, the chamberlain assisted Hadrian with his toga and crown of golden laurel, then lead the emperor back across the carved wooden bridge and toward the imperial palace, where the sound of silver cups filled with wine could be heard clinking over the music of flutes and lyres.

Now, safe within the villa fortress of his own design, the grief that had deadened his senses for so long began to burn away, leaving in its ash a fury and rage that seemed to sear his brain. It was the fury that burned through him in Palestina, the rage that told him how to handle Fuscus and Servianus. The pitying eyes of the spirits he had wronged forced him to face the reality that his time was short, the edge of the cliff he was headed for was coming into view, and he had so much to do before then. As he walked through the Courtyard of the Libraries toward the steps of the imperial palace, Hadrian felt a sudden sense of urgency in regards to the succession. Lucius Commodus was to be Caesar's successor, but first there was the matter of Pedanius Fuscus and Ursus Servianus to contend with. Sabina too would have been an issue had she lived. The dispatches presented to Hadrian by Urbicus and his Frumentarii since the emperor's arrival gave proof of Fuscus's movements in the city to secure his position as heir. Behind him was Servianus, pushing him, no doubt, into the right circle of senators who despised Hadrian. With confiscated documents that bore the names of Fuscus and the senators who had sided with him and signed confessions coaxed on to parchment by the Frumentarii, Hadrian was preparing his final move toward securing the succession.

Deep in thought as he walked toward the grand nymphaeum that stood before the Ionic Porch, Hadrian stopped to examine the handiwork of his Greek artisans. Architecturally designed as a copy of the great nyphaeum in Antioch, this grotto held portrayals of the great rivers of the empire in the form of bearded men surrounded by boyish nymphs. Hadrian's dark thoughts were temporarily swept away by the beauty of the rendering and the humor it portrayed. His amusement vanished as he realized the figure of the Nile bore an uncomfortable resemblance to himself. The joke, as it were, was on him. With a fleeting glance at Ophelos and the guards that accompanied them, Hadrian turned and, with a determined stride, moved on down the corridor toward the stairs that lead toward the grandeur of the imperial palace.

As they made their way down the marble pavers that wound their way through the open gardens flanked by innumerable Corinthian columns, Marcius Turbo caught sight of the small retinue and announced the arrival of the emperor. A great commotion was heard as the assembled guests rose in unison to greet their sovereign upon his entry into the tablinum. Tipsy cries of "Ave Hadrianus" filled the cavernous hall and echoed off the broad expanse of marble that covered the walls. The flickering light from the clusters of gilded oil lamps cast a golden glow on the faces of the guests and reflected off the polished marble sculptures that lined the walls. Taking his place on a couch that stood at the entrance of the rear peristyle, Hadrian dismissed an offered cup of wine and settled for spring water in a beaker of misty amber glass. As the conversation flowed around him, Hadrian studied the pattern of the floor—a dizzying array of marble rectangles and squares with lozenges of semiprecious stone. His preoccupation was interrupted by the arrival of two pages, one bearing a massive silver ewer of scented water and the other, a silver bowl with a linen cloth draped over his smooth pale arm. As he washed his hands, he studied the two kneeling youths—one slender and rosy cheeked with hair the color of chestnuts, the other blond, fair and Germanic. The golden torque around the neck of the fair-haired boy told of a noble bloodline, and his slightly reserved manner confirmed it. As Hadrian washed his hands over the bowl held by the rosy-cheeked youth, he bent his head slightly and spoke to him. "What is your name, my beautiful young Eros?" The blush of his cheeks deepened as the boy spoke in barely a whisper. "I am called Martialis, son of Dannotalos, my lord." The Latin he spoke was barely discernible, yet it did nothing to detract from the youth's obvious charms. "From your speech, I would guess you are from northern Gaul," Caesar replied with a smile. "I am, great Caesar," the youth replied and returned the emperor's smile with a timid glimmer of his own. "And you, my golden Apollo, are you from Germania?" inquired the emperor. Hadrian was pleased to see the slight haughtiness of the youth replaced with a blush. "Yes, Caesar. My people are from the Chatti region. I am Adalwin, son of Ewald." The youth could not help a flush of pride, reminding the emperor of why Germania was so difficult for Rome to keep all these years. The beauty of the youth also reminded Hadrian of a golden boy who had caused a riff between himself and his cousin Trajan years ago. *So many memories. So many mistakes.*

Despite the heavy accents that affected the two youth's Latin, Hadrian found the conversation pleasant. Even more pleasant was the fact that it kept the usual stream of favor-seeking senators and courtiers at bay. They used their invitations to the villa to extract influence and prestige from the emperor, as well as lands and wealth. On the days he was in a generous mood, the pickings were good. But recently, those days had been few. Now, as Hadrian took pleasure in the company of these two pages, handpicked by members of the court, the eyes of that court looked on expectantly. As much as he attempted to retain the *gravitas* of his station, Hadrian found himself succumbing to the charms of the two youths. Too many concerns weighed on his mind, and that mind needed a release. Motioning to the low-cushioned stools near his couch, Caesar offered the ephebes places to sit and converse. While the court and guests continued their socializing, all eyes were, at one time or another, carefully scrutinizing the emperor.

Defying the vastness of the hall and its openness to the cool night air, the heated floors of the tablinum had made the chamber stifling, and the mixture of heady perfumes of the mingling guests assaulted the senses. Hadrian looked out onto the apse garden behind him and decided to continue his conversation there. Rising from his couch, he motioned the youths to follow him onto the peristyle and to the enclosed garden. The slaves that had kept watch on the emperor's needs rushed down the flanking porches and lit braziers that sat on low pedestals ringing the courtyard. The flames flickered off the smooth faces of the youths and illuminated a magnificent sculpture of a naked Apollo, the gilded bronze bow in his left hand glistening in the firelight. It was a copy of an ancient Greek bronze Hadrian had seen in Ostia that legend said been done by the great Leochares. Hadrian had gracefully turned down the Ostian's offer of the piece, knowing full well the great pride they felt for it. Instead, he commissioned a copy from one of the many Greek artisans in the city who supplied sculptures for the wealthy there and at the resorts farther south. With that commission were the emperor's orders for where it was to be installed. Yet, as Hadrian contemplated the masterful work as it stood proudly before the granite pilasters of its garden apse, he saw a copy of beauty, not beauty itself. Just as the multitude of likenesses of Antinous he commissioned were mere copies of the perfection now vanished, this likeness, he knew, was an echo of Leochares's vision.

Hadrian turned from the sculpture's gleaming form and looked again at the youths before him. Martialis and Adalwin had left him to his contemplation and wandered off to dangle their feet in the splashing fountain. An occasional change of water pressure caused the bronze dolphins to send their spray farther at times; the surprised laughter of the youths mingled with the cascading water resulted in a concert of unrehearsed joy. But Hadrian was an observer of this emotion, not a participant. The beauty before him was a copy of what he once had, and while the youths remained preoccupied with their play, Hadrian slipped silently from the garden and past the granite columns of the side porch toward the thermae that hid his private palace from view.

As he stood before the entrance corridor of the now-darkened thermae, he became aware of the two Praetorian guards who had kept in step with him at a respectful distance since he left the garden. They took his hesitation at the entrance as a desire to enter; one of the guard's proceeded toward the porch of the frigidarium and entered, lighting with his own torch the iron torches that lined the walls along the way. The second guard followed the emperor onto the porch, and through the many rooms, he seemed to wander aimlessly through. Deep in his own memories, Hadrian took no further notice of the guards as he ran his fingers along the smooth marble walls that gleamed in the torchlight and reflected off the intricate mosaic floors. The pictorial mosaics underfoot gave way to simpler patterns in broad slabs of stone, which in turn turned to reticular and mixed patterns that echoed the use of the rooms.

All of this was to keep his mind busy. He remembered too much to allow his mind free rein and let the memories flow. Across these floors, he heard the fleet footsteps of athletic ephebe, led by a raven-haired youth. Laughter rang through these rooms as Antinous and his companions chased each other from the imperial palace to the sprawling chambers of the thermae. It was off-limits to the rest of the guests then; Hadrian had gifted the youth with the lavish building and created a private playground away from prying eyes. As he entered the *sudatio,* he saw in his mind's eye Antinous standing there in the light that poured through the oculus, scraping the cleansing oil from his broad chest and suntanned arms. The deep vermillion of the walls gave life to the chamber's frescos and set off the ruddy skin and fur of an amorous satyr and the pale flesh tones of flirtatious, frolicking youths. Antinous's laughter and chatter continued as he and his companions ran towards the frigidarium, creating waves of havoc as they plunged into the clear chilled water. From the heated pool, Hadrian would listen to the laughter continue as the youths splashed and frolicked before moving on to the caldarium, bypassing the tepidarium that Antinous always dismissed as unnecessary. The companions joined the emperor in the heated pool in a more restrained manner, flush with the chill of the cold water and their run across the delicate mosaics. Only Antinous laughingly ran to the basin and fell with a great flourish into the water and his lover's arms.

Hadrian's return to the present was brought about by the splash of water in the bathing pool that he now sat beside. It was as if he had sleep walked through memories and found himself here. The recollections were dreams, but the sound of the splash was real. Opening his eyes, the emperor saw in the torchlight a naked Adalwin wading through the tepid water, the heating fires having gone out hours ago. The youth had his back to Hadrian, his smooth round buttocks glistening in the light. A splashing sound behind him made him turn and, at the sight of the emperor, smile hesitantly. His former self-assurance gone now along with his clothing. The golden torque around his neck caught the firelight, as did the muted gold of his hair now flecked with droplets. As the glistening youth made his way toward Hadrian, he reached up to brush away a lock of hair that had fallen into his eyes. This gesture exposed the pale gold under his arms, matching the color of the damp mat of pubic hair as it came into view. Though not yet fully erect, pale flesh had begun to slowly unsheathe itself, leaving Hadrian, who remained seated, enthralled by the seductive performance the boy performed almost effortlessly.

With a sigh inaudible to the youth, Hadrian ignored his age and aches, succumbing to his desire for the radiant young god before him. Removing his tunic, he slowly entered the water and stood before the youth. Though not as hot as it would normally be, the warm water lent some relief to the emperor's stiff back and let his body relax. Reaching out to Adalwin, he pulled him close and covered the rose-colored mouth with his own. The cool reserve Adalwin had shown in the banquet hall melted in the warm water and the intense excitement he now felt. Nipping his neck playfully, Hadrian slid behind the youth and eased him toward the edge of the pool. Unsure of Adalwin's experience and his own readiness, Caesar took his time as he deftly positioned the ephebe for penetration. The youth gasped slightly as Caesar's hardness eventually found its mark and slowly entered. Holding the lithe, hard body tightly, Hadrian used his years of experience to pleasure the young Germanian. Reaching down between the youth's strong legs, he found the evidence of passion he hoped was being felt in return. Burying his face in the damp golden hair, Hadrian continued his thrusts until he heard the youth breathing sharply as he whispered the words of climax faintly in his native tongue. Hadrian felt the youth release himself in the tepid water at the same time the older man knew he could hold back no longer. Both ended the tryst gasping and slumped over the edge of the pool. Hadrian rested for a moment against the youth's smooth sturdy back before slipping backward into the basin's depths. Still catching his breath, Adalwin remained by the marble edge of the pool and hesitantly turned toward the emperor. Hadrian smiled at the youth's sudden timidity and, gliding swiftly toward him, took him in his arms and knowingly gave the reassurance the youth desired.

Soft woolen sheets had miraculously appeared, carefully folded, on a small stone bench by the entry of the caldarium. Hadrian walked to the bench and retrieved one for him self as he playfully tossed the other at the youth. Adalwin's soft laughter whispered off the high walls and broke the awkward silence. The entire exchange had been played out without a word spoken. And just as silently, Hadrian took the youth by the waist, led him from the thermae and down the path that led toward to the privacy of his small island sanctuary. A spark had been, even if briefly, rekindled. And as the swing bridge of the small circular palace swung out of reach of the court and its prying eyes, Hadrian was prepared to enjoy a rare night of unbridled contentment and dreamless sleep. Such a night was not to be.

Chapter Thirty-Seven

The New God Speaks

Thunder and lightning tore through the sky that night as the light of lamps and sacrifice poured from the windows and oculus of Apollo's temple in the villa compound. The temple priests had led a young goat from the *zooteca*, leaving the rest of the sacrifice animals to shuffle nervously in the vast hall. The priests had experienced storms before, but this one had the mark of the gods on it. As they offered the slaughtered creature as an appeasement, the smoke from the altar followed the lamplight through the blank stare of the oculus to the heavens. The uneasy priests chanted their ancient prayers and tossed spoonfuls of myrrh into the sacrificial flames while the night sky continued to defy the dark with each crackle and crash. As long as the gods refused to slumber, there would be no rest for the priests.

Not far from the temple of Apollo, the storm's reverberations were also felt in the emperor's private world. Buried as he was in the pile of plump pillows of the huge bed, Adalwin heard nothing of the storm and slept the deep sleep of youth. But at the first crash of thunder, Hadrian left his bedchamber and, after throwing on a woolen cloak, stood in the curved inner porch, gazing out through the fluted columns of the atrium. Each flash of light reflected off the still water of the canal, which in turn cast that reflection onto the gleaming marble walls and bold, polished mosaic floors of the palace. At the eastern side of the palace, in an H-shaped court, a small staircase carved in rough cut tufa and hidden behind a tall panel of travertine led to a rooftop porch covered by the palace's bronze-tiled dome. Gilt bronze grillwork filled the arched openings that looked out over the immense complex. As the lightning illuminated the vast array of marble structures, Hadrian cast his gaze over the roof of the Hall of Philosophy and the sprawling *pecile* with its many chambers, toward the double road that led to the main vestibule. There, beyond the walls of the pecile and along that road, he could barely make out the tip of a red granite obelisk that stood between two temples. The obelisk stood as his personal compass in this world of his own design. His northern star, his guiding light. It was in the *Antinoeion* that his beloved now rested, his embalmed presence enclosed in the alabaster sarcophagus, ready to be sealed within the Sanctum Sanctorum. Perhaps Antinous was ready, but Hadrian was not. As long as the sun's light revealed the contents beneath the sheet of rock crystal, Hadrian had no strength to leave the coffin in its final place of rest. All was in perfect order, except the state of his emotions.

As the lightning continued its fierce rampage across the sky, Hadrian's emotions began to become unleashed. With each crash, a roar of anguish escaped Caesar's still too human form, as if this demigod defied the gods themselves to out mourn him. *Or is this your voice my Beloved, accusing and angry, tearing the black sky with fire and shaking the world with each deafening crash?* Hadrian looked up into the darkness and breathed deeply the acid stench the lightning left behind. Each crash released another anguished roar, until the crashes became rumbles and the roars, moans of acceptance.

The peace and quietude that followed the storm was felt by nature, but not shared by the emperor. He remained in a heap on the floor of the porch, his head covered by the heavy cloak of purple wool. Slowly, he revealed himself and inhaled the clear night air. It was all like some terrible dream, except the ending of that dream was the same even when awake. Hadrian stood up and walked with unsteady steps to one of the arches. Resting his head against the cool bronze grillwork, he tried to sort out the intense emotions that had raced through him. With all that was needed to be done, in whatever time he had left, he could not afford the luxury of grief.

A slight sound behind him brought him out of his thoughts. As he turned, he saw Adalwin standing hesitantly in the shadows, his flaxen curls glowing dimly in the moonlight that caught them. There was a mixture of awe and fear in the youth's face as it peered from the heavy blanket of leopard pelts he used to shield himself from the cold autumn night. Despite the woolen cloak, Hadrian shook with cold and something more. "You shiver from the cold, my lord Caesar," Adalwin said softly, as if to a wounded animal. He approached the emperor and with one deft movement draped the blanket over his shoulders. Hadrian saw the youth wore nothing underneath, and even in the blue-white light of the moon, his pale skin glowed golden. Removing the blanket from his shoulders, Hadrian gently wrapped the youth in the leopard skin. "It is not cold that shakes me, but memories that can never be warmed," Hadrian spoke gently and took a step back to examine the beautiful youth. With the leopard skin wrapped heroically around him and the golden curls that framed his proud face, the youth was the vision of Alexander, the great Macedonian. "Why is it that I am still seduced by godlike youths?" he mused aloud. Adalwin did not answer; he was wise enough to know there was none. Keeping in mind the pride of an emperor, Adalwin resisted any solicitous impulse and simply bowed, turned back to the stairs, then disappeared. Impressed by the Germanian's courtesy and respect, Hadrian straightened up his aching body and followed the youth's descent.

As Adalwin, snug and comfortable, drifted of to sleep once again in the vast bed, Hadrian lay awake and pondered the next day's events. The sanctuary of Antinous would be consecrated, and his mummified remains would be sealed in his tomb. The idea that Hadrian would never see the face of his beloved again sent a shiver through him. The golden youth beside him stirred from his slumber, and Hadrian wrapped a reassuring arm around him. The sun was beginning to peer through the window and passed the drapery that hung heavily from the carved cedar bedposts. Reaching slowly for the hem of one of the embroidered panels, Hadrian tugged it and sent it sliding along the wooden pole, its bronze rings clattering softly. The panel blocked the rays of the rising sun and delayed for a time the oncoming morning for the sleepless emperor and his slumbering companion.

Chapter Thirty-Eight

A Man of Some Comfort

The morning did begin eventually, heralded by the sounds of the servants busily laying out the morning meal. The morning sun was higher than Hadrian had expected, meaning he had drifted off to sleep after all. Rising slowly from the deep cushions, partly to not disturb the still sleeping Adalwin, and partly because his body would not allow swiftness, Hadrian eased his way from the bed to the basin and ewer waiting on a bronze and marble table across the room. Glancing briefly at the haggard face in the polished bronze disk over the table, the emperor left the sleeping chamber for his private latrine before heading across the inner porch for the *caldarium*. There, his manservant waited to attend to his bath and dressing as two slaves arranged the last of the seasonal fruits around platters of bread and cheese. A cup of warm mead was kept steaming in the crisp air on a small bronze warmer as a glass pitcher of spring water stood nearby. Hadrian slipped through the haze that lingered over the heated bath and motioned for the mead to be brought to him. It was then that he noticed there was no provision for that evening's guest. *Dear old Ophelos would have known what to do without being told. Another piece of my past has fallen away.* The aged imperial chamberlain had been discharged from his services shortly after the return to the villa. Ophelos demurred at first, unable to accept the idea of being out of the imperial presence. But after seeing the small but luxurious suite of rooms his master had provided for him within the imperial palace, along with a servant of his own, he relented and tearfully accepted the comfort of his long overdue retirement. It was two days later that he was found dead in his sun-filled garden, seated in a comfortable chair with his favorite work of Cicero lying open on his lap.

Hadrian left his seat in the bathing pool and rubbed himself down with a linen sheet. He had intended to bring on a new man for the chamberlain position with Ophelos to instruct him. But as usual, fate had stepped in and thwarted his plan, and it appeared it would take longer than he had wished to replace the old gentleman. However, on this morning, Hadrian noticed a man amongst the servants who was slightly older than the rest. It was the same man who had escorted him from his private palace to the festivities night before. There was an assured but soothing quality to the man that appealed to the emperor. Hadrian was about to summon the man when he noticed the servant was already approaching him. With a deep bow, the man waited for the emperor to address him. "What is your name?" Hadrian asked. "I am Theos of Lydia, my lord Caesar," the man replied in a voice that familiar and sang of Greece—soft yet able to carry well in the stone clad room. "What is it that you wish to say?" Hadrian inquired. In a softer voice that was audible only between the two of them, Theos spoke in confidence. "Would my lord Caesar wish his servants to provide for his highness's companion when he awakes?" Hadrian was somewhat taken aback by the man's knowledge of the youth's presence, but then remembered the previous evening did not evolve without witnesses. The emperor approved of the man's respectful discretion as well as his silent presence. "You may direct the servants to provide for my guest when he awakes." Hadrian continued, "As you know, my chamberlain has recently passed on after many years of service. I was used to him and he with me." "The respected Ophelos was Caesar's worthy servant. I am from the same village he came from; we share the same culture and dialect. This was the reason he brought me on a few years ago to become familiar with the villa and be of service to my lord Caesar," was Theos's reply. Hadrian smiled at the continued dedication of his deceased chamberlain. Ophelos had thought ahead in order to be of service even after his own demise. "Ophelos seems to have already chosen his replacement and continues to serve me, even in death. I will respect this and give to you the position of imperial chamberlain. Make yourself his worthy successor." Theos was elated by this declaration, but took the honor in stride. *An honor, yes, but also a fearsome responsibility.* He knew, through Ophelos's reserved comments, this was not the strong, benevolent man the old chamberlain had started with. The death of the beloved had changed all that, and while the intellect had remained intact, the emperor's dark side had cast a mist of paranoia and bitterness over the court, as well as the senate itself. This was not a position for a weak man, nor a wise one for that matter. But Theos had always dreamt of an imperial position he could write proudly home about. He had been trained to be silent, efficient, and invisible when necessary. It was these attributes that drew Ophelos's interest in this one of many servants and led him to groom the man for the position he himself had been honored with for so long.

Theos had never met the emperor's beloved, the god Antinous. But he had worshiped at some of the small temples the new god shared with Apollo or Venus, and he had acquired his own small talisman—a gold portrait on a long golden chain that had cost him dearly. He had seen too the many sculptures of the young god; his naked likeness graced many of the baths throughout the empire, provoking devotion and admiration as well as lustful thoughts. It was in the temples, far from the flirtatious laughter and splashing of the baths, that Theos preferred his god. Solemn and mournful, the Antinous of the temples exuded an aura of the gods themselves. And now he was to serve the lover of the young god himself. The emperor, true. But more importantly to Theos, the mortal *erastes* of the blessed one.

Chapter Thirty-Nine

Into the Shadows

By the time Adalwin had risen and was searching the small palace for Hadrian, the emperor was long gone. The youth was surprised to be met by the palace slaves and the new chamberlain; the deep blush of his cheeks betrayed that surprise. His embarrassment was qualled by the respectful demeanor of the chamberlain as well as the slaves, and as he settled himself into the bath, he pondered the events of the previous night. As much as it had unnerved him to see the emperor in such a state, he imagined it was even more unsettling for Caesar. It was not wise for a person in the youth's station to be witness to the mortal side of an emperor. He feared for his future, yet he took comfort in the realization the reception he received from the serving staff was nothing less than respectful.

That realization was enhanced by the sight of a new set of garments that lay on a low marble bench inside the changing room. The tunic was not of the Roman style that he arrived in, but in the Greek style and of the whitest linen. As one of the slaves hurriedly assisted Adalwin with the jewel-studded fibulii that would pin the garment's shoulders, the other stood ready with a heavy himation of equally white wool with a border of acanthus leaf done in deep blue thread. As this was being done, Theos girded the youth's waist with a wide leather belt, then stepped back and cleared his throat. The confusion on the youth's face was apparent and certainly understandable. Theos explained the situation to Adalwin with a clipped, business-like instruction. "We are behind schedule, but you will be able to join the procession from the imperial palace through one of the connecting passages." "What procession am I joining and why?" an increasingly confused Adalwin replied. "The sanctification of the Antinoeion and the internment of the great god into his final resting place is today. It is a deeply solemn day, and you have been instructed by our august Caesar to participate," Theos replied as he guided the youth toward the outer porch of the palace and the waiting swing bridge that was already in place. Waiting also was Lucius Didus, much to Theos's chagrin. If the Praetorian praefectus was here, that means he was sent by the emperor, which also meant the emperor noticed the youth's absence. *How was I to know the boy would sleep so late,* thought Theos. *This is a sorry way to prove my worthiness for this position.*

The chamberlain hurried the youth across the bridge and together with Lucius and the two guards who accompanied him the small group proceeded toward the access path that would connect them to the procession from the palace already in progress. As they reached the long cypress-lined alley that lead to the Pecile, Adalwin was met by the heavy scent of incense and the sight of seven dark-skinned Egyptian priests with shaven heads, sun-bleached leather caps, and leopard skins draped over their shoulders. Set between the ivory fangs of each of the leopard's gaping mouths was a scroll of papyrus tied with a strip of red leather. Each priest carried a shallow bowl of iridescent Egyptian glass that from time to time they would raise to the sky with a deep-throated chant that would startle the birds nesting in the cypresses.

The lines of those Cypress gave way to a grove of young willows, sacred to Osiris, attempting in vain to shade the sweating priests. Behind the priests, pairs of slaves carried braziers of gilded bronze suspended from two thick poles of oak that they bore on their shoulders. The smoke from the burning embers billowed thickly as the censers swayed back and forth, their chains clicking in time with the music behind them. The music emerged from an array of ancient harps of different string counts and the bee swarm drone off flutes, pipes, and horns, each elaborate in their composition and eerie in their tone. No innovation had changed the structure of the music in over a thousand years, and the ancient spirits seemed to hover and float along with the thick smoke of the censers. Adalwin's own senses were so overwhelmed by the array of exotic sights, sounds, and smells that he failed to notice the arrival of the emperor.

Two dark-haired youths bearing splendid harps of ebony and gold and set with costly stones walked several paces behind the ancient din that filled the air. That din went suddenly quiet and in the calm that followed the clear pure voices of the boys could be heard as they sang a discussion between the gods and the living from the ancient Egyptian "Book of the Dead. "Oh great Thoth, where is the hunter?" the first began. "The hunter is in the water and shares the scepter of Anqet," replied the second. "Oh great Isis, where is the hunter?" To that question was the reply, "He glows beneath my hands as my magic makes him whole." To the next god was the question, "Oh great Anubis, where is the hunter?" The reply was heard, "The hunter is whole as I guide him to the afterlife." Then to the final ancient god, the question was, "Oh great Osiris, where is the hunter?" And in response, "The hunter travels beside me, his brother, in the forests of the afterlife." The music still remained silent except for the ebony harps of the dark-haired boys. That too ceased and the first youth sang to the new god in a clear, trembling voice, "Oh great hunter, where are you now?" The second voice replied, "I am a god in the afterlife, golden and ageless, who waits for his lover."

The priests had turned and from golden cruets poured precious oil into the braziers, sending clouds of scented smoke toward the sky. The musicians again took up their ancient tunes, and the procession continued toward the processional road. Through tear-filled eyes, Aldwin saw the gilded *fasces* of the lictors as they marched behind the *imaginifer* who carried the standard bearing the image of the emperor. Beside him marched the *aquilifer* bearing the standard of the golden eagle with outstretched wings. Behind the lictors came the twelve *signifii,* each of whom bore the standard of their individual centuria. The many silver medallions and commendations clattered noisily on their spear shafts as the sun flashed off the golden open hand that attested to each soldier's oath of loyalty. The message was clear; just as the ancient gods welcomed this new god, the power of the emperor made sure it was so among mortals.

There was a break in the procession, where Aldwin finally saw the emperor. As was typical of the Hadrian of old, he was on foot, his silver parade armor flashing from beneath his purple cloak in the thin autumn sunlight. The emperor had chosen to wear the golden diadem embedded with the costly sapphire intaglio of Hermes/ Antinous he had received from Damaris Elektra in Syracuse and set in the diadem by his now-deceased wife. The great amethyst, carved with the image of Antinous and set in a heavy gold fibula, sat securely pinned to the heavy cloak, bedded in a sea of purple. From his position beside the Germanic youth, Lucius saw the gilded face of Antinous, the embossed image peering from Caesar's silver cuirass over the quilted *subarmalis* that seemed to fit too loosely on the aged emperor. *Today will be all things Antinous*, thought Lucius as he ran his finger over the carnelian image in his ring. Lost in his own thoughts, the praefectus almost missed Caesar's sharp gaze as it flew toward him, a look of annoyance tempered by grief. Without a word, Lucius took Aldwin by the arm and directed him toward the procession. Another stop in the procession afforded Lucius and Aldwin to take their places just behind the emperor at his right. Hadrian mutely acknowledged the praefectus's salute and the Germanic youth's deep bow, then returned to his own thoughts.

Marcius Turbo watched the small drama from the corner of his eye. His bronze parade helmet, plated with silver with a gilded sphinx beneath a plume of red horsehair, had been presented to him during his time in Egypt. Its elaborate design and great immensity had become a private joke between the praefectus and the emperor. The helmet's great weight was such that Turbo rarely wore it, and while he regretted wearing it today, the honor he was showing the new god did not go unnoticed by the emperor. Yet Turbo could not help notice Lucius's elegant but sensible helmet, a silent mockery of Turbo's gilded proof of his far-reaching ambitions. But Lucius Didus's mind was not on the highly wrought helmet that obsessed his comrade. As he observed Turbo carefully watching him as they marched toward the processional road, he could not shake the feeling that a number of chapters would be closing this day, and they had not dressed just for the funeral ceremony of the beloved, but also the demise their own careers.

The emperor's behavior was becoming more and more erratic and unpredictable. The suspicious nature he always hid under a cloak of civility was coming to the surface more often and with seemingly sinister results. A number of senators had already vanished in the dark of night, and while Lucius could not believe the stories that Hadrian was personally involved in their disappearance, fear of his power made wise men cautious. The history of Rome was filled with stories of men who stood in the way of the will of emperors and lost. Lucius knew this, Marcius knew this, and with a brief glance at each other while keeping carefully in step, they both knew they knew.

As Adalwin walked alongside members of the court and the other young favorites of the nobility, he detected a heavy scent that began to compete with the exotic fragrance of the incense. He sensed it was coming from behind him, and as he turned to glance in that direction, his gaze fell on a strange old woman in extravagant but somewhat garish attire. Her hair was piled high in the latest fashion of Roman ladies of the aristocracy, the elaborate braids entwined with ropes of amethysts and pearls. Pale green peridots were paired with large amethyst cabochons, and the cluster was ringed with gold-and-pearl beading. These served as earrings suspended by gold wires, while a massive gold necklace studded with rows of the same gems weighed down the sagging flesh of her neck. Her eyes were heavily lined in black kohl in the Egyptian style, the eyelids coated with a green pigment that glistened as if wet and set off her piercing green eyes. Her face, whitened with a paste of chalk and tin oxide as was the fashion, was subjected to the bright blush of red ochre brushed liberally over her high cheeks. The skill of the woman's *cosmetae* was clearly apparent, but no amount of time or skill could conceal the ravages of age. Adalwin had made his observation through a number of furtive glances; one was simply not enough to take it all in. His second glance recorded her garment—a flowing silk himation in the deepest blue he had ever seen with a wide border heavily embroidered with gold thread and seed pearls. The shoulders of the robe were held in place with two gold fibulii studded with more amethysts and peridots that peered out from a heavy fur-lined cloak of blood red wool. The overall effect was that of an ancient Roman matron gone Egyptian, and Adalwin continued to cast glances toward her. At the fourth glance, he caught sight of an irritated emperor's steady gaze. The youth blushed deeply, the heat of that blush warming him against the sudden autumn chill. At the sight of the youth's embarrassment, Hadrian's anger subsided somewhat, and he turned back to his own thoughts.

Hadrian too had caught the scent of the woman behind him. The aroma was a perfume called Judean Balsam, and without turning to look, he knew the source. Julia Balbilla had arrived the day before and remained sequestered in her suite of rooms until the emperor called for her. He took his time in the hopes he could avoid an audience, but knowing Julia as he did, she was not one to put off for long. He was struck by how much she had aged since he had last seen her. This was not the aristocratic, lyric poet who escorted Hadrian and Sabina throughout the empire, nor mystic seer she proved herself to be at the Colossi of Memnon in Egypt. An old woman had appeared before him in the great hall of the imperial palace, skillfully painted to resemble her former self. *But not skillfully enough,* was the emperor's thought. The magnificent jewels she once wore with such elegance and grace now seemed to simply weigh her down. The lavishness of her clothes mocked her age, and the layers of cosmetics failed to hide the sallow tone of her loose and sagging skin. But her eyes. Her eyes had not dimmed or lost their brittle glitter, nor their ability to cut through the viewer to the truth. Hadrian never felt comfortable in the presence of an inquisitive Julia Balbilla. There was brilliance to her deceit, an honesty to her artifice. He always felt stripped naked before her; all his armor melted in her gaze. She wore her royal descent far more comfortably than the lavish robes that now draped limply over her ravaged frame.

It was Julia's arrival at the villa that moved Hadrian; the fact that she left the body of her friend, his wife Sabina, to be here to honor his Beloved. The wraith that now hobbled in the funeral procession was not the woman he had felt so physically moved toward so many years ago when she was married to the politician Marcus Junius Rufus. She had brazenly rebuffed his advances then, but courted them later during her second marriage to an aristocrat whose name Hadrian could never remember, despite his amazing sense of recall. It was at that time he had met his Antinous, and the importance of rest of the world seemed to vanish. The pedigree and glamour of the woman no longer held sway, but their friendship remained despite her connection to the empress. Now, the fact that Julia made the obviously strenuous journey to grace the Beloved's internment ceremony with her presence endeared her somewhat to the emperor, who chose to overlook her outlandish appearance. But as scent of Judean balsam continued to permeate the air despite the thick smoke of incense that trailed behind the priests, Hadrian looked forward to the end of this long march to the Antinoeion.

The procession turned at the corner of the pecile and came upon the double paved road that led toward the entrance arch of the Great Vestabule. But the pageantry was to end before it reached the arch; the *Temenos* that contained the temple complex was at the beginning of the thoroughfare. Here, within the pristine white marble architecture, the visitor could not help but reflect on the godly presence of Antinous. Just as a *lararium* was always placed at the entrance of a Roman house as the shrine its god, the Antinoeion was to remind visitors upon arrival that here was the god of the Villa Adriana.

Low walls of white marble lined the perimeter of the temenos and contained on three sides the courtyard of the Antinoeion, while twin sycamores flanked the entryway to the complex. It was believed twin sycamores stood at the eastern gate of heaven from which the sun god Ra appeared each morning. Willow evergreens surrounded the rectangular space that contained two small temples that faced each other; one in the Greco-Roman tradition and the other in the Roman-Egyptian. The iconic-style temple with its triangular pediment was dedicated to Antinous and Hermes; the other, with its curved pediment and roof, was devoted to

Antinous and Osiris. The Greek and Egyptian gods, both guides to the underworld, were now Antinous's constant companions. Between the two temples, an obelisk in deep pink granite soared toward the heavens and above the temple structures. The obelisk had traveled with Hadrian from Egypt and had been carved by Roman artisans upon its arrival in Rome.

Hadrian noticed with annoyance slight marks in the marble paving of the courtyard, betraying the fact that the cranes used to raise the obelisk had recently finished the installation and left just in time for the dedication. His annoyance faded as he gazed up at the great marker and read the hieroglyphic inscriptions. As he read his own words done in Egyptian symbols, the sacredness of the place began to manifest itself. On the principal side of its four surfaces, Antinous is depicted before the god Ra-Harakte, praising in lengthy passages the qualities of Hadrian and Sabina and asking the god, now spoken to as Father, to protect them. *Too late for Sabina,* thought the emperor ruefully, *but a nice diplomatic touch just the same.* As Hadrian walked toward the Osirisantinous temple, he turned to read the facing panel of the obelisk. Again, it evoked a god who, in the form of Thoth, the god of the moon as well as happiness and life, promises Antinous, "I will give you feasts for thousands of years." This was followed by the proclamation of his deification and a great mystery religion that would spread throughout the empire.

As Hadrian continued to read the Egyptian text, he felt the presence of Julia Balbilla as she stood reading the text in the slender shadow of the stone pillar. Her flair for the dramatic had not left her as he watched a soft breeze ripple the length of black gauze that now veiled her face. She sensed his stare and shifted her position slightly to return it. "An improvement over the painted mask you've chosen to wear in daylight," Hadrian remarked, tugging slightly at the thin fabric. "I wear it out of respect for the blessed eromenos. And to blur the mistakes in the hieroglyphic text," was her dry retort. Hadrian paused, then angrily ripped off the black gauze to come face-to-face with the aged gorgon. "What, in the stench of Hades, do you know of proper Egyptian texts?" he snarled at her with a fury that made her even paler under the paint. "This is Rome, not the east. As long as I can read the text, all is done well. It is the message that matters, not the linguistics." Julia stepped back and stared back at the emperor, her eyes alert and cautious. Since the death of the boy, the rational man she once knew no longer existed. And she could no long rely on an empress's friendship or status to protect her. With the memory of her battered lip in Rome still fresh in her mind, she motioned for her slave to retrieve the fallen veil as it fluttered across the marble courtyard. With her veil back in place, she bent her knee with some difficulty before the emperor, then walked slowly toward the steps of the Osirisantinous temple and seated herself in a sedan chair her slaves had carried with them. Drawing closed the curtains, she settled herself in the thick cushions and waited for the next act of the drama to unfold.

The sun had moved the shadow of the obelisk to create a path of shadow for the rest of the court to follow into the complex. The Egyptian priests proceeded toward the sanctuary of Osiris as the Greek priests made their way to the Temple of Hermes. The court milled around the courtyard, uncertain in their role as witnesses and mourners. As the chants of the priests began to fill the air, they seemed to meet at the obelisk as it continued to move its shadow like the gnomon of a sundial. The chants became louder as the priest emerged from their temples and, marching four abreast, met the emperor on the path to the small bridge that gave access over the water canal to the tomb. Hadrian followed the priests across the bridge toward the wide exedra faced with the purest marble and lined with Ionic columns of gray Egyptian granite and black Lucullian marble.

At the portal of the *Sanctum Santorum* was a great door of gilded bronze and Judean cedar inlaid with carved braids of ivory and studded with oval moonstone cabochons. Set in the center of the door was an oval medallion bearing a life-sized portrait of the golden youth carved in ivory, surrounded by a frame of precious amber. On plinths flanking the entry to the tomb were two funereal sculptures of Antinous in the guise of Osiris in pharaohic garb supporting a horizontal pediment and carved from single blocks of black marble, their darkness gleaming against the pale gray columns and walls of stark-white marble. All seemed to be as it should be. Yet as Hadrian crossed the small bridge, he noticed the niches he had designed for the tomb's façade were empty. The resting place of his beloved was still not finished as he had wished, and his anger returned. In an effort to calm himself once more, he glanced down into the rippling water of the canal and for a short time watched the lotus, the *Antinoo*, bobbing gently on lush green leaves, the deep red of their pedals absorbing the autumn sun. As the divine nature of the space released his anger, Hadrian left the warmth of the sun and entered the darkness of the tomb to be with his Beloved for the last time.

Chapter Forty

The Final Farewell

While the actual repository for the sarcophagus seemed too intimate a space, the fact was, Hadrian intended the tomb to be sealed when the ceremony was finished and Antinous was finally at rest. As he gazed at the alabaster coffin, he mourned the denial of such a masterpiece to the light of day and the eyes of mourners. But he knew too well the evil of men and the greed that would lead them to desecrate the tomb and steal the sarcophagus for their own use. Better to seal the tomb and never allow access to another human. The burial vault was the shape of a small Greek temple with four columns in front of the portico and a *naos* or cella behind it. The cella was lined with pale pink marble from Gaul, a favorite of Hadrian's, and the same stone that lined the walls of the sleeping chamber of his small palace. It was this stone that was the backdrop for the emperor's first night with his new eromenos, naked and hesitant yet with longing eyes for his new lover. But Hadrian was no longer the eager erastes from what seemed to be another lifetime ago, but the mourning Pontificus Maximus who would lead his young god into immortality.

There was little reference to Rome in this sacred plot of land. Roman society resisted Hadrian's attempts to deify his Beloved, and once again, as he did throughout his life, Hadrian turned his back on that city and its people. The design of the memorial complex was Egyptian first, then Greek—two cultures who embraced the new god and honored him to Hadrian's satisfaction. Antinous's death was believed to have ended a draught in Egypt, ensuring his god status there. And the youth was of Greek origin, a land showered by his lover with wealth and glory and inhabited by a people eager to return the honor they have been blessed with all these years. While the ancient mysticism of Egypt legitimized Antinous as god, the ancient glory of Greece sanctified it. There was, in Hadrian's mind, no need for Rome. *Rome has always needed me more than I have ever needed Rome,* thought Caesar. *I have given much, but they will not have my Beloved.*

In the light of the many oil lamps that hung from the rafters of the small temple, Hadrian peered through the thick slab of rock crystal. The mummified youth remained frighteningly intact, as the pain that tore through Hadrian could attest. The face remained fresh, the hair thick and dark, the mouth still full and lush. Beneath the transparent lid of the coffin, time stood still, and the youth truly did appear immortal. A shadow in the doorway reminded Hadrian he was not alone. Marcius Turbo remained on the portico, but Lucius Didus had entered the small temple as if unwillingly drawn to the object within. Hadrian recalled the Praetorian's devotion to the youth and the ring he now wore in his memory. His helmet gleamed in the flickering light as he held it tucked beneath his left arm, its scarlet horsehair swaying slightly with every breath. Hadrian noticed for the first time a bronze medallion embedded in Lucius's leather breastplate, a portrait of Antinous in profile. This surprising detail moved the emperor, and he looked at his praefectus standing in the shadows as if for the first time. "Come and gaze at the face of our god for the last time, Lucius Didus," Hadrian offered quietly. There was a hesitation on Lucius's part, but he knew he could not resist this one last chance to see the face that still haunted his dreams. He moved closer to the sarcophagus and let his hand run over the smooth transparent stone. The sight startled him, for the youth was still the same. Death had not sullied the beauty nor lessened its impact on the viewer. In a gesture that was pure impulse without thought, Lucius bent down and kissed the lid of the coffin. Then, as if to regain his soldierly composure, he saluted the emperor, bowed deeply and backed slowly out of the small temple. Upon reaching the portico, he turned and caught the eye of Marcius Turbo, preparing to scowl at what was sure to be a smirk from the man. But Turbo simply nodded his head in somber acknowledgment and stepped aside to let him pass.

The chanting priests of two cultures had entered and seemed to compete for the attention of their god as the mournful droning began to vibrate in the emperor's head, and the sacrificial smoke from their censers filled his lungs. Motioning for the priests to cease, Hadrian sent them to the portico and waited for the air to clear and become breathable again. As he knelt before the sarcophagus, he rested his head against the deeply carved narrative and absorbed the coolness of the alabaster. As his mind cleared, prayers began to replace the smoke as the pain of his loss renewed itself. "I offer to you my soul, charred and withered as it is," he thickly murmured, tracing the naked figure of Antinous the hunter in the stone. Sitting in a heap on the mosaic floor, he whispered prayers for forgiveness to the carved figure. Part of him wished for the tomb to be sealed with him in it, leaving him forever alone with his beloved. Yet just as this thought entered the dark corners of his mind, the horror of it sent a shudder through him. Shadows began to close in on him, and the tomb seemed to vibrate with the ancient spells of the priests. Shaken and covered with sweat, Hadrian left the tomb even more damaged than he arrived.

In his role as Pontificus, a haggard Hadrian consecrated the tomb; and in the thick smoke of burning incense, he watched as the door was sealed with lead. The aged man who left the sanctuary shocked his praefectii as well as the recently arrived commander of the Frumentarii. Publicus Urbicus stood beside Julia Balbilla's sedan chair and watched the end of the drama, bemused but concerned. Wild stories were circulating throughout Rome about the emperor's behavior, but Urbicus had never personally seen anything to lend credence to the myth. But the grief-stricken man who was crossing the narrow bridge from the small temple was not the man he had seen weeks ago. The armor was shining and pristine, his mourning robes of rare purple in perfect array. But the general air of this once fastidious man was distracted and disheveled. Hadrian had raised his hand to shield his eyes from the glaring sun as he read the inscription on the granite panel. "This god we find here, Antinous, rests in this place that stands on the property of the lord of prosperity, prince of Rome." Hadrian murmured the words he knew by heart as they traveled down the obelisk in their ancient text. As he finally reached the plinth that served as its base, he stood and stared at its restrained carvings as if unable to accept that was all to the story. The court had waited outside the boundaries of the temenos and faced the Antinoeion in silence. Hadrian gradually walked around the soaring symbol of Egypt, past the low hedges that had been hurriedly planted and through the entry toward the double road that led to the Great Vestibule.

Chapter Forty-One

The End of Two Stories

There were whispers and furtive looks as Caesar abruptly took his place in the procession that headed toward the official entrance of the villa. While the weary court walked the length of the roadway that led to the imperial palace, the priests had been left behind at the Antinoeion, keeping watch in their respective temples. As the court crowded into the great dining chamber, Hadrian made his way to the throne room followed by Marcius Turbo, Lucius Didus, Publicus Urbicus, and at a farther distance, Julia Balbilla. Theos, the royal chamberlain, met the small group beneath the soaring portal of the throne room, bowing low as they approached. Adalwin had stayed behind and was sitting forlornly in the dining chamber, unsure of his future in the court. But his connection with the emperor gave him a certain distinction, and he was treated with a cautious deference.

Hadrian took his seat on the carved wooden bench that served as his throne. Carved from oak, it had been gifted to him by the people of Athens many years ago after he had restored the Temple of Zeus at Dodoni. It was an ancient piece that legend said came from a section of a tree sacred to Zeus that had been struck by lightning and had once belonged to the great Pericles over six hundred years before. The idea that he sat in the seat of the great statesman, general, and orator had inspired Hadrian over the years. Now, he found it to be just a hard, uncomfortable place to sit. From his place in the vast throne room, the weight of all his imperial endeavors seemed to suddenly weigh down on him. His travels had brought him to thirty-eight of the empire's provinces, and his arrivals resulted in building and restorations, a prudent strengthening of existing administrative structures instilled with practical Roman virtues and considerable honor and wealth to those who appreciated the emperor's fruitful benevolence.

None of this seemed to matter at the moment. As the court assembled around the raised dais with its purple canopy and gleaming gilded eagle, Hadrian looked out at the crowd and wondered just what was going through their minds. He had poured out all he possibly could to the empire and the people of Rome, who despised him as much as he, them. But those who gathered at the Villa Adriana knew the value of being in close proximity of the imperial presence. Still, he knew his presence was becoming mercurial and arbitrary, and in their eyes, he saw they saw it too. His disheveled appearance revealed an equally disheveled psyche, and his disgust for life was apparent to all who ventured near him. He felt, with the courtiers milling about him, like a rock in a swollen stream—hard and unmoving, but wearing down. "My life has been reduced to this bleak comedy," he suddenly said aloud. The court froze. The black despair was seeping through him like blood through skin. And with that despair came a barely concealed savagery that the court learned to shield itself from. "I gained an empire, brought it to its highest glory, only to lose the one thing I cherished. Why am I still here?" The answer was as well known as the question was often heard. But none dared to give that answer. The sacrifice of the golden ephebe had assured a long, but not necessarily pleasant, life. Was it love or despair that lead to that death in the muddy waters of the Nile? As the courtiers gazed warily at the morose, decaying man in the seat of Pericles, they remained uncertain of this drama's finale.

Through the windows of the throne room, one could see the presence of Apollo was leaving for another day; the shadows he left behind were being vanquished with braziers and lamps. Shadows were not welcome here. As man-made light replaced the divine, Hadrian lifted his head and stared across the immense hall toward a figure that stood quietly in the flickering light. The flecks of quartz in the pure Parian marble shimmered in the lamplight and lent a sense of movement to the silent statue. Larger than life, the portrait of Antinous as Dionysus looked not toward the throne but through the space of the window beside it. How often Hadrian caught the youth staring far into the distance, lost in his own thoughts. Now that moment was carved in stone, making him as unapproachable now as he was in mortal form. The glided crown of ivy caught the lamplight and reflected on the upraised arm that held a gilded bronze thyrsus—a staff of giant fennel covered with ivy vines and leaves, topped with a pinecone. A divine weapon lazily sheathed in ivy. In his right hand, the figure held a high-handled kantharos of the same metal, an offering of wine no mortal would ever drink. "Pierce my heart with your staff and fill your cup with my blood. Release me and end this mockery of a life!" The words poured out thick and bitter from the old man's lips.

He had not intended those words to be shared, having forgotten for a moment the presence of the court. In an effort to regain some decorum, Hadrian motioned for Marius Turbo to approach the dais. The chamberlain had rehearsed this moment and was at the emperor's side with a packet wrapped in kidskin and a flat sheet of parchment. In a voice of commanding power that defied his age, Theos, the young Chamberlain, spoke, saying, "The Imperator Caesar Traianus Hadrianus Augustus, son of the Deified Emperor Traianus Parthicus, grandson of the deified Nerva Pontifex Maximus, Father of his country, holding the tribunician power for the twelfth time, consul for the fourth time, before the assembled court and selected senators, award a military diploma of honorable discharge, for his service to the imperial sovereign and the empire, to Marius Marcius Turbo, Praefectus of the Praetorian Guard, Military Commander in service to the Imperator Traianus and Imperator Hadrianus, as well as Proconsul of Rome, on the fourteenth day before the Ides of November . . ." The proclamation went on to list the honors and privileges presented to Turbo as well as the lands and properties to be awarded him. The bronze tablet itself was to be fixed to the wall behind the temple of the deified Augustus near the shrine of Minerva.

Turbo's head swam with the meaning of the proclamation and the sudden severing of his career. Hadrian's Pax Romana and the tranquility and wealth it provided the empire owed much to the mastery of Marcius Turbo. The terms were gracious beyond belief, but deep inside, he had hoped to eventually serve yet another emperor. He had accrued many accomplishments during his lifetime in military and political circles—accomplishments he had intended to continue promoting for even farther-reaching goals.

Retirement had never been his goal, but he was now face-to-face with it, an edict etched in bronze and soon to be posted for all of Rome to see. The provisos of his retirement included a villa at his birthplace, Epidaurus, in western Greece, plus a munificent stipend to allow for a lifestyle worthy of his achievements and service to the empire. Epidaurus was especially dear to the emperor due to its healing centers of great renown, and he had bestowed much gold into the restoring of the city's many temples. Yet for Marcius, the goal of the emperor was to position his former praefectus as far from Rome as possible without his true intent being obvious. Nevertheless, with the likelihood of a major political upheaval within Rome in the near future, perhaps it was just as well.

The proclamation was ending with an acknowledgment of Turbo as a loyal, assiduous, and vigilant man, truly worthy of his emperor's benevolence. An emperor, Marcius noticed, who at that moment was looking directly at him. Turbo regained his composure and thanked Caesar for the honors he bestowed upon him, then for what would possibly be the last time, saluted his emperor. Hadrian rose from his seat and, with an expression that revealed a complete absence of emotion, stepped down from his dais to clasp Turbo's hand with both of his own. For a moment, a discernable mixture of sorrow and resignation appeared like a shadow on the emperor's face as he stood before the man who had truly been his comrade. But the moment passed and a weary Hadrian made his way back to the dais.

As Marcius stepped back into the lengthening shadows of the throne room, the chamberlain began the salutation of another proclamation. It was Lucius Didus's turn to face the closing moments of his career, but for him, the end was a welcome sight. He witnessed the decline of the emperor's health, the mental being more frightening than the physical. He had traveled the empire in Hadrian's service and been there before and during the bright days of the golden youth as well as the blackness of the years that followed his death. Lucius was now eager to leave this realm of gloom and decay. The proposed declaration of Lucius Commodus as Hadrian's heir would come to no good end, and there were already grumblings from the senate and Roman society in general. Lucius had enough of court intrigue to last him the rest of his life. The good years ended that morning on the banks of the Nile, and they could never return.

The proclamation was coming to an end as another bronze tablet was revealed from its kidskin wrap. The mention of Antinoopolis brought Lucius out of his thoughts, and he studied more closely the parchment he had been handed. He had been given a villa in the new city of the new god, and it too came with a stipend to assure a life of privilege. Lucius looked up at the emperor as he descended the dais once again. As Hadrian clasped the man's hand with both of his, a glimmer of his old self shone through the gray haze in his eyes. "Old friend, you have been witness to so much. You had seen Antinous as a boy, then honored him with warmth and respect as a young man and my Beloved. Then . . ." His voice broke before continuing his sentence. "Then as a body caught in the nets of fishermen. You have honored his god presence with tributes on your own person; I have noticed these things, and they fill me with deep pleasure and gratitude." "Great Caesar, my life has been honored by the inclusion of your august majesty and the adored Antinous. My service is yours for as long as your life is your own." Lucius found words that had lingered in his heart for so many years. At this moment, the prospect of leaving the service of the emperor never looked less appealing. "Lucius Didus, the rest of my life's journey is short and one I must travel alone. You have done more than should be expected from one man. You will always be remembered when I reflect on the brighter moments of my life." For a moment, Hadrian's face returned to that of the man Lucius once knew and revered. The memory of those brighter moments in his life reflected in his features and erased, for that brief moment, the pain and grief that had stained them. Lucius felt the pressure of the emperor's grasp tighten for a moment, then vanish. The broken old man resurfaced and returned unsteadily to his ancient throne.

Lucius felt the gaze of Marcius Turbo as he reread the proclamation of tribute and its list of rewards. Glancing up at the man who moments ago outranked him, Lucius was surprised by the look of bemusement that stared back at him. Gone was the haughty gaze tinged with arrogance. But to Lucius's surprise, there was also not a trace of disappointment. If anything, there was the look of a man who was looking ahead toward the future. But what Marcius saw as the future was going to have to wait until the next emperor; this emperor made it clear the Praetorian's time in Rome was over. Lucius and Marcius each reached for cups of wine offered by passing slaves and, after raising them toward each other in a gesture of salute, drained them down.

The angry voice of the emperor cut short the wordless communication of both men. Julia Balbilla had been hovering around the throne during the tributes and now found her chance to approach Hadrian. She had traveled to the Villa Adriana to inform the emperor of the plans concerning the burial of Sabina and her deification. Learning she had been in contact with Ursus Servianus as well as his grandson Pedanius Fuscus to plan the funereal ceremony, Hadrian discarded the mask of civility toward her and replied to her questions with the full fury of his rank. The court froze in a mixture of fear and curiosity. But the emperor regained his composure and, after some brief words in Lucius's ear, stalked angrily from the hall, the echo of his outburst still reverberating in the air. Instead of heading toward the banquet chamber, Hadrian went to the side porch of the palace and was now walking slowly down the path toward the sanctuary of his private palace. There, he would spend the night surrounded by memories before preparing for the next day's journey to Rome.

Chapter Forty-Two

A Debt Repaid

Although the court was roused early the next morning, they were still not ahead of the emperor in preparation for the day. Hadrian had not slept much that night; his own preparations for Sabina's deification needed to be embellished beyond what he had originally planned. The ceremony Julia, Servianus, and the others conspired to present to the senate were more fitting to the late empress's status, but not what Hadrian wished for her. Now he would have to contend with an ascension and consecration of a deified Sabina, as he had done for the much more worthy Plotina. The circle of Romans who venerated Sabina were well known to Hadrian and carefully watched by the Frumentarii. They were the same who were plotting for Servianus's ascension to power upon the emperor's death, and if he should take too long to die, then Pedanius Fuscus's ascension. Neither were pleasing options for Hadrian now that he had made up his mind about Lucius Commodus. His return to Rome would be more complicated now, thanks to the meddling of Julia, his tiresome brother-in-law, and the sycophant court that goaded them on. Adalwin slept little the night before. He had spent the evening in the banquet hall waiting for the emperor's arrival, as did most of the courtiers, guests, and scholars. But Caesar never appeared, and Adalwin was left to wonder about his fate. The other pages were already gossiping about the young Germanian whose future had seemed as golden as his hair. Watching him as he sat forlorn and alone, the courtiers who had begun to fawn on him in hopes of finding favor with the emperor began to distance themselves, and the youth's influence began to diminish as the night wore on.

The arrival of Lucius Didus gave a rise of hope to Adalwin, believing the emperor would be not far behind. But Lucius was followed by the stern Praetorian Turbo, and both had the look of having had an unpleasant experience. It was Lucius that Adalwin saw coming toward him, his face kind but somewhat apologetic. After accepting a cup of wine, Lucius settled down beside the youth on the couch he had to himself for most of evening. "The emperor sends his regards and hopes you are enjoying the banquet, Adalwin." Lucius's face colored a bit, because Hadrian had not made such a statement. Lucius was told to let the youth down gently, but he was not to visit the emperor again. But there was more Caesar had told him. "I expected the emperor to arrive soon. He is well, I hope. Should I go to him?" the page spoke and rose from the couch expectantly, yet seemed to sense the change in the air. Lucius took the youth by the arm and pulled him back to his seat. "Caesar has retired to the island palace alone and wishes to remain that way. He will not be asking for you . . ." Lucius refrained from saying the word *anymore*, but the implied message was clear to Adalwin. Fighting back tears of humiliation, the boy laid back on the silk cushions and feigned interest in a silver platter of candied figs. Lucius suddenly felt protective of the youth at his moment of rejection and, sitting up slightly, took a better look at the page. The light blue of the tunic he had changed into set off the boy's golden curls and pale skin of his sturdy legs. The man recalled another fair youth in Britannia years ago when he had accompanied Hadrian there as a young centurion. The idyllic times he had shared with the young Briton ended when the emperor set his eyes on the youth. The lad willingly moved on, and Lucius was left with memories.

Lucius watched Adalwin fighting back tears as he silently toyed with the honey-drenched figs, and he gave in to his urge to take the youth in his arms to comfort him. By now, the court knew of the former praefectus's retirement and the youth's rejection by the emperor; they sat invisible to the eyes of the opportunity-seeking courtiers. Adalwin too seemed to sense he no longer mattered to this gilded crowd. He turned to look at Lucius and, in the lamplight, noticed for the first time how handsome the man was even at forty-one. He gazed questioningly at the retired soldier before finally speaking, "I am sixteen years old today, my lord praefectus. This is not how I imagined my birthday to be, but I am glad to be here with you." "I wish you good health and a bright future for your birthday," replied the man, "and please, call me Lucius. I have been retired by the emperor." "But," he added subtly, "the pension and privileges I received reflect the emperor's esteem and will serve me well at my new villa in Antinoopolis." At this, Adalwin smiled slightly as if the fates had suddenly revealed their plan, and he found that plan very pleasing. "I have always wished to see Antinoopolis," was his reply. "And so you shall," Lucius promised. Upon saying this, he sealed the promise with a kiss, the last words of the emperor still whispering in his ears. *What I stole from you in Britiannia, I replace and gift you with now. Salve Lucius Didus.*

Chapter Forty-Three

A Begrudging Tribute

Hadrian viewed arrival of the day's new sun from the gardens of the Antinoeion as he walked from the Temple of Osiris to the Temple of Hermes. He paused for a moment at the base of the obelisk and read once more the prayers that the sun slowly uncovered on the pink marble surface. He continued on to the Greek-style temple and, climbing the stairs of the podium, soon came to a stop at the devotional sculpture rendered in a pinkish white marble from Gaul. The stone was the color of Antinous's pale body in the winter, bereft of the summer sun that would tan it to a golden hue. The pink veining of the stone gave the sculpture an eerie trueness. The strength of the youth seemed to breathe in the body's portrayal, but it was the innocence of the face that was astounding. The great mane of curls seemed to push his head down and forced the deep-set eyes to greet the viewer, which at the moment was Hadrian, seated on a low giltwood bench placed before the altar and reflecting on the image of his Beloved.

He was not there long before a young priest entered silently from the portico and hesitated before beginning his daily offerings to the new god. Hadrian turned and acknowledged the priest, who bowed deeply. Unlike the Egyptian priests, the guardian of the Temple of Hermes was not exotic in the emperor's eyes. The loose *chlamys* he wore, of pure white linen, was elegant but unadorned. The priest's hair was long and thick, unlike his shaven brethren across the courtyard. Even the offerings had a familiar smell as they began to smolder over the newly lit coals. This temple instilled a peace in Hadrian, in that it represented the youth's birthplace and life, while the temple across the courtyard represented his death and deification. As he gazed through the doorway of the temple cella, Hadrian noticed the sun had begun its ascent and the day had begun in earnest. He rose and returned the bows of the priests before leaving, passing through the portal and out into the cool morning air.

The imperial barge was waiting at the dock when the emperor reached the canal, and at the sound of the centurion's *Ave Caesar*, his guards sprang to attention. He would use the barge for most of the journey, then disembark at the dock near the Porta Flaminia. There he would mount his horse and enter Rome in a manner more appropriate to the emperor of Rome. The ceremonies of deification for Sabina were to take place in the massive new Temple of Venus and Roma that had been completed that previous spring. Her clothed and anointed wax effigy had been waiting there for nearly two weeks, and it was reported, a great many citizens paid their respects daily. Hadrian was careful to have an *aureus* minted, as well as a memorial denarius struck in silver, to commemorate Sabina's ascension while a great marble relief had been carved for her consecration altar to portray the event. Hadrian was determined to wipe away the taint of rumor that surrounded her demise, and he would do so with fine art and ceremony. A number of portrait sculptures were commissioned—one for her altar in the temple of Venus and Roma and the others to accompany her installation at the still unfinished mausoleum across the Tiber.

While Sabina would be given the full honors due an empress, deep inside Hadrian resented, not the expense and lavishness of these honors, but the public's participation and acceptance of them and her deification. Hadrian's attempts to deify Antinous in the very same temple he had personally designed, funded, and built were thwarted by the senate and secretly mocked by much of the public. But he would have the final word against his wife and her supporters. As the barge left the confines of the canal and floated down the Aniene toward the Tiber, Hadrian unfolded the plans for a new temple that even now was being raised in Rome. With a sardonic smile, he ran his fingers over the innocent-looking parchment that had caused a firestorm in Rome. As with the rest of the empire, Hadrian would use his power and position to force the Roman people to accept his new god as one of their own.

Sabina's last gesture of defiance against her husband was contained in her will. She had left much of her wealth to her older half-sister Mindia Matidia, herself already an enormously wealthy woman. At the time of his betrothal to Sabina, Hadrian expressed his preference for Mindia as a wife, but Plotina would hear none of it. After the marriage, Mindia vanished from the court and occupied herself with her considerably vast landholdings in Africa, Asia Minor, and southern Italia. The brickyards Sabina had willed her half-sister were once a portion of her mother's estate that had been divided between Sabina and Mindia. Sabina's sizable estate in Velleia was left to Mindia also and, like the brickyards, formerly part of her mother's estate. These were of no interest or concern to Hadrian who still favored the older Mindia. But Sabina willed one piece of property that was a direct affront to her husband. Her mansion, nestled in the wooded slopes of the Palatine not far from the rest of her family, was willed to the family of Apollodorus, the brilliant architect who as a genius Hadrian admired but as a man he despised for years. The aged draftsman had insulted Hadrian since the time of Trajan and too often had the insolence to describe the domed buildings Hadrian favored and designed as "pumpkins." Only the man's unequaled brilliance kept him from banishment after the death of Trajan. The final insult Hadrian was willing to tolerate was Apollodorus's contemptuous remark that the seated statues within the cella of the Temple of Venus and Roma would hit their heads if they attempted to rise from their thrones. The derisive comment hit its mark and stung the already volatile emperor of Rome. Now, with a few strokes of his stylus, Hadrian confiscated the mansion and its property and banished the hapless family of Apollodorus back to his birthplace of Damascus. Just as the architect's sudden disappearance years ago ignited a blaze of speculation that the emperor had the aged man executed to put an end to their long-running feud, a story spread like Nero's fire through out Rome that the family had been executed. The flurry of rumors had barely subsided when, much to the outrage of Sabina's supporters and family, the ancient mansion was torn down and the property leveled. The new structure that was rising from the ruins was a pristine temple in the Greek style, a temple to Hadrian's obsession and the god Rome refused to accept, Antinous.

Wrapped up in his thoughts, Hadrian continued to examine the plans that lay draped over his lap, until Theos approached him to announce their arrival at the boundaries of the city. As the long panels of the purple canvas canopy snapped sharply in the autumn wind, Hadrian noticed the crowd that had gathered to catch a glimpse of their Caesar. Despite the senate's smear campaign against the emperor over the years, the populous still adored the man they credited with upholding the *Pax Romana* that ensured the secure lives they now enjoyed. As the crowd cheered at the sight of the imperial purple of the barge's enclosure, Theos assisted the emperor with buckling his silver cuirass with its gilded portrait medallion of Antinous over the thick-quilted subarmalis. As he struggled to pierce the heavy woolen cloak with the large cumbersome fibula, the chamberlain suppressed a gasp of pain as the sharp point of the fastener pricked the palm of his hand. To his horror, he noticed a trickle of blood running down the massive amethyst intaglio, blurring the engraving of the Beloved. Using the pretense of adjusting the heavy cloak, he deftly tugged a fold of the purple wool and wiped clean the placid image in the deep violet stone. Hadrian was too preoccupied with the reaction of the crowd to his arrival to notice the diminutive drama that had just occurred, literally, under his nose. After placing the golden laurel crown securely on the emperor's head, Theos stepped back and bowed deeply. As he observed Hadrian leave the shelter of the vast canvas pavilion, he saw a sickly old man suddenly transform into the emperor the people expected to see. With regal strides, he disembarked and stood on the stone pier, all the while absorbing the cries of adulation, the salutations of "Ave Hadrianus!" With his chestnut steed following behind, the reins gripped tightly by a young centurion, the emperor proceeded down the pier toward the riverbank. There, behind the forest of military standards and massive *textilis anguis* that swayed in the wind on their gilded staffs supported by able-bodied *draconarii*, Hadrian allowed himself to be hoisted with great effort onto his saddle. After regaining his dignity, he emerged from behind the banners back into public view and made his way toward the Porta Flaminia.

The crowd that greeted the emperor at the river was thin compared to the group that gathered at the gate. There was a strange energy that greeted Hadrian there, the reason for which would soon make itself known. Lucius Commodus awaited his former lover and now adopted father at the ancient gateway and was, to Hadrian's relief, on horseback and not a litter. The young man's beard glistened in the feeble sunlight, and he looked, if not robust, at least in good health. A look of concern past fleetingly over the handsome features as he greeted the emperor warmly. The time had depleted Hadrian's health, and despite his best efforts to conceal his poor condition, it showed itself to those closest to him. But now, riding side by side with Lucius on this crisp autumn day, Hadrian felt a forgotten sense of euphoria, as if for a few moments the past had embraced him and its warmth soothed the ache in his bones. The wind has swept away the smoke and stench that usually hovered over the city, and the hills shimmered in the sun like mounds of green silk in the distance. As the emperor and his adopted son made their way down the Via Flaminia, they nodded to the priests who lined the marble steps of Augustus's *Ara Pacis* with its continuous pillar of sacrificial smoke, then proceeded toward the *Arcus Hadriani* that loomed over the Via Lata. As they approached the arch, Hadrian examined the workmanship of the structure and the marble reliefs that flanked the opening. "Still unfinished," he mused aloud. "So much to do and so little time remains." Lucius glanced apprehensively toward his mentor as they approached the Quirinal Wall and advanced toward the Capitoline. Hadrian seemed to take little notice of the crowd that cheered his name, but Lucius did take notice that *his* name was never uttered. In spite of all the gold pieces Hadrian lavished on the senate and the populus, the acceptance of Lucius Ceionius Commodus Verus was still met with resistance. The senate's approval was given grudgingly—the result of gold and threats. Lucius himself could not help dread the day he would formally receive the adoption and be named as successor to the throne. Although he had served as a senator for a number of years, he had no military experience, nor the inclination or health to pursue one. He prayed daily for the continued life of the emperor—daily, fervently, desperately.

The imperial procession continued on toward the Porta Quirinal and past the gleaming grandeur of Trajan's Forum, its massive column soaring high above the marble architecture to the height of the hill behind it. Had it not been for the luminous sight of his Pantheon in the distance, Hadrian would have felt a pang of regret at the sight of his adopted father's magnificent edifice. But Hadrian left his mark all over the empire, not just in Rome. And even here he had been more than generous. As they made their way down the Sacra Via that cut through the ancient forum, the gilded roof tiles of the double temple of Venus and Roma came into view. Any regret Hadrian might have felt vanished at the glorious sight before him. Even the emperor Nerva's sprawling amphitheater just east of the temple could not dwarf its magnificence. The enormous statue of Apollo, once known as the Colossus of Nero before its features had been reconfigured, stood like a gilded beacon between the temple and Nerva's masterpiece. As Hadrian dismounted at the southern foot of the man-made knoll and climbed up to the immense gleaming sanctuary, he stood beneath the row of columns supporting the outer porch and turned to take in the view of Rome, his Rome. The Rome he had lavished with radiant temples, villas, and basilicas. The Rome that gave little in return. He honored Rome just as he was about to honor his departed wife. And neither deserved the tributes he bestowed.

Upon entering the temple, the procession wound its way to the left of the temple to enter the cellae of Roma Aeterna, the personification of the city. It was not lost on those present that the empress' wax effigy was lying in this temple and not the cellae of Venus Felix, the goddess of love. At the foot of the great, seated figure, the effigy seemed to float on a silk draped bier surrounded by a forest of white marble columns. Wrapped in blindingly white linen, the wax face and hands were modeled and painted with a realism that disturbed the emperor. The coffered half-dome ceiling of the apse glittered with gold leaf that covered the carved stone and inlays of gold-flecked glass and lapis tiles that caught the light of the many lamps, sprinkling their reflection from its great height to the image below.

The lamplight also illuminated Sabina's jewels carefully chosen before she died, with the subtle coaching of Julia. Ancient family pieces mingled with imperial regalia, combined to narrate the story of the empress's life. Hadrian observed the jewel-encrusted image with some amusement. He knew Sabina's taste, and he knew Julia's. His wife had no use for the heavy, ostentatious imperial jewelry or the heavy rings that now adorned each finger. He was also aware that Sabina's will dictated that her postmortem regalia was to be removed and presented to Julia before cremation. Turning to look at the wily old woman at the foot of the bier, Hadrian could almost hear her taking a mental inventory of the fortune covering the empress at her urging. As he began to turn away from Julia in anger, he caught the eye of Mindia Matidia. A small smile crossed her lips as they shared the same thoughts. Mindia crossed the foot of the bier behind Julia and eased her way next to the emperor. "Let old Julia get her due in gold and jewels," she whispered. "Perhaps after she's suitably weighed down, she'll go for a swim in the Tiber." A hoarse laugh escaped from Hadrian, and the cough he used to disguise it was barely convincing.

The priests had begun to drone on, and the incense was billowing toward the vaulted ceiling as Hadrian took his place on a throne of inlaid cedar. The aroma of the fragrant wood enveloped him as he settled himself against the high back and with great satisfaction marveled at the grandeur of the place. But this sense of fulfillment did little to ease the tightness in his chest or the dull throbbing in his head. *Too much incense and death,* he thought bitterly as his face took on a pallor that disturbed his chamberlain. Theos, having been observing the emperor since their arrival, knew all was not well and summoned the pages who had been readied with a ewer of spring water infused with the zest of summer lemons to refresh and bitter herbs to sharpen the senses. As one page poured the flavored water in a beaker of milky white glass, the second crushed the bitter herbs into a shallow bowl of beaten silver held by a third. The bruised aromatics cut through the sickly sweet odor of the incense and revived the emperor. With a possible disaster averted, the pages bowed and stepped away as the consecration ceremony continued on for what seemed like an eternity.

Hadrian again stood beneath the vast colonnade as the sun was turning westward and the day drew to its end. He stood like a rock in a stream as the processional participants flowed around him, down the marble steps and back onto the broad boulevard that lead to the forum of Trajan. A group of senators, led by Servianus, stood a few steps below the emperor and in a lengthy oratory declared the empress officially dead, consecrated and received into the pantheon of the gods. At the end of their dissertation, the senators joined the procession as the crowd watched Hadrian as he slowly descended the temple steps and followed the bier on foot. As he passed, soldiers handed out the newly minted *aureuii* to the people closest to the procession and tossed silver coins with the empress's portrait to the populous behind them.

The lavish procession of priests, knights, senators, and nobility led by legionnaires in full parade dress awed the Roman crowd, as did the sight of the emperor in full regalia walking quietly behind the supine image of his wife. His stoic, expressionless features were impossible to read, yet age and ill health gave him the look of a husband in mourning. Hadrian's physical presence alone seemed to dispel the rumor that he had driven Sabina to suicide. Clearly, this was a man who was suffering the loss of his wife; and in an odd release of emotion, the crowd cheered loudly for Caesar who walked silently past them. The gold and silver coins the soldiers were dispersing also helped the mood of the crowd. The portrait of the empress was a noble one, while on the reverse of the coin, the ascension of deified Sabina borne on the back of an eagle proclaimed her rightful place with the gods. For the citizens of Rome, all looked as it should, but a few still recalled the youth that once walked alongside the emperor and missed his golden presence.

There were no noble thoughts in Hadrian's mind as he mutely followed the artificial body of his wife. Urbicus had kept him well informed on the mood of the Roman people, and the Frumentarii kept an extensive dossier on the rumors the spread throughout the aristocracy and the senate, as well as the source of those rumors. At the root of all the rumors were, of course, Servianus and his grandson. The lavishness of Sabina's consecration and the public honor Hadrian lavished upon his dead wife far outshone the plans Servianus and Julia had presented to the senate, to the point that they seemed miserly in the eyes of those who had supported them. The senate had no choice but to bow to the wishes of the emperor when he presented a far more elaborate scheme for the recognition of his respected and popular wife. In a relatively short about of time, he had conjured up a magnificent posthumous portrait statue of Sabina and a grand altar for her official cremation. The grandeur of Antinous's shrine was momentarily forgotten as the emperor showed his dedication to the memory of his wife and empress. Once again, Servianus had been pushed into the shadows of the emperor and along with him went hopes of his grandson gaining favor with the senate as heir to the throne. The old man had hoped to showcase his grandson at the funeral proceeding and prove his worthiness for the crown to the people and the senate. Now, as he walked with Fuscus, lost in the crowd of lesser dignitaries, he raged inside at the thought of his plans being thwarted by a man he knew he would have to outlive.

The pain that racked Hadrian's body as he traveled the long road to the senate was mollified by the knowledge that Servianus had been slapped down once again. But the pain also instilled a darker edge to Hadrian's plans for the old man and his petulant grandson. Sabina's death had merely delayed Hadrian's final solution for this never-ending problem. After the smoke from the altars had cleared and the crowd had spent their gold and silver images of Sabina, blood would be spilled, and Gaius Servianus and Pedanius Fuscus would be out of his way forever. It was a bitter thought, but the necessity of this plan was clear. Lucius Commodus would not be safe on the throne if Servianus was allowed to survive Hadrian's death. Fuscus was of little consequence without his grandfather, but Hadrian knew the young man's death would lead to his grandfather's. And Fuscus would prove easier to eliminate than Servianus. One would lead to the other, and Hadrian's heir would be secure.

The procession passed through the Forum of Augustus and approached the Arch of Trajan with its magnificent bronze statue of that emperor in a four-horse chariot. The marble paved courtyard of the forum, for all its vastness, was proving too limited in size to contain all the mourners who had gathered there. Rows of torches lined the long porticos and illuminated the faces of a crowd expecting a brilliant oration by the emperor and a grand spectacle to surround it. Hadrian wished for nothing more than to return to the Palatine palace and find solace in the arms of *Somnus* and let the god of sleep give him respite from the exhaustion and pain he was fighting so hard against. The day had been long but was far from over. From the forum, the procession would journey to the Campus Martius for the cremation, then to the mausoleum across the Tiber. It was the knowledge that Servianus still lived and the senate was still not fully behind his choice for an heir that kept Hadrian motivated as he walked past the fluted columns of purple marble that supported the porch of the Basilica Ulpia, past the monumental Column of Trajan, and ascended the steps of the Temple of the Deified Trajan to address the crowd.

Adalwin felt little of the gravitas that filled the crowd gathered at the steps of the temple. Nor did he pay much attention to the oratory that held the crowd in rapt attention. To the Roman world, the man who addressed the masses was the emperor; but to Adalwin, he was a commanding, moody, and bitter man. The memory of his time with him had dissolved after his first night with his new lover. Caesar's forceful, demanding lovemaking had been exchanged for the gentle yet powerful passion of Lucius Didus. The former praefectus was still respected by the members of the imperial guard and was allowed to view the funerary proclamation from beneath the massive columns of grey Egyptian granite. But it was the memories flooding his mind that held Lucius's attention, and even the warm presence of his new eromenos could not erase the allure and power they held for him. When the lengthy oration had finally finished, the crowd began to separate for the emperor, court, and senators as they made their way down the broad steps and retraced their path through the forum on their way to the Campus Martius. Lucius turned to Adalwin and smiled at the beautiful, pale face that looked up at him. "Do we have to go to the campus for the rest of the funeral?"

the youth asked with a slight frown. "No. I think we've done enough of our duty for today," replied the soldier. "We need to make our way to Ostia where our ship awaits. In the morning, we leave for Antinoopolis." The prospect of the long sea journey filled the youth's eyes with an excitement that satisfied Lucius. One life was to be left behind, and another was just beginning as his heart, long silent, would learn to speak again.

Chapter Forty-Four

An Empress in Flames

Hadrian had called for his horse in order to undertake the journey to the Campus Martius with less effort and more dignity. He had dressed in the cumbersome robes of *Pontifex Maximus* with its heavily gilded *pallium* weighing heavily on his shoulders. Under the heavy wool that draped his head, the imperial diadem flashed in the light of hundreds of torches while the sapphire intaglio seemed to float in the sea of gold. With the assistance of two Praetorians, he mounted the steed and rode with rigid majesty toward the campus. The crowd had not lost its enthusiasm for the spectacle, and its outpouring of praise and tribute for both the dead empress and the emperor on horseback had not waned. From his perch on the strutting stallion, the crowd did not seem as overwhelming to Hadrian, and he could actually realize some pleasure from their adoration. As the grand monuments that housed the ashes of imperial families over the years since Augustus's time came into view, so did the *ustrinum*, the cremation site where the funeral pyre that would serve as the final resting place for Sabina's effigy boldly stood. The priests, senators, nobles, and family members gathered around the massive gilded wood structure while the musicians continued their mournful noise and the crowd kept at bay behind the walls of the campus sang their cacophony of grief and praise. The music could not drown out the unpleasant din, and the emperor was grateful when the priests began their own chants and quieted the crowd.

The massive *rogus* soared three stories high, and the gold leaf that covered its ornate carvings glittered in the torchlight. Garlands of flowers draped the pyre and wound their way through the statues of piety, modesty, and, strangely enough, marital harmony. Hadrian ruefully acknowledged the irony before him, as well as the many official gifts of respect from all corners of the empire. The practical Hadrian had designed thick wooden bowls that had been soaked in water as receptacles for the gold and silver gifts, separating the precious metals as they melted and making their retrieval orderly and secure. The *rogus* itself was a masterpiece as well as a strong retort to those who questioned the emperor's devotion to his wife.

As the fire began to take hold of the delicate wooden fretwork and silk drapery, Hadrian remembered the collection of jewelry that covered the wax figure—jewelry coveted by the manipulative Julia. In the corner of his eye, he could see the aged woman flailing her arms and wailing, held back by Sabina's sister, Mindia. To the uninformed, the antics of the old woman were born of uncontrolled grief and loss. But for those in the know, it was a fortune in jewels going up in flames that brought her to such a state. Hadrian could not help the slight smile he fought to suppress. The gods were getting in the last word as the fires took hold of the resinous mixture under the robes of the effigy and blazed toward the heavens. The thick smell of beeswax mingled in the air with the bitter scent of burning metal as the gold and silver offerings turned molten in their wooden bowls. The top tier with its gilded columns and carved-winged children came crashing down through the second tier, then landed into a pile of fiery splinters. The mourners began to nervously move away from the conflagration as the pyre roared with what was to Hadrian, all the pent-up rage Sabina had carried within her during the years of their marriage. The emperor's horse reared violently as the charred figure of a winged child fell from the platform to the ground below and rolled toward Hadrian. As the emperor steadied his steed, he recalled Sabina's bitter claim that she had aborted a child from his seed because she refused to bring his spawn into the world. Looking down at the smoldering figure, so lifelike and tragic, he found his hate for the woman was as strong now that she was dead as when she was alive. She had cheated him of an heir and boasted of it. Silently, he prayed to Pluto to open the ground and swallow the blazing tribute, sending it straight to the bowels of hades. But nothing happened. The rest of the once magnificent *rogus* blazed brightly for a while, then crashed with a great display of sparks into a smoldering pile on the stone platform below. As the roar of the blaze subsided, so did the chants of the priests and the horns and lyres of the musicians. Soon, only the crackle of burning embers could be heard as the crowd finally returned to their homes and taverns to relive the event in breathless conversations. The pageantry went far beyond the public's expectations, and the sight of the emperor still and silent upon his stallion, his crown and armor blazing in the light of the pyre, was the prevailing topic of discussion during the days that followed.

It was a weary Hadrian that pulled his horse on to the road that would lead to the Pons Aelius; its monumental span reaching across the Tiber to the mausoleum that loomed in the distance. There he would dedicate the shrine and massive altar to Sabina and officially begin the cult dedicated to the new *diva*. As he passed the temple of his mother-in-law, Matidia, that stood a ways back from the main road, he watched the litter of her daughter, Mindia Matidia, as it was carried toward the small edifice so a sacrifice of tribute could be made. Hadrian knew he too should stop to pay tribute, but in his exhaustion, he wanted only to put an end to this day, and the end was at his mausoleum.

A majority of the court took to streets that led to their respective palaces and villas, leaving the emperor with his soldiers and inner circle of courtiers. Mindia remained at the temple of her mother, and old Julia Balbilla was nowhere to be found. Hadrian found comfort in the small band of brethren who now accompanied him to Sabina's ashes. As they crossed the great stone bridge, the gilded peacocks perched proudly atop the travertine pillars supporting the metal grill fence began to catch the light of the processional torches. The apotheosis of the empress was embodied in these gilded birds as the eagle that stood proudly over the entry arch signified the ascension of the emperor. *In due time,* thought Hadrian as he gazed up at the symbol of his own demise. *In due time.*

Beyond the entrance of the central drum of the tomb, a corridor led to a large vestibule. The niche in the center axis now held a larger-than-life statue of the emperor in the heroic stance of a naked god. To the left of this vestibule was the shrine of Sabina, its marble altar gleaming in the lamplight. Hadrian entered and approached the altar to examine the newly finished relief of the empress's apotheosis. The ancient allegory was traditional at first glance, but Hadrian had included figures that he knew would shock many of the senators, had they made their way to the tomb. In the usual symbolism of the apotheosis, Hadrian is portrayed to the right, seated on a throne and gesturing upward. But his gaze is not directed toward the winged figure above him, but toward the seated figure at his feet—the figure of Antinous. Behind the emperor is a bearded figure that appeared to bear the likeness of Lucius Commodus. The portraitures were not obvious at first, but in the lamplight, they bore the uncanny resemblance to Hadrian's two beloveds. Hovering above the three figures was the winged figure of the apotheosis who bore from the funeral pyre the figure of Sabina, barely seen behind the massive wings, her head nearly hitting the stone slab above her that served as the altar table. Hadrian smiled at the final swipe at his wife; all that was due her was given, but according to his design. "She is barely in the picture, Father," whispered a voice beside him. Hadrian turned and saw Lucius's pale face in the lamplight as if for the first time. "As you were today, Lucius," replied the emperor sternly, but with a look of concern. "You left your horse and took to your litter." Lucius's presence was not as Hadrian had hoped on this auspicious day, but the thin sheet of sweat that glistened on the young man's face worried him. "I left my litter when I was able, my lord." Lucius's voice faltered. "Did you not see me?" "I saw little today," was Hadrian's terse reply. "I went as a blind man led by his servants. You are still not well?" "As well as I usually am these days. For what it's worth," was the quiet response. "Well, a drafty tomb is not the best place for us to be on a night like this. We will be here soon enough," Hadrian spoke coldly and regretted his words as soon as they left his lips. A dry, hollow laugh escaped from Lucius, followed by a cough that echoed through the massive emptiness of the tomb. Hadrian pretended not to notice the blood that stained his newly adopted son's lips. Suddenly, Lucius and his elegant garb reminded Hadrian of his wife's effigy—pale wax-covered with all too fragile finery. Hadrian changed the subject and spoke in a manner too hearty to be believed, saying, "We need the warmth of the baths tonight. Winter is well on its way." With a sudden need to get away from all things that smelled of death, the emperor returned to his horse and rode away leaving Lucius's litter far behind.

Lucius Commodus had taken the name of Lucius Aelius Verus Caesar upon becoming the adopted son and intended successor of the emperor. It had taken an enormous amount of gold and influence on Hadrian's part to persuade the senate's approval of the choice, and even now there were still rumblings among the members. Many believed Lucius, despite having been a senator, had no military experience and was a poor choice as heir. The more vocal in the senate, Servianus in particular, suggested the reason for Hadrian's choice was due to Lucius's beauty and their past relationship. But the die was cast, and now it was necessary to prove the choice was correct. Lucius, however, was not making matters easier. While his marriage to Avidia Plautia had been a public success with two sons and two daughters to prove his devotion to his wife, his true nature had not changed with marriage. His love of luxury, extravagance, and handsome young men was a constant liability and threatened to financially undo him at times. But charm and powerful connections saved him whenever the emperor would refuse to do so.

The ride to the *Domus Flavia* on the Palatine afforded Hadrian time to consider the situation of Servianus and Fuscus. The Frumentarii had reported enough activity on their part to justify the emperor's actions against the man and his grandson. For Publicus Urbicus, the time to act would be the next day before sunrise when the two aristocrats would feel the most secure. Fuscus would be thrown into the Tullianum Dungeon, to emerge after a short time, floating in the Tiber. Servianus would not be so easily disposed of, but the emperor knew that once the dead Fuscus was no longer viable for the succession, the old man would no longer see the purpose in living. Hadrian's decision was made before arriving at the palace; having been given the approval to carry out the next day's proceedings, Urbicus departed without a sound. As a weary emperor entered the palace, Theos met him at the great double doors and led him down the shining corridor to the comfort of the baths.

Late in the night, the wind shook the leafless trees as they clicked their empty limbs together. The sound was like that of the loom weights of a weaver's loom, a sound that brought Hadrian back to his childhood. Late at night, as he lay awake in his small room in the family villa, his nursemaid in the next room would weave the fleece thread she had spun that morning. The sound of the clay loom weights clicking together lulled him to sleep on those nights when his mind would not shut down. Yet that was many years ago, and the innocent vision he recalled was being replaced by the image of brittle bones tapping out a rhythm of death. Surrounded by the grandeur of his bedchamber in the Palatine palace, he longed for the simple joy of youth, when life was new, and all things seemed possible. Now, as the fates whispered reminders of his mortality in his ears, the clicking branches suddenly became the sharp sheers of those fates severing his lifeline. At that thought, the sound became the comforting image of eternal rest, and just as the sun began to peer over the horizon, Hadrian drifted off to a dreamless sleep.

Chapter Forty-Five

Clearing the Way

That same sun soon rose over the hills of Rome and turned the forums, both ancient and new, a radiant gold. The sun's reflection off the polished bronze roof tiles of the emperor's many creations seemed determined to find its way through the heavy draperies that covered the windows of the bedchamber. The golden light washed over the sleeping figure submerged in the thick bed cushions, picking out the silver that flecked the damp reddish curls of his beard. As he lay there absorbing the sun's warmth, he felt no desire to move more than was necessary to breath. The wind of the previous night had ceased, and now, all was quiet. Yet despite his desire to lay motionless, his mind began to stir and announce each task the new day would bring. As the roster of obligations continued to unroll, the emperor could hear Theos's discreet cough as he laid out the heavy wool of the imperial toga and smoothed out the gold thread of its thickly woven border. The steam from the bowl of thick porridge that would be part of the morning meal carried its scent of honey-sweetened wheat to the emperor nostrils, filling him with a sudden hunger. His lack of desire to move from his bed was replaced by the sudden need for sustenance. The warmth of an autumn morning's sunlight could not replace years of discipline and regimented order. Duty arrived on the wings of the new day, and there was no way to deny it entry.

As he slowly devoured the breakfast prepared for him, Hadrian took in the view afforded him from his expansive porch just outside the bedchamber. The clear light washed over the polished slabs of marble that clothed brick buildings and the columns that created a forest of shadows. The oaks had recently given up their brightly colored foliage and stood naked and black against white marble. The acorns from these trees were unusually large and ample this year and were being devoured by the wild boar that roamed the wooded areas, their greedy grunts echoing in the crisp air. The thick wool of his toga kept out the chilled, thin breeze that reached him, as did the felt and leather boots that wrapped his feet. *The trappings of an old man,* thought Hadrian bitterly as he picked up a piece of the soft cheese and pressed it against a chunk of still warm bread. Taking a sip of mead from a rare cup of translucent sardonyx, he studied the vessel as if for the first time. Despite its constant presence during his many years of journeying, the masterfully rendered intaglio of the Judgment of Paris never failed to arouse Hadrian's admiration for the unknown craftsman. Cradling the cup in his hands, he turned his gaze back to the panorama before him. The gardens of the vast estates clinging to the hills showed off their box hedges, skillfully clipped to resemble urns, spheres, and a menagerie of fanciful creatures. Beautiful villas inhabited by the vulgar and the greedy.

And yet, so many of those villas were empty, their owners having gone south to Naples, Baiae, or Capri. Others, mostly senators and wealthy aristocrats, simply disappeared. While Hadrian had no part in their vanishing, the rumors implicating him ran riot throughout the capital. True, his anger manifested itself more often these days, but time is short, and so was his patience. He had never been on good terms with the senate despite his constant overtures to win them over. The four senators who had been mysteriously murdered at the beginning of his reign were not of his doing, but the stain remained. The Frumentarii were constantly in touch, warning the emperor that the Jews of the city were an ongoing danger to his safety. They would never forgive him for Palestine, nor would he forgive them for their constant uprising. And of course there were the Christians, reeking of sweat and indignation as they preached their heresies in front of the sacred temples. Hadrian was tired of them all. But remembering Antinous's abhorrence at the sight of the crucified that lined the Tiber those many years ago, he had stopped the practice and was far more benevolent than they gave him credit for. But there were two his feelings of goodwill would no longer reach. And if all went to plan, they discovered their plight long before the sun had risen that day.

Even as the *princeps* of Rome sat gazing out over his city, Marius Gnaeus Pedanius Fuscus Salinator, grandson of Gaius Julius Servianus, was sitting in the damp and mold of the Tullianum Prison. He had been here before and lived to tell of it. But that was when the empress still lived and his grandfather still had power. Neither defense existed anymore. The empress was dead, and his grandfather's influence had withered since the senate, bowing to the will of Caesar, ratified the new heir apparent, Lucius Aelius. As he sat at the edge of the massive cistern, gazing twenty feet up at the morning sky that filled the hole in the roof he had been lowered through, then down at the sewerage that flowed thickly toward the Tiber, Fuscus knew his time was now finished. Pulling his fine woolen cloak up over his head to help warm his ears, he did not hear the dull click of the lock and the muffled groan of the ancient hinges as a hidden iron gate gave way to the two centurion warders who entered. Nor did he see, until it was too late, the braided silk garrote as it slipped over his head and, in the able hands of a veteran soldier, served its purpose swiftly. The body of the twenty-three-year-old went limp, and when the soldiers attempted to lift the corpse from the ledge in order to attach the rope that would lift it through the oculus of the dungeon, the lifeless body slipped from the woolen cloak and fell silently off the ledge of the cistern toward the running stream of muck below. The centurions stared down in horror as they watched the pale naked body disappear into the sewer of the Cloaca Maxima, knowing it would end up on the banks of the Tiber and, to the anger and embarrassment of the emperor, public view. The soldiers made their way through the iron gate, and as one relocked the rusted latch, the other clanked his way up the narrow steps of worn tufa leading to the upper level and from there to the ancient Forum. The second centurion caught up with the first and together with soldiers of lesser rank, they mounted their horses and made their way down the Sacra Via, past the Temple of Saturn, and toward the river. They knew the Cloaca emptied out opposite the Tiber Island, which slowed the speed of its contents, a part of which was, in this case, the body of Pedanius Fuscus. The soldiers sped past the carts that were hurrying into back alleys and enclosed courtyards in an effort to conform to the daylight curfew, quickly coming in sight of the slow-running river. Upon reaching the river, the centurions slide from their horses and stumbled down the muddy banks to the grating that enclosed the mouth of the sewer. Placed there hundreds of years earlier, the iron grate had rusted away at the waterline, leaving a gap wide enough for the corpse of a thin young nobleman. As they stood and peered into the reeking darkness, they saw the faint image of a pale mass floating toward them. The turbulent water tumbled the limp body pitilessly until it slammed into the rotting iron grate. The soldiers yanked at the iron bars that crumbled in their grasp and pulled the lifeless body up onto the bank. One of the two soldiers who remained with the horses made his way down the embankment with a woolen cloak the centurions had left behind. Wrapping Fuscus's body once again in his own cloak and tying the ends with pieces of rope they had brought with them, the centurions carried him up the embankment and tossed the corpse, without ceremony, over the rear of one of the horses. Mounting up quickly, they took the quieter back streets to the Palatine Hill and the palace of the dead empress—the Domus Augustana.

As Hadrian made his way from the Flavian palace toward the more official Domus Tiberiana, he was met by Publicus Urbicus whose face was even more dour than usual. "The situation with Pedanius Fuscus is resolved." The commander spoke firmly and with an undertone of anxiety. "It did not go quite as planned, but it is finished." Hadrian stopped short and, after waving away the courtiers who were following at a close distance, inquired tersely, "What part of your plan did not occur?" "According to my sources," replied Urbicus, "after the work had taken place, the body fell into the cistern and headed toward the Tiber. There it was recovered and brought to the Domus Augustana." Hadrian froze for a moment. The image of a lifeless body being dragged across a muddy riverbank was too much for him at this moment. Earlier that morning, he had recalled a few days before would have been the birthday of his beloved. He would have been twenty-four, too old in the eyes of society to continue to be the eromenos of an emperor. Perhaps too in the eyes of the emperor. But the memory of the beautiful boy lying on the banks of the Nile still grieved Hadrian. And the idea that another was found along the Tiber was too painful to think about. But while Antinous was alive, Fuscus had proven himself a competitor at best; at worst, an enemy. Added to that, he was the puppet of one that was much more lethal, Gaius Ursus Servianus. With the puppet gone, the puppeteer had nothing left to live for. Or so Hadrian hoped.

The emperor ordered that the body of Pedanius Fuscus be delivered to his grandfather. The official report was that the body of the emperor's grandnephew was found floating in the Tiber and, due to its status, brought to the residence of the empress. Upon receiving word of the death, the emperor commended the body into the hands of Servianus. This was the report that would be spread by the Frumentarii for public knowledge. What was not known was that even as the citizens were digesting the official report and bracing themselves for a major scandal, Servianus was being summoned to the Domus Tiberiana for a private audience with his old adversary. Servianus had barely composed himself at the loss of his grandson and heir when the summons arrived. The response, he was told, was to be swift and immediate. After dutifully serving three emperors, two as consul, one as governor of two provinces, Servianus was being summoned like a common courtier. Repressing a rage that was beginning to build inside him, the ninety-year-old old man called for his litter bearers and, wrapping his cloak tightly around his boney shoulders, stepped out into the cold light of day. Although it was clear to him what the circumstances were surrounding Fuscus's death, he would have to be diplomatic and servile when he stands before the emperor. Since the death of the Greek youth, Hadrian had become more erratic in his behavior, and his private inclinations began to cloud his judgment. Servianus had hoped to ease Fuscus into the emperor's life in any manner possible. But the golden Greek was far too beautiful to be overthrown, and once gone, too godlike to be replaced. Fuscus had neither the looks nor the allure of Antinous, and Hadrian held no interest in the youth, other than that fact he was his grandnephew. It was Lucius Commodus that Hadrian returned to. And Lucius, despite being married and a father, willingly returned to the emperor's bed. Or so went the rumors. After the death of Antinous, the gold dust in Lucius's hair and beard seemed to glitter even more brightly. Now, with the death of Fuscus, the succession of Lucius as adopted son and heir was almost completely secure. *Only I have enough power to stand in the way,* thought Servianus, *but even that may be taken away soon enough.* Despite years of service and the power that came with those years, Servianus was astute enough to know his hour had come. Just how that hour would end was the only mystery. His dreams of outliving Hadrian and seeing his grandson Fuscus on the throne were about to be snuffed out. And in a palace not far away, the glittering young man who was the reluctant reason for his defeat was just awakening from a fitful sleep.

The citizens of Rome, though charmed by the elegant, luxury-loving aristocrat, were a practical people who saw a dim future in the emperor's choice for an heir. Added to that the delicate state of his health, and Lucius Ceionius Commodus, now Lucius Aelius Caesar, seemed to be more of a liability to the empire than an asset. Impeccable breeding did little to hide the fact that, despite his tenure as praetor, consul, and senator, Lucius was ill prepared to take on the heavy mantle of *imperator* of Rome. Sycophants aside, no one could fool them selves to feel otherwise. And even the over 300 million sesterces Hadrian showered on the populace could not completely win them over. It was the army's love for their soldier emperor that kept them in agreement with the choice of heir, but for how long after his death would that last?

Chapter Forty-Six

The Removal of a Thorn

Hadrian startled the court as he strode in wearing a blinding white toga, its capacious folds and the gilt-encrusted border weighing heavily on his stooped shoulders. Lucius Caesar stood beside the gilded throne of his adopted father and struck a pose of casual elegance. He had decided to forgo the usual dusting of gold in his hair and had gone lighter than his accustomed dousing of his favorite perfume. Even after all these years and his personal relationship with Hadrian, the emperor's austere majesty still sobered the vivacious beauty into a more subdued version of himself. During the time of Antinous, Lucius had enhanced his delicate, elegant looks to no avail. As long as the exotic Greek existed, all other beauties mattered little in the eyes of the emperor. Now, despite the whispers that his adoption was Hadrian's "last insult to Rome," Lucius reveled in the reflected glory of his adopted father and his newly won title of heir. As a senator was extolling the virtues of the emperor's reign with a seemingly endless stream of superlatives, Lucius busied himself by counting the seed pearls sewn into his toga's golden embroidery. The lavishness of the garment was an affront enough for the staid senator, but the young heir's lack of attention to his oratory was beyond the pale. "Forgive me, Caesar," announced the senator as he interrupted his own discourse. "I seem to be boring our young Lucius Caesar to distraction." "Forgive my young friend, Gaius Martellus," Caesar replied as he cast his gaze irritably toward his adopted son. "He is always uncomfortable with the sound of praise . . . when it is directed toward someone other than himself." The jest was one that was worthy of Lucius himself, but the court's laughter stung and the message struck home. The rest of the proceedings held his abject attention despite their monotonous nature. It was only at the arrival of Ursus Servianus that his attention was truly captured.

By the time Servianus had arrived at the palace, the rumors of Fuscus's death had already taken hold of the city and filtered into the court itself. The vast halls of the Domus Tiberiana hummed with the excited whispers that echoed off the marble slabs adorning the walls and sailed toward the occupants on the royal dais. *The final scene in a play that's gone on much too long,* thought Hadrian, as the guards cleared out the lesser members of the court through one wing of the throne room, and a smaller contingent surrounding an elderly man entered through another. As they assembled before the throne and the two adversaries faced each other, the smell of hate prevailed. Publicus Urbicus stepped forward and at a sign from the emperor began to read off an inventory of offenses leveled at the aged senator and his grandson. When the list was finished, Hadrian handed another proclamation to the commander who, for all his years and experience, flushed slightly as he read the sentence of death for Marius Guaeus Pedanius Fuscus Salinator. When Urbicus had finished, he closed the leather folder that held the decree and returned it to the silent emperor. Servianus too was silent. What more was there to be said? Hadrian finally broke the dense hush with words barely audible to the soldiers who stood a short distance from the steps of the dais. Words that would end the grudge match he had harbored for years against the scheming old man. Leaning toward his ancient adversary, he spoke, saying, "Mark well these charges against your grandson, Servianus. They are your property too. The coup he imprudently attempted was done with your full knowledge and guidance as you and I well know. I counsel you to go home, settle your accounts, and join Fuscus as soon as possible. I expect the next full moon to find you only as ash." The old man glared at the emperor with all the detestation he had concealed over the years. With Fuscus dead, he had nothing left but a life without purpose, a life that had proved itself far too lengthy. Finally, from his smoldering anger, a curse spat from his lips, "My only prayer for you is that your life will be an agony that lingers so long, you will pray for a death unwilling to take you." Hadrian showed no emotion at these words, his face a mask of stoic determination and bitter resolve. With a wave of his hand, he dismissed his brother-in-law with the knowledge they would never meet again.

The torches along the pathway illuminated the breastplates of the Praetorians as they escorted the *princeps* past the massive arched walls supporting the Domus Tiberiana on to the Domus Flavia that loomed in the distance. Darkness was falling earlier as winter approached, and below the hills, the masses of citizens could be heard heading in litters and on foot toward the baths. Hadrian too was looking forward to soaking in the steaming warmth of his own bath and perhaps, not alone. He looked forward to the lively company of Lucius Aelius to help him push aside the memories of the problems he faced that day. But then, Lucius himself was a problem. The young man had become more petulant than charming, with his own ill health chipping away at the bright sparkle of youth. But imperial prerogative prevailed, at an enormous expense but also great satisfaction. "Yes, what is left of Lucius's charms will suffice for my comfort this evening," mused the emperor aloud without realizing. "My lord?" replied one of the Praetorian guards who had kept within reach of his ageing master, ready to prevent a sudden stumble. "What? Nothing. Nothing at all," Hadrian replied dismissively. *With every day come more habits of an old man,* he thought with bitter rancor. As the emperor and his retinue made their way up the southern crest of the Palatine toward the Flavian, he stopped to look down at the fountains and stadium attached to the Domus Augustana, remembering the woman who once lived there. He recalled a day when he and Antinous paid a visit to the empress and found her sitting, not in the shadows of her musty rooms, but in the garden surrounded by the sparkle and music of the fountains. Musicians attended her and her court while a sizable table was draped with layers of silk and set with heirloom gold plate and delicate glass goblets. The court chatted and laughed, and occasionally above their merriment, Sabina's own bright, brittle laugh could be heard. Hadrian never cared much for her laugh and did little to encourage it. But that day, something was different. Suddenly uncomfortable, he took Antinous by the arm and turned to go, but the youth resisted and took from his tunic a package wrapped in pale kidskin and tied with a fine silk cord. He handed it to the emperor. "It is the empress's birthday, Hadrian," the youth murmured. His eyes were wary, searching his lover's for a sign of displeasure at the trick played on him. "I have never gifted my wife for her birthday and have no intention of starting now," Hadrian replied with a terseness he could not help. Nor could he help but smile at the youth's gentle ruse and the kindness that provoked it. *So true to his nature.* "However," he continued, "you may present it to her. It will be better received coming from you." Together, they stepped into the sunlight of the garden as the music abruptly ceased and the court was rendered speechless. The empress rose and, with frozen features, bowed gracefully to her husband. "Long life and health, Sabina," Hadrian greeted his wife, not unkindly. His salutation actually had a ring of truth to it. "Long life and health, *Augusta*," was Antinous's greeting after the empress nodded to him in recognition. "You are, as always, most welcome here, Antinous." She was tempted to add, "More so than my husband"; however, propriety forbade it. But more importantly for Sabina, it would be an inexcusable affront to the beautiful youth before her. The folds of his linen tunic did little to hide the athletic chest and sturdy arms of the young man. And his face was, as usual, that of a god just roused from slumber. Antinous presented the wrapped packet to the empress, which she accepted with a gracious gesture, yet also a slightly girlish eagerness. With nimble fingers used to the task of embroidery, she unraveled the silken cord and found inside a thick chain of finely woven gold. From the chain, clasped by silver lion's paws, hung a gold medallion commemorating her ascension to the supreme position of Augusta. The medallion was surrounded by cabochons of moonstones and blue topaz, Sabina's favorite gems. "I had it crafted for you in Alexandria when we were there this past spring," Antinous explained. "I've carried it with me since." *No mention of whom he had intended to have it presented by,* thought Hadrian. *Just as well. It would ruin the pleasure of the gift for her.* Yet Hadrian saw immediately the significance of the object to Sabina and was taken by benevolent nature of his beloved's choice. There was a familiarity here that was thought provoking, but the emperor put it aside and chose instead to enjoy the moment.

The musicians had resumed their playing as Sabina gestured to the marble garden seats near her own, having shooed away two ladies in waiting who wisely kept hidden their indignance. As the three sat in the dappled sunlight, Hadrian was both annoyed and beguiled by the exchange of pleasantries between Sabina and Antinous. Again, he heard her laugh, this time slightly deeper and somewhat flirtatious. Her bracelets clinked in time to the fluid gestures of her hands as she spoke to the youth who gave her his undivided attention. Occasionally, Antinous would turn to include Hadrian in the conversation, which he would respond to politely and with as much interest he could muster. Despite himself, he found the afternoon a rare delight.

Later on, Antinous had gone to exercise his dogs around the stadium that was visible form the garden and attached to the Domus. His laughter, combined with the joyous barking of his tireless greyhounds, filled the air; and for a few golden moments, husband and wife experienced the joy of watching the one perfect thing they shared in their life, golden moments they would never have known otherwise. Hadrian pondered those memories now as he gazed down at the fountain garden, desolate and abandoned now in the rising moonlight.

"Stubborness and pride," he said quietly into the darkness. "Love has been wasted on me." He stood for a moment more and watched the moon's reflection play on the surface of the great reservoir beyond the Domus Tiberiana. As he turned and faced the Capitoline Hill and its gleaming temples, there was a hollow feeling inside that Caesar could not quite identify. Great pain, both physical and emotional, had rendered him immobile for a moment, until a chilling emptiness replaced it. It was the sound of the Praetorian's heavy boots shuffling in the night's chill that brought him back to the present; he ended the torment of his memories, ascended the steps of the palace, and was greeted by Theos his chamberlain who stood vigilantly in the doorway.

Chapter Forty-Seven

Duty after Pleasure

The salutation of "Viva Imperator" could be heard in the peristyle courtyard below as the Praetorian guard maneuvered into their evening formation. *Viva indeed,* thought Hadrian. *And if Servianus's curse has any merit, it will be a viva filled with pain.* Theos assisted the emperor with the removal of the bulky toga after he had handed the royal regalia of diadem and scepter to the knight of the treasury. After the voluminous robe was removed, the heavy cuirass was unstrapped and the thick subarmalis detached and removed, Hadrian peeled off his sweat-soaked tunic and reached for a cup of wine on a nearby table. As he did so, his imperial signet slipped off his finger, and after clattering on the bronze surface, fell with a thud to the mosaic floor. As he stooped down to retrieve the ring, Theos noticed a thin cord of wool wrapped around the inner band. Caesar had been noticeably losing weight since the death of the empress, and the ring had slipped off during a number of occasions. The strip of wool was no longer enough to secure the ring, and Theos made a mental note to discreetly replace it with another.

Hadrian was too exhausted to care about the ring as he watched his chamberlain reverently place the object on the table. After a servant wrapped a large cotton sheet around the emperor, Hadrian made his way down the broad staircase toward the cavernous bath, his privacy there ensured by his imperial household. As he left the bedchamber, Hadrian alerted Theos to the possibility of a visit by Lucius Aelius, then he disappeared, in the company of a slave, through the forest of marble columns. Along the corridors, his reflection haunted him in the highly polished walls and pillars, a legacy of Tiberius himself. Unlike the paranoid Tiberius, Hadrian was an emperor with no fear of death and therefore no desire to know what was lurking in every corner. All he saw was the specter of his failing self, a specter that slowly dissipated as he reached the caldarium, the steam of which blurred the offending reflections. Hadrian slid the cotton sheet from his shoulders and let it fall to the rim of the sunken pool. Steadying himself on the arm of his slave, Hadrian lowered himself into the soothing waters, grateful for what he had come to regard in his later years as the greatest of Roman inventions. Set in the center of the enormous rectangular chamber, an elongated, oval basin was bisected by a circular bulge that held in its center a massive, triple-tiered fountain, its circular bronze bowls rising from the steaming waters. On the backs of dolphins, which appeared more irritated than ferocious, plump, gold-winged boys in pink marble tormented the gray granite beasts as they doused each other with jets of water. The gilding on the bronze and the riotous behavior of the children would have been dizzying had it not been for the steam from the pool, which served to soften the effect.

Hadrian turned and rested his arms on the thick marble rim of the basin and set his gaze on the more soothing row of double columns that supported the shallow peristyle surrounding the chamber.

Their pale marble shafts and the lyrical scrolls of their Ionic capitals were a calming contrast to the overblown monstrosity in the pool and much closer to Hadrian's taste. But then, he thought with some satisfaction, they were his own contribution to this cavernous chamber. Replacing the blank, windowless walls that were once there, this addition had cost him a fortune, but the peristyle transformed the atmosphere of the caldarium from Roman to Greek and was well worth the expense. The view of his own design was soothing to Hadrian, and as he sat on the stone ledge beneath the steaming water, it lulled him to a state of semi sleep.

The emperor woke to the sound of a lyre that echoed softly throughout the chamber. In Caesar's semiconsciousness, this resonance of the lyre, together with the floating clouds of vapor that filled the vast space, created an odd sense of peace and confusion. "Have I finally died?" he whispered to himself, a whisper that carried though the thick mist and reached the source of the music. "Ave Caesar," replied a soft voice in a Latin that was tinged with a slight Greek inflection. "I hope my playing did not disturb you, sire." Through the haze, Hadrian could barely make out the form of a youth seated a stone bench not far from the steaming pool. "I thought I had died, and a winged god was here to lead me to the heights of Olympus or," he added with some trepidation, "the lowest depths of *Tartarus*. "Tartaros," replied the misty figure, the Greek pronunciation slipping more easily from his tongue, "is for those who must be punished. You have done nothing to deserve such an end. And besides, you seem to have suffered enough." Hadrian gripped the side of the pool and whispered, "Then I *have* died, and you are here to take me to my

Beloved." "No, Caesar, I have no wings to make that happen. Alas, I am only a simple page with a lyre, sent to please you in any way I can." Quietly, the figure rose, emerged from the mist, and knelt before the emperor. Hadrian saw the youth was sandal-less and, due to the heat, had untied the upper laces of his chiton revealing a smooth, bare torso. The youth's garment was shorter than the customary knee length and revealed thighs more suited to an athlete than a musician. His ample head of hair was thick and the color of chestnuts, a long braided lock revealing his youthful status. Around his neck, a golden bulla hung from a braided leather cord and glistened in the lamplight. The finely worked charm was a subtle mark of distinction, the sign of a highborn youth. Hadrian walked up the steps of the pool, sat on its edge, and gazed at the glistening face of the boy, as the youth looked questioningly back. "What is your name, lad?" he asked, suddenly tired and overwhelmed by such beauty. "I am Adelphos, my lord Caesar," the youth replied, suddenly shy at the sight of the naked emperor. "Adelphos. That means 'sibling born in the same womb' in your native tongue," Hadrian replied. "Have you a twin?" "I did, my lord. He died, along with my parents, nearly a year ago." A shadow passed across the pale features as the youth turned away, leading Hadrian to regret his question. Taking the youth's chin in his hand, Hadrian turned the boy's face toward him and saw the tears that were beginning to fill the dark, almond-shaped eyes. *Almond-shaped dark eyes filled with tears. How often did I witness those in the past and ignore their meaning?* A sudden stab of grief and regret tore through Hadrian's gut as he turned away to keep from frightening the youth. For a moment, he felt he would lose consciousness as he fought to retain control of his emotions. Age was weakening the defenses that had served him well in the past.

Forcing his mind to clear, the pain had subsided, and Hadrian was able to face the youth again. "Come, Adelphos," Caesar spoke with a forced levity that masked both his ache and that of the beautiful youth at his side. "Join me in the bath, and we will let our sorrows float way on clouds of steam." As he walked back into the soothing waters, he watched Adelphos slip out of the rest of his chiton, leaving it in a linen heap along the water's edge. With a grace that needed no wings, he crouched then thrust himself with one fluid motion into the clear, warm liquid, creating a splash and ripple that reached the central fountain and sprayed the marble buttocks of the frolicking boys.

The *princeps* of Rome silently watched the young Greek swim the length of the deep basin, stopping only to examine the gaping mouths of the granite dolphins. Climbing on to the back of one of the beasts, Adelphos's fair skin shone brighter than the marble boy beside him, as the fountain anointed him with water. Suddenly, the youth stopped his playful antics and, after a moment's hesitation, slide off the fountain's base and walked slowly toward the emperor. Hadrian had totally submerged himself to wash away the sweat from his face and hair and, upon reemerging, wiped his eyes and found himself face-to-face with the youth. The water had straightened Adelphos's loose curls, and his dark hair clung limply to his slender neck. Droplets of water clung to his thick lashes and then flew away with every blink of his inquisitive eyes. The youth's mouth had escaped Hadrian's notice at first—not as full as his Beloved's, but still the seductive pout, the tender stain of pomegranate. The exhaustion that had threatened to shut down his body not that long ago was slowly being replaced by something more familiar, more welcome. In a gesture he had become so used to with another Greek youth, he reached out and drew this one to him, tasting his mouth without asking. As Adelphos gave no resistance to his advances, a question whispered in Hadrian's mind. *Where did the youth come from, and how was he allowed entry to the palace?* As they made their way to the steps leading from the bath, Hadrian posed the question to the youth. Unfazed by the query, the Greek youth answered simply, "I was sent by my lord, Lucius Aelius Caesar. I was instructed to please you as once he did." He hesitated for a moment before adding, "I hope I am pleasing to you, Majesty." Hadrian smiled ruefully at this small attempt at modesty. *Surely this youth has more suitors in pursuit than hounds after a stag.* But he simply smiled and nodded. After drying himself, Adelphos slipped on his tunic, leaving the upper section untied and draped around his waist. As he retrieved his sandals and lyre, the emperor wrapped the sizeable cotton sheet around himself as a makeshift tunic and, after gesturing the youth to follow, made his way to the bedchamber.

As always, Theos was waiting for his master at the entrance to the imperial suite. The servants had just finished laying out a meal, which was, Hadrian noticed with amusement, for two. It was Lucius, not Theos who would be this presumptuous. "Was it Lucius Aelius Caesar who directed all this, Theos?" Hadrian inquired with feigned annoyance. The chamberlain had followed the emperor and the young Greek into the sitting room that often served as Hadrian's private dining room. "Yes, my Caesar. He arrived here with his servants and assured me you would welcome the meal and be pleased. It is, in my humble opinion, beautifully prepared, Majesty." With this statement, the chamberlain bowed in anticipation of the emperor's reply. "It *is* well done. Thank you, Theos. I'll have no more need for you this evening." The chamberlain withdrew, drawing the quilted silk draperies that discourage both drafts and gossip and leaving the two Praetorian guards to protect the night.

The meal was deceptively simple, contrary to Lucius's usual flair for the dramatic. On gilt trays, nestled between mounds of plump grapes and even plumper figs, sat small fragrant venison pies wrapped in a buttery, flakey pastry and ground, seasoned lamb contained in bite-sized packages of blanched lettuce leaves. A true Lucius touch was the glass *tazza* bearing translucent green grapes glistening with gold dust. In all, the contents of the trays were created to be eaten effortlessly with one hand. When Hadrian had questioned the same presentation years earlier, Lucius's coy reply was simple: *This is a meal meant to be eaten between kisses.* Unlike Antinous, Lucius had the effervescence of a courtesan and the expensive taste to match. Antinous was the earthy hunter, as solid as the eastern land that bore him. Lucius was the height of western decadence. Antinous carried a golden aura within him, while Lucius sprinkled gold in his hair. Yet Hadrian had loved them both for their own worth. *I've lost one and fear the other will follow soon,* thought Hadrian as he surveyed the small feast before him. Shaking off the gloom of these thoughts, he focused on the lad beside him who examined the food with a hungry curiosity.

The meal had been placed on a contraption Hadrian had invented years earlier for his private palace at the Villa Adriana. With a slight push, the table glided silently on its leather-wrapped wheels from the anteroom to the bedchamber and came to rest beside the bed. With a smile, Caesar took his young Greekling by the hand and followed the table's path.

The elegant respite prepared under Lucius's direction turned out to be more of a sedative than an aphrodisiac. Upon consuming a healthy amount of the small pies and lamb wraps, some fruit, figs, cheese, and a cup of wine, Adelphos curled up beside the emperor; the soft growl of a snore signaled sleep had come to the ephebe. Hadrian smiled softly at the slumbering figure pressed against his body, grateful for warmth and comfort of the beautiful youth as well as the rest he now afforded him. In the flickering light of the brazier, Hadrian watched the shadows that danced hypnotically across the polished walls. Soon the purr of his companion and the crackle of the burning embers lulled the emperor to a gentle sleep. For a brief moment, the fates took pity on the ailing man and gave him a state of peace worthy of a Caesar.

A sharp sound jolted the emperor awake, and his eyes followed the naked figure that moved silently in the room. Adelphos was stirring the dying embers with an iron poker and adding coals to the dwindling pile. Sitting up in the sprawling bed, Hadrian watched the youth as he brought life to the sputtering fire and sat back to contemplate his success. Hadrian was about to commend the youth on his skill, when a spark flew from the brazier and flew toward the boy. With a yelp, the youth leapt from his place on the floor and landed on the bed with thud. Startled, Hadrian went quickly to Adelphos's aid, but he could see a small mark already forming on the boy's stomach where the spark had made contact. "You can afford a small imperfection, little one," he said in an attempt to comfort him. "It will disappear in time." And with a kiss near the point of damage, Hadrian pulled the youth back toward the many pillows, holding him closely as the fire of his own desire began to burn within him. Adelphos smiled as the pain of the burn was forgotten, and the original purpose of his visit was about to come to fruition.

The youth was certainly experienced, yet his submission was hesitant, gentle. He did not show off his skills but waited for them to be called upon, and upon doing so, gave them willingly. It was not the athletic romp of most youths his age, but a dance of exploration that Hadrian found intoxicatingly innocent. Their lovemaking lasted longer than Hadrian had expected, and he was left pleasantly drained of desire but not exhausted. Adelphos's gentle nature continued as they remained entangled, and he kissed the many scars on Hadrian's hands and arms. A chill had set in as the brazier began to die down once again. But not one to tempt fate twice, Hadrian prevented the youth from stoking the fire and instead reached for the thick blanket of bear fur lined with soft crimson wool. The massive pelt, filled with memories of his travels in the northern provinces, evoked a special comfort for the aged hunter. The familiar scent, together with the warm, supple body pressed against him, sent him once again into the blessed realm of sleep.

Morning arrived at the appointed time, but what little sunlight it brought mercifully remained behind the heavy curtains that covered the windows of the royal bedchamber. The weather was typical of the beginning of December—cold, gray, and dreary. Snug within the covers of heavy silk, wool, and fur, the two continued to indulge in sleep. It was Hadrian who woke first; his mind alert, then his body. The young Greek beside him continued to purr softly; the scent of his skin was strong and earthy yet sweet. As Hadrian wrapped his arm around the slender waist and pulled the youth closer to him, his hardness pressed against the full mounds of flesh that had filled him with pleasure the night before. The soft purring ceased as a hand reached over to pull Hadrian closer. Raising his leg slightly beneath the covers, Adelphos guided the rigid flesh to the place they both desired it to be. Hadrian entered slowly and with deliberate strokes took control of the youth who gasped and moaned as Caesar brought him to a bursting climax. Hadrian continued until he too was released, and for a time, both remained still and silent.

Despite the unaccustomed joy he was feeling, Hadrian knew it was time to leave this warm paradise and face the day. Rome would not excuse this indulgence for long, and just outside, at the foot of the Palatine, the city awaited his arrival. As he slipped from out of the covers, the morning chill was bracing but welcome. It cleared his mind as he began to rehearse the day's events. Soon, he would be standing on the Rosta Augustus before all of Rome to formally accept the recognition of the citizens and the senate for his son and heir, Lucius Aelius Caesar.

Chapter Forty-Eight

The Lamp Still Blazes

Peering out of the window from behind the heavy silk, Hadrian scowled at the sunless sky that greeted him. The cloud cover was thick now and forbidding, defying the sun's weak attempt to break through. With a quick prayer to the gods, he strode across the vast marble floor to the room beyond, leaving the joy of his previous night behind. Theos was waiting for the emperor as he entered the anteroom; he hid his surprise at the princeps's healthy stride, and he was grateful to observe a healthy appetite. The chamberlain had offered the usual morning meal of bread, cheese, fruit, and a vegetable broth that today contained small shreds of poached chicken. Caesar usually ignored all except the broth and a small piece of bread. But this morning, he tore hungrily at the crusty loaf and devoured the soft steaming middle, then reached for the cheese and broth at the same time, devouring the creamy chunk and downing the bowl of broth in a few gulps. Theos stood transfixed at the sight of the man who, only yesterday, seemed so close to death. Hadrian looked up from his bowl and saw the glistening eyes of his faithful chamberlain. The show of emotion unnerved him, and he spoke jokingly, "There used to be fresh sausage in the broth at one time. Are we economizing, Theos?" The chamberlain failed to grasp the humor at first and went slightly pale, before noticing the slight smile on Caesar's face. "If you promise to eat as well in the future as you have today, sire, I assure you there will be fresh sausage from now on," replied Theos with a smile of his own. "I will hold you to that promise," responded the emperor with a slight raise of his brow; then added, "You have become a great comfort to me, Theos." With that, he scooped up a handful of blood-red grapes and a cup of honeyed wine, then headed for the treasury chamber where his imperial robes and regalia were waiting.

The chamberlain stood still for a moment as he watched the emperor disappear among the many polished columns, then turned at a sound behind him. Wrapped in a massive bear pelt, the sturdy pale youth with tousled hair from the night before stood hesitantly in the doorway behind him. Theos bowed slightly and gestured to the table laden with the morning meal. "Caesar has already invaded the table and created havoc," the chamberlain said with a gentle smile, "but I will have more brought to replace what he has eaten. I'm sure Caesar's young guest has the appetite of an athlete after such a night . . ." His voice trailed off, shocked at his own impertinence. Adelphos blushed slightly and thanked the man. "I see plenty there to make for an ample meal, there is no need to call for more. Allow me to dress first, then I will accept your offer." Again, the chamberlain bowed slightly, then left the chamber to resume his duties.

As Hadrian prepared for the day's events, three scribes took dictation for proclamations, the consecration of an altar to the legionaries and auxiliaries who had perished in Palestine, and the acceptance speech for Lucius after the recognition of the senate.

The day would be difficult and filled with political intrigue. But the one possibility Hadrian had braced himself for never happened. The deaths of Fuscus and Servianus caused a ripple from the senate to the back alleys of Rome, but little else. The retribution he had expected failed to materialize; even Urbicus seemed baffled by the lack of response from the powerful families who had once supported Servianus's ill-fated coup attempt. His Frumentarii scoured the city for any growth of dissention, only to find a frozen silence. The might and severity of the emperor, both real and imagined, silenced the citizens of Rome. Imperial prerogative prevailed. However, Caesar saw little to trust in the populous. All his generosity in both the private and public realm amounted to little more than a sullen respect. Rumors of his capriciousness, cruelties, and even assassinations filled the reports that littered his desk. He had gifted Rome with temples, monuments, and schools of learning, yet they remained petty and bitter. He was done. Today, the brutal might of Imperator Caesar Traianus Hadrianus Augustus would be paraded down the Sacra Via and flow to the very steps of the senate.

The proclamations were to be presented in the *Aula Regia* of the Domus Flavia, much to Hadrian's relief. His euphoric burst of energy earlier in the morning had dissipated; the rush of adrenaline bowed under the weight of age. His body ached as he made his way through the peristyle courtyard toward the audience hall, the heaviness of the embroidery on his toga picta, as well as the burden of the heavy purple wool itself, competed with the circlet of golden laurel leaves, its sharp points occasionally poking his scalp through his thinning hair. The ivory scepter with its heavy gold eagle lay cradled in his left arm, and as he walked, he tapped the reddish-gold oricalcum handgrip impatiently with his imperial signet. But his face betrayed no emotion, and the tapping of his ring was deadened by the strip of woolen cord Theos had earlier wound around the back of the ring to prevent it from slipping off Caesar's finger again. Uncomfortable and tired, an irritable Hadrian was in no mood for conflict and dissent. This was not a portentous way to begin what promised to be a very long day.

The procession made its way through the lofty portals of the royal chamber and past the walls of marble veneer with their vast array of columns, the Phygian marble shafts reflected in the polished stone slabs. The gilding on the Corinthian capitals that crowned the forest of columns caught what little sunlight that made its way through the clearstory windows into the vast hall. The path to the apse that loomed in the distance seemed endless to the emperor as he gazed at the painted frescos and coffered ceiling studded with rosettes of gilded bronze. The dais could finally be seen, and after ascending the three broad steps, Hadrian settled gratefully into the thick cushions of the ivory inlaid throne. The lectors bearing gilded fascii lined up on either side of the dais as the Praetorian guard assembled in a semicircle along the curved walls of the apse. From his throne, Hadrian looked out over a sea of marble and porphyry of every known color as the court and guests made their way past endless niches filled with bronzes of gods and heroes. The palatial hall was designed to impress, and the faces of the guests confirmed the architect's success. Rabirius worked wonders for the emperor Flavious Domitianus, and even after the Aula Regia was filled with the entire court, toga-clad senators, knights, rich merchants, and visitors from every corner of the realm, its immense scale seemed undiminished.

The first guest to be presented was Hadrian's distinguished and wealthy friend, Herodes Atticus. The prefect had arrived from the Asian provinces earlier that day and had hoped to gain access to his friend and mentor in a more private setting. But as he looked up at the age-worn man on the canopied dais, he knew this was not the same friend he had known during their glory years in Greece. So many years had passed since a young man stood tongue-tied before the new emperor, unable to announce his ascension. As he approached the throne, Herodes searched for a look of recognition on the emperor's face. The eyes seemed to be that of a statue—sightless, empty, an ivory Zeus in an ancient temple. Suddenly, Hadrian seemed to return from his inner thoughts, and those same eyes blazed with recollection. Rising from his seat, the emperor descended the steps and met his younger comrade with an embrace. For a moment, the years melted away, and the two great patrons of Greek culture were united once again. More than once, Hadrian had soothed the ruffled sensibilities of the Athenians who resented the domineering philanthropist, despite the generosity of his contributions. From Athens, Corinth, and Delphi to Thessaly and Peloponnesus, Herodes, with the blessing and support of the emperor, filled the land with baths, theaters, and stadiums. The Athenians, grateful for a Roman emperor who was there to embellish their city and not to loot it, gave Hadrian free rein as he restored ancient buildings while adding schools and temples in the Greek, not Roman, style. They were not as patient with Herodes who, they felt, acted as if he was their better and often tore down to build, rather than restore and honor the past. But all this mattered little as the two men embraced before the court. "My dear friend," whispered Hadrian as he embraced the thin shoulders of the man. "It has been too long. My soul bleeds, and I . . . I have lived too long." Herodes was appalled by the darkness of the words but took them in stride as he replied, "Majesty, you need to visit Athens again to restore your soul. This city can rob you of it piece by piece over time, I am sure." A bitter smile eroded some of the solemnity in Hadrian's face as he seemed to seriously consider the invitation. But a cloud passed over once again as he replied, "There are far too many memories there, my old friend. You will have to fight your Athenian brethren alone from now on." Herodes knew he needed to come to the point of his visit quickly, while he had his volatile friend's attention. "Our friend Arrian of Nicomedia is still governor of Cappadocia, as you know. But he visits Athens often and hopes to be made an honorary citizen. After such a brilliant career in Roman government, he would be," added Herodes," a welcome addition to Athenian society and could find an important office there. I could use an ally to assure the continuance of your vision." Hadrian's attention was focused now as he called for a scribe. When none could be found, a centurion stepped forward with his *optio* who, as always, carried with him a set of wax tablets at the ready for orders and announcements. The emperor was in full command as he dictated a lengthy proclamation ending, with full honors and monetary compensation, Arrian's governorship at Cappadocia, while at the same time granting the people of Athens the privilege of bestowing an honorary citizenship on Lucius Flavius Arrianus. "Now he will have more time to write," commented Hadrian as his dictation wound down. "Another handbook on military tactics against nomads, perhaps, for the next generation of soldiers." The face of the soldier emperor was flushed and vigorous as the task of honoring his old friend and issuing orders restored his sense of purpose. The court stood in rapt attention as they watched the transformation of an old man to the commander of Rome and her empire. Those for whom Hadrian was still beloved, rejoiced. While those who had hoped to be witnessing his final days had their fear of his power and volatility rekindled. The emperor returned to his throne after sending for a bench to accommodate his old friend. As the court settled down and waited for the next proclamation, the military flavor of the proceedings continued with the presentation of one hundred auxiliaries who had reached their twenty-fifth year of service. They included infantry from Gaul and Germania; archers from Syria, Scythia, and Crete; and finally, cavalry recruited for the northern tribes. Hadrian noted with satisfaction that, despite their varied places of origin, the auxiliaries were purely Roman in appearance and discipline. To present to these men the Roman citizenship they had worked for as they're due reward was empowering for the emperor as well as the soldiers. Behind him, Hadrian could hear a slight commotion within the veteran *triarii,* as they shifted in their iron *lorica segmentata*, clicking a subtle reminder to this mass of soldiers of their presence. However, the auxiliaries were weaponless and about to be rewarded with paid retirement and citizenship. They were no threat to their imperator and the fully armored legionnaires that lined the apse had nothing to be concerned with. *It is the court they should be wary of, not these men,* thought Hadrian as he gazed down at the many devious, powdered faces.

As Hadrian stood to receive the troops, he motioned for two centurions to approach. As they did, they proceeded to unravel the draping of Caesar's toga picta, revealing a gleaming, muscled cuirass of silvered bronze with gilded medallions. A detail on the breastplate that could not go unnoticed was the gilded portrait of the Beloved positioned over the heart. Under the armor, he wore the usual quilted subarmalis of scarlet linen layered with thick felt. Tooled and studded leather straps hung from the armholes of the undergarment, while others formed a *pteruges* that hung from under the waist of the cuirass. Gold eagles with outstretched wings studded the leather tips of the skirted front and glistened in the light of hundreds of lamps that glowed overhead, as did the crown of golden laurel that remained on his head. A voluminous cloak of purple wool was then draped over his shoulders as another centurion appeared from behind the throne carrying a *hasta*, its banded shaft of ash over six feet in length. The head of the shaft was not the traditional iron but of the rarer *oricalcum*, glowing with a deep red hue. The soldiers who stood in frozen attention behind and in front of the *princeps* of Rome understood the meaning of this hue, as did the ashen-faced court before him. Every schoolboy knew that while the magical properties of this rare metal were mythological, the chemical properties were very real. The peculiarity of this ore was that the more blood the oricalcum absorbs the deeper the reddish hue. And the head of the staff held by the imperator of Rome was nearly black. It served as a silent testament to Hadrian's imperial power—unbridled, undiminished, and absolute.

The stunned silence in the vast hall was deafening. And while the assembled military stared at their imperator with the awe and reverence they had always felt toward their Caesar, the court, and senators, along with the many visitors who had traveled from the corners of the empire, stood pale before Rome's master. Some trembled slightly at the unearthly sight before them. True, they had all gone through the formality of declaring the emperor a demigod. But never had they seen Hadrian wrapped in such Olympian glory. As he stood beneath the soaring nave, its blazing lamps suspended like stars behind him, he was the living embodiment of the statues that filled the forum, basilicas, and temples. Slowly, the court lowered itself to its knees, followed by the visiting dignitaries, and then finally, more out of abject fear then reverence, the senators.

The sight of the emperor in full military regalia evoked the image of the great sculpture of Augustus Caesar that stood in majesty before his temple in the forum. For a time, Hadrian belied his sixty years and ill health and took full command of the situation. His oratory filled the immense stone hall, and it seemed the very oil lamps and braziers shook with the sound of his voice. "I, Caesar Publius Aelius Trianus Hadrianus Augustus, imperator of Rome, Pontifex Maximus . . ." The words echoed through the chamber and filled the ears and, for some, the heart as each soldier approached the dais and was presented with a diploma etched in bronze.

The *constitutio* was recorded on a large plate of bronze that would be lodged in the military archive in Rome, while the smaller diploma was inscribed on two thin sheets of bronze hinged together and presented to each of the honorably discharged. The *constitutio* was presented to the court for viewing as the soldiers each received their own double inscribed diploma, which had been folded together with the text inside and bore seven witness seals. These diplomas were of great significance due to the fact that they granted citizenship to each soldier's parents and siblings, as well their children. The generosity the endowed the terms of discharge were exceptional, due perhaps to the fact that this group of auxiliaries had served in Palestine and lost many of their brethren. The memory of that bloody, ill-fated conflict still burned in Hadrian's conscience and sickened him at heart. Here was the last group to be compensated, the final chapter of a tragic story. *So little given for so much lost.* Hadrian hoped to push the memory of that ill-fated land as far from his mind as possible.

Chapter Forty-Nine

An Uneasy Succession

The emperor's mood and energy remained steady throughout the duration of the ceremonies. The interaction of the emperor and his soldiers empowered him, as did the elevating of three commanders he knew well to the title of Praetorian prefect, and the promotion of four centurions for valor. The clatter of their gleaming uniforms nearly drowned out the musicians, yet for Hadrian, this was music in itself. The scent of leather and freshly polished metal soothed his senses, a welcome respite from the perfumes of the court. After two hours, the ceremonies ended, and the court prepared to leave the Aula Regia for the forum. As the crowd parted into two groups, the emperor and his Praetorian guards paraded past them, entered the afternoon light of the peristyle courtyard, and headed toward the forum and the monument dedication.

Caesars horse waited impatiently outside the Domus Augustana, greeting Hadrian with an eager whinny and stamp of his hooves. As much as Hadrian wished to mount the steed without assistance, he knew the weight of his dress armor would prevent this and result in an embarrassment he could not afford. Two centurions appeared discreetly by his side and assisted the emperor with a swiftness that avoided detection by all but the closest soldiers. The heavily armored infantry was already leaving the walls of the Domus while the emperor was busy mounting his horse and were met by a row of drummers followed by another row of musicians bearing long straight tubas. The low melodic bay of these horns was often the last sound soldier's heard as they were signaled into battle. Following these war sounds, the elite troops of Cohort I under the Primus Pilus marched 480 strong down the Sacra Via, followed by the Cohort VI made up of another 480 of "The Finest of the Young Men. A centuria of 80 men in scarlet tunics and gleaming bronze cuirass, led by a centurion, were the next formation, as the lictors with their gilded fasces marched behind the *imaginifer* bearing the golden image of the emperor on his standard next to the standard of the *aquilifer* with his winged eagle. Behind it all was the heavy thud of six thousand boots, the Praetorian guard's assurance of the imperator's personal protection.

The jostling crowd that had begun gathering since early morning was enjoying the spectacle but more eager to catch a view of the emperor. Rumors of poor health worried the populous, and they needed to see the truth for themselves. A row of *corniceii*, their curved horns wrapped around their bodies, sounded the *classicum*, a stirring timbre that could only be announcing the emperor and escort of the imperial guard. The crowd pushed forward as far as the line of soldiers would allow in order to catch a glimpse of their princeps, and at first sight of the ramrod figure seated high above the crowd, that crowd let loose a roar of approval. As he was before the court in apse of the Aula Regia, Hadrian appeared godlike in his shining cuirass and imperial purple. As the people pushed and cheered and flowers flew from the grand garlanded homes that lined the way to the forum, the sun too pushed its way from behind the clouds and poured down benevolently on the assembled masses. The people expected their imperator to be a demigod, and Hadrian did not disappoint. As he rode down the Sacra Via, the sunlight caught the crown of golden laurel as well as the Antinous amethyst set in the fibula that secured his cloak and reflected against his face. That same sun bathed the gems that studded the scabbard of his ceremonial sword and the bridle of his steed. Although Hadrian raised a salute to acknowledge the citizens of Rome, his face remained impassive. As the great Temple of the Deified Vespasian and Titus—the first destroyers of Judea—came into view, the plan that had begun to formulate in his head months before was about to unfold, a plan that would enable him to finish this day with dignity.

Waiting on the steps of the temple was Lucius Aelius Caesar, resplendent in a snow-white toga and a simple circlet of gold on his head. Wisely, and according to Hadrian's instruction, Lucius had forgone the usual dusting of gold in his hair and beard. Instead, he stood somber and regal on the steps of Trajan's temple waiting for his adopted father to arrive. Behind Lucius stood, again according to Hadrian's instruction, his wife Avidia Plautia, a well-connected Roman noblewoman from an ancient family, and their four children. As Hadrian drew closer to the temple compound, the sight of Lucius Aelius and his family was that of the ideal *Familia Romana*, the very thought of which forced Hadrian to suppress an urge to laugh. Instead, a broad smile greeted the family, and they in turn returned his with their own. Seven-year-old Lucius Ceionius Commodus fidgeted with the embroidered hem of his tunic as he gazed up in wonder at the man on the immense horse.

Curly haired and bearded like his father, this man was far larger and much more frightening. Be that as it may, Ceionius had been well rehearsed and, after releasing the hem, stepped forward and saluted with a loud and determined "Ave Imperator!" The crowd took notice that Caesar slipped with surprising ease from his mount and strode up the temple steps with a vigor that belied the rumors of age and illness. Embracing his adopted son, Hadrian then turned his attention to the young Lucius. The boy, now quite pleased with himself for being the center of attention, gave an encore of his salute to the obvious delight of the emperor. The crowd too took enormous pleasure in the precocious young prince and cheered this rare moment of warmth and family. Hadrian turned to Avidia Plautia who knelt and smiled as he nodded his approval. Together, they walked up the steps toward the altar that rose up before the temple; and with a signal to the temple priests, a sacrifice was offered to the deified emperors before the senate and people of Rome.

After the sacrifice had sent enough smoke billowing into the air, Hadrian continued on up to temple, through the great bronze doors, and into the comforting solace of the darkened cella. The temple priest, seeing the approaching emperor, prepared another chair next to the one Lucius had used while waiting for the imperial arrival. The crowd outside assumed the family had entered the temple to pay homage to Hadrian's deified adopted father, and while this was somewhat true, the emperor also needed to rest in silence and out of the public view. The priests who had performed the sacrifice returned to the temple and had joined the chants taking place before a colossal statue of Hadrian in full military regalia bearing a gilt, winged Nike in his upturned hand. The young Lucius Ceionius was awed at first by his adopted grandfather's image in stone, but soon found other objects in the temple to keep him occupied. The deep monotone of the chant was a soothing backdrop for the tired emperor, and the antics of the young Lucius Ceionius kept him amused. But soon, the prefect of the guard entered the temple and stood silently in the shadows. Hadrian knew it was time to continue his public duties, and now Lucius Aelius Caesar would join him in those obligations.

What was now an imperial family descended the steps of the temple and once again entered the public view. A folding platform had been set up beside the emperor's horse, and he mounted with a slow but steady grace. Lucius too mounted his horse, but without a platform, much to Hadrian's relief. A centurion lifted the young Ceionius to his father's arms, and much to the crowd's delight, the boy saluted the assembled legion. Lucius smiled proudly as he pulled his horse into position beside his adopted father and proceeded to the ceremonial site. The blaring horns and booming trumpets vibrated in the late autumn air as the drums kept the troops in a steady rhythm. Even the horses seemed to know this moment in time was golden but fleeting as the sun continued to anoint the day.

The gold-and-silver *phalera* mounted on the staffs of the legion's standards flashed in the sunlight as the procession reached the Tropaeum Hadriani. The monument was inscribed to commemorate the loss of Legion XXII during the Bar Kokhba and the subsequent expulsion of the Judeans from Jerusalem. It had taken three emperors and three wars to subdue the Judeans, and the final defeat was a brutal, bloody mess on both sides. But

Rome prevailed, and as the trophies from the final war were paraded around the Tropaeum, Hadrian watched with a mixture of revulsion and anger. So many lives lost for a land with so little to offer.

To Mars, god of war, Caesar the Imperator, son of divine Trajan, Trajanus Hadrianus Augustus, Pater patriae who restored Rome's honor, Princeps who defeated the Judeans, Ponticus Maximus who built on the Judean mount the great temple to eternal Jupiter, declared for the twelfth time tribune of the plebeians, declared emperor by the army for the seventh time, elected consul for the sixth time, dedicates this memorial monument to the memory of all those who perished while defeating the Judeans.

The inscription boldly declared a hollow victory, but the people had short memories and were content to accept the story carved in the metopes that lined the circular, temple-shaped monument. The elegant tall structure was raised on a stepped podium and topped by a gilded, bronze-tiled roof supported by thirty fluted columns crowned with simple capitals in the Doric style. An incense altar stood in the center of the edifice under an oculus that would accept the rising smoke of the burning sacrifice. The altar was of golden Jerusalem stone, polished and carved with garlands of grape clusters and wreaths of laurel surrounding shields emblazoned with the standard of the Legion XXII. And piled upon the altar were the broken swords of the defeated. While the decoration of the altar was conventional and somewhat benign, the *metopes* along the entablature displayed the wrath of the emperor. The destruction of Jerusalem and the expulsion of the Jews were graphically depicted in the reliefs, as was the slaughter of the rebels at the gates of the city. The Roman legions were depicted ascending the heavens on the wings of Nike as Hadrian watched the burning city. All of Hadrian's hatred for that troublesome land was on display in the marble narrative that swept across the frieze. And although the losses and bloodshed on the part of the legionaries were staggering, the end result was what he celebrated here—Roman heroics and a vanquished foe.

The smoke from the altar was still billowing from the oculus of the monument when Hadrian set off for the senate basilica and his final duty for the day. The short walk gave him time to consider the tact he would need when accepting the senate's affirmation of Lucius as his son and heir. The consecration of the war monument went well enough that he felt there would be little resistance to his choice. Hadrian had paved the way with coffers of gold and then presented to Rome the ideal family. True, Lucius's health was about as secure as his own, but if the gods deemed it, he would live long enough for the young Lucius Ceionius to come of age and rule as heir. After three emperors in the Nervan-Trajanic dynasty, there would finally be a prince of the blood on the throne, and the *Pax Romana* would be secure for at least another generation.

The senate had spent day bracing itself for this event. From the clouded beginning of Hadrians's reign that led to the assassinations of four powerful senators, to the frequency of his absences, to the recent deaths of Sevianus and his grandson, the senate had no warm feelings for this indomitable man. There were those amongst the senators who argued the fact that Hadrian had consolidated and strengthened the empire, vanquished or struck treaties with her enemies, and had been a fair and generous ruler. The very state of Rome as a city bore witness to his benevolence as the fresh, gleaming marble of new temples, schools, and forums could attest. At the end of the day, those who still wished to vilify Caesar had not changed their minds, but had been persuaded to keep silent. And those who witnessed the majesty on display that day were now more cautious about crossing the still potent emperor and more willing to agree to the terms regarding his heir.

The senate was prepared to offer Lucius Aelius tribunician power and the governorship of the northern province of Pannonia as well as eventual consulship in Rome. His time as a senator was less than brilliant but better than most, and his circle of influential friends had grown immensely. The senate had been worked into a level of comfort that would allow for obedience to the emperor as *tribunicia potestas* while retaining its air of authority. As with the emperors before him, Hadrian ruled by personal prestige, and his authority as supreme ruler and emperor was absolute. Of course, the unwavering devotion of the military could not be underestimated. In Hadrian's mind, the confirmation of his heir was preordained and the senate approval, an afterthought.

The walk to the basilica also gave Hadrian an opportunity to speak with Lucius for the first time after many weeks. But speaking was difficult due to a persistent cough Aelius attempted to hide behind the fold of his toga he held to his mouth. After a time, the cough subsided, and Hadrian caught glimpses of the man between nods to the cheering crowd. By the time they had covered the short distance to the senate, Caesar had little opportunity to brief his young heir apparent. "Say little. Nod and smile," advised Hadrian. "Appear distracted by your children and let me address the

senators." "I pray this ordeal will be brief and your life will be long, my dear father," replied Lucius. "The senate will appreciate brief," acknowledged the emperor. "And as for my mortality, one who is no longer here took care to assure its longevity." Lucius grew pale at the allusion to the Beloved. *Will the boy never release his hold on this man?* he thought bitterly.

But Hadrian had a specific agenda in mind when he arrived at the steps of the senate. The senators who gathered beneath the massive columns of the basilica were somewhat startled by the mass of military that surrounded the emperor. With the dedication of the tropeum completed, there was no need for this many legions in attendance. But a number of the senators knew the plan and watched with great interest as the emperor played his final and most convincing card. Descending from his horse at the foot of the steps, Hadrian walked up to the Rosta Augusta, the midday sun setting a shimmer to his cuirass and crown of golden laurel. A blast of trumpets tore through the air as the assembled legions took their formal formations at the steps of the senate and saluted their emperor. A herald from one of the cohorts stepped forward and in a voice that rivaled the trumpets announced the military's second imperial acclamation of the emperor for the hard-won victory of a war recently ended. The second blast of trumpets could barely be heard over the mighty roar of the military whose assemblage intimidated the crowd as well as the senate. The few senate members who had been made aware of this planned show of strength ahead of time smiled at Hadrian's stoic acceptance of the military's acclamation, knowing full well this was his final blow to the senate's sense of authority and dominance, as well as any remaining reluctance to acknowledge his heir.

The emperor motioned for Julius Servus, Publicius, and Haterius Nepos, the most high-ranking officers in the Judean campaign, to follow him into the confines of the senate. There he presented each the *ornamenta triumphalia,* the supreme military honor not seen presented since Trajan bestowed the *ornamenta* on three of his commanders from the Dracian Wars on this exact spot. The significance of these awards was not lost on the senate as Caesar proceeded to present the rank and file that had survived the war with the *dona militaria.*

"I, Publius, Aelius Trajanus Hadrianus, Imperator and Princeps have, from the *Fossatum Britiania* and its great sprawling wall to the olive groves of Baetica, kept the empire secure and prosperous. With prudence and efficiency, I have retained the military as the *Machina Romana* that keeps the world in balance, and I have gifted all corners of the empire with the cultural advantages of Rome and the security of her strength." With these words, Hadrian addressed the senate, reminding them of his power and worth as an emperor and the debt they owed for the *Pax Romana* resulting from those attributes. His oratory was of the crisp, factual military style and not that of a lengthy senatorial discourse. His presence filled the senate hall as his voice carried past the walls and into the still air outside where the expectant crowd stood unaccustomedly quiet. They listened as Caesar presented the legacy of his lifetime and reign in preparation for the formal announcement of his heir and its ratification by the senate. The outcome was clear. Gold, and a dazzling display of military might, assured an answer favorable to the emperor. As the final words of his oratory faded in the autumn breeze, the senate rose in ovation and applauded politely, but the crowd outside the basilica erupted into a tremulous roar of approval. The ground-shaking sound of the crowd and the presence of an armed and devoted military aside, the speech did have a convincing affect on the senate. The venerable Vibius Silius Africanus rose from the cushion that warmed his stone bench and made his way to the open floor of the basilica to address the emperor. "Ave Caesar. Viva Imperator and Santus Pontificus. The Senate of Rome salutes you and praises your glorious contributions to the empire." The aged Vibius had known Hadrian since the days before Trajan's ascension as emperor and had served as prefect in Alexandria during Hadrian's visit with Antinous. The sight of the man was bittersweet for Hadrian and a reminder of his own mortality. In a low steady voice, Vibius solemnly confirmed on behalf of the senate, the emperor's choice of heir, Lucius Aelius Verus Caesar.

Earlier in the day, Lucius Aelius had ingested a mixture of mint and cherry resin mixed with wine to calm his chronic cough and a mound of chicory wrapped in lettuce to ease his stomach problems. Luxurious living had its price, and even in his young age, Lucius was paying dearly. His servant had passed him another draught of the wine mixture to prepare for his address to the senate. The pain that slowly crept through his bowls had forced him to be seated during Hadrian's discourse. This did not escape the emperor's notice, and as Hadrian listened to the senate's proclamation, he searched his brain for an excuse to leave without Lucius's having to address the assemblage.

After Vibius Silius finished his oratory, Hadrian acknowledged the senate's gesture before he seemed to go suddenly pale and slumped into his chair. A cup of wine was offered but refused as the emperor appeared to recover from the mysterious attack. Rising from his chair, Hadrian walked to the larger-than-life-size sculpture of his adopted father that stood at the entry of the senate chamber and stood in silence. Although the gesture was anticlimactic, the senators took this as a sign that the ceremony was over and, after bowing to the emperor, began to file out of the hall while talking quietly amongst themselves. Lucius and his family joined Hadrian as he silently acknowledged the departing senators. When they were gone, the emperor ordered a litter to be waiting on the porch of the basilica for Lucius to discreetly slip away in. For his part, Verus appeared distraught at his own failure and the disappointment in Caesar's eyes. But Hadrian chose to be kind. "All went nearly perfect," he spoke quietly so that only Verus could hear. "The ending was dismissive and of no consequence. They were eager to leave my presence anyway." Hadrian spoke lightly, yet deep inside, Lucius's failure disheartened him. Nevertheless, the confirmation was made and the documents signed. But as with Judea, it was a tainted victory and not without cost.

Chapter Fifty

A Gift of Beauty and Pain

Winter had come to Rome, and Rome, or Romans who were financially capable, had come to the Bay of Naples. Located on the west coast of the Gulf of Puteoli, Baiae was one of the choice resort destinations for the nobility and wealthy, as well as the choice for the emperor of Rome. Hadrian had purchased a villa from the estate of Silius Italicus, who in turn had obtained it from the estate of Cicero. Silius had been a renowned orator, a prudent politician under Nero and proconsul of Asia. Hadrian had long approved of the Stoic-influenced verse of Silius despite his own preference for the archaic Greek style and was pleased to own one of his homes. Hadrian also owned another of Cicero's villas—the lavish estate in Formiae that had awakened the child in Antinous as he dug through the many years of ruin in search of treasure. The memory of the youth's delight was too painful now, and the villa remained in a frozen state of preparedness for its owner's return. Besides being decadent, hedonistic, and self-absorbed, Baiae was also the site of warm mineral baths directed from natural sulphur springs and known for their medicinal properties. While Hadrian had once seen Baiae as a "vortex of luxury" and a "harbor of vice" as described by Seneca the Younger, he now enjoyed the restful baths and springs that held his interest, as well as the architecture such as the Temple of Echo whose dome had inspired the architect in him to design the dome of his Pantheon. Rest for his body and diversion for his mind would bring solace to the aged man's final days. Or so he hoped.

Hadrian left Rome just before a light snow had dusted the dirty streets. He arrived at the Portus Julius, the homeport of the western imperial fleet, with a flotilla of his own. The lavish villas were already aired out and fully staffed while the rows of shops along the main streets were doing a brisk business. Servants from the villa kitchens crowded the *vicus tuscus* for spices and herbs, the *velabrum* for the general goods, and contended with the fly-infested stench of the *Forum Boarium* where meats from all over the empire were offered at prices only the affluent aristocracy could afford. The alleys of wine shops shook with rumbling carts loaded down with barrels and amphorae destined for the villas that clung to the terraced hills that overlooked the bay.

While their slaves and servants shopped the basics for the kitchen larders, the wealthy themselves went by litter to the *forum cuppendinis* and *saeptia* where the wealth and scope of the empire was on display in the form of an overwhelming array of luxury items—perfume merchants, silk and jade from China, linen from Egypt, furs, shoes, and other leather goods from the north and eastern provinces—all to be had for the plentiful coinage of the well to do. And a majority of that coinage bore the profile of Hadrian. Society matrons were well aware of that profile as they prepared for the opulent parties that they had planned months in advance while still in Rome. In the past, the attendance of the emperor to one's event was an achievement of the highest order. In the days of the exotic Antinous, Caesar was charm and benevolence as he basked in the glow of his love for the golden ephebe. Villas rang with music of gold and silver dinnerware at feasts that lit up the night, then deteriorated into the infamous orgies that lasted until the sun began to illuminate the yachts moored in the sparkling bay.

While the invitations to the emperor were many, they were sent more as a formality than in the hope he would attend. The honor of receiving an invitation to the imperial villa was far more preferable. The expense of entertaining the emperor was enormous, while being a guest was a way to display one's wealth and outdo one another with their luxurious gifts for the royal host. With Caesar's presence in Baiae, the center of Roman government was shifted to the seacoast where the marble villas of senators and the nobility clustered like many pale moons around the imperial sun. Near the imperial villa was the getaway of Julius Caesar, while farther up the steep slope was the villa of Nero with its massive swimming pool that took, according to legend, two hundred soldiers an entire day to fill. The neighboring towns of Stabiae and Puteoli competed in terms of luxury and licentiousness, but the royal presence in Baiae made it the reigning queen of the bay.

In his younger days, Hadrian had preferred Puteoli due to its lively harbor and the massive Flavian Amphitheater. Here too was another of Cicero's many villas, a favorite of Hadrian's and purchased by him in the year Trajan became emperor. Located by Lake Lucrino with a view of the harbor to the west, it was part of a sleepy hamlet that overlooked the volcanic crater that still steamed in the distance. It was there, in a grand suite of rooms that served as the royal apartments, that Hadrian placed a sculpture of his Beloved carved in the purest Parian marble in the eastern window that would capture the rising sun each morning and another before the western window to catch the golden glow of the setting sun. But the villa at Baiae was grander and more impressive with its many columns of Phrygian marble in imperial purple that stood on an endless sea of polychrome stone in every color the empire could provide. In the reception room's wall mosaics portrayed birds in flight and peacocks displaying their finery, while in the triclinium, satyrs pursued maidens through wooded forests or slumped drunkenly against tree trunks. Here too was a floor mosaic of cupids vintaging and fishing while surrounded by swirling acanthus scrolls with heads of feast animals and garlands of flowers. Hadrian had lavished the villa with furnishings that reflected the Greco-Roman style he appreciated at an enormous expense, incurring the wrath of Trajan for his extravagance. Again, it was Plotina who came to the rescue and smoothed out yet another dispute between her husband and her favorite. Hadrian spent many pleasant evenings with Plotina surrounded by cedar and ebony chairs, stools and cabinets inlaid with mother of pearl and gilded bronze ornamentation, as well as bronze and marble tables, braziers and lamps. Each piece had been personally chosen by Hadrian, and each was exquisite and expensive. The extravagant water clock Plotina had gifted him with was still in the original location the empress had placed it so many years ago, its finely wrought silver figures still twirling and ringing their tiny golden bells to mark the hours.

But it was in Baiae that Hadrian rested in the warm natural spring the thermal bath had been built around, while his chamberlain was preparing for the banquet that would be held that night in the massive triclinium. Theos had spent much time in the kitchen directing the cooks whose slaves who were busy roasting and boiling, over the open fireplaces and charcoal stoves, the meats and fowl that would grace the tables that evening. Smoke from the bakery ovens billowed from the chimneys as the pastry crusts of small meat and fish pies slowly turned golden brown. The kitchen shelves were quickly emptied of beautifully crafted cookware and utensils as pots, pans, and kettles were filled with rich sauces, braised meats, and sweetened custards. Although quite a distance from the main residence, the odor of the cooking meal could be detected throughout parts of the villa, and slaves waved enormous fans to keep the aromas at bay.

It was said that Romans become Greek when at their country homes. The same was true for the atmosphere at seaside villas. The floor plans followed the Greek ideal as did the mode of dress for both sexes. Hadrian embraced his inner Greek at every opportunity and so took the lead in promoting the Grecian affectation of Rome's elite. As two servants positioned into place the oblong linen of Hadrian's snow-white chiton, another fastened the golden fibula set with the ever-present amethyst of Antinous. Hadrian inhaled deeply as a girdle of tooled leather studded with diminutive golden bees was wrapped around his midsection and secured with small golden buckles. The effect was uncomfortable yet flattering; even age and tragedy did little to wither his vanity. With that done, a special slave whose job was the fine art of tending to the emperor's himation stepped forward. With a flourish that was both businesslike and haughty, he wrapped the generous amount of finely woven wool, arranging the drape and folds to a state of perfection and elegance. The minister of the imperial coffers arrived with a cloth-lined tray arrayed with various pieces of jewelry—chains of state, the imperial signet and other assorted rings, and a variety of golden cuffs and bracelets studded with gems. Hadrian studied the collection for a moment before choosing a simple circlet in the form of a wide band of gold studded with amethysts and moonstones, the golden signet, and an inconspicuous bracelet that had once belonged to his wife Sabina and for a brief moment, his Beloved. After draining a cup of honeyed wine, the *princeps* of Rome prepared himself to greet his first guests of the season.

Caesar crossed the Grand Corridor on his way from his private apartments, through the first set of public rooms where the inner circle of his entourage joined him on his way to the triclinum. As they reached the peristyle, Lucius's two young sons were heard, then seen, as they emerged from the guest rooms. As they ran through the peristyle gardens, they were followed by a muscular youth of sixteen or so. The two princes had hidden themselves in the waist-high boxwood shrubs, giggling as they watched the youth call and search for them. At the sight of the emperor's approach, the dark-haired youth froze and fell to one knee, causing the boys to turn and cease their giggling. Hadrian stopped to address the boys as they rose from their bows and ran toward their adopted grandfather. In the corner of his eye, Hadrian watched as Lucius Caesar wandered from the guest quarters, the setting sun catching the golden hem of his tunic and the many rings that adorned his hands. The emperor noticed, with some amusement, the quick pat of Lucius's hand against the backside of the dark-haired youth as he made his way past him and across the courtyard. "Dearest father, I salute you and pray you are well," was Lucius's jovial salutation that sent the roosting birds flying from the trees to the safety of the rooftops. "And I, you, my dear son," replied Hadrian. "It appears the change of climate as well as the sea air has done wonders for us both." After the dark-haired youth reached the young boy, he stood silently behind Lucius where Hadrian noticed his bright blue eyes as well as his budding muscularity. Lucius caught the emperor's appraisal of the youth and blushed slightly beneath his beard when their eyes made contact. "This is Nikomedes of Athens. He is related to your friend Herodes Atticus, I believe." Lucius was curiously sheepish as he spoke. "I have taken him into my household as a page." *I'm sure you have taken him in*, thought Hadrian with a slight smile. "My son is a man of such fine tastes," Hadrian said to no one in particular, as he turned to Lucius and took his arm. "Walk with me to the feast. I could use some youthful company. *Nikomedes*. That translates from the Greek as *to scheme of victory*, does it not?" Hadrian could not help ask, knowing full well that even with Lucius's feeble grasp of the language he could not avoid the translation of the youth's name. "It does, my lord," replied Lucius with a sly smile. "Perhaps I should be on my guard. I would not want him to take me for more than I offer him." And so, wrapped in the warmth of familiar banter, the emperor and his heir arrived at the banquet hall to begin another gilded season to the blare of trumpets.

The Patrician societies at the resort towns were grateful for the early date of the first imperial banquet. Propriety dictated that any official feasts before the first royal event were frowned upon and an insult to the emperor's status. Hadrian was well aware of this and wished to get his own obligation, and himself, out of the way of the society matrons. In the past, it was Sabina who arranged for these feastings, and her husband's only obligation was to attend. It now fell upon Theos to arrange the appropriate order of things, a responsibility he took seriously and carried out with more flair than the empress. Although unseen by Hadrian was Lucius's imaginative but spendthrift hand. As the emperor entered the triclinium, the vast hall vibrated with anticipation for the new season. The question on every tongue was, "Would the presence of the emperor add a luster to the season or cast a shadow?" The answer lay in the sumptuousness of the feast and the richness of the setting—a true indicator that the golden age still existed.

With the emperor settled in the thick cushions of a finely wrought *lectus* of glided bronze and ivory, an army of slaves entered through the forest of columns bearing silver trays weighed down with rich egg dishes, stuffed shellfish, fish cakes, and raw vegetables marinated and drizzled with a thick cream sauce. The clatter of silver and ivory spoons replaced the chatter of idle gossip, and the slurping sound of tender garlicky snails being sucked from their shells threatened to drown out the reedy music of the aulos and the shrill sweet sound of the kithara. As Hadrian picked at his food, he received a seemly endless stream of nobility, aristocrats, and a scattering of newly wealthy merchants who appeared as overawed by the grandeur of the imperial residence as they were by the imperial presence. One in particular seemed extremely eager to present the emperor with the gift he had brought with him. Paetas Vibius had arrived early and created a stir with the massive crate that was wheeled in behind him. The soldiers had detained him and were about to have him ejected from the villa until he not only presented them with his invitation but also opened the suspicious crate. As the soldiers stared into the pine container, they knew this man would be a bittersweet guest for the emperor.

Hadrian was somewhat irritated by the fawning man before him who seemed to sweat from every pore. His thinning hair was arranged in curls that were as damp as the carefully trimmed beard that did little to hide his numerous glistening chins. The guest's constant bowing only directed the odor of his voluminous robes, soaked as they were with sweat and an expensive perfume that did nothing to mask the offending stench, directly toward Caesar. Theos, standing protectively nearby, understood the situation swiftly and sent for servants to fan away the odious fumes. Vibius was well aware of the necessity for swiftness if his plan was to succeed. With a flourish, he directed the emperor's attention to the tall draped object that stood in the courtyard of the oval peristyle beyond the tablinum. Hadrian had not noticed the object before and was suddenly curious about both the object and the distasteful man who drew his attention to it. "Almighty Caesar, I am Paetas Vibius, and I beg your indulgence. Come with me and allow this humble servant to honor your magnificence." With a sigh, Hadrian motioned for his cup to be refilled before rising from his couch to follow the odd man with the slightly Greek accent. As they drew closer to the draped object, the crowd of guests began to grow silent with anticipation. Most of the guests knew of Vibius. He was from a class of former *mercatores* emerging in this close-knit society on the strength of their vast wealth and purchased influence. Although most found him physically repulsive, they respected his affluence and exquisite taste. The guests too had noticed the draped figure but assumed it was part of the night's entertainment. As the emperor approached the mysterious object beneath the columned entry to the gardens, the guests noticed from the curious expression he wore that he too had no knowledge of its nature. Vibius reached the object first and with a great flourish clapped his hands as a signal for the slaves to remove the draping. With a tug, the thick silk covering whispered as it slid off the object and revealed a sculpture in pristine white marble. A collective gasp was heard in the crowd as the image of a naked Antinous came into view. The rendering of the work was undoubtedly Greek—the grace of the pose, the fine finished quality, the sensitive modeling of the facial features. Those who had known the beauteous boy were struck by the very Roman-like accuracy of the portrait. But unlike many Roman sculptures, the subject was a work done in its entirety and not a stock body with a portrait head added on. The body was a younger Antinous in repose—soft, slightly fleshy, not yet fully matured. The features too spoke of an earlier youth—petulant yet intelligent, innocence a recent memory. The crowd cautiously applauded Vibius's gift to the emperor, but the man was too concerned with the reaction of the emperor to notice. Hadrian stood frozen before the life size image of his beloved as it stood on its marble plinth. The stone seemed to hold a life of its own, an inner light. He drew closer and examined every detail, finding nothing unfamiliar. But it was the sculpture's face that drained the blood from his own. It was the boy. The deep-set eyes, the proud nose, the full lips. The unruly locks of hair were a labor of love. Hadrian stood transfixed before the glistening image of the young god, unaware of the tears that streamed down his face. The whispering guests again went silent as they watched a young man walk up to the emperor and place his hands on the man's shoulders, squeezing them gently. Hadrian composed himself and turned to face his consoler.

Lucius had watched the drama unfold from his couch beside the emperor's. His aversion to Vibius's strong odor kept him from accompanying Hadrian as he followed the merchant to the mysterious gift. But as the silk draping began to reveal the masterpiece beneath it, Lucius knew he would be needed to temper the reaction that would follow. "It is a thing of beauty, worthy of your god," Lucius spoke softly to Hadrian. He then turned to a very agitated Vibius and said, "You have outdone yourself in your homage to the emperor's beloved." "Yes, Vibius," the emperor managed a reply, "you have honored me and the memory of the boy. I am . . . overwhelmed by the beauty of your gift and will certainly find a way to express my appreciation." The extent of Vibius's relief left him shaken and weak. And after rising from his knees with the help of one of his slaves, he made his way to a nearby couch as another slave fanned him with a spray of peacock feathers—a look of relief and satisfaction on his face.

Hadrian's mood had grown somber, and it permeated the vast hall. As they turned to return to their couches, Lucius gestured for the musicians to play light tunes as the servants poured more of the warm spiced wine for the emperor. But for Hadrian, the enjoyment of the festivities was over, and he made little effort to socialize. Lucius and his wife continued to entertain as Hadrian drew deeper into himself. He found it impossible to take his eyes from the silent sculpture that seemed to glow against the darkness outside. As he fought against the combination of the warm wine, the lilting music, and the sheer emotional exhaustion, he knew it was a fight he could not win. Motioning to his guards, he left his couch and made his way toward the entry of the triclinium and the pathway that lead toward the Grand Corridor and his private apartments.

The servants were still lighting the lamps that lead to the inner rooms of the royal suite when Hadrian appeared at the doorway. Theos had kept the braziers going since sundown, and their light and heat helped to make the rooms more welcoming. "No more lamps need lighting, Theos," the emperor instructed. The light from the braziers was sufficient for the single occupant of the rooms, and there would be no visitors on this night. The chamberlain had already turned down the layers of linen and wool sheeting before ordering a brazier to be placed closer to the bed. On a nearby table, a cup of honeyed wine infused with ground Henbane seeds waited to assure a full night's sleep. Sleep did come after a time, but not before Hadrian's mind reenacted the day's events; the scenes blurred like aged frescos as they passed before his eyes. The last memory before sleep was that of the silken sheet sliding off the exquisite statue of Antinous, revealing the perfection underneath. Hadrian fought off sleep in an effort to retain the image, yet the persuasive nature of the Henbane had already taken hold, and with a sigh, Caesar surrendered to its power.

Chapter Fifty-One

A Failed Plan

Rain had followed the days after the state banquet, but that did nothing to delay the construction of a small temple outside Hadrian's private apartments. The large fountain had been removed and a circular concrete podium installed, even as the emperor was still at work on his design. Modeled after a traditional temple of Venus, the new structure would house the graceful gift from Paetas Vibius. And as the rain splattered on the marble paving outside the library where he was busy at work, Hadrian poured over examples of fluted columns and their proper capitals, classical architraves and entablatures, and decorative elements in the Greek and Egyptian styles. As the concrete of the podium was setting and then clad with pale green and brown marble, Hadrian finalized his design and presented it to his builders. The final result was an regal structure that called to mind a traditional *phiale* with the sculpture being the centerpiece of the domed and open portico, rather than the usual fountain. The occulus of the dome was filled in with an inverted bowl of clear leaded glass panels that allowed light in but not the rain that, up until a few days earlier, had plagued the workmen. Hadrian ordered a shallow pool dug with a low wall of rusticated stone to surround the temple. A narrow bridge of the same stone lead to the temple, and Hadrian was standing at the end of that bridge overseeing the installation of the statue when he heard the sound of children behind him. Turning to greet his grandchildren, he saw Lucius Aelius and his young page followed the children as they emerged from the shadows of the chambers. The two boys bowed with a studied formality before looking up to check the emperor's mood. A smile from Hadrian sent the youths running to him, their impulsiveness warming him as he showered them with an unaccustomed enthusiasm. There was a smile too for the page, Nikomedes, as he fell to one knee and voiced a shy salutation. Only Lucius remained silent as he studied the new temple. "My dear father, your work is finally completed. The boy would be pleased," Lucius finally remarked somewhat dismissively. Hadrian took offense to the tone of his adopted son and replied, "Yes, the *god* Antinous is pleased. Look, the sun has left the shadow of the clouds to honor this moment." Indeed, the sun had emerged from the cloud cover and was now blessing the gleaming temple with an eerie winter light. Having forgone the fluted style column for a smooth shafted design, Hadrian felt compelled to crown them with antique Ionic capitals he had purchased in Greece and had set aside for another project at the Villa Adriana. He had sent for them, knowing the garland festooned volutes of the capitals would suit the simple marble shafts, and no other decoration would be necessary. The simplicity of the design suited the sculpture and, more importantly, the god himself.

Hadrian was still absorbed in the edifice before him when Lucius interrupted his thoughts. "My lord," he began," I am preparing for my journey to Pannonia to begin my consulship there." In a lower voice, he added, "Are you certain this is where you need me most?" Hadrian knew what Lucius was alluding to. The weather in Pannonia was far from pleasant, especially during the winter. This was a painful content in the emperor's plan for the succession, but vital. The parallels of experience drawn between Hadrian and his successor must be clear to all. "I was governor of Lower Pannonia before I was made emperor, and my villa in Aquileia is still being maintained," Hadrian spoke dryly and matter-of-fact. *So this is the reason for my son's bitter mood.* This realization shifted Hadrian's response from irritation to tact. "I have repositioned the Legion X Gemina from Vindobona to be at your disposal in Aquileia, while the XIV Gemina will remain in Carnuntum under your proconsul Vibullius Rufus. He will be under your command in Western Pannonia, while Publius Coelius Balbinus will be your man in the eastern province. All will be well," he added, with more hope than certainty. "Hadrian," Lucius gripped Caesar's arm and spoke with a familiarity that could only be whispered, "you know me. I am not . . . equipped to deal with such conditions. I should certainly wait until spring to undertake such a journey, let alone such a command." There was desperation in the man's voice that cut through Hadrian like shards of glass. But it was vital that Lucius assume this post as a stepping-stone to the eventual succession—vital in the eyes of the people and the senate. He knew too well the implications of the senate as an obstacle to an emperor's authority, and he could not pass that hindrance on to his heir. "Pannonia will make you more of a man," was Caesar's terse reply, as he broke from Lucius's grip and walked slowly toward the temple. "And my family?" Lucius called after Hadrian in a cold, acrimonious voice. "They will remain here for the remainder of the winter, then return to Rome," Hadrian replied, as he suddenly whirled around and in a voice that seemed to make the branches of the myrtles and pines themselves shudder, added, "By the gods, I have decreed it!" Lucius stared in disbelief, then fell to one knee in obedience. *The vicious bastard! He's sending me to my death and doesn't care that I know it.*

Lucius knew his own health was fragile and his life precarious at best. Deep inside him was the silent knowledge that he would never reach the end of the long road to the throne; his only hope for his family's future lay in his son Lucius Ceionius Verus. When faced with the indomitable will of the emperor and his own determination to live, Lucius knew he was no match. He accepted Caesar's dispatch to Pannonia without any further complaint and bitterly prepared his family for his absence.

Lucius was quite wrong regarding Hadrian's will to live. Despite outward appearances, the emperor's health was declining rapidly, and Hadrian was doing nothing to halt that decline. By the time of Lucius's succession, death was a welcome friend that stood in every shadow but refused to claim his victim. The attacks that beat Hadrian's chest like great fists were more frequent and becoming more ferocious. But each attack left him the same way, gasping in a pool of sweat, spitting blood, but still alive. The Henbane his Greek physicians prescribed no longer brought sleep, while the Mandrake brought his heart to a slower rhythm that eased his body but blurred his mind. The only foods he could digest now were soft eggs and porridge, which, as the weather turned from the mild but damp winter to a radiant spring, he ate in the garden outside his private rooms, staring intently at the pristine little temple and its marble god.

Spring had also brought the beginning of the end of the resort season, and from the columned porch of his villa that overlooked the sea below, he watched the many yachts beginning of their departure for Rome. The solitude that spread like a silent mist along the terraced hills was soothing for the emperor, and he was loath to leave it for the capital and its teeming masses and smoke-filled sky. Lucius's wife, Avidia Plautia, was eager to leave the quiet of the villa and follow the society whose adoration she had come to enjoy. Her position as a future empress raised her status even further in the aristocratic circles she had come to dominate. Any letters from her husband were presented to the society matrons and the snapping of the velum sheets in her fluttering hands became a familiar sight. Soon after the court's return to Rome, however, the letters became less frequent as well as less lengthy. For her, it was no great matter because in her mind her status was secure and irrevocable. But for Hadrian, it was cause for great concern. The fewer letters to Plautia was due to bad news in many letters to the emperor.

Winter had been cruel to Lucius despite the luxuries he had sent ahead of his arrival. The villa at Aquileia proved to be pleasant enough, but not to the standards Lucius was accustomed to. Snowstorms prevented him from venturing far from the villa, and his interaction with his proconsuls was through dispatches from messengers who braved the winter winds. Hadrian's postal service was swift and efficient as it sent a flow of correspondence to Lucius's wife at their villa near Baiae. Recounting the stories of the locals and the soldiers who guarded his villa, Lucius filled his letters with the adventures Domitia regaled her society friends with. But once spring had thawed the frozen Danube, tribal attacks forced Lucius to join his proconsuls and their legions at the northeastern borders. The attacks were repulsed with little effort or participation by Lucius Aelius, but that did not stop him from erecting an arch to commemorate the victories over the hordes at Vindobona, Brigetio, and Aquincum. From the heavily fortified *castrum* of Aquincum, Lucius could see the untamed lands of the Lazyges that led to Dacia, the lands Hadrian deemed not worth keeping due to the constant cost of military and funds. To Lucius, the land he was defending was not worth the effort either, but that was not his call. The city that grew up around the fortified base was kept in check with a legionary force of about six thousand men who defended the gifts the empire bestowed upon the inhabitants—central heating, public baths, palaces, and an impressive amphitheater to satisfy the Roman lust for blood sport. From his quarters in the large comfortable home of the *decurion* Marcus Antonius Victornus, Lucius wrote to the emperor for the funds needed to construct the victory arch, embellishing his role in the dispersal of the tribes with the assistance of Victornus. An arch would be a great political statement for Victornus as well as Lucius Aelius Caesar, and Hadrian was eager to present to the senate his announcement of victory as well as his decree that an arch to be erected.

The military jargon in Lucius's letters raised some suspicion in Hadrian, but it had the intended effect on the senate as it rose to the ceremonial approval of the funds. In a more private letter, Lucius asked his adopted father for gold to fund a temple to Mithras, a temple that would lie within the grand home of Marcus Victorinus. With this missive, Hadrian was soon able to piece the reality of the campaign together, along with the reports he had gleaned from his personal spies. They had filled him in on the adventures Lucius had conveniently left out of his writings. He had discovered a local mead-like brew called *sabaea*, and along with Victorinus, he had begun to spend more time at the baths and banquet rooms of the local merchants than the battlefield. Hadrian had hoped for more from Lucius, but the reports did not come as a surprise. As long as his letters painted the portrait necessary, Hadrian remained satisfied with his wild adopted son.

Lucius's time away allowed Hadrian to spend more time with Avidia Plautia and her children at the Villa Adriana. As he watched young Lucius Ceionius play along the canopus, the warming sun of late spring reflected off the water and sparkled in the sandy blond hair of the boy. As much as he tried to restrain himself, Hadrian spoiled the boy with gifts and what little time he could spare. The fact that the boy was born forty-eight days after the death of Antinous made a connection for Hadrian that elevated the seven-year-old in his mind's eye. He hoped to see the youth grow to be more responsible than his father, but Hadrian's lavish treatment of the boy was leading him down the identical path as his frivolous father. The stern Roman scholar Hadrian had hired, Marcus Cornelius Fronto, kept Ceionius in check, but the young Nikomedes was too eager to allow the emperor to influence the boy.

It was in Aquincum that Lucius began to weaken and cough blood again, the rigors of war being the least of the reasons. Summer and autumn had been mild, but the next winter proved to be more hostile than the last. Lying on thick cushions and propped up with pillows, Lucius made his way back to Aquileia by a covered carriage in hopes of gaining back his strength in the milder climate along the sea. But in truth, he wished only to return to Rome, as he sensed the flickering candle of his life was growing dimmer. Sitting by the fire that blazed in the sitting room of the emperor's villa in Aquileia, Lucius pondered his life as he wrote to Hadrian for permission to return to Rome. His plan was to take a ship to Ariminum, then take the Via Flaminia to Rome. Taking a ship through the Mare Hadriaticum and around the tip of Italia would be far less arduous, but in truth, Lucius was unsure of the time left to him. It was these thoughts he poured into his letter, hoping the emperor would comprehend the dire need for his return.

The letter reached Hadrian during a banquet at the Winter Palace within the villa compound the following week, and its content warranted a swift reply. Hadrian left the banquet hall to the dignitaries who had traveled from Aquitania in Gaul to present wagonloads of finely colored marbles from the mountains there. As he traveled down the long corridor to the staircase that led to the intermediate level, he reread the long, rambling missive, stopping near a blazing torch from time to time to make out a word or two in the hesitant handwriting. As difficult as the dispatch must have been to write, it was even more difficult to have to read. By the time he had reached his bedchamber, Hadrian knew the letter word for word and by heart. Rather than calling for a scribe, the emperor sat down and wrote a reply in his own hand. It was obvious the young man had to return, but in what condition would he arrive? Hadrian finished his reply and called for his proctor to prepare his personal ship for a voyage to Aquileia, staffed with the best physicians and cooks. The week-long voyage may be the perfect beginning for Lucius's recovery. *If it arrives there in time,* was the whispered thought in Hadrian's mind.

The *Adriana Augusta* took to the waters of the Mare Tyrrhenum past Rhegium and into the Mare Ionium in record time, as if the gods themselves wished for a speedy rescue for Hadrian's adopted son and heir. In less than a week, the ship was sailing the Mare Hadriaticum, hugging the coast of Dalmatia and its many islands and fast approaching the port city of Aquileia, where Lucius was anxiously awaiting the emperor's answer. He was sitting on the vast porch of the villa overlooking the water, so lost in his thoughts he failed to notice the majestic ship entering the harbor. It was only when a servant entered with a cup of honeyed wine and excitedly pointed out the vessel that Lucius was aware of its arrival. At first, the sight chilled him. *Had Hadrian himself arrived to rescue or chastise him?* The sight of the imperial yacht created a stir in the city as well as amongst the soldiers garrisoned there. But Lucius Aelius suddenly realized the imperial standard was absent from its usual place on the main mast, meaning, of course, the emperor was not aboard. A mixture of relief and disappointment rushed through the young man as he prepared to meet the envoy that was even now disembarking. A fit of coughing sent another stain of blood that ruined yet another cloth of embroidered linen which Lucius hastily tossed into the a small pile that filled a woven basket by his desk. A page was quickly by his side with a fresh cloth, neatly folded on a gilt silver tray. Lucius gazed for a time at the page, his favorite in the retinue. The boy was from Macedonia and claimed to be from the same lineage as the great Alexander, who himself claimed to be descendant from the gods. Lucius smiled at the thought. *We are all gods, yet we all suffer the pains of mortals.* Strangely though, the youth did bear a strong resemblance to the portraits of the ancient conqueror. Tall for his age and sinewy, with pale blue eyes and a mass of golden curls that took advantage of the slightest hint of a breeze; the youth was an alluring sight. Despite having just turned thirty-six on the thirteenth of the month of Janus, Lucius could still remember what it was like to be young and adored by an emperor. He was sixteen when he met Hadrian, the age of Antinous when *he* entered the emperor's life. But that golden ephebe was astute enough to depart this life early and carry the heart of his lover with him. As Lucius stared down into the pile of stained cloths, he felt as if he was seeing his own life as it faded away in a bloody heap. He had lived long enough to reach the throne, but would he live long enough to actually sit on it? Lucius Aelius looked again at the fair-haired boy beside him, then turned and made his way toward the receiving hall of the villa.

The envoy presented a packet to the head of Lucius's Praetorian guard, who in turn presented it to Lucius. Seating himself by the warmth of an open brazier, Lucius prepared himself for the worst. The opening lines were formal and official as a chill began to creep into Lucius's heart. But after the official salutations had finished, the missive took on a warm and fatherly tone.

> *My dearest son, it pains me to hear of your constant illness. I too suffer the indignity of illness, and were it not, so I would have arrived along with my ship. As it is, you must allow this letter and the comforts of my vessel to suffice until your arrival into Rome. Listen to the physicians as they attend to you. They are the*

disciples of Asclepious and the best I have to offer. Return to Rome quickly before I am in need of them myself. I miss your sparkling laugh, as do your wife and children. May the gods of the wind bring you back swiftly.

A relieved Lucius ordered his things to be packed and loaded on board the ship with greatest of speed, grateful to leave this cold, unforgiving place.

Chapter Fifty-Two

Homecoming for an Heir

As the great ship plied the waters of the Mare Hadriaticum, the gods of the wind did make themselves known. Boreas used his cold northern wind to drive the ship and its escorts swiftly down the coast until the city of Brundisium could be seen. As the flotilla followed the small peninsula south of Brundisium, Eurus flew in from Greece and his warm, wet wind gently guided the fleet through the Mare Ionium toward the cities of Rhegium and Messina, eventually losing his power as the ship entered the Tyrrhenum. The gifts of the two gods did nothing for Lucius's health as he remained huddled in his staterooms, the burning brazier his closest companion. It was only Zephyrus's warm western breezes that could coax the ailing man out onto the decks to mingle with the courtiers traveling with him. The promise of spring contained in these breezes cheered him, and by the time the ships passed Ostia and reached Portus, the great lighthouse at the entrance of the harbor was a sight Lucius could savor from the deck as well as the busy traffic of heavily burdened ships that bustled around his small fleet. Even the arrival of the heir apparent could not stifle the business of the empire.

Beyond the lighthouse, at the end of a high, narrow pier that protruded from the manmade island, was a colossal statue of Trajan—a not so subtle reminder of the builder of this magnificent port and the small city that embraced its grand design. As Lucius entered the harbor, his own standard, flying from the great aft mast, was still unfamiliar to the populace as they scrambled along the piers and docks of the hexagonal basin to catch a glimpse of the occupant. They knew this as the imperial yacht, but rumors had already circulated with the arrival that morning of the emperor at the great palace built by his adopted father. It was not long before the crowd became aware of the presence of the son and heir of the emperor of Rome, as hasty preparations were made to welcome him in a style due his station. But for Lucius, a hot bath and a bed that did not move with the waves was all he desired.

Hadrian had occupied himself with the business of state and commerce as he waited for the arrival of his son. The imperial palace was more an administrative structure than a private residence, and the emperor appreciated the convenience of its central location between the two large basins of the port. From nearby Ostia came merchants, engineers, and craftsmen to present plans and lists of materials for the never-ending building of the Villa Adriana. Receipts and lists of ships contents littered his desk as the squealing sound of ropes and pulleys extracted the contents from the bowels of those ships. The sound filled the air even as the emperor arrived at the palace and had grown louder as the day progressed. Finally, Hadrian had enough. "Is there a shortage of grease on those ships?" he asked sharply to no one in particular. But Thanos heard the familiar building of anger and irritation in his master's voice and used his position to send a message to the procurator, who in turn alerted the shippers and merchants in the outer rooms that they were angering the emperor. A flock of pages bearing large pots suddenly emerged from the palace and headed with due haste down toward the piers, and soon the squeak and squeal of the cranes and lifts was reduced to a muffled grumble. The sudden realization that the annoying sounds had ceased caused Hadrian to look up from his desk and gaze out the broad window that offered a picture perfect view of his predecessor's masterpiece. He was in time also to witness the arrival of the *Adriana* into the harbor. His *notarius* looked up from his wax tablet to know the purpose of the emperor's sudden silence and, following the direction of his master's gaze, knew the reason. All work would cease now. The emperor's son and favorite had returned home.

The procurator of Portus, Sixtus Didus, left his meeting with the emperor and slipped quietly out of the *palazzo imperial*, past the massive colonnade that formed part of the palace wall and took a short cut through the warehouse that flanked the palace. A storage building for fine arts from all corners of the empire, this building was where he usually lingered, running his hands on the smooth surfaces of the splendid sculptures and rummaging through the endless stacks of tapestries and paintings. But today he was on urgent business. He had to reach the pier where the *Adriana Augusta* was about to dock before the heir apparent disembarked. Lucius Aelius Caesar was not to be kept waiting, and the emperor was not well enough to meet his son at the pier. As the highest official for the harbor complex, the procurator was deemed worthy to greet the new arrival. The Procurator Didus had known Lucius when he was Aelius Commodus, and as he crossed the wide sandy space that led to the docks, he wondered how the name change, and fatherhood, had affected him. After the usual procession of aristocrats and courtiers, the elegant but gaunt figure descending the wide ramp was not what he expected or remembered.

Sixtus had met Lucius Commodus when Sixtus's older cousin, Lucius Didus was still the praefectus of the emperor's personal guard. It was during the year following the death of Antinous, and the emperor was still deep in mourning for the death of his beloved. The occasion was the arrival of Hadrian into Rome, as well as the arrival of the sarcophagus of Antinous. He recalled his cousin Lucius high upon his horse as he surveyed the crowd that gathered to watch the somber procession. Next to him on a pale gray horse rode a young man with golden curls, looking both mournful and triumphant. The elegant slender figure moved like a spirit through out the procession until he reached the emperor's side. A glance that passed between the two told the whole story, yet it would be years before Sixtus could decipher it. As the emperor passed the viewing stand where the sixteen-year-old Sixtus stood with his brothers, both Hadrian and Lucius turned to look in his direction. Sextus saw nothing in the emperor's eyes as he turned away, but a flicker of interest could be seen in the eyes of the golden man. Sixtus's father was a senator, which gained him access to the funeral ceremony in the great Pantheon. Finding his way as close to Lucius as possible, Sixtus managed to catch his eye once again; and the flicker of interest led to an introduction, with an eventual tryst that sealed the friendship.

The physical meetings between the two were brief but passionate. With the death of the Beloved, Hadrian began to reconnect with Lucius; and while Lucius reveled in the newly gained attention, it left him little time for this pleasant new pastime. But while the young man still amused and delighted the emperor, he was now of an age that made visits to the imperial bed unseemly. Instead, Lucius gave lavish parties; and along with the trays of delicacies that were passed around, a parade of beautiful youths was presented before the emperor at each gathering. Hadrian was more amused than insulted by Lucius's somewhat indiscreet purveying. He enjoyed the view but rarely show much interest, which flattered Lucius's vanity and eased the hurt of being too old now for his former lover. The afternoons spent with the athletic Sextus also filled the physical void as the youth displayed talents beyond his years. Despite the fact that gossip about his surrendering to the charms and endowment of the youth flowed like honeyed wine throughout Rome, it made no impression on Lucius. But it made Hadrian's job far more difficult when he began his campaign to make his former favorite his son and heir. When Lucius was faced with the choice of a lover or the throne, the lover was sent to a post in Ostia and forgotten, as Lucius polished his image as a proper Roman family man. Now, as Lucius descended the ramp and headed toward the litter that would bring him to the marble columned palace in the distance, he caught sight of the sturdy young man who came towards him, full of authority.

If Sextus was dismayed by the sight of the emaciated, bearded man, now called Aelius Caesar, he was too wise to show it. Lucius's veneer of breeding and refinement grew transparent upon close inspection, but the handsome features still prevailed.

Leaving nothing to chance, Sextus saluted the heir apparent and introduced himself as the Procurator of Ostia and Portus. A small smile appeared as Lucius Caesar appraised the young man before him. "These six years have not dimmed your beauty, Sextus," Lucius said with a touch of rancor. "The sturdy youth has become a marvel of a man since our last time together." "I left Lucius Commodus and now stand before Lucius Aelius Caesar," replied Sextus softly. "The years have been generous to us both." "More to you than me," was Lucius's terse reply. "I see you command not one basin of water but two. Two ports for one man; how do you manage such a task?" A low laugh escaped from the young man's throat before he responded. "It is more about keeping the merchants from each other's throats than managing the coming and going of ships. Besides," he added, "someday, as emperor, this will be all yours." *If fate allows me to out live the present emperor,* was Lucius's bitter thought. But aloud he said, "And you? Will you belong to me also?" "I come with the ports, my lord," was Sextus's thinly veiled reply. A myriad of witty but scandalous retorts flew through Lucius's brain, but with the close proximity of the soldiers and his couriers, he thought better of it. His father would be pleased. Changing the tone of the conversation, Lucius inquired about the emperor's whereabouts. "The emperor is at the palace, but state business and his health prevented him from meeting you at the pier. He is eager to see you." "And I, him," replied Lucius as he settled himself in the litter. It was a short distance to the palace, but it would not do for him to be out of breath after such a short walk. Better to allow the people to think it was vanity that demanded the use of the litter and not necessity. As they proceeded to the palace grounds, Lucius leaned back against the cushions and allowed his eyes to take inventory of the many blessings the gods had gifted the man who walked with great strides along side him. As handsome as the uniform was that wrapped Sextus's form, Lucius knew no clothing had a right to interfere with the beauty beneath. As the threat of a cough interrupted his thoughts, they changed course, and Lucius examined once again the carefully chosen words he would relay to the emperor.

Hadrian sat by the window that overlooked the port and watched the small drama that unfolded between the thin elegant man and the fine-figured procurator. Even from this distance, Hadrian could make out Lucius's flirtatious movements toward the man, subtle though they were. *Would Antinous resemble this sturdy man had he lived to his age?* The thought of an older Antinous with a face of stubble and a family sent a chill through the old man, and he shook off the image. In his hand, he toyed with a golden bracelet he had chosen for Lucius as a welcome home gift. At each end of the thick twisted curve was a lion's head, each studded with ruby eyes and a collar of lapis. The piece had traveled with him from Lydia and had been intended for Antinous. But on the morning Hadrian chose to present it to him, the boy was found dead by the banks of the Nile. Hadrian could not bear to look at the piece after that, but neither could he part with it. As he watched the procession of the litter and the strapping man beside it, he began to feel the bracelet seemed to portend bad omens and dark endings. Leaving his chair, he returned the piece to its silken pouch and placed it back into the carved cedar box that had served as its home all these years. Hadrian returned to his desk and waited for his son to present himself.

The litter deposited its passenger at the top of the broad marble steps of the palace, and Lucius sailed serenely past the succession of columns, evoking healthy thoughts and the sparkling witticisms that were expected to fall effortlessly from his mouth. With Sextus beside him, he did feel a surge of energy and well-being, and that surge sent a somewhat healthy glow to his face. The Lucius that appeared in the doorway of Hadrian's study was a warming sight and dispelled some of the emperor's misgivings. As he rose to greet the young man, Hadrian's hand went instinctively to the carved box and withdrew the fated bracelet he had dismissed earlier. The full beard Lucius wore was somewhat disconcerting, but Hadrian saw instinctively it was an attempt to emulate his adopted father and brought their physical similarities closer. *His new look will ruffle a few togas in the senate,* thought Hadrian with more than slight satisfaction. "Ave Imperator. Viva Caesar," was Lucius's slightly mocking salute to his father and former lover. Hadrian's face lost color slightly from the jest done in the presence of the court and officials, but his joy at the sight of a seemingly healthy Lucius overcame his disapproval. "Welcome home, Aelius Caesar. It seems the sea air agrees with you. I half expected to see you arrive wrapped in a shroud." The sudden paleness of Lucius's face caused Hadrian to immediately regret his cruel jest. "The sight of you does my heart good and proves my prayers to the gods for your safe return reached their ears." Hadrian's words restored some of the color to Lucius's features, as did the small pouch the emperor handed to him. But the color did not remain for long. As Lucius removed the object from the scarlet silk, he recognized it immediately. He had been there in Lydia when Hadrian drew out the design for the piece and chatted eagerly with the artisan he prodded with gold pieces to finish the work quickly in time for their departure. Even then, Lucius saw the inappropriate nature of the piece. As finely wrought as it was, it would still serve as a reminder to Antinous of Hadrian's prowess and the young life he saved from the lion in Libya. Lucius witnessed Hadrian's elation as well as Antinous's humiliation at that event. *It would not have been well received,* thought Lucius as he examined the gleaming wristlet. But all that is past, and Lucius looked up at Hadrian with a smile and words of thanks for the precious gift. The welcoming ceremony concluded, they all proceeded to the dining room where the wife and children of Lucius Aelius Caesar were eagerly waiting for his arrival.

Chapter Fifty-Three

A Marriage of Convenience

Avidia Plautia and her three children had not seen Lucius in over a year, and although the children seemed oblivious to the physical change in their father, Plautia's regal composure slipped at the first sight of her husband. His beard did little to hide the gauntness of his face and actually aged him far beyond his years. But her pleasure at seeing him overtook any apprehension as they embraced with heartfelt affection. Plautia had given her husband four children in four years, and with a mutual consent, they kept the number at four. Lucius resumed his position as the emperor's favorite as Plautia took her place as the center of Roman society. Sabina, the empress and wife of Hadrian, had all but retired from a society she had rarely interacted with, believing her imperial status far removed from aristocracy and merchant classes. Yet Plautia lived in the empress's omnipresent shadow until illness, and the emperor's adoption of Lucius eased her into society's highest realm. Her husband's transfer to Pannonia did little, at first, to change that position; the attentions and honors bestowed her and her family by the emperor ensured her position. But Lucius's refusal to call for her to join him and the rumors of his illness began to erode Plautia's influence. Despite Hadrian's arranged engagement of her daughter, Ceionia Fabia, to the fifteen-year-old aristocrat Marcus Aurelius, it was clear to her that she should began to steer her eldest son toward the emperor in the guise of grandson and heir to his ailing father. The return of Aelius Caesar to his wife was welcomed in Rome, but his new look and the state of his health began the circulation of a fresh round of rumors. Yet, for a brief time, the image of the perfect *Familia Romana* warmed the winter chill as society settled in to wait for the coming spring.

It was the beginning of December when Lucius Aelius arrived at Portus, then Rome. He made himself at home in the small opulent palace Hadrian had built for his adopted family at the Villa Adriana. Lucius's taste for the extravagant had not diminished, but his physical ability to keep up appearances had. As the emperor began to sequester himself at his small island palace more and more, and Lucius was forced by coughing fits to miss state banquets, Plautia began to take on a more active role as royal hostess, her eldest son at her side. The seven-year-old Lucius Ceionus Verus grew up quickly in a court haunted by an ailing emperor, an absent father, and an increasingly bitter, insecure mother. Plautia began to notice the increased presence of the highborn wife of the recently returned proconsul of Asia, Annia Galeria Faustina. Faustina was the daughter of Marcus Annius Verus and the consort of Titus Aurelius Antoninus, who was also one of the four proconsuls chosen by Hadrian to administer Italia a number of years before. Plautia resented the seemingly blissful marriage of Antoninus and Faustina and the beauty of their children, as well as Hadrian's high regard for the sturdy, level-minded Antoninus. But the death of their third child, Aurelia Fadilla, two years before, and the recent deaths of their two sons, Marcus Fulvus Antoninus and Marcus Galerius Antoninus, had softened Plautia's animosity toward the couple. Faustina's elegance and skill at navigating the diplomatic pitfalls related with visiting dignitaries was a welcome relief for a wife who was watching her husband, and her position in court, slowly die. Young Lucius Verus observed the drama that surrounded him before slipping away to his grandfather's little palace to watch him scratch away on endless parchments, his version of the life he had lived, the way he wished the world to remember it.

Hadrian felt the eyes of his young grandson examining him as he edited the acceptance speech Aelius Caesar would present to the Senate. The reluctance of Aelius to appear before the senate was evident in the contents and flavor of the speech. Brief and unembellished, it was the address of a military man and not the oratory of a future emperor. "So Lucius did learn something during his time in Pannonia, after all," commented Hadrian aloud as he translated the military jargon of the speech into a language suitable to the occasion. "What did you say, Grandpapa?" Young Lucius Ceionius left his drawings that littered the small table Hadrian had made for him and moved silently to the emperor's side. The familiar name he used to address the *imperator* both warmed and amused Hadrian as he placed his arm around the young shoulders. Already, at seven years old, the boy had acquired the sparkle of his father in younger days, a striking contrast to the somber demeanor of the emperor he had grown to adore. Born in the year of Antinous's death, Lucius Ceionius carried a certain significance to Hadrian, a significance that gained strength in the emperor's waning years and was fostered by the child's mother. The boy's tutor, Nicomedes, also promoted the image of Lucius as Antinous reborn, despite the glistening blond of his curls. The emperor's devotion to the boy ensured the position of both mother and tutor. For his part, the boy's devotion was built on his view of his grandfather as the emperor of Rome and a demigod. His youth spared him from the judgmental complexities and intrigues of court and allowed him to simply worship the heroic figure looming over him.

A strong sense of foreboding hung over Hadrian as he finished the oratory Aelius Caesar would present for his official acceptance of the senate's recognition of his title of heir to the throne. This conformation was the fruition of great effort, arm-twisting, and many coffers of gold coinage. Yet something whispered in his head that this event would never occur. Not that the senate would rescind its promise, but that the fates had already written their own version of the future. His adored Lucius was becoming weaker in body and spirit, despite the presence of best physicians who tended to him daily. Hadrian's own body was failing, but it seemed Lucius would precede him to the grave. Forcing these dark thoughts from his mind, the emperor finished the speech just as a light tapping could be heard from the outer hall. Hadrian looked up and saw Lucius standing in the semidarkness, his golden hair and beard catching the light of the lamps filling the study with light. In this light, he resembled the Lucius of the early days—the lithe, elegant figure and wicked dancing eyes. He had just left the banquet in honor of Herodes Atticus, a banquet Hadrian had promised to attend. While his wealthy philanthropist and philosopher friend understood Hadrian's aversion to the lavish spectacles that wore him out, Lucius felt it was an insult to himself as host, as he too had little strength to bear the burden of these events. Wine and fatigue rendered him short tempered, but he chose his words wisely. "Your old friend does not grow younger as he waits on your arrival, my lord." He spoke with a measured restraint, but his words hit their mark. "I must finish this oratory before I can allow myself to entertain a friend who is used to waiting for me," was Hadrian's terse reply, before quietly adding, "You look worn out, or is it too much wine?" "*Too much*? I've never heard of such a thing!" was Lucius's laughing retort. He abruptly retreated into the darkness of the corridor as a fit of coughing followed the hollow laughter. Hadrian saw the boy beside him stiffen with concern for his father, and he put a comforting hand on the golden head of curls in a gesture of comfort. But the specter of death lingered in the shadows as fear whispered in the wind that blew in the darkness outside. Putting down the stylus, Caesar instructed the *notarius* who had been seated on a low bench by the desk to copy the speech in a clearer larger hand and file the original in the library. "Have the copy delivered into the hands of Aelius Caesar in the morning," Hadrian commanded as he took his grandson by the hand and left the study. Taking Lucius by the arm, the three headed for the banquet chamber—an emperor, a future emperor, and one for whom the throne was within reach, but would never be attained.

The early winter morning was milder than the previous days, and Hadrian silently thanked the gods for their benevolence. The soldiers had gone on ahead, before the imperial barges left the pier, to beat the thin crust of ice that had formed on the canal the night before. Wrapped in a woolen toga and heavy furs, Aelius Caesar and his family boarded the lavishly appointed barge as it prepared to follow the emperor's craft for the journey to Rome.

Behind them came the physicians, knights, and courtiers who looked forward to continuing on to the warmer resort towns along the Bay of Naples. Even as they settled themselves amongst the cushions that circled the crackling braziers, preparations were underway in Rome at the Domus Flavia to receive the royal visitors. Hadrian sat under a canopy of purple canvas emblazoned with the imperial eagle and heavily draped with panels of thick wool embroidered with golden bees on a field of purple. A large chuck of charcoal pumped out heat like a great burning heart within a bronze brazier that rested on the backs of three gilded griffins. Wrapped in a cloak of bear fur, Hadrian recalled the image of the Beloved sleeping peacefully on the massive pelt on the floor of a tent, somewhere in Greece. The memory of his pristine beauty, naked and servile, brought an ache inside him—an ache that became the prelude to another attack. Silently clutching his chest, Hadrian slumped in his chair and covered himself with the thick fur. As sweat poured down his face, he prayed that this would be the end. *If the gods be merciful, I will reach death before Lucius and cheat the gloating senate of their victory. Antinous my beloved, will you greet me in the afterlife?* But the pain subsided as the attack passed, leaving Hadrian dejected and sweat drenched. The end he prayed for every day had once more eluded him and as he listened to the splash of the oars on the icy canal as they eased the barge onto the Tiber and brought him closer to the fog covered city of Rome.

Chapter Fifty-Four

A Vaporous Succession

The arrival of the emperor's barge was greeted with muted reaction. The senate had been busy with its campaign to besmirch Caesar's reputation as well as his legacy. Quiet rumors, readily believed, filtered throughout the city, from the marble villas on the hills to the cramped quarters of the lower class apartments. Only in the barracks of the soldiers did the rumors fall on deaf ears; this was the soldier's emperor who for years had eaten the same food as them and slept in the same tents. The lurid tales spread by a soft, corrupt aristocracy held no sway here. To underscore that sentiment, the lusty cheers and salutes echoing along the riverbanks came from the throats of the enlisted men who vocalized their reverence for the emperor of Rome. Glares from these men toward the silent crowd enticed the citizens to add their own lackluster voice to the greeting. Deep within his canopied shelter, Hadrian listened silently as he gathered his strength for a regal arrival into the city.

Aelius Caesar too was gathering his strength for his first appearance in over a year before the people. The physicians had concocted numerous potions for strength and to lessen the severity of his cough. As they left the barge, their many bottles and vials clinked and clattered in the leather pouches that held them. The dark-clad medical men were kept at a respectable distance from the emperor and his heir so as to not draw attention to their presence and add fuel to the existing rumors. The regal bearing of the aging emperor evoked the proper respect and enthusiasm from the crowd as they witnessed what the emperor wanted them to see—a still virile and robust ruler of Rome. The emergence of Aelius Caesar did not exude the same assurance and strength, but the family by his side made up for his lack of a dynamic presence. Gone were the many rings and wide gold bracelets that usually adorned his hands and wrists. Gone too were the heavily embroidered borders on rich silks. The pristine white of his woolen toga with its narrow purple border glowed in the winter light, while Domitia's rich but modest dress complimented her regal bearing. As the children tumbled out of the barge assisted by their personal guards, the young Lucius Verus stepped purposefully down the ramp, already well aware of his royal status. The stylized image of a perfect Roman family was well received by the citizens who watched from the riverbanks; the aura of security and peace surrounded the image and was as reassuring to the eye as the presence of the emperor. The sight of the emperor and what appeared to be two generations of successors to the throne seemed to assure the Pax Romana and warmed the winter chill. The excitement of the crowd grew as the small group clustered together, surrounded by a daunting flank of red-cloaked centurions, and proceeded toward the Sacra Via, where open litters awaited the family and horses stood ready for Caesar and his heir.

Aelius Caesar looked longingly at the well-cushioned litter his wife had made herself comfortable in, but a sharp glance from Hadrian sent a clear message; the horse that stood waiting for him was the correct and expected transportation to the palace. Hadrian knew the public needed to witness the connection between emperor and heir, as well as his son's fitness for the job. Yet deep inside, the discomfort on Aelius's face wounded Hadrian. The man was *not* fit for the responsibilities he would face, and at some point, his body would betray that to the world. As Hadrian returned the salutations of the crowd, he glanced at another man in the retinue who seemed to be sharing the same thoughts. If the man felt the steady gaze of the emperor upon him, he made no acknowledgment of it. Keeping at a respectful distance, he rode with a measured ease. He had learned to bide his time and wait for the fates to reveal their intentions.

Titus Aurelius Antoninus had returned the year before from his proconsul position in Asia, where his tactical handling of the provinces reinforced the emperor's high regard of him. He had returned, at the age of fifty, to accept a position as senator and had been cautiously welcomed into the imperial circle. Clear-minded and purposeful, Antoninus took his place in the royal court and quietly built a foundation of friends and allies, both within the court and in the senate. The favor the emperor showed him came without the taint of gossip, and the fine breeding instilled in him by his highly cultured maternal grandfather, Gnaeus Arrius Antoninus, served him well. The fates seemed to keep watch over him through out his life, even to the point of his marriage to Faustina, whose mother was the half-sister to Vibia Sabina, the now-deceased empress and wife of Hadrian. As Antoninus watched the drama between Hadrian and Aelius Caesar drawing to a close, he prepared himself for the emperor's next move. The stars were quickly aligning in his favor, and despite his wife's misgivings, they were about to shower him with a crown.

From the comfort of her litter, Annia Galeria Faustina too had her thoughts on the drama that was slowly unfolding in the imperial circle. While her beauty had always attracted attention, the rising star of her husband had kept the eyes of all levels of society focused on her every move. The loss of two sons and one daughter during the past two years gave her an aura of gravitas and deepened her commitment to the poor and disadvantaged. This only served to heighten public regard for her and added a luster to Antoninus's reputation. The only shadow in her life was the wife of the new heir to the throne. Plautia knew her position was precarious as it balanced on the teetering health of her husband. She was well aware her future was in her children, and her husband only needed to outlive the emperor, his adopted father, to secure the throne for their eldest son. Her daughter's continued engagement to Marcus Aurelius showed promise due to Aurelius's favor in the eyes of the emperor, but Plautia's hopes lay in her son as she pushed him closer to the throne. All this was common knowledge to Faustina, who preferred to continue her social work and observe the political manipulations from afar. Unlike her husband, the throne held no allure for her.

As the court arrived at the gates of the palaces, the political maneuverings continued. Hadrian and his immediate entourage were made comfortable in the emperor's personal residence, the Domus Flavia, while the family of Aelius Caesar and his courtiers were installed in the Domus Tiberiana, the emperor's state residence. Antoninus and his wife and household were given the Domus Augustana, the former residence of Flautina's aunt, the empress Sabina. A light snow began to dust the capital as the families settled down in their drafty marble palaces, their glowing braziers working valiantly to keep the cold at bay. Despite the heating system beneath the palaces, the December cold still found Aelius, who sought refuge in the more intimate bath of Hadrian's palace. It was there that Hadrian announced succinctly the purpose for the winter visit to Rome. And even in the sweltering heat of the bath, Aelius felt a chill run through him.

Hadrian knew he had to plan his succession carefully and expediently. With his own time running out, he needed to face the situation head-on without regard for feelings. The confusion of the senate regarding his choice was understandable, unaware as they were of a promise made long ago. To bring the promise to fruition, a great deal of influence and gold had been spread about to turn Lucius Commodus Verus into Aelius Verus Caesar. While Aelius had served capably as senator and was well connected, his lack of military experience and ill health made him a less than perfect candidate. But for Hadrian, a promise was a promise; one used seven years earlier to convince the then Lucius Commodus to marry and provide heirs for Hadrian's throne, a throne that would go to Lucius first as Hadrian's adopted son. Although initially reluctant, the entry of a new favorite into the imperial circle finally convinced Lucius of the wisdom of complying with Hadrian's wishes. The appearance of Antinous caused a stir in the tight-knit entourage, even while invisibly sequestered in the paedagogium on the hill. The twenty-seven-year-old Lucius could not compete with the sixteen-year-old beauty from Bithynia. It was then that Lucius accepted Hadrian's pledge of eventual adoption and the inevitable throne—a pledge that would come to haunt the emperor in his final years.

It was the implementation of that agreement that was being discussed in the heavy air of the marble bath. The acceptance oratory Hadrian had requested from Aelius and worked on for days was to be presented in person to the senate after the emperor's birthday on the twenty-fourth. Hadrian wished to see another year of his life pass and had chosen the day after the new year for Aelius to address the senate. He needed the acceptance speech to be presented to the senate and the decision confirmed before the court retired to the Bay of Naples, where, he hoped, he could die in peace. But he was suddenly roused from his thoughts by the sounds of a coughing fit that was wracking Aelius's frail body. *By the gods, I'll outlive him yet. The fates will defy my wishes for sure!* Aelius gamely recovered from this bout, but Hadrian still noticed blood in the water that had sprayed from his sickly son. The sight of his weakened state forced the emperor to silently acknowledge the next step that needed to be addressed with stealth and speed. With Lucius Verus being too young to rule, Antoninus, with his successes as praetor and proconsul of Italia and Asia, was the logical choice after Aelius, but with stipulations. After Antoninus would be Marcus Aurelius beside Lucius Verus. The succession would address any problems that could arise and secure a peaceful empire for generations.

Hadrian left the bath and quickly dressed in his woolen tunica and a heavy cloak, making his way to the Domus Augustana.

There, with Faustina present, he presented Antoninus with his plan of succession, which included the adoption of Aelius's son, Lucius Verus and Marcus Verus, or *Verissimus* as Hadrian fondly called him. The serious, intellectual Marcus was "most truthful" as Hadrian's nickname implied and an interesting counterpoint to the already frivolous Verus. Faustina listened impassively as Hadrian discussed the terms of Antoninus's succession and thought back on her own sons who had died too soon. The fates had been fickle, but the gods had still kept watch. After a time, Hadrian rose and, with Antoninus by his side, made his way to the Domus Tiberiana and the court that waited for the emperor to begin the evening's festivities.

Theos of Lydia, the imperial chamberlain, met the emperor at the massive double doors of the palace. The day had been long and draining for Hadrian, and the mask of energy and health was quickly slipping from the aged man Theos met at the portico. As the small entourage continued to the banqueting hall, Hadrian sought the comfort of the lavishly decorated cubiculum with its hanging oil lamps and a glowing brazier creating a sense of welcoming warmth beside the thickly cushioned bed. Theos closed the heavy drapes in the doorway before offering a cup of warm honeyed wine to the emperor, who gratefully accepted it before sinking back into the deep cushions. "I need some time to recover, Theos," Hadrian whispered. "Tell them to begin the banquet, and I will be with them soon." Theos bowed and slipped out of the room and, after issuing the emperor's orders, stayed close to the drapery in the doorway to wait for the emperor's next command. Hadrian closed his eyes and reflected on the day, as well as the days that would follow. The birthday of Mithras would arrive in a few days, and with it, the subsequent banquets during the following days. Hadrian looked forward to the end of the year and the journey to his villa at Baiae. But there were things to deal with before then. Willing his mind to shut down, he allowed his eyes to wander over the elaborate frescos in the cubiculum as the restful views of gardens and lounging musicians lulled him to a light sleep and the music from the nearby dining chamber filtered through the drapes in the doorway.

Hadrian's entrance at the banquet was belated, but his renewed energy delighted the guests and seemed to revitalize the gathering that earlier seemed to be winding down. As he took his place on a couch that stood beside Aelius, he noticed wine and the medication his heir had been prescribed were mixing too well and bringing on sleep. But while this fatigue showed in his eyes, it relaxed the haggard features, and the proud cheekbones were flushed above the pale blond of his beard. Hadrian motioned away the slave that had come forward to renew Aelius's wine cup. "No more wine for you, Aelius. It would be unseemly for you to fall asleep in front of our guests, my son," Hadrian spoke gently to prevent a defensive response, but Aelius was far too overcome by the wine and doses of opium poppy to object.

While the assembled guests drank and laughed, seemingly oblivious to the fact that their host was nearly incapacitated, Plautia sat across the room with a frozen smile on her face. The frosty stare from her eyes competed with the rows of ice blue topaz that ringed her neck and glittered from her ears. The façade of tranquility and domestic harmony witnessed by the public had vanished once the couple had crossed the threshold of the palace.

Their marriage had never easy, and she thanked the gods that her fertility enabled her to produce four children from the few conjugal visits her husband had paid her. But she had married for wealth and social status and because the emperor deemed it to happen. For a time, she felt her aspirations would bear fruit. Yet now, as she found herself closer to the empress's crown than she had ever imagined, she also seemed to be watching it slip further and further away, along with the life of her husband. As she picked at a glass bowl of ripe figs, she turned her gaze to Faustina and her husband, deep in conversation with a senator and his wife. Antoninus had the respect of the senate, and his wife, the respect of the people. It seemed to her he had grown more regal in stature, and Faustina, in gray pearls and heirloom emeralds, appeared to be posed for her portrait on a coin. Antoninus too had chosen to be bearded like his emperor and now looked like the image of the Hadrian of old. The gossips had long been busy questioning the emperor's choice of Lucius over Antoninus. Now, Plautia too began to question the reason for his choice. And as she watched the slaves assist the Hadrian's thin, frail heir from the room, her eyes followed the emperor as he made his way toward the small group presided over by Antoninus and his wife. Although in the same room, Plautia suddenly felt she was on the outside looking in. Rising slowly from her couch, she crossed the vast chamber and disappeared through the towering doorway. No one noticed her departure.

Days of celebration arrived with Mithra's birthday. Hadrian had greeted these days with some apprehension, yet most had gone smoothly without incident. He had dressed with care on those mornings, the amethyst-studded fibula nestled firmly in the purple folds of his imperial toga. After a light breakfast, he walked to the

Domus Tiberiana and followed the standard bearers and lictors into the immense reception hall, their heavy boots clattering on the marble floor. Waiting for him there were foreign dignitaries, knights, and scholar from his court and a scattering of senators, their white togas and red sashes setting them apart from the rest of the court. Hadrian nodded to the senators as he passed, his face impassive but his eyes cold with disdain. The absence of the majority of senators was quite obvious to the assembled court, but the slight was not one they dared to discuss. Whispers of death warrants issued for a number of senators filtered through the palace, but not loud enough to reach the ears of the emperor. Hadrian's increasingly erratic behavior lent itself to a number of stories, some more believable than others. But for today, the mood was to be festive and celebratory as Hadrian faced what he prayed would be his last celebration of Mithras's day.

The presentation of gifts and honorary proclamations seemed endless, but eventually, the line of guests dwindled, and the participants left for their homes or the baths. Hadrian left for the Domus Flavia where he too made his way to his private bath. After a time in the frigidarium, he took the narrow corridor to the steaming waters of the bath. For a time, he sat along the side of the pool and read a section of the *Punica*, a work by Silius Italicus whose seventeen-volume poem held a place of honor in the library at the Villa Adriana as well as in the great library Hadrian built in Rome. But the work could not hold his interest on this day, and the pain that lingered in his body distracted him further. Slipping into the steaming basin, Hadrian sat on the stone ledge under the water, rested his head against the pool's marble edge, and waited for warmth of the water to ease away the ache. From somewhere in the distance, the sound of a flute and a lyre filtered into the vaulted chamber and mingled with the splashing of the fountain along the far wall. In a niche over the fountain, a sculpture of Antinous as a naked Hermes. The god figure stared down into the spray that glistened in the glow of the many lamps hanging from the ceiling and the torchieres that stood before the columns of pink marble. The mystical feel of the light and the sweet sound of the distant music lulled Caesar into a light slumber, as the aroma of the scented water added to the sensual aura.

As he drifted in and out of the murky vapor of conscious and unconscious, another scent could be detected—a familiar one that he had not experienced in years. A heady aroma that recalled nights in Macedonia after a day of hunting, darkened chambers filled with precious volumes in Athens and still afternoons on cushions by the Canopus at the secluded villa. The taste that followed that scent was clean sweat and intoxicatingly smooth pale skin. It was the unique aroma of the boy, the golden youth, the Beloved Antinous. Hadrian's eyes opened slowly, as if to unveil a dream he could not believe, yet prayed, was true. Had he died? Did he fall asleep and drown in the warm, steaming pool. As he opened his eyes further, he saw the same room he had entered earlier, the same lamplight, the same fountain. But the niche over the fountain appeared empty of its sculpture.

The soft padding sound of bare feet brought forth a shadowy figure appearing in the haze of steam—naked, glistening, pale. A mane of dark curls, damp and shining from the dense mist crowned a noble head with dark eyes and full lips. The thick lashes that shaded those almond-shaped eyes held moist droplets that fell in slow motion to the broad pallid chest and ran down a firm, taut stomach. Between firm thighs swayed a manly phallus, untouched by the barbarism of circumcision. The gleaming image strode boldly toward the half-submerged Hadrian, fell to one knee and, bending toward him, kissed him gently. "Forgive me and release my soul," Hadrian pleaded to the vision before him. "I will come to you soon, my love, when I know you have suffered enough," the ghostly image whispered softly. With a small smile, the young god rose to his full height and slowly entered the pool. Wading toward the center of the basin, the firm, full buttocks that had captivated Hadrian so long ago caught the light of countless flames before melting into the steaming mist. Splashing handfuls of water on his face, Hadrian looked again in the direction the youth had vanished. There in the niche above the fountain stood once again the statue of Antinous-Hermes. Hadrian closed his eyes, sank back against the rim of the pool, and wept bitterly.

Time had flown swiftly after that and the emperor's servants began to whisper nervously to each other. Theos, however, dared to enter cautiously and found his master still in the pool. Hadrian had composed himself by this time, but the swollen redness of his eyes betrayed him. Theos had brought thick cotton sheets for drying and a long woolen tunic that he assisted the emperor into. Another servant entered with mulled wine served in a cup of thick, embossed glass. The young cupbearer's hand shook as he presented the drink to the emperor, the rare glass cup rattling on the gilded tray. Hadrian took the cup and studied the down turned head of the youth. The youth's dark curls sent a stab of pain through Caesar as he took the boy's chin in his hand and raised his head. "Look at me, boy," the emperor spoke firmly but not without warmth. The dark eyes slowly traveled up to the older man's face, and as they settled there, a mixture of fear and curiosity moved the emperor. "Thank you for my wine," Caesar said softly as he ran his thumb over the youth's soft mouth. Tapping the boy's smooth cheek gently, Hadrian sighed and reached for another cotton sheet to cover his head before making his way to the bedchamber. He turned to look at the youth once more. *No, those days are through,* he thought regretfully. Turning again, he disappeared into the darkened corridor and, after saluting the guards at the doorway, retired to his bedchamber for the night.

And so the birthday of Mithras passed quietly in the palaces on the Palatine. The *imperator Caesar* remained in residence, and Aelius Caesar was confined to his rooms, both due to ill health. The underground temples of the Persian god hummed with the festivities that surrounded his birthday celebrations, as did the dining rooms of many of Rome's citizens. Ironically, the Christian sect of the city also celebrated, but it was a day they claimed as the birth date for *their* god. Hadrian eventually ignored both and spent the remaining days within his darkened bedchambers and haunting the corridors that connected those rooms to the library and bath. The visit of Antinous in his dream the previous night still obsessed him, and the embittered words he spoke were too prophetic for comfort. Racked by violent pain and haunted by his own dark deeds, the dream did not bode well. Immersing himself in his work, Hadrian finally finished the speech Aelius was to give before the senate just after the New Year to accept his position as adopted son and heir to the emperor of Rome. Yet even as he finished polishing the closing line, he could not shake the feeling these words would never be spoken, at least not by Aelius.

Chapter Fifty-Five

Golden Dust

It was the first day of the new year, and a small army of physicians clustered in the private rooms of Aelius Caesar, their faces taut with apprehension and discomfort. They had been summoned to prepare the emperor's heir for his presentation to the senate. But a persistent cough and shortness of breath had kept him confined to his bed for the past week, and on this auspicious day, he was no better. None of the physicians present wished to be involved in this intervention, but the emperor's summons came with an escort from his private guard, a convincing response to their reluctance to attend the patient. As they surveyed the situation, the emperor suddenly appeared beside the bed. Expecting the worst, the physicians attempted to vanish into the shadows, but Hadrian would have none of it. After a thorough interview, Caesar picked two Greeks who professed knowledge of the proper pharmaceuticals that would prepare Aelius for his day.

Together, the physicians produced a costly theriac based on an old recipe attributed to Andromachus, the personal physician to Nero. The combination of castor oil, cinnamon, frankincense, ginger, and honey was combined with myrrh, pepper, and saffron. These potent ingredients were added to an even more potent opiate mixture and presented to Hadrian in a small vial with a golden stopper in the shape of a lion's head. After, the physicians requested a glass beaker of water and honeyed wine and a small amount of the theriac was dissolved in the liquid and given to Aelius. After a time, his cough ceased and he seemed to rest easy. Satisfied, the emperor returned to the Domus Flavia and prepared for the next day.

That evening in the Domus Flavia was spent perusing Lucius's correspondences from Pannonia and comparing them to the dispatches from the proconsuls Rufus and Balbinus. Vibullius Rufus had joined up with Lucius's Legion X Gemina in a skirmish near Vindobona where, according to Rufus, Lucius had proven himself an able commander. While Rufus's Legion XIV Gemina carried the bulk of the fighting, Lucius's tactics showed a judicial use of his legion's ability and strength. While the skirmish was not the rugged battle Lucius had portrayed in his letter, his accomplishments were not as embellished as Hadrian had first suspected. His lack of experience did not deter him from making an impression on the troops—a statement made numerous times in the dispatches of Rufus and in those of Publius Balbinus in the eastern sector. In reading these letters, Hadrian realized it was not Lucius who let him down, but Lucius's body that had let them both down. His performance in Pannonia was a side of the man Hadrian had never seen, and never would. A realization passed over the emperor; had he waited until the spring or stationed Lucius in a more southern climate, perhaps things would not be as they are right now. The youth Hadrian had known and loved had become a man, yet the love of the youth had continued without his former lover even noticing. Another life was slipping through

Hadrian's hands, and like the first time, he was responsible for its departure.

Hours had passed, and a polite cough interrupted Caesar's thoughts; he looked up to see Theos standing hesitantly by the doorway holding a small velum packet. "A messenger from the Domus Tiberiana, my Caesar." The worried look on Theos's face told Hadrian that, as always with servants, the man knew the contents of the message before the letter was opened. Breaking the seal, Hadrian immediately recognized Plautia's handwriting, unsteady as it was. She urged him to come with haste to Lucius's bedside. Time was slipping away. Sensing there was no time for the intricacies of a toga, Hadrian called for his tunic and cloak, preparing himself for the worst. The cool-minded Plautia would only call for him if the end was near. The ground seemed to shift beneath his feet as he made his way through the snow-dusted courtyard to the palace. Aelius's ragged breathing could be heard even before Hadrian reached the royal apartments. The firelight within the bedchamber cast shadows over Plautia's profile as she stood in the doorway, worry and fear aging her beyond her years. The sound of his boots caused her to turn and then fall silently to her knees. Hadrian stopped and lifted the woman as she raised her head to address him. "The gods have ignored our pleas, my lord." She then added urgently, "Is there nothing you can do?" "If the gods wish this, there is little I do in this matter," was Caesar's rather terse reply. Though hurtful, it was the only way he could maintain control. Gripping the curtains that framed the doorway firmly for a moment to retain his emotions, Hadrian entered the chamber and walked slowly toward the heavily draped bed. The black-robed physicians gathered there scattered like chastened crows at the sight of the emperor. The bravest of the group stepped forward and spoke hesitantly, "Great Caesar, the theriac seemed to provide some healing and comfort, and he seemed revived for a time. He had risen from his bed and was writing when another attack occurred." He added, "We have given him another dosage, but I fear . . ." His voice trailed away, unwilling to state the obvious. Hadrian walked to the table where he saw the speech of thanks, its reworking covering page after page in Lucius's own writing. Collecting them in his hands, Hadrian turned to approach the bed once again, this time taking a seat beside Aelius's frail body before reading the spidery handwriting. Aelius cast his eyes on the pages, then raised them up to search Hadrian's face for a response. After finishing the last page, Caesar closed his eyes for a moment and searched for words, not to critique the content but to convey the emotions that pummeled him like great leaden fists. "You used my suggestions wisely yet found your own voice. You have become your own man after all." He wished to say more, but his mind seemed to be frozen in grief. Lucius Aelius felt tears of relief fill his eyes as he gazed at the man he had loved and lived to please all these years. But it was disappointment and regret he felt now, not love. "I might as well have written them in dust," was his hoarse reply. Time was too precious now to hide the bitterness he felt. And that bitterness flew at Hadrian like poisonous arrows, each hitting its mark. "I did what I could and kept my promise to you. I had no idea the cost." Hadrian too had feelings of bitterness and regret, but his were too cruel to pour on a man with only moments to live. And besides, they were the product of his own foolish defiance of the fates. Before him lay dying the plans for his succession, dearly paid for with a river of *sesterces* that flowed to the senate and the bullying presence of the army. So much time, effort, and money went into fulfilling a promise that sated his ego yet went against all logic, as well as the will of the senate. The senate could be appeased, but logic and the fates won out. Gazing down at his dying favorite, Hadrian chastised himself for being too indulgent over the years and providing for his every whim. He had built a marble temple on a foundation of mud, and now he watched as it slowly sank into oblivion.

The rancor and regret in Hadrian's eyes forced Lucius to turn away. Words were useless now, a waste of precious breath. Yet, as his gaze fell upon his golden haired son beside his bed, a ray of light appeared. Raising a thin pale hand, he pointed to Lucius Verus and said softly, "There, Hadrian. There is my legacy and your hope. Watch over my son, and through him will I live and fulfill your promise." As Hadrian turned to gaze at the boy, he heard a small gasp, and a shadow passed over the youth's face. Turning back at the fragile body beside him, Hadrian saw that Lucius Aelius Verus Caesar was no more.

Chapter Fifty-Six

Death Begets an Heir

The first day of the new year was a foreboding one. As the body of his heir lay cold and silent in the Domus Tiberiana, Hadrian dictated letters to three *notarii* at once—one to the senate, one to Titus Antoninus, and one to the widow of Lucius Aelius Caesar. The nature of each letter was vastly different in motive, effect, and emotion, and each needed to be worded with strength and diplomacy. Not wishing to disturb the senate or the public during the holiday, the letter to the senate would wait until the day after which would have been, ironically, the day they were expecting Aelius's visit. After the senate, a public announcement would be formally released. Hadrian would present Titus Antoninus as his adopted son and the new heir. This decision was unseemly and abrupt but given the prestige of Antoninus's lineage, his success over the years in the offices of quaestor, praetor and proconsul, and his personal reputation within the senate, Hadrian expected no resistance to his choice. The most influential member of the senate, Marcus Annius Verus, was Antoninus's father-in-law. When Verus's son, Marcus Verus the Younger, died nearly fourteen years earlier, the elder Verus adopted his grandchildren, Annia Faustina and Marcus Aurelius, the same Aurelius who was betrothed to Aelius Caesar's daughter Ceionia Fabia. As Hadrian dictated the senate's letter, he smiled ruefully at the tangled web of pedigree and political intrigue he was introducing. If the senate confirmation of Lucius as Hadrian's heir was nearly at knifepoint, his sudden replacement came with everything but giftwrap. But buried deep within that tangled web was the young Lucius Verus, the key to Antoninus's ascension to the throne. Through him, Lucius Aelius Caesar would be vindicated, and Hadrian's wish would be fulfilled.

The letter to Titus Antoninus reiterated the conversation that took place at the Domus Augustana. His ascension to the title of Titus Aelius Caesar Antoninus would depend on his acceptance of all Hadrian's conditions, and he had raised no objections to those conditions during their meeting. At this point, with the crown only one step away, Hadrian knew there would be no hesitation. With the astute and respected Faustina on one side and his revered father in law on the other, Antoninus had judicious, as well as influential, council. For Antonius, the adoption of Marcus Aurelius to take the place of his dead son, Marcus Aurelius Fulvus, was one of fate's mysteries. As for Lucius Verus, that adoption would be a small price to pay for a throne. And yet, as Hadrian dictated the final pieces of the puzzle, his satisfaction dimmed at the prospect of the missive to be sent to the widow of the tragic Lucius Aelius. In this game of crowns and empires, she was the only one who would be left with next to nothing.

Avidia Plautia, once so close to the title of empress of Rome, was now a widow of little consequence. As she kept vigil beside the body of her husband, she waited for the appearance of the emperor. She was astute enough to know he held her future and that of her children in his hands. She had anticipated this day, despite her stubborn denial of its arrival, and had done what she could to present her eldest son to the emperor in a favorable light. Accustomed to a world where her destiny always seemed preordained, Plautia now sat in the drafty dark palace and awaited her fate. A servant's muffled tapping at the door announced a messenger from the emperor who held in his hands a folded packet emblazoned with the purple wax of the imperial seal. Presented to her without a word, she knew that contained within it was her future.

Hadrian's letter had taken on a formality that hid his sorrow and sense of loss. It was an official correspondence that would become public, and the public had no right to see into his heart. As Plautia read the letter for the second time, she heard the sound of boots on the marble floor of the corridor leading to the bedchamber. She rose from her chair and greeted the emperor before lowering herself to her knees. Hadrian came to her quickly, raised her up again, and embraced her. Plautia offered the chair she had been using, but a servant was close behind the emperor with a chair of gilded wood. Hadrian refused both and moved toward the body, seating himself on the bedside.

Plautia's moment of reflection allowed Hadrian a chance to observe the new widow's elegant features. The lamplight sent shadows across her pale skin as she looked pensively at the corpse of her husband lying on the low bed. Everything about her look was studied, carefully arranged, and executed. The succession of blood-red cabochons circling her slender neck caught the firelight and sent crimson flames across her face. Hadrian had gifted her with these rubies, the size of plump grapes, to celebrate the birth of Lucius Verus and to make up for the fact that her husband paid her little attention during her pregnancy. Plautia had always held a fascination for Hadrian, yet she had proven to be as tragic as her husband. She had always been a beautiful compliment to her spouse—elegance with elegance. Hadrian studied the refined features, the high-swept tresses, the delicate profile that would never gain immortality on a coin. All she was, all she aspired to be, would go to the grave with her husband.

And as with her husband, Lucius Verus, had become her saving grace. Beyond her own son, she held no sway, wielded no influence. She had planned for her son to keep her relevant, but the future would not go according to her plan. A simple imperial signature would end even that influence. Upon Hadrian's demise, Antonius's adoption of Lucius Verus would remove him from his mother's grasp, and herself from any sphere of influence. As Hadrian continued to gaze at Plautia, he realized he was witnessing the end of any meaning in her life, a life she thought she had planned out perfectly. The self-assured little girl who once told him she would become an empress one day was now a widow of *no* consequence.

Plautia sensed Hadrian's gaze and looked up to see the pale gray eyes lost in thought. Raising her head proudly and returning the penetrating gaze, the empress that would never be smiled warmly and addressed the emperor. "My future lies here with my husband, and I relinquish both to the fates with a calm heart. Life has taught me my aspirations were shallow and ill conceived. My only wish now is to vanish into the shadows and watch from afar my eldest son's ascension. As his star rises brightly, mine falls into the sea and is extinguished. I am content." In one statement, Plautia bowed to the will of the emperor and ensured herself a comfortable retirement. By assuring Hadrian that the adoption of her son would not be challenged, Plautia secured his gratitude and benevolence. Hadrian's instinct had not failed him. The cold, formal letter had clearly sent the message of what the future held and allowed Plautia to decide for herself where she would fit in that future. Her statement set all that to rest. Hadrian rose and stared down at the bed where his most misguided object of affection lay. Here, in the silence of this death chamber, he could almost hear the crackling of parchment as the last chapter in this slim volume of a life ended and the book closed forever.

On the second day of the new year, the senate received the emperor at the newly restored basilica. Funded entirely by Hadrian, the building the senate convened in would be a constant reminder of the emperor's power and presence. As they waited for that imperial presence, the senators sat silently on the cushions that warmed their unforgiving marble seats and pondered the consequences of their acceptance of the emperor's choice of an heir. Only Gnaeus Arrius Antoninus sat placidly in the front row seat he had occupied for many years. The senators noticed Gnaeus's adopted son Antoninus was missing, a deviation of the norm that was obvious even to the preoccupied patricians who were now becoming restless in their seats. Their impatience vanished as commotion outside the senate basilica signaled the emperor's arrival and the senators prepared themselves for their official acquiescence to the emperor's will.

Caesar arrived with Titus Antoninus at his side. Yet, while this struck the senators as odd, it was the emperor's garb that turned blood to ice. Clad in a black, purple-bordered *toga pulla*, the emperor's face was strained and solemn. Without waiting for the ceremonial greeting of welcome from the senate, Hadrian seated himself on the ivory throne and waited for the rest of his personal guard and entourage. Those already assembled anxiously noticed that Titus Antoninus, standing beside the emperor, was dressed in the same toga pulla. Once the clattering guard was in position, silence had settled in the vast hall and in that silence the brittle chill seemed to grow more intense as the Imperator rose slowly from his throne and began to address the assembly.

The announcement of the death of Aelius Caesar shook the senate to its core. Despite the initial resistance to Hadrian's choice, the decision had been ratified, and they had begun to plan their strategy accordingly. The sudden death of the emperor's heir threw confusion into those plans and rendered them useless. But as the emperor continued his oratory, it became increasingly clear that he had already laid his own strategy, a backup that must have been in place for some time. The presentation of Titus Aurelius Antoninus as the new heir produced another shockwave, but this time, it was a wave of excitement that rushed through the chamber. Gradually, the senators began to realize why Gnaeus Arrius was neither surprised or perturbed by the sudden events. The elder Antoninus had been privy to the backup plan all along and had merely waited for the time to arrive.

The emperor's speech was drawing to a close, and the senate was now digesting the gravity of the situation. There was a sense of relief at the offer of another heir apparent—an heir they approved of and were grateful for. Caesar returned to his seat, and Antoninus rose to address the emperor. "Salutis Adriani Caesar, Father of his Country, Pontifex Maximus, heir of Divine Augustus, son of Divine Trajan and Plotina, husband of Divine Sabina, Keeper of the Flame of Antinous, Archon of Athens, Protector of Britannia, Gaul, and Parthia, Pharaoh of Egypt, and Father of Titus Aurelius Antoninus. Your son salutes you with all humility and lays at your feet his life and that of his family . . ." By the end of Antoninus's testimonial of thanks and gratitude to his adoptive father, Aelius Caesar was all but forgotten as the senate rose as one to confirm the emperor's choice. His affirmation as adopted son and heir followed Hadrian's proclamation quickly. Antoninus's sober acquiescence and his eloquent reminder of his adopted father's overwhelming attributes left the senate in a rare state of respect for their emperor tempered with an awe for his indomitable power and sense of purpose. From his marble chair, the elderly Gnaeus Antoninus basked in the glow of his former adopted son's new status, as well as his own, while his fellow senators clustered around him and quietly offered their congratulations for this turn of fortune. From his throne, Hadrian watched the more opportunistic senators elbowing each other for a place by the two generations of Antoninus. *Old dogs fighting over a new bone*, thought Hadrian. As he watched the two men take their new status in stride, Hadrian felt a morose sense of completion, as if the story of his life was now finally drawing to a close. With the line of succession stabilized and the senate's full approval, he could deal with Lucius's burial, and then watch as his own days dwindled down.

The public announcement of Aelius Caesar's death was greeted with shock and confusion. The citizens were never fully aware of the extent of his precarious health, and after the recent display of the perfect *Familia Romana,* the public had begun to perceive their future with a new regime. After the initial confusion, dark suspicions began to arise. Hadrian had already anticipated this shift in the public's mood and used the skills of the Frumentarii to plant the right stories among the gossips. Within a day, the public's mood had shifted once again, and the new choice of heir was embraced with little effort and great acclaim. The Antonine family was revered and respected, and pius Faustina's renown invoked adoration among the masses. In Roman opinion, finally "one of their own" was about to grasp the reins of power, and a bright new day would soon be dawning.

The following day would see a delegation of senators appear before the emperor at the Domus Tiberia to offer an official proclamation of mourning for Lucius Caesar and a commemoration of his life. The sight of the imperial family unnerved many of the senators as they approached the dais in the colossal throne room. Seated stiffly in his gilt bronze and ivory throne, Hadrian presided over the closest image of a family the senate had ever witnessed. Approaching the dais with royal proclamations in hand, Gnaeus Arrius smiled slightly as he observed Hadrian's final stroke of genius. To the right of the emperor's throne stood Titus Antoninus, now Titus Aelius Antoninus Caesar. Seated beside him was the revered Annia Galeria Faustina. Beside her stood Faustina the Younger. To the left of the throne stood Lucius Verus, with Plautia seated beside him. Marcus Aurelius stood beside Plautia's daughter Ceionia Fabia, his betrothed. This collection of royalty, as well as three generations of imperial succession gathered under an eagle-emblazoned canopy of deep purple created an aura of unbridled majesty and continuity in the vast marble hall. The senate's position as a ceremonial body was made clear, just as Hadrian's display of dominance, permanence, and power was unmistakable. While the late morning light from the high windows of the chamber continued to anoint the enthroned royals before them, the senate's delegation presented their proclamations in an atmosphere of hushed reverence.

The salutation and official address of condolence were what Hadrian expected from the delegation. But the senate's offer to deify Aelius, being that he was the son of the emperor, was unanticipated, as was the lack of scorn he would have expected to accompany that offer. Unexpected too was the proclamation of a special assembly of the senate for the purpose of eulogizing the deceased. Hadrian saw this as the perfect setting to further cement the line of succession and assure Lucius Verus's right as an heir to Antoninus, while the inclusion of Marcus Aurelius along side that succession would sweeten any remaining bitterness the senate still clung to in regards to the emperor and his departed son. The final pieces of the succession were easing into place; the fates were finally smiling down on Hadrian.

From under a veil of black silk gauze, Plautia's gem-studded diadem quivered slightly as the senate announced the offer of deification. Being the widow of a deified prince would elevate her status to one almost equal to Faustina. With her son now the legal charge of the new heir, her connection and sphere of influence was minimal at best. She was merely a wealthy widow who could be forced into a politically advantageous marriage and never heard from again. But the deification of Lucius would protect her from being cast aside. As she considered her prospects, she absentmindedly ran her fingers over the ruby strand the emperor had gifted her with. The addition of a black ribbon had made the gift more appropriate for the occasion—a gift that would remind the emperor of his duty to her. Plautia was no fool. The main piece of the dynastic puzzle depended on her son, and to degrade the mother would be to degrade the son. As the senators filed by and bowed respectfully, Plautia sat rigid and regal, the image of the empress she would never have the chance to be.

Hadrian sat silently as the knights, courtiers, and ambassadors joined the senators in their expressions of condolence. Wave after wave of dignitaries filed by and expressed their regret. But Hadrian was no fool. He saw the relief in their eyes and felt a pang of guilt in the relief that whispered silently in his own mind. For all his efforts, passion and politics did not mix, and Lucius had been the victim of Hadrian's attempt to do so. As he sat on the hard throne clad in his heavy black toga, the diadem of gold laurel leaves and clutching the paraphernalia of state, Hadrian felt as if he was already turning into a wax effigy of himself, prepared for the fires of immortality.

The next day was typical for the month of Janus—cold and gray with the bitter smoke of innumerable cooking fires lingering thickly in the air. The cold did no good for Hadrian's aching body, and he went by litter, with some unwillingness, to the senate. It was nearly a week since Lucius's death; it had taken that long to polish the final documents that formally proclaimed his decision.

The acceptance needed to be unanimous; the compliance, unequivocal. Once the official documents were signed and sealed with red wax before the senate, he wished nothing more than to disappear into a mist, far from the reach of the fawning, crafty faces that greeted him at the doorway of the senate basilica. The tributes he provided to the senate over the years were sickening to him now. He had worked so hard to glorify the city of Rome with temples, monuments, and villas, but the patrician class he had come to loath never accepted him. They worshiped his august father and would probably do the same for his new heir, but what they would do to his own legacy; he cared little. His life had become a black pit he wished to sink into, eternally floating in a void of darkness—mindless, painless, eternal.

Antoninus had accompanied the emperor to the senate, but walked the distance from the Palatine to the basilica. By horse, he would have hovered unacceptably over the royal litter; and by litter, he would have appeared to the crowd, fragile and aloof. Hadrian smiled at the courtesy, yet felt suddenly so much older because of it. As Antoninus walked alongside the litter, he thought of the warm embrace his wife had given him before his departure. Faustina was on her way to visit Plautia at the Domus Augustana to pay her respects to the widow who seemed to never leave the ashes of her deceased husband. Antoninus knew his wife would much rather be at one of the many hospitals she had founded to assist with the poor and afflicted. He knew that even as empress, the poor would be of more importance to her than the tiara. Antoninus smiled slightly at the thought, and for the first time, saw hope in the future in the Rome that spread before him.

Hadrian too was deep in his thoughts. But his were not so warm and full of hope. His visit with Plautia that morning was less than pleasant. He had told her of his decision to refuse the senate's offer of deification for Lucius. Despite Lucius' status as the son of the emperor and heir, the process of deification was far too costly and, moreover, inappropriate. With Lucius no longer a part of the equation, the succession could not afford his shadow upon it. Hadrian settled back into the cushions as he recalled Plautia's blue eyes go from a regal widow's tears to a wraith's icy stare as she began to comprehend the significance of his words. With a single decision, Caesar had wiped out her chance at elevated social status, and with it, any influence she might enjoy. "I have lost my husband and my son, and now you take from me any respectability that could come from those losses." Her whisper was more of a hiss as she tried to compose herself before the emperor. "You have not lost your son. I have put him in line for the throne after Antoninus. He is of more value to you now than if he were still in your own home," was Hadrian's blunt reply. "You have status as his mother, as well as estates, income, and three other children to keep you company. Be content with your life and live it wisely." With his patience nearly eroded, Hadrian had left abruptly after that. He had seen the widows of soldiers left destitute and childless, so this pampered woman had nothing to complain about. He left Plautia alone to contemplate her future, as he went forward to secure that of his empire.

Chapter Fifty-Seven

Loose Ends Are Bound

With the events of the past few days still fresh in their minds, the sight of the ailing emperor carried into the senate by litter did little to fool this administrative body into thinking he was weak of mind. With the imperial succession at stake, the old lion was more dangerous now than in his younger, more hopeful years. Time was too precious to bother with diplomacy; he would wield his power with less precision, perhaps but with more lethal results. As the senators examined their numbers in the vast hall, they noticed certain faces were missing from their ranks. Rumors of death sentences issued from the emperor seeped through these ancient, hallowed halls like the cold winter drafts that chilled their marble chairs. A number of their fellows chose to vanish in the night for their villas in Greece, Egypt, or Gaul—anywhere the roads from Rome could not reach them easily. Many were the surviving allies of Servianus, still bitter and hostile, their moment of revenge vanquished like smoke. Even in death, the old man proved to be a formidable adversary, ready to cut the line of succession at its weakest link. But Hadrian had positioned his players well, with lineage, reputation, and respectability as his main weapons, and no mention of the past, golden as it was.

Yet the specter of Lucius Aelius Caesar did linger in those august chambers. The announcement of Lucius Verus as one of Antoninus's heirs created agitation in the chambers, yet the grumblings were short lived as quick glances toward a placid Gnaeus Antoninus proved this decision too was preordained and so was to be accepted. As Hadrian had hoped, the inclusion of Marcus Aurelius sweetened the deal, and Caesar could sense the senate was settling into this new vision of the future he had arranged for them. In the presence of the presiding magistrate, along with senators, knights, and Hadrian's new son and heir, the line of succession was secured as the manifest was folded and a massive wax seal was poured and stamped with the ancient crest of the senate along side the imperial insignia. Copies of the now-sealed document were issued on two sheets of bronze, one to be secured to the wall of the senate and the other to the dividing wall of the Temple of Roma and Venus. As Hadrian descended the steps of the senate and returned to his litter, he knew he was hearing behind him for the final time, the closing of those ancient doors. With this chapter finished, the ink dry and the sacrosanct seal in place, Hadrian had no further use for Rome and no strength to finish the world of his own creation north of her ancient walls. Turning his back on Rome, he was also turning his back on the Villa Adriana. It was this epiphany that sent a wave of melancholy through the imperator of Rome—the realization that he had truly relinquished the right and desire to live.

Upon his return to the Domus Flavia, Hadrian summoned the chief priests, architect, and builders who were visiting from the sacred city of his Beloved, Antinoopolis. As they were ushered into a small chapel across the courtyard from the imperial apartments, they found the emperor seated on a gilded chair at the foot of a sculpture of a young Antinous as Apollo. The pale marble of the sculpture was in stark contrast to the sheets of shimmering lapis that covered the wall of the vaulted apse that contained it. In his role as Pontifex Maximus, the snow white of the emperor's toga and the cloak that draped his head competed with the stone, and the effect was dazzling despite the dull, midwinter light. Beside him stood a slightly nervous *flamien maior,* who clutched his fringe-edged cloak tightly and tried to ignore the tightness of his leather skullcap. Hadrian had reinstituted this ancient priesthood to promote the cult of his Beloved and invested lavishly on all those who entered its realm of worship. The *Collegium Pontificum,* beholden to the emperor's benevolence and protection, said nothing as Hadrian used his status as Pontifex to assign to the deified Antinous an honor usually designated only to the major gods of the religious pantheon. They had timidly suggested the use of a *flamine minor*, used for the more obscure gods of the pantheon. But the fit of imperial rage that ensued forced the rescinding of that suggestion and the immediate designation of *maior* as well as the honors and rites connected with this pronouncement. Through the influence of the Egyptian and Greek beliefs, Hadrian had made Antinous the son of Jupiter and Ra as well as the brother of Apollo and Osiris. At this level, he was a *divus*, entitled to a priest of the major rank. All this because Hadrian's knew too well that a translation of *Pontifex* was "able to do," and so he did.

The chief priests from Antinoopolis gazed with curiosity at the antiquity of the flamen's garb—the long fringe of the woolen cloak, the bronze studded chin strap of the skullcap, and the small spindle of olive wood that protruded from the cap from a small fluff of white wool. Hadrian had conjured up the most ancient of traditions to legitimize his young god and, through sheer force of will, made them real. The chief priests too made quite an impression with their eyes heavily lined with kohl and their exotic Egyptian garb—a long linen tunic, leopard skin cloak, and scarab-incrusted jewelry. Beside them walked acolytes who bore bowls of painted alabaster filled with sacred incense from the main temple of Antinous/Osiris. After bowing deeply, the chief priest made a motion to add to the incense already burning on the small altar, but Hadrian stopped him with a small gesture. His head was already aching from the scent of the present offerings, and he was too familiar with the heady, pungent odor of Egyptian fragrance. The emperor's small slight was eased by the appearance of a large domed coffer, masterfully carved in cedar and studded with gilded bronze stars. Hadrian motioned to the centurion bearing the obviously weighty box to place it on the stone table beside his chair. With some effort, the centurion did so and then undid the bronze latch, which responded with a dull click. As the hinges chirped from the weight of the heavy wood of the lid, the glittering contents slowly revealed themselves as slaves hurriedly lit more of the numerous oil lamps that hung from the high ceiling. The sight of such an offering brought the Egyptian priests to their knees, as the rest of their entourage followed suit. "A gift for my Beloved's temple and his guardians." These were the first words emperor had spoken to the visitors, and they were directed toward the head priest, who bowed his head further, until it rested on the cold stone floor.

At these words, the architect who had been in charge for the building of the sacred city stepped forward and presented a massive portfolio filled with painstakingly rendered drawings of the architectural wonders of Antinoopolis. The head priest and his brothers rose from their prostration and stood silently as the emperor spoke intently with his architect. The head priest was named Abdju, after the sacred city he was from, in valley of the same name. As descendants of the Vizier Nespeqashuty, one in each generation of his family served at the Temple of Osiris the Great since the reign of Psammetichus I. Having been passed over for this honor in deference to his older brother, the priesthood in the temple of the new god born from the River Nile was a gift from the gods and, it seemed, the emperor of Rome. The wealth that flowed into the gleaming white city of Antinoopolis was staggering, as were the tributes that enriched the temple of Antinous-Osiris. As he stood and watched the emperor slowly examine the pages of heavy parchment, Abdju took the opportunity to study the interior of the small chapel. Although lavishly appointed with rich stone inlay and heavy gilding, the diminutive scale of the sanctuary shocked the priest. He had heard that Rome did not eagerly embrace the new god as did the rest of the empire, nor did they approve of the emperor's devotion to the youth whose death had devastated him. There was a mixture of practicality and arrogance to Rome that chilled the priest more than the bitter damp that prevailed in every corner of the city. Not a part of the distant conversation between emperor and architect as they discussed the young god's city, the priest's thoughts drifted to the ship that bobbed in the harbor of Ostia, eager to return to the warmth of Egypt. With his task completed so quickly and without a single word of request, the priest hoped that return would now be hurried along. His thought were suddenly distracted by the slight movement of the acolytes as they fidgeted from boredom and the cold that rose from the marble inlay of the temple floor. As Abdju gazed at the slender beauty of the youths, his mind drifted from his desire for Egypt to his desire for other things.

The hum of conversation had ceased and the chief priest returned to the matters at hand, motioning for the gifts that had traveled from the land of the Nile to be presented before Caesar. A painting of Antinous done in the Roman/Egyptian style, a bust of the Beloved in the guise of Osiris done in pink granite, a small golden coffer bearing a large turquoise scarab resting on earth from which the temple of Antinous/Osiris rose. A large papyrus was unfolded and revealed the night sky done in brilliant inks and showing the position of the star of Antinous within the constellation of the eagle. As the chief priest unfolded the papyrus, the young acolyte, in a voice pure and strong, began a song of praise for the golden young god. "Hail to you who are in the sacred desert of the West! Osiris knows you and knows your name; may you save us from those snakes which are in Rosetjau, which live in the flesh of men and gulp down their blood, because Osiris knows you and knows your name." The chief priest then joined in the chant, as did the lesser priests in the entourage. "You are the Radiant One, the brother of the Radiant God, Osiris, brother of Isis, son and mother Isis have raised you above your enemies. Praise be to you who sits with Osiris, the firstborn of the company of the gods, eldest of the gods, heir to his father Geb. You are Antinous-Osiris, lord of persons, alive of breast, strong of hinder parts, stiff of phallus, who is within the boundary of the common folk." As Hadrian sat spellbound during the hymn of praise, the doors of the sky seemed to open, and a torrential rain poured down as if in response to the sacred chants. A clap of thunder shook Hadrian out of his reverie and brought him back into the present. The lightning illuminated the Parian marble form that loomed over him, briefly making the pure stone translucent. "You are the pure lotus which went forth from the sunshine, which is at the nose of Re; you have descended that you may seek it for Horus, for you are the pure one who issued from the marshland." The storm and chants seemed to go on endlessly, and as they began to meld into one, Hadrian felt himself succumbing to the blackness that was slowly slipping over him. The centurion that continued to stand beside the emperor caught him before he could reach the chapel's marble floor.

The death like sleep that enveloped Hadrian that evening lasted until morning. After emerging from the faint he had fallen into while in the sanctuary, he awoke in his bedchamber, weak and chilled with the sound of chant and thunder still in his head. Somewhere in the distance a lyre was being softly played along with the splashing of rain that could be heard as it fell to the stone pavement outside. The heavy drapery over the windows prevented him from knowing the time of day. Not that it mattered. Sleep descended once again, and with the dark came a dreamless sleep.

The darkness and rain did not lull Plautia to sleep that night. With her husband's ashes interred at his family's estate and her son now living with Antoninus Caesar and Faustina, the true situation of her life seemed to overwhelm her. Most of Rome's society was already settled in their villas along the Bay of Naples, but Plautia knew the gossip regarding her loss of status had traveled quickly to the lavish halls and lush gardens from Cumae, Baiae, and down the Via Campania to the Isle of Capri. All the villas where she had been lavishly entertained in the past and would surely never visit again.

After pacing up and down the hard marble floors of the arcade that surrounded the inner courtyard's gardens, Plautia suddenly felt the weight of the past month's events come crashing down on her. Making her way to a stone chair beside one of the columns, she sank wearily between the two carved arms and gathered her woolen cloak around her for warmth. The previous occupant of the chair had left a small pillow there; Plautia was grateful for the small comfort it provided her. She curled up, catlike, on the smooth stone and rested her head on the silken cushion, watching the drops of water falling from the arched passageway above her. Although the rain had stopped, the torchlight caught the succession of drops as they still fell to the wet marble steps that led to the sunken gardens. As she listened to the hypnotic rhythm of the dripping water, she found herself tapping her ring in time with the beat. She stopped and examined the ring for a moment, as if for the first time. A braided band of gold held a wreath of stylized peacock feathers surrounding a lustrous cabochon amethyst. Although it was not to her taste, she smiled slightly as she recalled its origin. It was the ring Lucius had given her on the day of their betrothal. He called his choice of stone a glimpse of the future, so sure was he that Hadrian would choose him as son and heir. She was unaware then of the agreement between the two, an agreement that sent Lucius away from the emperor he loved and to the marriage bed she knew he never felt completely comfortable in. Caesar tried to groom Lucius to become the perfect Roman, complete with the perfect Roman family. How bright the future seemed on the day she received this ring, how seductive the lure of its smooth purple jewel. But purple was not to be her color after all. All she could do now was watch from afar as the world, and time, hurried past.

The next morning was bright and clear as the three palaces hummed with activity. The emperor and his entourage were preparing to leave the Domus Flavia for the gentler clime of Baiae, while at the Domus Tiberiana, Antoninus's household was packing for their journey to his grandfather's villa in Putoli. Faustina was grateful to leave the drafty palace and its miles of marble halls. She had requested the Domus Augustana as the official residence when they needed to return to Rome. Hadrian's response when presented with this request was somewhat cryptic. "By the time you return, all of Rome will be your husband's. You will have to bring up the matter with him," was all he said. After the senate's confirmation of Antoninus as son and heir, Hadrian seemed to lose interest in anything that concerned the state. Faustina watched him withdraw more and more from the court and, indeed, life itself. Each morning's light seemed to find less and less of the man who seemed to gradually wither away beneath darkness of his *toga pulla*. From her window, Faustina watched the imperial litter leave the palace grounds on route to the frigid waters of the Tiber, her husband walking solicitously beside it. He had now, at the urging of Gnaeus Antoninus, turned his attentions to his newly adopted father, despite the fact that Gnaeus's health was just as precarious as the emperor's. But the old man was eager to see his grandson take on the reins of power as quickly as possible.

After all, who knew who would win the race to their final rest, himself or Caesar?

Faustina had sent servants to the elderly man's villa at the foot of the Palatine to assure his readiness for the journey to Putoli. The former imperial flagship, the *Felicitati*, would carry the heir and his family and lead the small flotilla bearing the entire court to the Bay of Naples followed, finally, by the *Adriana Augusta*, where they would then depart for their respective villas. Hadrian had disrupted the social season in the southern resort towns with his delay, but this had never been a concern of his before and would certainly not begin to be one now. The society matrons, and indeed, society in general, were already missing the exuberance of Aelius Caesar and his fun-loving wife. The austere Antoninus and his pious wife had little interest in the parade of lavish banquets and revelries that flowed like a wave up and down the villa studded hills. And as each social grandee received her letter of regret from Plautia announcing her decision to forgo the social season along the bay, the season began to look even bleaker. But the more resilient of the social climbers used these breakdowns in the social order to climb another rung up the ladder. More wine was ordered and more exotic entertainment planned, as little by little the hills began to hum with the festivities of the season.

Chapter Fifty-Eight

Death, Will You Not Come?

On the broad portico of Cicero's restored villa, a barefoot slave was valiantly struggling with a large amphora of Falerian wine as he poured the thick red juice into a fine bell crater of Greek origin. Another slave stood by with a three-handled *hydria* filled with spring water, chilled and ready to dilute the wine already splashing about in the mixing bowl. When this was finished, a young slave, himself of Greek origin, used a gilt silver *oinochoe* as a ladle to remove some of the wine mixture and pour it into a *stamnos, a* smaller crater set aside for the emperor. The deep gurgling sound of the wine pouring into the Greek boy's jug brought Hadrian out of his state of reflection on the view before him and returned him to the present. He watched as the youth poured a thick stream of amber-colored honey into the mixing bowl of wine, the fine musculature of his slender arms straining as he lifted the bowl and swirled the mixture to blend the contents. Hadrian watched with wry amusement at the boy's intense concentration as he accomplished his task and poured the sweetened wine into a shallow silver kylix. With an almost poetic grace, the youth took the cup in both hands and presented it to the emperor. Despite having no desire for the wine, Hadrian could not refuse, after all the care involved, the offering from the pale, dark-eyed youth who knelt before him. After all this time, the tousled hair, the almond-shaped eyes with their thick lashes, and the lush red mouth send a familiar rush of recognition through the emperor, as did the graceful gestures of the cup bearer. As he reached for the cup, Hadrian's fingers touched those of the youth, who blushed at the contact. *To have such beauty before me at this time in my life is cruelty itself,* was the thought that whispered dimly within the emperor's mind. The youth hesitated for a moment, expecting perhaps an invitation of some kind. Unlike the wine, Hadrian had a shadow of desire for the youth, even if his body disagreed. Inviting the youth to sit on the low footstool beside his chair, Hadrian sank back against the thick cushions and studied the youth's dark curls while sipping his sweetened wine. This mood of rare contentment that was slowly washing over Hadrian vanished quickly with the sound of his guests as they made their way to the columned portico. The youth rose quickly from his footstool, his grace and discretion a tribute to his breeding. The youth stood quietly by Caesar's chair, and the guests began to arrive.

If Antoninus noticed the attractive youth beside the emperor's chair, he gave no sign of it. He had arrived with Faustina and Marcus Aurelius, who Hadrian still referred to as Verissmus, or "the truest." The emperor's fondness for the youth raised some suspicions at first, but Marcus's stoic qualities and natural reserve, as well as his fine conduct in the positions the emperor had placed him in, swept away the gossip, and positioned him as the perfect heir of Antoninus. Clad in his *toga virilis,* the slender youth approached the emperor and knelt before him with a quiet reverence. Repositioning himself painfully in his chair, Hadrian reached out and touched Marcius's cheek, noticing that at seventeen, there was still no sign of a beard. "Verissmus, I'm told you take your religious duties very seriously, just as you take all things." The emperor spoke with gentle mocking, knowing Marcus was as thrifty with his humor as he was with his possessions. "I wish only to serve with the best of my ability," was the youth's quiet reply. After one last light pat on the youth's cheek, Hadrian repositioned himself in another unsuccessful attempt to find comfort for his aching body. Giving up, he rose from the heavy chair and began to pace the marble floor of the portico. There were times when the bloodless nature of the youth chilled the emperor. The Stoic philosopher Apollonius of Chalcedon had a great influence on Marcus—far more than on the more worldly Lucius when he was still Ceionius Commodus. While Lucius slowly turned away from Apollonius's teachings, Marcus embraced the philosopher's view of life with an almost religious fervor. Despite the warmth Hadrian had always shown the youth, he never felt anything more in return than a distant regard and respect. *As warm as my wife had been*, thought the emperor as he stopped to gaze at the sparkling bay in the distance.

Winter had quietly slipped away, and spring graced the hills with a dense floral carpet. The aroma of the flowered fields mixed with the sea's salty breeze creating a heady perfume that again distracted the emperor's thoughts. There were no pressing issues now, no question of an acceptable heir and successor. No ambivalence regarding the future. "I have no reason to be alive. No purpose. No place left in this life," Hadrian murmured to the scented air. "You are still the imperator of Rome, my father," came a reply from behind him. Antoninus had followed his adopted father as he made his way down the colonnade. He had watched Caesar's state of mind deteriorate along with his physical being since the line of succession had been secured. Already the rumors of his attempts at suicide had filtered throughout Rome, as well as over the clatter of gold and silver plates in the lush villas from Baiae to Puteoli. Dark tales floated along the steep terraces overlooking the bay. One rainy afternoon before entering his bath, Hadrian forced a dagger into the hands of his servant and ordered him to plunge it into his heart. The servant took the dagger, ran from the changing room, and hid in the wooded section of the estate. It was here that Antoninus found the frightened man and heard the story. Hadrian's rage at being defied thundered throughout the villa, and Antoninus moved into the residence soon after to prevent the emperor from taking revenge for the servant's betrayal. Shortly after, Hadrian commanded the imperial physician to provide a draught of poison, leading the horrified man to take his own life, rather than be responsible for the death of his emperor. After Antoninus had walked in on his adopted father's attempt by his own hand, the dutiful son began to shadow the emperor during his waking hours and had servants stand watch during his few hours of sleep.

Antoninus knew the ramifications of the emperor's suicide on his own future and pleaded with his father to accept his fate and not put his son's future as emperor in jeopardy. "The Roman people can forgive and ignore many things, but a parricide as emperor would be more than they could accept," he told him one early spring day. The day had been sweet smelling and mild; the usual body aches and throbbing in Hadrian's head had become more bearable, allowing him to listen with some empathy to Antoninus's plea.

The winter had turned to spring, and spring too was about to turn into summer, a summer that was to find the emperor resigned to a life Antinous had drowned in the Nile to preserve.

On the first day of summer, Antoninus's grandfather and former adopted father, Gnaeus Antonius, died in Rome while attending a session of the senate. He died as he would have wished. Having just reprimanded a group of willful junior senators for nearly an hour and set into motion Antoninus Caesar's right to rule by proxy in the emperor's continued absence, Gnaeus Arrius Antoninus sat back down in the seat he had held for more years than the junior senators had been alive and quietly died. The senate went on as usual, unaware that their elder colleague's spirit had passed on. The senators were used to the distinguished gentleman's habit of napping after a particularly satisfying victory, and the still smiling Gnaeus, slumped in his seat with eyes closed, was a familiar and slightly amusing sight for the members. It was not until the senate had finished and the consul unsuccessfully attempted to wake the man that the assembled group realized that Gnaeus's long and honorable life had ended before their eyes.

As Gnaeus Antoninus's only heir, Antoninus Caesar became one of Rome's wealthiest men. As he prepared for the consecration and burial of the noble man, many memories and emotions ran through him, as well as a slight sense of guilt for not being at his grandfather's side at the time of his death. But Antoninus knew the old warrior's fierce love for independence and his passion for a good fight. "There is more danger and reward in the senate chambers than on any battlefield," he would often tell his grandson. And after winning yet another of his countless victories, he died in the marble senate chair that was his battle-scarred saddle. As Antoninus placed the plain bronze urn containing the ashes of the elder statesman into a niche in the family tomb beside the Via Appia, another chapter of his life came to an end, and his trusted mentor was gone forever.

From under the portico of the ancient family mausoleum set on a small knoll just outside the city walls, Antoninus could see the setting sun wash the marble buildings of the forum with a warm amber light. In his heart, he had hoped for a satisfying career as a senator, then a long and equally satisfying retirement. But the death of an heir and the will of an emperor changed the course of his life's plans. At the age of forty-two, the idea of being heir to the throne of Rome filled him with a desolation he never thought possible. Hadrian was not a man one would chose to follow in succession. With his grandfather by his side, Antoninus had become a stable advisor to the emperor and enjoyed the distinction of being a member of the imperial inner circle. Hadrian had always treated him with high regard, as he did with his grandfather and Faustina. The good Hadrian was enlightened, indomitable, and wise. In those days, Antoninus saw the empire through a golden light that seemed to emanate from Caesar himself. The imperial entourage entered city after city through magnificent gates and arches built especially for the emperor's arrival. And in return, he showered the splendor and benevolence of Rome upon the welcoming people. To be *with* Caesar was to be one with the gods. To *be* Caesar was to be a god. All that ended along the muddy banks of the Nile. The beauteous boy Hadrian loved and dominated had, the rumors whispered, sacrificed himself for the life of his lover. From the shadows, Antoninus saw things differently, but said nothing. Not even with his beloved Faustina would he share the things he had seen—the great man's jealousy, vanity, and ability to cruelly toss aside the people who loved him unequivocally. The youth had become too old for the emperor's purposes, as he and all the love Caesar had given him would soon be cast away. Only after Antinous's death was Hadrian aware of the pure essence of the youth's tenderness and devotion for him. Kneeling in the mud of that sluggish, ancient river, Hadrian held the fruit of his own selfishness and pride. And he wept. Antinous would have wept too had he known then what his lover's future without his beloved would bring. Guilt and pride had mixed within the emperor and poisoned his spirit, slowly unleashing a rage that, empowered by his crown, would prove deadly. Antoninus clung to his values and purity of intent like life raft in a violent sea. More a plow horse than an equestrian showpiece, Antoninus stayed the straight and true course in a turbulent and sometimes deadly journey. "You are my rock in this raging river of sorrow and pain," Hadrian once whispered to Antoninus one summer day as they stood before the tomb of the Beloved one. *A rock,* thought Antoninus as he gazed at the city of marble. *A man must be stone to rule Rome. By the grace of Mithras, may this glory thrust upon me not turn my soul to lime in its blaze.*

Chapter Fifty-Nine

The Beloved's Final Gift

Summer settled sweetly upon the terraced hills of Baiae, and its balmy breath wafted through the darkened corridors of the royal villa, infusing its cold marble and creamy alabaster with a warming glow. Was it Apollo or Ra who traced the inlaid geometrics of the stone floors that lead to the imperial apartments? Whichever sun god it was, he was determined to shed his light on the old man who was slowly being prepared for the new day. Hadrian's life had become a strict ritual carefully watched over by servants and guards eager, for reasons that escaped him, to keep their emperor alive. No one wanted Caesar's death to occur on their watch, least his successor accuse them of acquiescence to the pain-racked emperor's wishes.

Despite the warm July breeze, Hadrian shivered under his linen tunic and urged his servants to hurry with the toga of finely woven wool. As he waited for them to arrange the snowy folds into a perfect drape, he ran his fingers absentmindedly across the heavy embroidery of the tunic's collar, tracing the palmette pattern over and over as a blind man would examine a familiar face. His mind drifted away to another time, when he had traced the same pattern on a tunic worn by his Beloved. A favorite of the boy's, it had been washed countless times, and the linen weave had been broken down to a buttery softness. As the youth napped beneath an umbrella pine beside the great pool at the villa, Hadrian would trace the Greek palmette pattern along the hem of Antinous's tunic, occasionally veering off the fabric to run his fingers along a tanned, muscular thigh. The youth's hand would brush his own in a halfhearted attempt to stop the wandering fingers that had found their way beneath the hem. Hadrian would watch as the youth's dark eyes slowly opened, the full lips parted in silent consent. The creaking of the pine sang in time with the flickering shadows of its branches. It was summer then, the allure of love seemed endless, and the Nile was still a year away. In his reverie, a poem revealed itself and sang softly in his ear.

> *Love is no sweet confection,*
> *But a bitter fruit,*
> *Best left on the tree.*
> *Lest the blood of that fruit*
> *Seep into our veins*
> *And poison our hearts.*
>
> *Love makes a mockery of life*
> *There is cruelty in its brevity.*
> *In its taste,*
> *The freshness pales*
> *Then fades.*
> *Its fresh flow is as dust.*
> *Yet life is a shadow at best*
> *Without this bitter tonic,*
> *This vague writing*

On a faded page.
A prescription for an existence
That is but a brief illness.

Sink your words into me
As knives through my flesh
Make me feel each wound
Fresh, bloodied.
For, as long as I suffer
You are not truly gone.

The whisper of a poem written years ago in Egypt, as he stood before the Colossus of Memnon. It contained in its lines all the bitterness he had come to know. All the ache that would never leave.

Hadrian's reverie was broken by the weight of the diadem as Theos the chamberlain positioned it gently on his head. It was the crown that had created for him to hold the sapphire intaglio of Antinous/Hermes. As Theos tied the purple ribbons in back to tighten the wide golden band, Hadrian's mind again wandered to another time. Memories of the youth in the presence of the empress flooded his mind with a golden mist; the sternness of Sabina's features softened by the boy's beauty. The same softness she showed when complimenting the crown with the sapphire. It was the last of the few pleasant memories he had of his wife. A light breakfast waited for the emperor after his dressing had finished, but the shadow of an ache was forming in his head like thick smoke. He dismissed the servants and slowly drank the potion his physician had prepared for him earlier. Sitting under the small portico outside his private chambers, Hadrian finished the potion and placed the cup of rose-colored glass on the small table beside the chair. The sky had changed from the color of the glass to a stronger orange that would soon give way to the yellow heat of midday. On a small piece of parchment, he had begun to scrawl a few verses that had been whispering in his brain. *Animula, vagula, blandula Hospes comesque corporis* . . . "Little soul, roamer and charmer Body's guest and companion . . ." The potion had a calming effect that soothed the ache in his head and legs, but it lulled him to sleep at the same time. *Quae nunc abibis in loca* "Pale, naked. Where are you now?" Sleep continued, fitful but calming. *Nec. Ut soles, dabis iocos* . . . "Who will you play with, tender soul, now that I am gone . . ." A dull clanging and the sound of distant drumming interrupted his brief slumber. Hadrian woke, and for a moment, confusion muddled his brain before he noticed the diadem had slipped from his head and gone crashing to the floor. That explained the clanging, while the sound of distant drumming was, to the emperor's chagrin, the great sapphire rolling on the smooth travertine. The stone had dislodged after the crown struck the stone, its broad bezel of soft gold giving way to the force of the blow. Anxiously, Hadrian retrieved the jewel and examined it for damage. To his sorrow, he found a crack had developed, running across the gem and through the portrait of Antinous. A wave of anger rushed through him as he felt suddenly blinded by the pain that raged in his head. Falling back into his chair, he forced himself into a sense of calm as a servant silently appeared with another cup of the medicinal potion while another stooped to reverently recover the damaged crown. Thanos too appeared, ashen faced and begging forgiveness for the mishap. "I feared tying the ribbon too securely and bringing on your aching head again," explained the frightened chamberlain. "I beg Caesar's forgiveness." Hadrian had little strength to either reprimand or forgive. With a small smile, he waved the chamberlain and servants away resting for a time and clutching the damaged gem.

The ache in his head eventually subsided, and he slowly began to make his way through the atrium and walked into the morning sunlight. Standing in the shadow of the columns that stood guard along the entry porch of the villa, Hadrian recalled the day he received news of his adopted father's illness. *Was it this day? Yes, the tenth of July. On a day in Syria much like this one.* Trajan's wife, Plotina, had alerted him of the situation in a letter from Parthia where the emperor was fighting, promising her influence with her husband naming him son and heir. His relationship with Trajan had soured over time, as the old man grew more aware of his declining years. Despite their closeness, Trajan had always seen Hadrian as a competitor in both the battlefield and the bedroom. Too many boys caught the eye of both men, with Trajan using his crown to lure them in, while Hadrian used his youth and vigor. While Syria was a vital province and the position of governor was an important one, Hadrian could not help thinking he had been sent there to be out of the way. But less than a month after Plotina's letter arrived, Trajan succumbed to edema in the port city of Selinus along the coast of Cilicia. With the diamond ring of Nerva as a promise of succession, the endorsement of the senate and the Syrian armies at his command, Hadrian secured the crown with little political opposition. *And much bloodshed,* thought Hadrian as he recalled the four senators who paid for their dissent with their lives. He always denied involvement, but the stain of suspicion remained with him for years and crippled his relationship with the senate. Nor was Hadrian's order of dismissal of the dissenting Lusius Quietus a death warrant, yet it became one for the Berber commander who had crushed the Judean rebellion. Publius Attianus, Hadrian's former guardian and the Praetorian prefect before Turbo, had cleared the way for the succession in a brutally efficient way. *Blood spilled in my name but not by my word.* The throbbing in his head had been reduced to a mild irritation as Hadrian made his way across the courtyard to the temple he had built to Antinous. The midday sun reflected off the glistening marble of the new structure, intensifying its glare to a blinding brilliance. Clutching his cloak in both hands, Hadrian pulled the woolen wrap over his head as he ascended the steps towards the bronze entry of the temple. Giving the heavy door a push, he entered the dark coolness with a mixture of reverence and relief.

The votive statue that greeted the emperor seemed to float in the shadow and light created by the thin panels of alabaster that defused the gaze of the sun. The pure white Parian marble seemed to absorb the light and bring the figure to life as the inset eyes of jasper and onyx gleamed disinterestedly into space. The sculptor had chosen the Agathodemon or "good genius" to render this portrait of the Beloved, the iconic snake winding its way up a tree trunk and past a bunch of lush grapes. The artist had portrayed the youth immodestly draped from his thighs down, but the portrayal had beguiled Hadrian with its bodily perfection, bringing back memories he had long sought to suppress. As the sun's light washed over the chaste stone, oiled and polished by the young god's reverent priests, Hadrian stood at the foot of his god and ignited the sacrificial spices with the oil lamp beside the altar.

While the smoke began spiraling toward the oculus of the domed temple, Caesar's head once again began to throb, his eyes burning from the smoke of the smoldering offering that seemed to grow thicker and darker than usual. The form of Antinous appeared to move as if under murky water, pristine white wrapped in a sooty wave.

As Hadrian looked up at the face of his personal god, the mantle covering his head slipped off, revealing the ravaged face of a dying old man. The sculpture seemed to come to life; the snake crawled up the trunk, past the cluster of grapes, and nestled around the neck of the youth. The youth's head turned, the jasper eyes glowing with firelight as they gazed down at the enraptured man. As Hadrian gazed in wonder, the ache in his head began to grow into a stabbing pain that opened like a blossom inside his brain, its burning petals releasing themselves into his blood until they wrapped around his heart. His body, having sustained a number of hemorrhages in the past, could not withstand one of this magnitude. As the pain ripped through him, he straightened himself to full height and, with his gaze locked upon the face of his Beloved, met death not as a foe but as a savior. A final explosion tore through him, and he fell without a sound to the marble floor.

Epilogue

The story of the *Imperator Caesar Divi Traiani filius Traianus Hadrianus Augustus* did not end on the floor of Antinous's temple. Before he was to become *Divus Hadrianus,* his cremains were to continue that wanderlust the emperor had reveled in, and then was cursed by, during his lifetime. When the body of Caesar was discovered by the priests of the temple, they sent a messenger to the imperial guard to announce the death. They in turn paid a visit to Hadrian's adopted son and heir, Antoninus, at his villa in Puteoli, to present the imperial signet ring. Antoninus removed Nerva's diamond ring of heir presumptive and replaced it with the heavy imperial signet—a promise fulfilled.

Antoninus ordered sacrifices in Hadrian's memory, and the body of the emperor was escorted to the great courtyard of the temple in Baiae surrounded by his adopted family and the knights and courtiers brave enough to appear. Musicians and dirge singers were collected and masked actors representing Hadrian's ancestors sat on low chairs before the rostra as Antoninus gave a brief eulogy. The body was cremated with great pomp and ceremony in the protected privacy of the courtyard, far from the critical eyes of a mostly disinterested populous the emperor had tried so hard to appease. After this rather lack-luster ceremony, Antoninus took the remains of the late emperor of Rome to the royal estate in Puteoli, another that had once belonged to Cicero. There they rested in a temple of Hadrian's design, until Antoninus was prepared to return to Rome and formally accept the crown. Once there, Hadrian's remains were to rest in the Gardens of Plautia until his massive mausoleum was finally finished the following year, and he was laid to what was supposed to be his final rest.

Hadrian died unloved and unmourned by the populous and the senate. Only the military recalled the glory days of their emperor who mingled with them as one of their own. It would be a year before Antoninus would be able to sway the senate to deify their former master. His grandfather, Gnaeus Arrius Antoninus, was now deceased, but his name and prestige was still felt within the senate walls. Antoninus uses these, and the sudden reappearance of knights and senators supposedly murdered at Hadrian's command, to his advantage. With temples, proclamations, and lavish gifts, Antoninus Pius, as he was now known, glorified his adopted father and himself at the same time. Posterity would proclaim Hadrian as "one of the five good emperors," and his mark on the history of the empire would remain indelible. But in the lengthening shadows of the days end, one cannot help but wonder if the story of the man who was Hadrian would have been different had a beautiful youth not ended his own life in the muddy waters of the Nile. Grief and guilt are forces powerful enough to change history. Then, of course, there's love.